BEAR MEDICINE

G. ELIZABETH KRETCHMER

Dancing Seeds Press
Friday Harbor, Washington

www.gekretchmer.com

Print ISBN: 978-0-9961038-6-2
Digital ISBN: 978-0-9961038-7-9

Cover art by Julia Hayes-Siltzer
Cover design by Maria Aiello

ALSO BY
G. ELIZABETH KRETCHMER

Set largely in Alaska and narrated from the afterlife, *The Damnable Legacy* is a story about love and survival, exploring the importance of attachment, place, and faith, and asking how far we should go to achieve our goals—and at what cost.

Women on the Brink is a collection of loosely linked stories in which women aged thirteen to ninety must wrestle with family dynamics, self-esteem, socioeconomic status, maternal obligations, and a compelling desire for independence.

Please turn the page after you've finished *Bear Medicine* for samples from these works.

I've dreamt in my life dreams that have stayed with me ever after, and changed my ideas; they've gone through and through me, like wine through water, and altered the colour of my mind.

—Emily Brontë, *Wuthering Heights*

ONE

Brooke

August 2017

LIFE HAD ALREADY grabbed me by its enormous jaws, its fangs scratching at the surface of my sanity. Carson had no time for me anymore. Delaney hadn't spoken to me for months. And my dear husband, Shane? Let's just say he was the main reason I was 800 miles from home in the middle of Yellowstone National Park. I had needed to get away, to capture some time for myself. To run, to think, to be me.

When my alarm disrespectfully serenaded me before dawn on this particular fateful day, time was still a limited resource. At least this morning's run would be short and easy, I thought as my eyes fluttered open. I'd been training hard for the Portland Marathon until now, so a lighter workout was in order. I hauled my rebellious bones and muscles out of bed, collected them into some semblance of a human being, and drove to Biscuit Basin. Steaming geysers and bubbling mud pots, awash in eerily magical tempera paint colors, greeted me.

I made my way across the Little Firehole River bridge, followed the boardwalk, and found the trailhead. The path steered my feet into the forest, but my mind began to wander. As I ruminated—yet again—about what had brought me here, my thoughts straddled that thin line between self-respect and remorse. Eventually I found my training groove. I sailed past a hodgepodge underbrush of grasses, shrubbery, and the occasional wild raspberry, and navigated my way over a patchwork of fallen logs. This place was nothing like my garden back home, where concrete pavers were mathematically spaced, a lighted waterfall spilled into a blue-tiled reflecting pool, and artistically arranged pots of varying sizes and shapes overflowed with strategically colorful plants. This, right here in Yellowstone, was the type of landscape I'd always loved, and it also represented the exact opposite of who I'd become in all the years I'd spent with Shane.

Besides training, my goal for the morning was to snap some photos I could send to Delaney. The communication embargo my daughter had imposed on me was wearing me down. A text or Facebook message with photos could serve as another pathetic plea for reconciliation. Keeping a watch out for interesting subjects, I thought I saw something out of the corner of my eye—a dark shadow of sorts—but when I turned there were only branches swaying in the breeze and the distant rushing of Mystic Falls. I remember stopping anyway, thinking that spot was the perfect photo op. I remember lifting my phone and framing the river between two lodgepole pines. I don't recall tapping the shutter, but the file of photos on my phone verifies that I must have done just that.

And then my memory becomes muddled. The brain can do strange things in desperate times, and I may never be able to fill in some of the blank moments. I may also never know which of my so-called memories is accurate, or which was formed by stories others have offered, or which might simply be imagined. At any rate, this was the moment when life's fangs did more than scratch at my sanity. This was when life really shook things up.

A horrible stench. A distinctive blend of musk and rot. A slow-motion image of my phone being jettisoned from my hands, bouncing down an embankment, and landing against a fallen pine. The subtle taste of sandy dirt. And then the stabbing penetration into each of my hips, blinding pain, liftoff from the ground. Heavy and helpless, I was hefted into the air like a tree stump raised by a bulldozer.

It's a wonder that, in the midst of all my agony, I had enough wits left to figure out what was happening. But I did.

I'd been attacked by a bear. A very big bear.

There's not much you can do to fight off, or otherwise protect yourself from, a wild beast when you're hanging from its jaws. In a way, it's like childbirth; at some point you have to give in to nature and let everything run its course. Whether it shook me like a Raggedy Ann for hours, minutes, or seconds will forever remain unknown, but eventually the damn beast dropped me onto my stomach—hard. I felt a sharp swipe down the right side of my face. Claws raked deep into my right arm and leg. And then a jagged clamp crushed my right leg. Not once, not twice, but three separate times as the bear chomped away, its teeth penetrating all the way to bone.

I'm pretty sure it climbed on top of me, too, as Carson did when he was small, declaring victory over his kingdom. I have a foggy recollection of air being pressed out of my lungs, although that memory could have become mixed up with others—memories tend to get misfiled at times like these. Years earlier, I'd been trapped under a canoe in a river and had inhaled too much water. I thought I was going to die then, too, but obviously I didn't. This time, I was certain I would.

TWO

Anne

August 1877

THOMAS LAY ATOP me, his hips squeezed between my thighs, when I awoke on the hard ground in our dreadful tent. His snake of a tongue slid down my neck, and he began to thrust. I remained in the good wife position, waiting for him to finish our obligatory marital congress, while any possibility for my own joy seemed hundreds, perhaps thousands, of miles away.

Asking him to stop would have been futile and dangerous. *I am your husband*, he often reminded me, as though I would ever forget the vows I had so naively taken—vows that neglected to mention the promise of gentle behavior on his part in the course of these intimate affairs. Closing my eyes, I turned my head to the side and waited. While he proceeded, I listened beyond his moans to the sounds all around us: a swan's honk, a loon's wail, an ever-so-slight drumbeat. I felt the ground rumbling beneath my back and could not imagine the source of this quiver, which clearly had nothing to do with Thomas's exertion. As he thrust harder, the vibrations intensified. When he finished, he collapsed on top of me, panting. But the land beneath us continued to convulse.

Earthquake? I had heard about such phenomena. But no, this was something else. This was surely a stampede. A buffalo stampede.

"Thomas!"

I pushed at him while at the same time scrabbling to get out from under his weight. He came to his senses, reached for his rifle, and hurtled himself out of the tent, his trousers wrapped around his knees and his man parts exposed in all their glory. I fumbled about for my blue frock amidst our tangle of bedrolls and blankets and pulled it over my head without bothering about my corset or bustle. As I dressed, I imagined the reprimand I would receive from Thomas later—if we lived through this. It had been at my insistence that we set up camp there, after traveling on horseback for hours across open grasslands. Every ounce of my being ached, and when we finally came upon this little lake, with its refreshing water and crystal blue surface, I reined in my horse and refused to go farther.

Now I seized my bonnet, my sketch-book, and my pencil pouch—as well as Thomas's pistol—and I clambered out of the tent, my feet still barren of stockings or boots.

It was then I heard the frenzy of whoops and hollers and realized what had caused the earth's quake. The morning sun illuminated a dozen or more Indians and their mounts, charging directly toward us. Thomas quickly pulled up his trousers, and as he haltingly stepped away from the tent, I ducked down, already mesmerized by what I saw beyond his figure amidst a cloud of dust. Indian men with smooth, bare chests and war paint on their faces. Chestnut horses patched in white with expansive, strong flanks. Enormous feathers and braided leather ropes decorating both man and beast. I had read stories about these people and their spectacular regalia back home, but I'd always thought them the folly of fiction.

The Indians were circling Thomas. He forced a weak smile onto his visage, but none of them returned a warm expression. Shivering, I crept behind our tent and lowered myself to the ground, determined to become as invisible as possible. Once again, the ground began to shake.

Soon another set of riders trotted toward our camp-site, and I peered around the opposite corner of the tent to watch their arrival. This group included two more decorated Indians, three white men, and two white women—one of whom must have been near my age. She rode side-saddle, while the other was much younger and likely quite uncomfortable straddling her horse. They were both clad in dust, their clothing torn and blood-stained, their faces adorned with fear more vivid than the paint on the Indians' faces. The poor dears appeared ready to collapse, and I had half a mind to run to them with a canteen of fresh water and a bar of lye soap, but I caught myself, only later fully understanding the two thoughts that had held me back. First was the selfish realization that it would be foolish to endanger myself for strangers when the success of any rescue was improbable at best. The other was more troubling: I had been tempted to help those women, yet I had no such inclination for Thomas.

None of the visitors had noticed me thus far, and at present, there was a mild fracas among the Indians—an argument, it seemed, about Thomas. The white women cowered as the Indian men waved their hands about and their horses danced in place. It would only be a matter of seconds, I fretted, until someone discovered my presence, so I did what any rational and cowardly woman would do. I dashed like a frantic doe, up a slight incline from the camp-site into the timber, and hid behind the thickest trunk, clutching my bonnet and pencils and sketch-book—and Thomas's gun—to my bosom.

THREE

Brooke

I AWOKE, UTTERLY disoriented, to vibrations beneath me and the sound of a child's scream. For an instant, I thought I was back home nine or ten years ago, waking to the sound of Delaney's squeals as she jumped onto my mattress. But the pain coursing through my body enlightened me: I was lying on a forest floor amidst a pandemonium of voices. The vibrations were caused by footsteps shuffling all around.

As a tentative hand touched my shoulder, a voice asked if I was all right. *Far from it*, I thought. I wasn't able to speak.

Another voice cried out, panic-stricken. "Oh, dear God! Don't let the children see this!"

"They already have, dear."

The sound of retching. A maelstrom of other voices in tones ranging from worry to disgust to something akin to awe.

"Let's get some pressure on these wounds."

"She's shivering. Probably in shock."

"Look at her hair. It's beautiful."

"A ginger."

"Must've been a bear. A sign back there said to beware of bears. Was she out here all alone?" Murmurs. "Foolish." More murmurs.

Something was placed over me—a jacket, maybe.

"You sure you want to do that, honey? I don't know if the bloodstains will ever come out."

"Margaret, I can't believe you said that."

I tried to make sense of where I was. What was happening. To whom these voices belonged. When a gentle hand swept my hair away from my face, and I opened one eye—only one eye *would* open at first—I tried to move but couldn't.

A man's face, a set of sparkling green eyes, and a khaki shirt appeared in my line of vision.

"Let's give her some space here, folks," the man said, and then he told somebody to apply pressure to my leg wounds. He leaned his face close to mine, his breath warm on my face.

He said his name was Palmer. He was a National Park Ranger. "Looks like you've run into a bit of bear trouble. Can you tell me your name?"

It took a while to recall who I was. And to part my lips. You never appreciate how easy it is to talk until you can't. Intense pain shot through my jaw as I tried to form my mouth around the letter *B* to tell him who I was. A whisper made its way out.

"Blake?" the ranger said. "That's a pretty name." My name wasn't Blake, but I didn't have the mental capacity or physical fortitude to correct him.

He asked me some other questions, about what happened and whether I was alone, but again I couldn't think or speak well enough to answer. He barked orders at bystanders—tourists, I later learned. A zipper scraped open. Fabric ripped. Every time someone touched me, or even my clothes, a torrent of agony rushed through me. Layers of weight piled on top of me—more jackets, maybe, for people to worry about ruining.

"She's losing a lot of blood."

The tip of a plastic bottle mercifully appeared at my lips, but before I could taste its sweet relief, the ranger swatted the bottle away. He wore a grim smile.

"Nothing to drink yet," he said. "Wait for the medics."

I was so overwhelmed with fatigue that I couldn't rebel. Even now, the mere memory of that day exhausts me.

"Stay with me," the ranger said, over and over. I liked the sound of his voice, soft as fur. I liked that he wanted me to stay.

I didn't want to wake up, but someone was being insistent. It must be Saturday, I thought. Shane was pushing for me to get up and out of bed. *You can rest when you're dead.* But it wasn't Shane's voice. I forced what seemed to be my good eye open.

An unfamiliar man knelt beside me, his face down at my eye level. He looked like a blurry, one-eyed alien. He said he was a medic. His name was Joe.

"She's been in and out of consciousness," that kind, green-eyed voice said in the background.

"Bear?" the medic asked.

"Grizzly. 'Course you'll see what I mean when you see her wounds. She's lucky to be alive."

Somebody lifted a flap of jacket, or blanket, or whatever had been covering me, off my right leg. A breeze cut across the wound like a machete. Not that I knew how a real machete would feel.

"Jesus. How long ago did this happen?"

"Not sure. Maybe two hours. Maybe longer."

"I'll have to immobilize you," the medic said to me. "This might hurt a little."

As I was lifted and set back down onto an extremely uncomfortable board, I squeezed my eye shut. He'd lied; that movement hurt more than *a little*. He bound me to the board like a load of debris tied down on a flatbed truck and, when he tightened the straps, the f-word squeezed out from my lips.

"Helicopter's waiting at the trailhead," the medic said to the ranger. "You coming?"

"No can do," the ranger said. "Got a bear to track down."

Joe and a second medic lifted me off the ground. I wanted to thank the ranger, before we left, for saving me, but all my energy was devoted to surviving the pain; the board I lay upon was about as comfortable as my dining room table.

"It's only about a mile back to the trailhead," Joe said. The stretcher jostled as they began the hike out, and I moaned with each step. I tried to focus on a memory of Delaney in front of her new dorm in a black, strappy top and tiny denim shorts, tanned from a long summer in the sun, Ray-Bans resting on top of her head, her long red hair blowing in the wind.

"Shit! Oh, shit!" Joe said.

Once again I detected the scent of musky rot. Then came a hiss of spray. I opened my good eye once again, but all I saw were tree branches high above me.

"You sprayed it too soon," the medic behind me said. "You dumbass."

"Fuck. Got any more bear spray?"

They set me down roughly. I cried out. The straps wouldn't permit me to turn my head in any direction, but even so—even in all that pain—it didn't take a genius to know what was happening. I lay on the ground, vulnerably attached to a dining room table like a feast for the grizzly bear, while Joe and his partner argued about who was supposed to have packed the second canister of bear spray. I started to hyperventilate, then remembered my own canister. I tried to force two simple words—*back* and *pack*—from my mouth.

"What did she say?" Joe asked.

"Back path. She said back path," the other medic said. "Maybe there's another trail we can take."

I tried again.

"She said backpack," Joe said. "Backpack, you idiot."

I tried to spit out the word *spray*.

"Spray? Did she say spray? Check her backpack for bear spray."

I think I lifted my left thumb.

After a flurry of activity, I heard a zipper. I also heard the bear's huff.

"Got it."

"Hurry up," Joe said. "She's circling around behind us. And closing in."

"I'm going as fast as I can. Shut the fuck up."

I squeezed my eye shut again, knowing that my next breath could be my last. Then came another long hiss of spray. And the distinct smell of cayenne wafting toward me.

"We got her. Hell, yeah. Look at her run!"

They hesitated for another moment, celebrating their victory the way guys do, before picking me up again as ungracefully as the first time. They jogged now, the jostling worse than before. But as long as they got us to safety, I could endure. Even in my near delirium, I felt guilty about these two men having risked their lives for me.

Whirring helicopter blades soon chopped through the distant air. The medics' footsteps clip-clopped on the wooden boardwalk I'd jogged upon earlier that day. I snuck one eye open, long enough to see bystanders staring down at me as we rushed past. Once more, my thoughts drifted to Delaney. And to Carson. And finally to Shane, whose blood would be so boiling hot—hotter than the steaming mud pots and geysers we passed—when he heard what I'd done.

FOUR

Anne

CROUCHED AMIDST A cluster of pine trees, I tried to rein in my disorderly thoughts and scattered emotions. I knew I should go to Thomas and stand by his side, if not because he was my husband then because I had no desire to be here in the woods alone. Before we had embarked on our overland journey to Yellowstone, my dear brother-in-law, Edgar, had warned us about the perils of traveling in these parts—not only the wild animals and all the hardships but also "the horrible savages" who lived out west. He had told of Indians attacking travelers and doing "unspeakable" things to white women. I had been clearing away the china from the table after dinner that evening, and Thomas, having just lit up his cigar, waved his hand in the air to brush away Edgar's admonitions.

"Stop filling my wife's head with nonsense," he told Edgar. He sniffed his brandy. "This will be an adventure like no other. Furthermore, my dear friend General William T. Sherman of the United States Army assured me that we will be perfectly safe so long as we stay within the boundaries of the park."

Yellowstone National Park had been created by our government a few short years earlier, and those we knew who had already visited came home with remarkable stories of stunning vistas, fantastic geysers, and magnificent wildlife. I had also seen one of Thomas Moran's paintings and understood why this land was known as Wonderland. Initially I had begged Thomas to take me there, completely naïve to the dangers that, according to Edgar, lurked behind every tree.

"Maybe we should hold off on this trip," I said as I opened a window to let the cigar smoke out into the night. I was having second thoughts.

But Thomas had already put good money down on our itinerary, and money was as necessary for his survival as the very air he breathed.

"Now don't be silly, darling," he said. "Don't listen to a word old Edgar here is saying. We'll proceed with our plans, and you'll be just fine. In fact, you'll be the envy of all your lady friends: camping out in nature, riding horses, fishing for our suppers. Roughing it, as they say. When else will you be afforded such an experience? You'll love it, my dear."

His dark eyes bore into mine, reinforcing his words. "Now run along. This discussion is over."

So sayeth my Lord.

Thomas, however, was wrong. I did not love it out here in this mysterious and remote country. From the moment our stage-coach crossed into the park, I was ready to turn around and make haste for home. The late August sun melted us by day, the mosquitoes devoured us in the evenings, and the howling wolves and yapping coyotes kept me awake all night. There was no place for a proper bath. No privacy whatsoever for a woman's personal needs. And, instead of the fine, civilized tourists I had anticipated, we had encountered only vagabonds—trappers, miners, and derelict outlaws—traversing the park, men who had seemingly not bathed or even shaved in months.

And now Indians. As I hid in the woods picking pine needles and splinters from the soles of my bare feet, both my hatred for this wilderness and my sinful animosity toward my husband swelled in my heart like a fever. But before I had a chance to ferret out my thoughts any further, another commotion brought my attention back down to the lake.

Fifty or sixty new horses trotted into our camp-site, also from the west. They were followed by scores of Indian women and children who rode in rickety old wagons or walked alongside horses laden with baskets and blankets. And guns. I had never seen so many guns! They crowded into what had been a peaceful, idyllic site just yesterday afternoon, and when the last wagon rolled in, I spotted a small Indian girl lagging behind it, a rifle in her arms as long as she was tall. Beautiful black hair and large, sorrowful eyes, and she could not have been more than four years old.

Despite this large congregation of strangers and the additional men and weapons, I felt ever-so-slightly less afraid than I had moments earlier. I believe it was because of all the women and children now gathered around.

Until I heard gunshot.

I startled and yelped, immediately slapping my hand over my mouth and freezing in place. Thomas would reprimand me harshly if he knew I had uttered a peep. My eyes searched for him, but I could no longer see him amidst the savages and their wagons and the swirling dust.

A volley of angry voices drew my attention eastward when the cloud of dust commenced to settle. Two Indian men were arguing with the white men, who were presumably hostages. Something about horses and flour and sugar. And guns. There was a lot of pointing and shouting. The two white women began to weep. I still could not find Thomas in the ruckus but also did not spot anyone bleeding or dying, so I made the assumption, if only for my own sanity, that the gunshot had either been an error or a warning.

Meanwhile, a few Indian children discovered our tent, only yards from where I hid. They snooped around it, paying no heed whatsoever to the fact that this was not their property, and I most certainly did not like the way those ragamuffin spies invaded my makeshift home; indeed, I found this highly insulting and inappropriate. But what was I to do? My mood worsened still when one of the little devils came out of the tent with my underpinnings, laughing and waving them around in the air. I wished to shout out, I was so angry, and embarrassed, too. But wisdom took hold of me and silenced my voice.

Two more Indian children then went into the tent. One came out with my expensive, but terribly uncomfortable, boots. The other reappeared with my Parisian cosmetics case, which contained all sorts of lovely ointments and fragrances that Thomas had insisted we leave at home. I had won that argument, but now I watched helplessly as the band of scoundrels presented their treasures to one of the Indian men—an old man in full feather regalia. A chief, I presumed. He lifted his head and gazed out first toward the tent, and then toward the woods where I now hid. I stepped back behind a tree trunk and inhaled as deeply as possible to narrow my girth. When I could no longer hold my breath or my curiosity, I exhaled and peeked around the tree.

The old chief nodded and made some hand signs to the other warriors, at which time the youngsters tethered my cosmetics case to his majestic, glistening black horse. The two Indian boys returned to our tent, quickly collapsed it, and rolled it into a disheveled ball. All of my belongings—including every last stitch of clothing I had brought on this trip aside from the flimsy frock I now wore—were contained inside the heap of canvas they dragged through the dirt and heaved into a wagon.

The Indian chief who acquired my cosmetics let out a whoop. The others echoed his cry, and a flock of birds shot out from a clump of shrubbery along the lake's edge. Soon the entire group of several hundred nomads moved along on their merry way eastward. Again, dust kicked up everywhere, making it difficult to see anything or anyone. I spotted the two white women, but no Thomas.

I finally caught a glimpse of him riding one of the two horses he had rented for us. The other horse—the white mare I had ridden—trailed behind. Thomas glanced over his shoulder toward the flattened grass where our tent had stood moments earlier, and then he lifted his face—his chin, his dark mustache, and his eyes—toward the woods where I hid, but only for a blink of a moment. I could not decipher the expression on his face, but when he raised his index finger to his lips, I knew I must stay put—and stay quiet. Then he kicked the horse's sides and rode off.

When he and every last one of the Indians had followed the trampled grassland trail into the brush and around the bend and were thus completely out of my line of sight, I collapsed to the ground, unsure whether to be grateful I was free and alive—or terrified that I still was.

FIVE

Brooke

I WOKE FROM an odd dream, something about dark eyes staring into my soul. Stiff as a block of wood when I tried to move, I discovered I was no longer strapped to the medics' stretcher. Now I lay on a slightly softer surface, my right arm and leg and much of my torso layered in gauze wrappings. I had been mummified.

At least I was alive; this I knew because of the machines chirping behind me and the IV needle taped to the top of my left hand. Also because of the agony radiating up and down the right side of my body from face to foot. I tried to interpret a montage of what I assumed were memories: whirring helicopter, restraining straps, ripping fabric. Voices—lots of voices. A man's green eyes. Excruciating, shooting, stabbing pain. And a horrible, rotting smell.

Recalling that stench made me suddenly nauseated. Which actually brought me out of my brain fog and into a clearer state of mind. I knew now that I was in a hospital, and I flailed for a call button once I discovered I could now open both eyes, hallelujah. But the flailing and searching was to no avail. I lay back and steadied my breath until the urge to vomit passed, and as I did a new barrage of memories—or dreams—flashed in my mind. Running on a trail in the forest. Lying on the forest floor, my arms wrapped around my head. And the face of a huge animal with hot, fishy breath in front of me.

Once again, a desire to barf arose. The machine behind me began to beep rapidly, and a moment later the pink curtain hanging from a ceiling track, which separated me from the door and the world beyond, slid open. A colorful bouquet of wildflowers appeared in someone's arms.

"Oh good, you're awake," a voice behind the flowers said. As the flowers were set down on a small tray across from my bed, a woman in scrubs asked how I was doing. She was short and plump, with a smart little pixie haircut and dark eyes that met mine head-on. Her expression seemed stern, and I felt as I sometimes did when Shane got mad at me, like I wished I could slip out of my skin and slink away.

"I feel sick," I said, my tongue as slow as if buried in fresh concrete. "Sorry."

"Waves of nausea? Pretty common; no need to apologize, dear. We've given you something for your pain. I'll get you some anti-nausea medicine, too. In the meantime, here." She handed me a plastic kidney-shaped bowl. "I'm Ruth, by the way. I'll be taking care of you here in the ER."

"ER?"

"Yep. You're at Snake River Medical Center in Idaho Falls, in case you're wondering." She walked behind my bed and tended to the machines. "We're a Level II Trauma Center. You're in good hands."

"Like Allstate?"

Ruth didn't laugh, but when she came back around into my line of sight, her eyes were smiling and her face had softened. "I see you're a feisty one. Good for you. Humor goes a long way around here."

She took a doll-sized paper cup from a dispenser near the sink and filled it with water. Thank God, I thought. I was dying of thirst. But she poured the water into the vase.

"You've got a husband? Or boyfriend?"

"Husband."

"Beautiful taste in flowers."

"I doubt he knows I'm here."

"Here," she said, handing me the florist's card after pulling it out from the envelope.

As I reached out, I winced.

"I'll check with Doctor about more pain medication, too."

I thanked her, then read the florist's note.

"Well?" Ruth asked, as if she had a right to know who'd sent the bouquet. It was a nice collection; I especially liked the sunflowers.

"It says 'Palmer.' I don't know anyone named Palmer. Are you sure they're for me?"

She showed me the florist's envelope. It read *Grizzly Bear Woman*.

"Do you know why you're here? Do you remember anything?"

"Not exactly." I threw my left arm over my eyes to block the overhead fluorescent light. "I'm getting snippets of flashbacks. Or dreams. Can't tell which."

"You had a run-in with a grizzly bear, I'm told."

I listened to the faucet running again and asked for water.

"Not yet, honey. Not until we hear from Doctor." She poured more water into the vase, then adjusted my pillows and my drip line. "Anything else I can do for you?"

"Track down my husband," I said. "Make sure he knows where I am."

"I'll go see about that right now.

I lay there for an interminably long time, rolling in and out of sleep. I recalled the time when Carson had gotten hit in the head with a flying baseball bat and we'd rushed him off to the ER. He lay on a gurney for hours, complaining not of pain but of how bored he was.

I wondered if Ruth would be able to reach Shane. And if he would call the kids. Not that I wanted them to worry. Carson, in his senior year at Indiana University, was undoubtedly already in the thick of classwork, and Delaney was still getting settled into this new phase of her life as a freshman co-ed. I wouldn't want to upset them, and there was certainly no need for them to come out here and miss classes on my account. Unless I was dying.

But Shane? He'd surely take time off work for an emergency like this. He'd want to be certain I was getting the best care. On the other hand, if he didn't come, I could avoid feeling ashamed for abruptly leaving him, the way I had that night. I could avoid the need to apologize just yet. And I could suppress the guilt that was already simmering about this bear attack, which I already knew was somehow my fault.

My ruminations were interrupted by two doctors entering my room. One—the shorter one with neatly cropped blond hair—came around to the left side of my bed and introduced himself as Dr. Redstone, a surgeon. The other was Dr. Hill, the attending doctor in the ER who stood a head taller than Dr. Redstone and had obsidian black hair and eyes. He stood to my right. Both of them looked like they belonged on the cover of GQ, right down to their hands.

"I'd like to say welcome to Snake River Medical Center," Dr. Redstone said. "But I suspect you'd rather be anywhere else but here."

The two doctors smiled at each other—a rehearsed line no doubt. I tried to smile, too, but as my lips began to curl, my right cheek immediately felt as if it were being shredded.

"It looks like you've had quite an ordeal," Dr. Hill said, placing his hand on the bedrail beside me. "But we're happy to report some good news. We think you're going to make a full recovery."

"I am?" Now, instead of nausea, a wave of relief coursed through me.

They nodded in unison.

"Still, a trip to the operating room will be in order," Dr. Redstone said. "Tonight."

"Surgery?" The only time I'd ever gone under the knife was to have my wisdom teeth removed.

"I'm afraid so," the tall doctor said. "For one thing, we need to debride and irrigate—deep clean—your wounds. Infection is a major concern with this sort of injury, and we need to avoid any chance of sepsis. Lucky for you, Dr. Redstone's one of the best surgeons around."

Dimples appeared on Dr. Redstone's magazine cover face.

"Also, we'll need to do some surgical repair work on your right leg. An orthopedic surgeon will be here momentarily to talk to you about that."

"All of these procedures are pretty routine," Dr. Redstone said. He stepped a few inches closer.

"What about my face?" I had no mirror, but I knew. "And my eyes."

"Actually, your face wounds are relatively superficial," Dr. Redstone said. He drew one of those lighted pen things from his pocket and told me to follow the light. "Your eyes look fine to me but I can send a specialist in if that will make you feel better."

I told him how I had only been able to open one eye at first.

"That may have been from the immediate trauma; there aren't any lacerations within a couple of centimeters of your eye. But like I said I'll have someone come in to verify. Overall, I'm quite confident you're going to be fine. Any residual scars should be minimal and can be addressed with surgery down the road. Nothing to worry about at this point."

I couldn't help but wonder, even in my medicated state, what he meant by *relatively superficial*. Or if these doctors really knew what they were doing, despite what Ruth had said. I asked if they had much experience with bear attacks.

"We get maybe a couple of maulings a year. Which means we've probably got more experience than anyone else around."

"So Ruth was right? I'm in good hands?"

"Just like Allstate," Dr. Hill said.

An involuntary smile tried to surface.

The orthopedic surgeon showed up next. It was practically a party, with everyone squeezing into my small space. She looked fresh out of medical school but exuded confidence and authority. After introductions, she said she'd just come from examining the X-ray and CT results. I didn't even remember having those tests.

"Your right fibula was snapped. The tibia was also fractured. It's common for both of these injuries to occur at the same time. We'll go in, have a look around, and probably place some rods or plates and screws in there to get you fixed up. Oh, and the X-ray showed a darkening of the fatty tissue-filled space in front of your Achilles tendon. If it's ruptured, we'll take care of that as well."

"My Achilles?" I said. "Ruptured? That can't be. I'm a runner. I'm doing the Portland Marathon in October. Besides, the pain is everywhere *but* in my heel."

The three doctors shrug-nodded at one another. Code for something I couldn't decipher.

"I *will* be able to run in the marathon, won't I?"

The orthopedic surgeon said I would run again. "But not so soon. You'll have to miss this year's marathon, I'm sorry to say."

A searing current raced down my leg, like a gossipmonger hurrying to spread bad news. This would have been my first marathon, and I'd trained hard. I'd also fought hard with Shane for the right to run it. Ever since *his* decision to run—for the House of Representatives in the next election—his political aspirations took priority over everything else. Perhaps rightfully so; after all, he was the primary breadwinner in our household. But the marathon had been *my* dream for years, so when he scheduled a fund-raising event for the same weekend, I balked and told him he'd have to go solo for that one. After sulking awhile, he said no. *There will be other races.* My place was at his side, he also said. I needed to get with the program. I should support him, given everything he'd done for me over the years.

"There's only one thing that would make me miss this marathon," I'd said. "Death."

Shane had laughed until he realized I was—maybe for the first time in our marriage— standing my ground.

"There will be other marathons," the surgeon said, echoing Shane. "The good news is that the bear's teeth and claws missed your femoral artery—barely. They also missed your organs and the nerves in your lumbar region. So you will heal. It'll take time, and hard work, but eventually you'll be fine."

Eventually.

"You've been through a major trauma. Give yourself a break," Dr. Hill said, handing me a box of tissues. I hadn't realized I'd been tearing up. "Get some rest now. We'll check in again shortly before the procedures."

I asked how long until the surgery and how long I'd be there in the hospital.

"We're working on pulling together the staff and everything we need for the surgery right now," Dr. Redstone said. "It shouldn't be much more than a couple of hours until we're ready for you. Post-op, we'll talk about wound care and rehab. We'll likely have you out of here in a couple of days."

I slept in spurts until Ruth returned.

She checked my vitals. "Looking good."

"I don't feel like I'm looking good."

"I know. But you will soon enough. We're going to fix you all up. As hard as it might seem right now, you're in a better place than the bear."

"You're going to have to explain that one to me."

"Whenever there's a bear attack on a human, everyone gets in a dither about what to do with the bear. It's not the bear's fault, honey. But it's not yours, either—don't get me wrong. You were both just in the wrong place at the wrong time." She adjusted something on a machine behind me. "It won't be long now till they come for you for surgery. Can I get you anything in the meanwhile?"

"Something to drink?" I was even more parched than earlier.

"Not yet, sorry. But I will get a sponge lollipop for you. Anything else?"

"Do you know where my stuff is? My backpack? Or my phone?"

"Let's take a look." She held up a plastic bag that had been stashed on a shelf under the hospital bed.

Only my shoes and phone were there. "Where are my clothes? My running tights? My top? Or my backpack?"

"They probably kept some of your belongings for DNA testing. I'll check for you."

"DNA?"

"Mm-hmm. Sometimes the park wants us to save clothes and other personal effects that might help them identify which bear did this. I'm guessing they also swabbed around your bite marks. Just like CSI." Ruth had a hearty laugh. A kind laugh. "Boy, I'll say one thing." She pulled a chair next to the bed. "You sure are a strong one. You've been through quite the nightmare today. A lot of patients wouldn't hold together so well at a time like this. By the way, I've been trying to reach your husband. So far, I'm only getting voicemail." She confirmed the numbers she'd been calling; they were accurate. "I'm sorry I haven't gotten through to him."

"Shane's a busy man."

Ruth nodded and gave me a half-smile. "I'll keep trying. But first I'll go get those lollipops for you."

After she left, I dozed on and off again. When I awoke, I realized I'd been dreaming about Ruth. She sat on a rock near a trickling creek, busily attaching feathers to a woven circle of yarns. The water was soothing, rhythmic, sensual—like water gurgling in a fountain at a spa. And then a bear approached, and I tried to call out to warn her, but she calmly gazed back in my direction. *Don't worry about Grandmother,* she said.

A woman with a clipboard full of forms charged through the pink curtain. She sat in the guest chair, crossed her shapely bare legs, perched the clipboard on top of her knee, and bombarded me with a bunch of questions about my medical history. I answered *no* to every disease and disorder she named. She didn't seem very happy with me, as if I were a student cheating on an exam.

"I can't help it," I said. "I'm incredibly healthy. Or at least I was."

She then asked about my insurance card.

"It's in my running pack," I said, "which apparently has been confiscated by CSI."

With no reaction to my latest attempt at humor, she handed me forms to sign.

"I promise I won't sue," I said as I scribbled my name. "But my husband might. He's an attorney. So don't screw anything up."

This woman could have been a champion poker player. Although I'd meant my comment about Shane as a joke, there was an element of truth. He was known as a formidable opponent in court, meticulously detail oriented in managing our finances, and vehemently opinionated about what he deemed right or fair. Moreover—and ironically—health care was one of his major campaign issues. I didn't look forward to seeing his reaction to my medical bills, even if our insurance paid for most of the expense.

I tried to resume that dream about Ruth and the bear after the forms lady left, but then a young man came into the room.

"Welcome to Grand Central Station," I said.

He peered quizzically at me through his wire-rimmed glasses.

"It's just an expression," I said. "It's been busy in here lately. No rest for the wicked, as my mother used to say."

"Sorry about that," he said. "Maybe this will help." He set up an iPod and dock. "Dr. Hill ordered this."

"Music? Before surgery?"

He laughed. "Yeah, I know. Kinda weird. But he believes in the healing power of music. So if you don't mind, I'll turn it on now."

He dimmed the lights, and as he walked out of the room, a flute began to play: breathy, spiritual, celestial—a sound I'd never tune into on my own.

No dance beat, no lyrics. It reminded me of both a wolf's howl and a bird's song. I listened with my eyes closed, and it seemed as if I were breathing in the notes with each inhalation and breathing out worry each time I exhaled.

Within minutes I felt at peace, suspended in that delicate, stress-free zone between wakefulness and slumber. I envisioned myself back home in my own comfy king-sized bed. But as luxurious as it had once been, it had lately felt toxic, with more and more conflict arising between Shane and me. The strife between us had developed gradually over the years, as I supposed it did for all couples, the same way a mattress gets lumpier over time.

I moved my thoughts into my little home office—a cheerful sunroom just off the kitchen, which I had set up for my online consulting business. I'd tacked postcards depicting my clients' artwork on a bulletin board and huddled various potted plants on a table in front of a side window. But thinking about my room and my business now drew Shane back into my thoughts. He hated the clutter on my desk. He interrupted me all the time when I was in there, even when I'd closed the door. Most importantly, he didn't seem to understand why I'd want to spend my time helping a group of starving artists. He called my business a *hobby,* as if it were something cute and insubstantial.

My thoughts progressed to Carson's room upstairs, decorated with posters of Olympic swimmers, and then to Delaney's, whose lavender walls had been lined with bookshelves since she was in elementary school. She'd held onto books about strong women, but the shelves once lined with romance novels were now barren. Since last spring, she'd been trying to make sense of relationships between men and women—a phase, I assumed—but in her refusal to articulate anything to me, I had been unable to understand exactly what went on in her brain. Parents of other teens assured me this reticence to share her thoughts with me was perfectly normal, especially for the college bound. Even so, I now pictured myself lying down on her bed and snuggling with her old Winnie the Pooh bear as she shared the events of her day with me.

"I see Dr. Hill has introduced you to his medical music theory."

I had nearly fallen back asleep when Ruth's voice startled me. She was dressed in street clothes now. "It won't be long until surgery," she said as she checked my IV and machines. "I'm off duty, but thought I'd stop by on my way out. Can I get you anything? Besides the water that I can't let you have?"

Maybe it was the pain and trauma. Or the long day without food. Or the feeling of being totally alone. Or something about Ruth and her generous spirit. Whatever it was, all emotional hell unexpectedly broke loose. This was not a trickle of tears. This was a torrent, and the more I cried, the more everything hurt.

Ruth pulled the visitor's chair toward the bed.

"I'm sorry, I'm not a crybaby," I blubbered. "I don't know why I'm suddenly losing it."

She patted my hand, although what I really wanted was a great big hug. A goddamn bear hug.

"I understand. You've been through a lot in just one day and you're probably nervous about the surgery. But soon that will be behind you and you'll be on your way home. By the way, we're still trying to get through to your husband."

"The thing is...my husband...Shane. We're...not getting along that well lately." Memories from what happened just before I came to Yellowstone flickered, like lights before a storm. "I don't know if I want to go home."

She squeezed my hand. It felt safe embraced in hers. "Maybe you shouldn't worry about that right now. I think Dr. Hill wanted you to calm down, not get riled up. We'll talk tomorrow, after surgery. All right?"

I knew she wasn't dismissing me the way Shane sometimes did, but when she said the doctor wanted me to calm down, I couldn't help but hear my husband's voice. *Calm down. Get a grip on yourself. We can't solve anything when you're like this.* When had he become so condescending?

Ruth released my hand, patting it gently, then stood to leave.

"Wait. Can I ask you something?" I said.

I told her about the weird dreams I'd had earlier: the one with the dark eyes staring into my soul, and then the one with her sitting by a creek telling me not to worry about Grandmother. "I don't really believe in dreams, and you probably think I'm crazy, but these have me kind of spooked. And like you said, I'm supposed to be trying to stay calm. Do you think they mean anything?"

"Hmm. I'm no expert," she said. "But there are people in these parts who might say those were the eyes of Bear looking into you."

"So the bear that attacked me is haunting me now?"

She held the pink curtain back and smiled. "Quite the opposite. Bear has been important in many native traditions and sometimes is seen as a protector. Also, I've heard that Bear sees and senses things that we humans don't. So maybe this is good that she's showing up in your dreams."

After I assured and reassured Ruth I had everything I needed, she left, and Dr. Hill and an anesthesiologist came into the room, along with another nurse. The anesthesiologist described what he'd be doing during the procedure. Dr. Hill asked if I was ready. The nurse confirmed the sedative was flowing.

"I'll see you on the other side," Dr. Hill said, placing his warm hand on my good arm.

I felt myself letting go of the conscious world as I remembered how Delaney used to drop her binky from her lips when she fell into a deep, hard sleep.

SIX

Anne

ONCE THE DUST—and my nerves—had settled, I placed my sketch-book and Thomas's pistol behind a rock and ran down to the water's edge, dodging the pine-cones and piles of horse excrement left behind and watching over my shoulder for any additional Indians. I immersed my poor feet into the lake and sighed. The cool water soothed my soles but offered little relief for my soul. My heart still raced. Thomas was gone, and I had to collect my wits. How I would do this, I did not know.

By now the sun had risen above the tree line, and it shone down on me like mercy from heaven. I turned to face it, withdrew my feet from the water, and found a patch of soil that had not been tilled by wagon wheels or feet. I lay flat on my back, and it felt divine, lying there by myself as the afternoon heat baked into my bones.

Presently I heard a rustle from behind, and a musky scent wafted toward me. I was no longer alone. Cautiously, I turned over onto my stomach, resigning myself to whatever fate now lay in store for me. To my relief, it was merely a small herd of elk that had come along to graze. They took no notice of me, and I did not fear for my life because these were women elk, and children, too. No antlers were in the mix. I watched them nibble here and there, then gracefully move to another spot, and then another. The sun shone down on them, too, and the scene was one of the most glorious I had ever beheld. A calf moved away from its mother; she made sure to follow close behind. Two elk rubbed their heads against one another as they flicked flies away with their tails. Overhead, two hawks circled the edge of the forest, and a light breeze rippled the lake's surface. Had I not just witnessed what I had, with the Indians and the captive white folk and Thomas being led away by the barrel of what I ultimately realized had been his own rifle, I might have thought I was in heaven, and I was certain that Mr. Thoreau would have agreed with me were he here. I wanted to retrieve my sketch-book from the forest's edge, but it was impossible to coax my body to move. I lazily crossed my arms beneath my head and dozed off.

When I awoke I was famished, and I recalled that Thomas had tied our food in a leather sack and hung it from a branch in the forest the night before. When I had inquired why he did this, he had snapped at me.

"Bears, of course."

He may as well have called me Stupid, given his tone. I wondered now how many bears there really were in these parts. And I also wondered, my mind darting around the way it often does, whether the Indians would be feeding Thomas anything. I cared about my husband, despite some of the awful ways he had treated me and the unrepentant demands he had made of me—and most of all the discomfort to which he had subjected me in our bed, day after day and night after night.

I made my way to the hanging sack, picking the softest path I could for my pitiful bare feet. After some difficulty—and cleverness on my part—I was able to lower the sack to the ground. I quickly devoured a small slab of dried beef, only to discover it made me profoundly thirsty. I was about to return to the lake for water when I heard yet another set of hooves heading in my direction, and I began to wonder if we had inadvertently chosen a highway on which to camp. So many travelers; so much for the peace and quiet of nature.

Soon the riders came into view. Men wearing uniforms. Three men. Military men. Rescue was forthcoming!

I dropped the food sack and ran toward the edge of the woods, my intention being to wave them down, when a small pine-cone affixed itself to the sole of my right foot. I stopped to extricate it, and the riders pulled up their horses at the edge of the water. I endeavored to adjust my dress for propriety's sake.

On the one hand, I so desired to unload my troubles onto them, like depositing an armful of heavy wet laundry onto a table, but on the other, there was something about them that I found unsettling. Their horses looked downtrodden, not like the frisky military horses one sees in parades. The men did not sit upright and proud, as one would expect of military men either. And even from this distance, I saw how their uniforms were disheveled. It was probably my imagination running wild, as Thomas always said it did, but I wondered if these were military men at all, or if they were bandits who had stolen the uniforms, horses, and ammunition from the real, and possibly dead, soldiers.

Indeed, a voice inside my head cautioned me to be wary.

One of them pulled a pistol from a holster and inspected it, reminding me of Thomas's gun. I had set it down, somewhere here in the woods. Now where was it? *Foolish woman.* Yes, Thomas would have been right to call me that now, for I had misplaced what could possibly be my only hope for survival. Not that I had the first inkling how to use it.

The men exchanged words, which I could not hear from my vantage point. One shrugged; another nodded his head toward the woods. *My* woods. Then they kicked their horses' sides and took off, quickly escalating into a full gallop, heading along the same trail that had taken Thomas from me. The entire incident happened quickly, and now as their mounts kicked up yet another burst of dust, it occurred to me they may have been my last chance for rescue. My last chance to see my Thomas again. Now—for the second time in one day—I had been left to fend for myself in this desolate place.

"Wait!" I called.

Thomas always said I was too slow. *You need to think faster, woman! Or life will pass you by!*

"Wait!" I called again. They either did not hear me, or did not want to stop, for they did not turn back.

It was well past noon by now. I collected the food sack and my sketchbook, and after locating Thomas's gun, I returned to sit by the lake. It behooved me to develop a plan. But what should it be: set up camp here, without proper shelter, and hope an honorable traveler would find me before I starved or froze to death? Or head eastward along the trail in Thomas's wake, to who-knew-where, unfamiliar with the terrain but hoping that, as this appeared to be a major trail, I might encounter a Good Samaritan, or Thomas, before my feet gave out or I expired? Or head westward along the trail, back in the direction from which we—and the Indians and unsavory military men—had come, the direction in which Thomas and I had seen hundreds of buffalo with enormous horns? Or try to find my way south to Old Faithful, which Thomas and I had visited earlier in this adventure, where other tourists would be congregated and rangers would be stationed to greet me, if I ever made it there?

I had no compass or map. No canteen for water. No shelter. No boots or slippers or stockings. I was utterly alone. Even the elk had moved on and the hawks had flown away.

I determined one more day here could be advantageous before changing locations. I heard my mother's voice: *if you ever get lost, stay right where you are so I can come and find you.* Mother had died two years ago, never having even seen my wedding day, so she was not about to come and find me now. Still, the sky promised good weather for a while, and at least water was plentiful at the lake. Given the apparent popularity of this location along the trail, it was likely somebody would come along. Eventually.

I took out my sketch-book and began to walk around the water's edge carefully in my bare feet. It was a small lake, by Chicago standards; Thomas had called this a pond and estimated it to be only twenty acres or so in size. It was calm and lovely compared to Lake Michigan, without great winds or pounding waves or deadly currents. The forest came nearly to the shore in several spots, and to the west a creek stole away some of the lake's water. A few careless clouds dropped their picturesque reflections into the water. I was reminded about an article I had recently read about a young artist named Julie Hart Beers, whose water landscape paintings were highly acclaimed. If only I could, one day, be so talented. And so recognized.

I took a seat on a log, fished my pencil out of my pouch, and endeavored to draw the setting in sufficient detail so that, upon returning home, I would have an adequate foundation for a painting. The new impressionistic style had been creating quite a stir in the artist community, and I decided to set the lake off center and include a cluster of wildflowers, bending in the breeze in the foreground. The gloriously colorful petals would be brightened by the penetrating sunlight while also casting shadows on the ground beneath. In my imagination I saw an exquisite masterpiece, and I was initially able to shut out all distractions.

Until I heard a rustling in the woods behind me. *What now?* I peered toward the creek, trying to discern tree trunk from shadow while at the same time encouraging my poor heart to remain calm and steady. It had experienced enough excitement for one day.

"Hello?" I whispered softly at first, as I did not wish to startle anyone, man or beast. When I received no response, I called again three more times, my voice becoming louder with each consecutive attempt, although it also crackled with fear. Still, the only reply returned was that mysterious rustling sound. I picked up Thomas's gun and proceeded toward the trees. "I have no intention of hurting you," I said to whoever or whatever was there. "I simply want to make your acquaintance."

There. Something moved, something large, several feet off the ground. I caught a mere glimpse, but it certainly was not just a fox or squirrel, given its height. I stopped, waited, and then heard the nicker of a horse. How fortunate could I be to have come upon a lost horse!

"Come here, darling," I said in the kindest voice I could muster. I had nothing to offer, no apple or carrot, but I nevertheless held my free hand out toward the horse as I proceeded forward. It stamped a hoof, twice, and soon

I saw it had the same lovely spotted coat as the Indian horses from earlier that morning. It was also covered with beautiful blankets, a saddle, and a roll of animal hides.

I was not twenty feet from it now and able to see a rope hanging loosely from around its neck. The animal was untethered, which likely meant it was lost or a runaway. Indeed! The most precious treasure I could ask for: a horse without a rider. I continued to walk delicately toward it, desperate to make its acquaintance and not frighten it away. When I came within ten feet, the horse shuffled its stance. It was then I discovered, just beyond the horse's belly, a pair of legs dressed in fringed buckskin. And a pair of feet wearing moccasins.

I slapped my hand against my mouth to contain another inevitable gasp.

The legs stepped cautiously toward the rear of the horse, so that I could no longer see them. I slowly raised the gun with my right hand and used my left to steady its shaking partner. I nestled a finger into the curve of the trigger and prayed to the Lord I would not need to pull it, for I had no idea how to aim nor what to expect if I did shoot. I took a step backward. I watched the horse's left eye, staring and blinking at me, for any telltale sign of impending action. I took another step backward, and then a third. On my fourth footfall, the arch of my bare right foot came down on an immensely sharp object. I bit my lip to stifle a cry. Then, when I endeavored to lift my foot from whatever had impaled me, all the while keeping the gun trained on my unidentified target, the confounded hazard—a tree branch with an end as sharp as a spear—refused to release its hold.

I urged it out from my skin. Blood spurted. I gasped, and a veil of heavy blackness descended upon me. As I collapsed to the ground, I heard an *oomph* fly from my lips, and I saw the Indian legs step out from behind the horse.

This was it. This was how my life would end: alone, twenty-seven years old, married with no children. I would perish in the Far West, and no one would ever know my story.

My last two thoughts were thus: I hoped I would not be scalped, and I also hoped no one would discover that, beneath my frock, I was completely indecent.

SEVEN

Brooke

THE ANESTHESIA HAD begun to wear off by the time I was delivered to my new hospital room after the surgery. The pain escalated throughout the rest of the night. Sleep was nowhere to be found.

The smell of coffee and the sound of voices drifted into my room from the hallway early the next morning. Lying on my bed, I strained to listen for Shane's voice. Even though I hadn't wanted him here before the surgery, I did now. I wanted to feel his strong arms around me, to see his perfect smile, to hear him say everything would be all right. But as I lay there waiting, and hoping, I found myself thinking back to all those other times I lay in bed waiting for him to come home from a long day at work. I'd sit up and read or watch TV, anything to fight off sleep, and I'd keep one eye trained on the window, watching for his headlights. Eventually his BMW would come speeding along, and my heart would skip like a little girl playing hopscotch in a playground. Delaney once said I was too dependent on Shane, that I needed him far more than he needed me. She was probably right. But I was devoted to him. And now I needed to know that he was devoted to me. So when footsteps stopped abruptly just outside my door—footsteps that sounded heavy and male—that little girl inside my chest skipped once again.

"Knock, knock," a man said. "Mind if I come in?"

It was a melodious voice. Not Shane's.

An overhead light flickered on, blinding me. When my eyes adjusted, I saw an older gentleman who held himself with authority, like he belonged there. Practically like he owned the place. A hospital administrator, perhaps. Except that he was dressed in a flannel shirt and jeans.

"Can I help you?" I asked. Dumb thing to say; obviously there was nothing I could do to help him, or anyone. Not in my condition. But what are you supposed to say to a strange and handsome—even if substantially older—man when you're lying immobile on a hospital bed, buried in gauze and practically strangled with tubes and hoses?

He smiled down at me, his eyes shining like my emerald earrings back home. There was something familiar about him, but I couldn't figure out what.

He extended his right hand toward me—a tanned, strong hand. "My apologies," he said. "You probably don't remember me. The name's Palmer."

Uncertain how to reply to this stranger, I said nothing.

"Your favorite National Park Ranger? You're Brooke, right?" He glanced at the white board in the room. My name had been printed on it with blue marker. The two o's in my name were shaped like little flowers. As he pulled the visitor's chair closer to my bed, a cart clanged past my door, once again leaving the fragrance of coffee in its wake.

He sat in the chair, crossing his legs and clasping his hands together over the top knee. His lopsided smile reminded me of Harrison Ford. I glanced down to make sure my lovely hospital gown wasn't revealing anything it shouldn't.

"I'm sorry, but I can't place how we know each other," I said.

"Do you remember anything from the bear attack? Anything on the trail?"

"Not really. Not much, anyway."

"That explains it. Why you don't recognize me, I mean. I was the ranger who found you." Looking toward the window, he drew in a deep breath and shook his head. "What a day. Wow. You have no idea what a shock it was to come upon you like that."

An odd thing to say, as if he was the one who'd been traumatized. People say the weirdest things in difficult times.

"Yes, I imagine it was. A shock, that is." And now I remembered those eyes. "I guess I should say thank you. For saving me."

He held his hands up, palms out. "No need to thank me. All in a day's work. I'm just happy, and relieved, to see you doing so well. There was a moment or two when I had my doubts. Anyway, it'll make for a damn good scene in my memoir."

"Your memoir?"

"Don't worry," he said. "I'll change your name if you'd like. But, sure, you'll be in there. As the chief expert on bears and wolves in these parts, I can't leave an incident like this out. My publisher would never go for that."

I admit, I was discombobulated. Instead of Shane, here sat a park ranger who'd come to visit me. And who, instead of seeming concerned for my well-being, seemed focused on his own experience. His demeanor was off-putting, and yet this was the man who had saved my life. I knew I should feel indebted to him.

"I'll look forward to reading it someday," I said to be polite.

He motioned toward the wildflowers on the table. "I thought you might like those."

"Oh, those were from you?" Now I remembered Ruth had read the card, signed by someone named Palmer. "Yes, they're lovely. Thank you so much."

"I know, I know. Sometimes I just can't help myself."

He stood up and rocked back and forth on his toes and heels, adjusting the waistline of his jeans and puffing out his chest. "Well, I guess I'll be off. Two hours, yes two hours, back to West Yellowstone from here, you see."

My pillow slipped off the side of the bed as I tried to sit up. His eyes landed on the pillow now on the floor, but instead of retrieving it for me, he walked over to the flowers and sniffed them. It was as if he was in his own world. I thanked him for the visit, and he waved back at me as he walked out the door, like a celebrity waving to fans as he exited stage right.

A barrage of people kept me busy during the remainder of that first post-op day: nurses, a social worker, the general and orthopedic surgeons, and a national park investigator determined to figure out what happened in order to see if the park needed to take any corrective measures.

"Corrective measures?" I asked. "Against me?"

"No, not against you." She laughed. "We need to figure out what motivated the bear to attack you. In case she needs to be euthanized." The park had determined by now that it was likely a female, given the size of the claw and teeth gashes. I told the investigator what little I could recall, which was primarily just a stinky bear staring into my eyes, saliva dripping down from her very big teeth.

Neither Ruth nor Dr. Hill came to visit me that first day, however, even though they both had said they would. Shane was a no-show, too.

Finally, just as *Jeopardy!* came on the TV, he called. He apologized profusely.

"We had a technology outage at the office yesterday. They still don't have the lines back up. And I dropped my cell phone yesterday and didn't have a chance to get to Verizon until just now, so I couldn't call. It was like *The Twilight Zone*, with no way to get through to you. By the way, when I finally got through to the phone people, I did find out that your data usage is finally under control. Thank you for that."

Here I was, lying in the hospital, and he was worried about my data usage? It could have been laughable, had I been in a different frame of mind. Instead, I gave him the *Reader's Digest* version of all that had transpired. Sounding genuinely concerned, his deep voice was the potion that I'd needed.

"I have to say I was a little peeved that you hadn't found a way to reach me over the last couple of days," he said. "I had no idea where the hell you were. Now I understand. But why on earth did you go to some Podunk hospital in the middle of nowhere?"

There. That was the sort of Shane comment that sent me into a tizzy. Always convinced he knew best, he had a habit of second-guessing everyone, including me. I often had to justify my decisions to him.

"I'm here because this is where the EMTs brought me, I guess. I didn't have much say in the matter. It all happened so—"

"We'll get to the details of what happened later. Believe me, because I'll need to know what our legal rights are. But first, we've got to get you out of there. No sense paying out-of-network hospital bills to a bunch of country bumpkins. I'll make arrangements to get you back to Portland right away. I know people here. I know a lot of doctors...*good* doctors."

There was nothing I wanted more than to hang up on him. He didn't even bother to ask whether I thought my care was adequate. And his attitude suggested that the kind people here, like Ruth and Dr. Hill, couldn't be trusted to be competent. I knew he meant well, but he was focused on all the wrong things.

"Shane. Listen to me. I was mauled by a grizzly bear, a wild animal five times my size. I've got a dozen lacerations all over my body that are susceptible to infection. My leg was broken in two places. My Achilles was ruptured. I doubt your doctor friends have any experience with that. And this hospital does. It's a Level II Trauma Center."

Another pause. More information processing.

"You're Achilles was ruptured? So...you're not running the marathon?"

"Right."

I knew he was thinking about his fund-raiser, and I hoped he didn't have the audacity to bring it up now. Putting on a sparkly evening gown and plastering a never-ending smile on my face—and spending a tabloid-worthy evening among rich people with egos the size of the Greater Yellowstone Region—was the last thing I'd want to do in lieu of the marathon.

"So when are you coming?" I asked.

"I don't think I can, Babe. I've got some commitments I can't get out of."

My body suddenly felt deflated, as if flattened by an overwhelming fatigue. What prior commitments take precedent over your wife's traumatic injuries? He didn't say anything after that. After you've been married to someone for a couple of decades, you know how to interpret these conversational lulls. This one wasn't because he wasn't sure what to say. This one meant he had become distracted by something else: an email notification, perhaps, or a touchdown on a muted TV. Or last February's swimsuit edition of *Sports Illustrated*, which kept resurfacing to the top of his magazine stack in the bathroom. After hearing he wasn't going to bother to come to the hospital, there wasn't any more reason to stay on the line.

"I've got to go, Shane. The doctor's here." I had never lied to my husband before. But things were different now. Although I'd experienced his distraction a thousand times before, I'd never done so in a situation like this. I was exploring new terrain.

I started to set the receiver down, but then remembered the kids. "Wait. Did you tell Carson or Delaney what happened to me?" Instead of hearing his reply, I heard a dial tone.

When Dr. Hill came into my room the next day, I was still miffed that he'd stood me up post-op despite his promise to visit. But I was also grateful he was here now. Something about him was so comforting. He sat down in the visitor's chair and leaned back, as if planning to stay awhile. I pulled my sheet up to my neck, wondering how bad I smelled. I had now gone three days without a shower. Sponge baths just weren't the same.

The doctor was tall like Shane, with dark eyes and thick hair like Shane. Except the doctor didn't pull his hair back into a ponytail. Despite Shane's conservative political stance, he'd always been proud of that rebelliously long hair and the reactions it drew. For me, that one wild streak had been evocative in our youth and, in later years, had mitigated the tension between us that grew out of his increasingly bullheaded viewpoints. Dr. Hill would have looked handsome with a ponytail, too.

"I heard you're about to be discharged," the doctor said.

My good spirits quickly disappeared, despite his warm smile. I suddenly felt like I was being abandoned, as if he was breaking up with me. "I'm not sure I'm ready to leave," I said.

"Your attending says you're ready."

"You mean my insurance company."

"That, too."

"Well, neither my attending nor my insurance company knows my full story. I've just started to get some rest. People have been buzzing around me for days, like social butterflies around sugar." As soon as I said it, I recognized my error. I could hear Shane's voice. *Honey, Brooke. You mean like bees around honey. You've got to stop confusing your idioms and metaphors.* And then he'd laugh. Even though love isn't supposed to laugh at mistakes.

"I don't mean to whine or sound ungrateful," I said. "I'm just exhausted. And on top of that, the pain's still really bad. I don't think they're giving me enough medication."

"I'll talk to the attending. Meanwhile, I brought you some music to transition by." He reached into a canvas briefcase and retrieved his iPod and its dock. I hadn't noticed before my surgery that the device was practically a collectible—possibly the first generation iPod. He set it on the table beside me and powered it on. Quiet drums, like heartbeats, began to fill the air, followed by soft whistling sounds, like wind breezing through a stand of reeds. And finally a lone—but joyful—flute.

"Brooke, it's normal for patients to go home exhausted from the hospital. And for the pain to be worse on the second day, when your tissues have swollen. And it's also normal for patients to feel uncomfortable—even wary—at the thought of going home. As long as you have someone with you, not only to help get around and take care of your daily needs but also to help with any emotional ups and downs, you'll be fine."

He pulled his wallet out, slipped out a business card, and wrote a phone number on the back. "This is my cell phone number. Call me anytime." He stood to leave, running his hands down the front of his slacks to smooth out the wrinkles.

Shane smoothed his wrinkles out the same way, always achieving an impeccable appearance. Normally I appreciated how put together he always was. But the last time I saw him do that was when he stepped out of the taxi that brought us home from the airport the day we'd delivered Delaney and Carson to college. Who cares how you look when you get home from a long, emotional trip? I was a frightful mess. I'd cried on the plane all the way from Indianapolis to Denver, and even after he upgraded me to first class for the second leg of the trip, from Denver to Portland, I sniffled and sputtered. It wasn't just sending the kids off to college; it was sending Delaney off without any sort of reconciliation between us. A mother can't just let go like that.

The rest of that evening turned out to be the beginning of the end. By the time we arrived home, my outfit was wrinkled, my sweater stained with spilled coffee, and my eyes red and swollen. Shane brought the luggage into the house. I stomped up the stairs. I ripped off my clothes, throwing them in a heap on the floor, and jumped into the shower. While I used up every molecule of hot water in the house, he ran out to a local gourmet market. That's what was so exasperatingly confusing about him: sometimes, he could be the best husband ever. He came home with king salmon and a bouquet of long-stemmed pink roses. He set the table with linen napkins and our wedding china. He opened a bottle of sparkling wine. I finally came downstairs in my running attire, unaware of all that he had done.

After handing me a glass of wine and toasting to our new empty nest, Shane took me by the hand into the garage to show me the surprise he had waiting for me.

I broke down all over again.

"Stop that," he said. "You should be happy for the kids and stop feeling sorry for yourself. It's time to focus on us again, as an empty nested couple. And on your marathon. And on my campaign. And oh, by the way, you could show a little gratitude while you're at it."

I told him I was happy, and grateful—the latter being a stretch—but that I was also still grieving. "It's the end of one stage in our lives to which we'll never return. And so much uncertainty lies ahead. You don't just flip a switch gracefully. Change is a process. It'll take time for me to deal with this new empty nest lifestyle. It'll take time for me to become comfortable in the role of politician's wife." I didn't say it would take time to get used to that god-awful vehicle. What made him think I'd want to drive a Corvette? And a red one at that?

We made our way to the dining room, solemn as mourners at a funeral. He brought the salmon in from the grill.

"I think I need to take a break," I said. "To go away for a while. Take a sabbatical."

"A what? What the hell are you talking about?"

I hadn't given this an ounce of thought and blurted out the first thing that came to mind, which, surprisingly, wasn't a trip to someplace exotic like Nepal or Machu Picchu or a week-long pampering session at a desert spa.

"I'd like to go to Yellowstone," I said. "Yes, I've always wanted to go back to Yellowstone, and now seems as good a time as any." In my previous life, before Shane, I had been quite the outdoors enthusiast, and for years I'd been trying to get him, and the kids, to go to Yellowstone, or Taos, or various other outdoorsy places. But they never wanted to go. "I think I'm going to go to Yellowstone, Shane. By myself. Without you. I'm going to take a sabbatical and train for the marathon there."

It had been a spontaneous decision and announcement. I had erroneously given zero thought to how he might respond. But even so, his sarcasm surprised me. When he asked since when did *housewives* take sabbaticals, something inside me snapped. All the years of diapers and Little League and college essays came tumbling back to me.

"Mothers deserve sabbaticals as much as anyone," I snapped back, and if he had replied any other way, I might not have been lying in a hospital bed now. But he smirked, and that did it. One of my hands, as if operated by an evil puppeteer behind a hidden curtain, picked up the vase of roses he'd just bought and heaved it at him. I don't even know if the vase hit him; I stormed out of the dining room and back upstairs. Less than thirty minutes later, I was out the door without a goodbye. And by the next morning, I was paying for my entrance pass to Yellowstone National Park.

We had spoken little since then. Neither of us had apologized. The thought now of returning home to him as an invalid, needing his 24/7 care, was simply unfathomable.

"I'm not going home," I now said to Dr. Hill, like a smartass teenager. "I'm sorry. I know this isn't your problem. But you can't make me go home. Isn't there a hospital social worker I can speak with? Maybe she can help me make other arrangements."

"Yes," he said. "There is. But hold off on talking to her. I have another idea."

EIGHT

Anne

IF ONLY I had been dreaming. Quite the contrary, I found myself lying next to a small camp-fire when I awoke, and an Indian girl sat beside me with my injured foot in her lap. For all I knew she was preparing to slice it off and roast it over the open fire.

I peered at her as best I could from my supine position. She was young—barely a woman—and diminutive in stature, with black hair that hung in two braids and a patch of red on her cheek. My first thought was that it was my blood, although I later concluded it was a sort of paint. Her hands were tiny but strong and graceful as she inspected my wound.

I tried to kick, but she held my foot so solidly, my only hope for immediate escape would be to leave my appendage behind. When I saw the large knife in a leather sheath hanging from her belt, I determined that my demise was imminent.

Our eyes quickly met, then darted away.

Although my heart beat like a rabbit running from a fox, an unexpected sentiment of awe arose in my mind. The girl's buckskin dress was so exquisitely adorned with glass beads and shells that I fancied her to be more of an artisan than a savage. She also wore a leather pouch around her waist that was not unlike my own for pencils. On the other hand, there was that knife, and also a strand of animal teeth and claws hanging about her neck.

It occurred to me, then, that we were not positioned where I had fallen. The girl had carried or dragged me from the forest to the lake. My sketch-book lay next to me, no doubt her idea of kindling. My bonnet lay beside me as well, already removed so she could scalp me, I supposed. What a prize she would have with my long, wavy locks!

Suddenly my foot stung as though bitten by a bumblebee. "Ow!" I said, again trying to kick free, and again succumbing to the girl's firm grip. Presently, I felt a moist poultice on the bottom of my foot. Poison, I assumed. When I tried to kick for the third time, she straddled me so that I could neither roll over nor otherwise escape her torture.

"Let me go!" I said. "Let me go, you savage!" Edgar had been right about those Indians.

She did not simply let go. She let my foot drop to the ground and promptly climbed off me. I rolled over and sat upright, now discovering that she had unsheathed her knife and held it out in front of her as she backed away from me toward her horse. Her breath was heavy, her face alarmed. She held one hand behind her back. Good, I thought. Perhaps now we were on equal ground. But then I realized this could be my third chance for rescue in one day. To let this one slip away would be foolish indeed.

"Wait," I said, as though she could understand me, while trying to recollect how Thomas had greeted the Indian we had encountered at Old Faithful.

"How," I then said, at first tentatively and then again with feigned confidence. "How." I raised my right arm and showed her my palm while trying to force a smile on my trembling lips as I cautiously stood. By now she had reached the horse, and as she reached for its flank, I saw what she had been holding behind her back. Thomas's gun! She had the knife, the horse, and my husband's gun. I had only my bonnet, sketch-book, and pencils.

She pointed at my dirty feet, where she had left a large shell. It was shaped like an egg but was shiny and curled tightly in on itself, with only a small slit for an opening. I had seen shells like that in a souvenir shop along the Atlantic City boardwalk, when Thomas and I traveled there for our honeymoon. Surely this girl had not been to Atlantic City! She then shoved her knife back into its sheath, clambered up onto the horse faster than I could climb onto my four-poster bed at home, and pointed the gun at me with a strong and steady hand.

I picked up the shell; it was still warm from her grasp. I sniffed it; the poultice she had been applying to my foot was inside. Perhaps, after all, she had been trying to help me.

"Wait!" I said. "How." I held my palm up to her again. "How, sorry."

The girl sat motionless on the horse, her blank face reminding me of Thomas's expression whenever he becomes perplexed about one of my many errors. Then she whispered softly—a word I could not understand—and the horse began to prance.

"No, please wait," I said, hobbling toward her. To lose her would be intolerable. "I am sorry. I am stupid. Please do not leave me here alone."

She gently tugged on the horse's mane. The animal stopped. Gun still aloft, she slid back down from the horse, keeping her gaze affixed on me as if trying to divine my motivation. Slowly, she approached. She crossed her legs and sat down by the fire. She opened her palm, an invitation for me to sit again. I obeyed.

After setting the gun at her side, she gently lifted my leg and placed it across her lap. She took the shell from my perspiring hand and tapped it against her other hand. A thick substance oozed from the slit in its side. She dipped a finger into the poultice and applied it to my foot.

"Ow." It still stung. But she held my captive foot firm and massaged the wound with the salve while keeping her eyes focused not on me but on something in the east, perhaps the trees reflected in the shimmering water upside down, or perhaps something well beyond them. She said something in Indian, a word or phrase with so many sounds and syllables that I could not have repeated it had she held Thomas's pistol to my head. Then she laughed, or at least I thought it was a laugh, but it sounded more like a puppy's yip than the laughter I knew. When she was done applying the salve, she wrapped my foot in a small piece of animal hide she produced from her leather belt and then tied the bandage together with a long piece of grass.

"Thank you," I said.

Presently, she handed my sketch-book to me, then proceeded to tend the camp-fire, adding small bits of dry wood bit by bit. I inched forward and picked up some slivers of wood to help, but she motioned me away as though I were a nuisance child—even though I was clearly much older than she. I retreated to my comfortable spot.

She moved with such purpose, such grace, neither too quick nor too slow, but with efficiency. As she did her work, I began to do mine. I liked to think of my art as my work, although Thomas would scoff if I called it that. *Child's play. That's what it is.* Using small, light strokes on my paper, I began with an outline of her entire form, and then I filled in shadows and details. I paid careful attention to her braids and the ornaments around the neckline of her dress, as well as the fringe at its hem. I became so engrossed in my project that I didn't hear her walk away. It was only when I heard her horse's galloping hooves that I realized she had left me.

Yet again, I was alone, the afternoon sun ready to leave me as well. It was not just fear I now experienced. Already, I was grieving for my new friend. I did not even know the little heathen's name.

A near eternity passed before she finally came riding along, with a small, skinned carcass impaled on a sturdy branch that was no wider in diameter than my thumb. Thomas's gun was tucked into her leather belt, along with a gray rabbit pelt. Without acknowledging my existence, she set about building up the camp-fire and arranging several large pine-cones on it. A rich, medicinal aroma arose. She was cooking the animal's innards.

When the liver was done, she set it aside and proceeded to balance the skinned carcass, once again impaled on the branch, over the fire. As it roasted, she took a bite of the liver, then handed it to me. It was tough, ugly, and bland. Some minced shallot, cracked pepper, and a splash of Sherry would have improved it immensely. But I was so hungry, I gobbled it down, and when the rest of the meat was done, we both ate as though we had not eaten in weeks. Once sated, she set to work preparing the hide by cleaning away what skin remained, stretching it over a platform she'd built from twigs, and sprinkling something white all over it, which she had retrieved from her saddlebag.

"What is that?" I asked, pointing to the white granules.

Her scrutiny of my face, every feature one by one, reminded me of Thomas when he sometimes suggested I might very well belong in an asylum for the insane. She poured some granules into the palm of her hand and proffered them to me. I dipped my finger in and touched it to the tip of my tongue.

Salt. Good old Onondaga salt. If only we had used it with the liver.

It was now dusk, and I had spent the entire day sitting by the fire like a good-for-nothing princess while the Indian girl had worked so hard, and for me. Even now, she was not finished. She retreated to the forest, where she set up a makeshift shelter of sapling trunks covered with a roll of animal hides she removed from the back of her saddle. She yanked tall blades of wild grass with feathery plumes out of the ground near the lake and sprinkled them on the floor of the shelter. Indeed, I was mesmerized as a child might be watching her mother tend to the myriad of household needs. It felt splendid to be nurtured this way.

She gathered all the remaining rabbit parts and stashed them into another pouch that she had plucked from a large saddlebag—which appeared to be an endless trove of tools and treasures. She tied the pouch closed with a rope, paced off a hundred feet from the shelter, then swung the rope with such precision that it caught a branch on her first try. Expertly, she raised the meat cache over the branch.

Upon her return, I gestured to the ground next to me, by the warm camp-fire. "Sit."

A leaf was stuck in her hair, and as I reached to remove it, she flinched, raising the elbow of her right arm as though to block me. I placed one of my hands on that arm, gently, and slowly reached for the leaf. When I untangled it from her hair, I showed it to her. She took it, smiled, then tossed it into the breeze. Together, we watched it flutter away.

"Look," I said. I held my sketch-book halfway between my lap and hers. "I want to show you what I worked on today."

I was not sure I wanted to reveal my work—I was usually much more tentative about doing so, especially because Thomas had little appreciation for my talent—but I wanted in some way to justify all the time I had spent sitting idly while she had worked so industriously. Not that artwork counted for much given all she had done, but the truth of the matter was that I had no idea how to live out in the wilderness. I could have already perished without her. Also, I believed showing her my sketch-book might develop a bond in the same way one does when sitting down to read with a child.

She took the book from me and opened it. The first few pages were sketches of Yellowstone that I had made on previous days: one of Old Faithful, one of an elk with many points on his antlers, and one of the trees silhouetted against a cloud-ridden sky. Then came the sketch I had begun at the lake earlier that very day, when the elk had come to visit, which was still unfinished. She ran her fingers across it gently, as one might run her fingers across a baby's face.

When she turned to the fifth page, she let go of my book as though it scalded her hand.

It was the sketch of her tending the fire.

"This is you. See? There you are. I drew this picture for you." I pointed to the braids in the sketch, then gently touched one of hers. I pointed to the V-shaped ornamentation on the dress in the sketch, then to hers. "See how beautiful you are?" I pointed to the face of the girl in the sketch, then tentatively touched her cheek. "Beau-ti-ful."

She pressed her index finger onto the sketch and ran it down from top to bottom, from braids to moccasins. I wished she would not press so hard; the pencil was beginning to smear. She held the page so close to her eyes that her nose nearly touched the paper, then pulled it away from her face, stretching her arms as far as they would reach. She tilted it from one side to the other. Perhaps she needed glasses, I mused. Or perhaps she could not see it well in the waning light. But then she placed one finger of her right hand on the knife sheath in the image as she placed all four fingers of her left hand against her breast.

"No pouch."

No pouch? She was right. I had forgotten that accessory. But it was such a little thing. I was indignant that, instead of admiring the work I had done, with all of its intricate detail, she had found the one mistake I made. And then I realized what had just happened.

She had spoken. In my language. Her fierce eyes glistened.

This new development gave me great cause for consternation. Our relationship had been clarified. This girl had not simply taken responsibility for our survival and tended to my medical needs. She had, all the while, withheld important information. She was clever. Cunning. The question was whether she could be trusted. I reviewed the events of the day in my mind, attempting to assure myself that I was not imperiled, and had nearly satisfied my endeavor until I recalled how I had previously referred to her. I had called her a savage.

You fool, I heard Thomas say.

Perhaps she had not understood that word, *savage*. Perhaps she only knew a few words in English.

"No, no pouch," I said, desperate to discover what she did and did not comprehend.

She stood, then extended her hand down toward me. "Come."

Another English word.

With moderate difficulty, I hoisted myself up from the ground. Together, we sprinkled dust over the dwindling fire. She carried the gun. With my sketch-book and bonnet in hand, I followed her into the woods, hampered only nominally by my injury. We came upon the modest shelter she had prepared. She gestured for me to lie down on one of the horse's blankets inside. I did as she insisted, and she flapped a second blanket over me. She curled into a ball alongside, on the barren ground, facing me. She smelled of wood and smoke. A mere six inches distanced our respective noses; our knees touched. Her knife and Thomas's gun lay between us.

NINE

Brooke

TWO ORDERLIES HAD carefully positioned me in the back seat of Ruth's Ford Explorer later that day, and now we were en route toward Yellowstone, where my adventure had begun less than a week but more than a lifetime ago. Dr. Hill had arranged for me to stay with his cousin Leila for a while. He'd also arranged for Ruth to drive me there. When I asked Ruth, as we drove out of Idaho Falls, how he managed to pull all this together, she said sometimes the universe just aligns like that. She also told me to stop scratching at my scabs, which were already beginning to itch like mad.

I liked Ruth. I also liked her reply. I'd always had a theory that the universe is destined to find balance. One person gains weight, another drops pounds. A person dies, a baby is born. Each war cry is echoed by a call for peace. And every wound is offset by an act of kindness. I didn't ask why they had gone the extra mile for me; I decided just to accept what was offered with whatever modicum of grace I could muster.

Dr. Hill did tell me that Leila had been living temporarily in West Yellowstone, Montana, while taking care of her aging grandmother. The old woman had recently passed away, and now Leila was sorting through all the belongings, getting the house in order, and otherwise settling the estate.

"She might only be there a couple more weeks," he told me. "But maybe that gives you enough time to collect yourself."

Collect? That sounded as if I were scattered all over the place. In a way, I guess I was.

I had tried to call Shane before leaving the hospital, although I still didn't really want to talk to him. There was too much that needed to be said. So when I got routed directly to his voicemail, I was relieved, and I left only the briefest possible message: I was heading back to Yellowstone. No forwarding address.

He called back while I was in the car with Ruth, while I still had cell service. He asked what the hell I thought I was doing, heading back to Yellowstone instead of coming home to Portland. I told him I wasn't sure.

"All my stuff is back there at the motel where I was staying. I need to collect it...and my thoughts."

His failure to reply prompted me to check my service. I still had four bars.

"You need to get your butt home right away," he said finally, the same way he had talked to the kids when they missed curfew.

"How dare you tell me to get my butt home."

"Well, listen to yourself, Brooke. You're not making any sense. What kind of drugs do they have you on?"

I held the phone away from my ear as he went off on me. When his voice started cutting out, I checked my cell service again. I was down to one bar. Thank you, Verizon.

The last thing I heard him say was something about how I couldn't expect him to run a campaign and household by himself for much longer. Clearly, the stress of the campaign was getting to him, which I'd been worried about from the start. Or maybe it was the stress of my absence. Maybe he really did love and miss me. A part of me thought I should be heading directly home to him. But then Ruth winked at me in the rearview mirror. Shane's worries about the household seemed pretty lame; we had gardeners and cleaning ladies to help. All Shane would have to do was his own laundry—which he usually sent out anyway because I didn't make his shirts look crisp enough—and water my houseplants and find a way to feed himself. Given that Portland was consistently included on the top ten lists of restaurants—it actually ranked higher than Chicago and New York in a recent *Washington Post* article—I was pretty sure he wouldn't starve.

I didn't know if it was a dropped call or if Shane hung up, but I didn't care. In fact, sitting there in the backseat of Ruth's car, in the wide-open landscape framed by mountains and dotted with antelope in the shadowy grasslands, I felt pretty good despite my post-op discomfort. I actually felt proud of myself for standing up to him, and standing up for myself, figuratively speaking.

Less than two hours after leaving the hospital, the sun touched down on the horizon behind us. Ruth switched on her headlights, and a few minutes later her turn signal. We pulled off the highway onto a remote gravel road nearly hidden by trees and brush.

"This is it?"

She nodded. "Welcome to Maggie's Place."

"Maggie?"

"Long story. I'm sure Leila will tell you about Maggie eventually."

Her SUV bumped over the gravel, and I felt every pothole in my wounds. "I'm going to need some more meds when we get inside."

The gravel road dog-legged to the right, and once we came around the bend, I spotted an old log cabin sorely in need of some TLC. A single window was lit up by an interior lamp. There wasn't even a porch light on to welcome us. This wasn't at all what I'd envisioned.

"I'll just run up to the door," she said. "Stay put."

Ruth had to be at least sixty, but she had the energy of a child. She hurried toward the cabin as if anxious to meet a long lost friend. I peered through the car windows at the surrounding property. The eastern sky was eerie and purple as amethyst. Finally, a porch light illuminated.

Ruth came back toward the car with a woman at her side. I guessed her to be seven or eight years younger than me. She was taller than Ruth, but nearly everyone was. Even in the dim light, I could tell she had long black hair and a slim, athletic build.

Ruth opened the back seat door. "Come, Brooke. Come and meet Leila."

The dome light revealed how stunning Leila was. She could easily have been a model. As she helped me maneuver out of the car and into the wheelchair with my big therapy boot, I was especially drawn in by her dark, expressive eyes. And her skin, smooth and blemish-free, except for a tiny silvery scar above her left eyebrow. She smelled minty, as if she'd just come out of the shower. I felt weak, germy, and completely inferior in her presence.

The cabin was much lovelier on the inside than the outside would suggest. Small and quaint, maybe, but clean and functional with pine and leather furniture. American Indian blankets draped over, and kilim pillows dotted, the sofa and chairs. Rugs of jute and other natural fibers were scattered atop the wide-plank floors. Original works of modern art in geometric designs hung on the walls, and one impressionistic painting of the Yellowstone grasslands, with dozens of bison, hung over the sofa. Shelves were filled with hand-thrown pottery, baskets, and books. The air was perfumed with a floral scent wafting from a candle, and all sorts of cacti and houseplants were positioned throughout. Shane, always preferring contemporary and maintenance-free simplicity, would have hated it. No rustic décor for him. Which made the new rebel in me love it all the more.

Leila invited us into the kitchen for chamomile tea, and my eyes were immediately drawn to the bank of windows at the far side of the room. It was nearly black outside by now, but the night was interrupted by a solitary light that appeared to be a hundred or so feet beyond the cabin. I wondered who, or what, was out there.

Ruth and I sat at the old pine table while Leila stood at the stove, waiting for her kettle to sing.

"Don't mind the mess," Leila said, pointing to two stacks of various-sized cardboard boxes next to the back door. "That's my project. And I've only just begun."

"Are you going through Emily's belongings all by yourself?" Ruth asked.

"Afraid so," Leila said. "You're welcome to help if you want. But I don't mind doing it by myself, really. It's helping me process everything."

"I wish I could," Ruth said. "But hospital duty calls."

Leila commented on Ruth's commitment to her nursing career, and I thanked Ruth for her kindness and compassion. Ruth shrugged. "It's just who I am, I guess. That sort of thing has been in my family's blood for generations."

After Ruth filled Leila in on my post-op needs, she retreated to the living room to make up the sofa with a set of sheets and blankets that Leila had already set out. Leila wheeled me into a guest room decorated with charming little-old-lady furnishings, including a dresser topped with lace under glass. The walls were lined with slightly faded Victorian-print wallpaper, and the windows draped with white lace. A few sketches from the Wild West hung on the wall, needlepoint pillows with Indian designs adorned the bed, and a string of what I presumed to be bear claws was looped around one of the bedposts. The room was Jane Austen meets Sacagawea—and I found it utterly fascinating, even though the bear claws were a bit unsettling.

She offered me a cotton flannel nightgown, a clean pair of socks, and a stack of fluffy towels, all of which smelled like fresh laundry soap. She asked if I'd like to take a sponge bath before going to bed since, obviously, I was a long way away from being able to take a full shower.

"I'd love to, but I'm exhausted."

It was true—I was tired—and I also wasn't ready to let a perfect stranger help me in such an intimate way. Not yet. The last time I'd needed any sort of help with private affairs, outside the hospital room, had been after giving birth to Delaney eighteen years ago. I'd need Leila's help eventually, but it would have to wait till at least tomorrow. For now I'd retain whatever semblance of private dignity I still had.

Which was all well and good...until I awkwardly tried to use the bathroom and couldn't even get my ugly hospital scrubs off with my one good hand. I called out the door for her.

"I'm not very good at this," I managed to stutter out. "I mean, needing help, and giving up all modesty. I'm sorry. Hopefully I'll be doing this on my own soon."

Leila reached out and touched me gently on my good forearm. "Don't be silly. This is why you're here. And this is what we do."

I didn't know what she meant by *we* but was too tired to ask, or even to care. We survived the toilet challenge, after which Leila cleaned my wounds and changed their dressings as professionally as Ruth—who was now snoring on the sofa—would have done. She didn't even flinch when handling my soiled bandages or seeing the underlying gruesome wounds. I was already hopeful that Leila could be not only an aide but also a friend. Finally, with a clean face and brushed teeth, I slid beneath thick downy covers. After dimming the lamps, she sat down in my wheelchair beside the bed.

"J.P. had some very nice things to say about you," she said. "And he made me promise to take good care of you."

"J.P?"

She laughed. "My cousin? Dr. Hill?"

"Oh. Sorry, I didn't know his first name. Or initials. Yes, well, it was kind of him to make these arrangements for me. And very kind of you to take me in. I feel a bit like a lost cat. I just hope I'm not too much of a burden."

"Not at all. Taking care of others is what we're all about here at Maggie's Place."

"Ruth said you'd tell me about Maggie."

"I will. But not tonight. There's a long history, but right now we both need our rest."

I asked for my oxycodone, and she brought it to me with a glass of cold water.

"Tomorrow we'll talk about this, too," she said. "We need to wean you off this poison as soon as possible."

I swallowed the pills and handed her my glass. She set it next to the medicine vial on the dresser, then came back and kissed me on my forehead the way my mother used to kiss me goodnight, and the way I'd kissed Delaney until only months ago, when she began to rebuff me. Leila's warm, moist lips felt comforting and caring, but the gesture was nevertheless unnerving given how we'd only known each other for a couple of hours.

"Sleep tight," she said as she left.

I dreamed about Leila, and when I awoke the next morning, I lay in bed thinking about her kiss. Even in the light of day, it both exhilarated and frightened me.

Not that I'd never been kissed by a girl; I'd had a lot of girlfriends when I was in high school and college, and we often hugged and occasionally kissed each other—platonically, like sisters. Surely Leila's kiss meant nothing more; I was probably just out of practice in the girlfriend department. I outwardly blamed my paucity of girlfriends on having been a busy mom for so many years, and then being the wife of a lawyer-turned-politician who needed my support and attention. But the truth was that, once Shane and I got together, my girlfriends started to slip away, even before the kids were born. Some left for natural reasons, like marrying a man from another part of the country or getting a job offer in a different state. Others left because I was less available. Shane didn't want me going out with my girlfriends *on his time*, and when I did, he insisted I come home by ten o'clock in the evening. I told myself, and my friends, that he set up a curfew because he loved me so much and worried about my safety.

Once, my friend Linda suggested that he was intentionally isolating me. We had gone out for coffee after he'd left for work and the kids had gone off to school. "He wants you to be dependent on him, and without a group of friends for support, you have no one to confide in about his abuse."

Her comment pissed me off. I blew on my latte so hard that the foam splashed out of my cup and onto the table. "Shane loves me," I said. Then, looking around to be sure no one was eavesdropping, I whispered. "He'd never hurt me."

"He's hurting you by controlling you," she whispered back. "Possessiveness, strict rules around the house—including a curfew for his wife? Expecting you to see things his way? Those are all classic signs of psychological abuse. All those to-do lists he gives you? The way he asks who you're talking to on the phone? His sarcasm? His idea of love is having someone who's devoted to him, Brooke. And that's not normal."

I saw then that I'd been wrong to share my marital problems with her. She had no idea what a wonderful man he was. "You're crazy," I'd said to end the discussion. "Nobody's perfect. He's under lots of stress at work. He just likes things to be orderly and predictable at home. And what's so wrong with being devoted to him? Maybe you're just jealous that your husband doesn't ask you to be home at a certain time."

I refrained from suggesting that maybe their sex life was subpar. Even after all the years, Shane still had desires. For me.

"In a healthy marriage, each partner wants the other one to be happy," she said, her voice soft but authoritative. "Each partner lifts the other one up. My husband doesn't impose a curfew because he knows how important my girlfriends are to me. He doesn't put me on a pedestal, as Shane does with you, because that's unnatural and unhealthy."

I couldn't tell if I was flushing because the coffee was hot or because Linda had discovered the warts in my marriage.

"I love you," she said, "and I only want what's best for you. You might consider calling the domestic abuse hotline, if you don't believe me."

I stood up abruptly, bumping the table. I picked up my cup and slung my purse over my shoulder. I knew she was right but couldn't admit it. Not to her and not to myself. Linda stood, too, and came around to my side of the table. She hugged me tightly. It was the last time we saw each other, but I never forgot what she said.

Now, one broken vase and a grizzly bear attack later, I was finally beginning to see things about Shane differently, like how inappropriate it was that he didn't come to the hospital as soon as he heard what happened. Or how he had been monitoring my cell phone data usage. These were not normal husband behaviors. I was also starting to accept something about myself that I had refused to see all these years, like grime inside my oven. I was desperately in need of friends. Women friends.

As I was thinking about all this, Leila came in to greet me and help me out to the kitchen where Ruth was working on breakfast. She scrambled fresh thyme into our eggs, Leila buttered gluten-free toast, and I mindlessly watched a raven perched on the edge of a fire pit out back. It screeched and flew off, and it was then I noticed a semicircle of small cabins beyond the fire pit. They were all dark, boarded up, and in various stages of disrepair, except for one, where curtains fluttered inside an open window and multicolored wildflowers surrounded the cabin's base. A gray cat lounged in the morning sun on the cabin's front porch. This was where that light must have been coming from the previous night.

"Does someone live there?" I asked, pointing to the cabin.

Ruth and Leila glanced at each other, and then Leila said a friend of Emily's had been staying there for a while.

Later, after Ruth had left for Idaho and Leila had retrieved my belongings from the motel where I'd been staying before all this stuff happened, I brought up the subject again about Emily's friend in the cabin out back. I asked if I could meet her.

"Let's talk about that some other time," Leila said.

I was the guest in her home—or in her deceased grandmother's home—so I was in no position to argue. Still, I was ever so curious.

Over the next several days, Leila and I settled into a routine. First thing every morning she'd come into my room, fresh from her shower, her long wet hair smelling of mint or rosehips, and help me into the kitchen, where she'd set me up with a mug of steaming coffee and an Indian blanket over my lap while she fixed breakfast. After eating together, she'd help me bathe, attend to my bandages, and make sure I had anything I might need while she ran out to do errands. I usually read or napped while she was gone. When she returned, she spent the afternoons going through Emily's belongings, and I watched. I also watched her culinary artistry as she made dinner, feeling as if I had my own personal gourmet chef. At day's end, we'd sit on the sofa to read, but invariably we'd get into a conversation about one thing or another.

One evening she asked about my kids. I decided to start with Carson; he seemed less complicated, for the moment, anyway. I told her when he was born, how tall he was, what his academic strengths were, and that he was a fabulous swimmer with Olympic dreams.

"I swear he's part fish," I said. "He's always been comfortable in the water. I have no idea why; it's not like we insisted on swim lessons or spent that much time at the beach. It's like he's drawn to it at some subconscious level. And now he swims for Indiana University."

"You could be right about him being part fish," she said.

There was something about the way her eyes latched onto mine. It was almost as if she was serious. I laughed. "I'm pretty sure he's got lungs instead of gills."

She laughed then, too. "What I mean is that there could very well be a subconscious reason he loves the water. Maybe Fish is his spirit guide."

Now I laughed. "I don't believe in stuff like that. I'm pretty sure Carson doesn't either."

For a moment it seemed that Leila stopped breathing, and I felt as guilty as if I'd told a priest I didn't believe in God. I tried to backpedal. "But if a fish *is* his spiritual guide, it would have to be a shark."

"Because?"

"Carson once wrote a paper for a science project about sharks. And about these little guys called pilot fish that swim in schools around the sharks, cleaning parasites from their skin. When Carson became a teen, he was always surrounded by a throng of girls. His teachers joked about his harem. We joked the girls were his pilot fish."

"Hmm. Could be. Shark is a good spiritual guide. Keeps you motivated, hardworking, moving forward."

The next evening, Leila made baked trout in parchment for dinner. I wondered if it had any connection to our conversation about Carson and fish. She dressed it with fresh rosemary and served it alongside an arugula salad and mashed sweet potatoes. I asked if she, by chance, had any wine.

"I do. But you can't have any as long as you're taking those nasty medications."

"I'm following a doctor's prescription; it's not like I'm buying drugs off the street. Your own cousin prescribes pain medications, doesn't he?"

"Yes, he does, but that doesn't mean I approve of them. And certainly not mixed with alcohol."

Scooping some mashed potatoes onto my fork, I thought of how Shane refused to eat a lot of the foods I prepared because they, in his opinion, weren't healthy. Potatoes were a big no-no because the starch converts so quickly to sugar. I'd tried on more than one occasion to convince him he was missing out on some of the greatest comfort foods, but he was rarely willing to shift his opinions to meet mine—which hurt, in part because he wouldn't eat the food I'd lovingly prepared but also because the message was that he was right and I was wrong. No one enjoys being wrong, but he didn't seem to get that. Moreover, I often questioned how often there truly is a right or a wrong. Wasn't it possible that we could both be right? Or that we could each have different priorities that were right, and valid, for us as individuals?

And now here was someone who, by all appearances, seemed fit physically, emotionally, and spiritually—who also enjoyed a helping of mashed potatoes now and then. I felt vindicated, about the potatoes. But not about the wine. Or meds.

"I guess everybody has their own feelings about what's healthy and what's right," I said to Leila, wishing I'd had the courage to speak those same words to Shane.

"Guess so," she said tightly.

Damn it. Now I was reminded why I hadn't said things like that to Shane. I hadn't meant to put Leila off. I should have been nothing but grateful for her care and hospitality, but now I found myself becoming defensive and annoyed that she was lording her opinions over me. One glass of wine wouldn't have killed me. Whatever.

I told her my orthopedic surgeon wanted me to get on a regular schedule of oxy before the nerve blocking medicine ran out. "Or else I'll be out of my mind in misery, she said. Don't worry, I intend to use the medicine as sparingly as possible, but I also intend to go with what my doctor says. Oh, that reminds me. She also wants me to take ibuprofen, so if you wouldn't mind getting some for me, I'd appreciate it. I'll give you some money before you head out to your errands tomorrow."

I dipped my fork into the fish, and the pink meat flaked delicately. I squeezed my eyes shut, trying to focus on the flavor and not on the silence all around us. The fish was moist, savory, nuanced. Like magic, it subdued the angry monster inside me. "This trout is amazing," I said. "You'll have to share your recipe with me."

"I don't follow recipes," she said in the same curt tone Shane always used whenever he said he didn't need maps or GPS. "I just follow my instinct." She took a bite of the fish and caught my eye as she chewed. "There are other options for pain management, you know. Ibuprofen isn't good for you either."

Sheesh. I appreciated Leila's concern, but she was treating me like a child. Or a junkie. Either way, my anger began to resurface and those little white tablets called louder.

"Have you ever been mauled by a grizzly?" I asked, setting my fork down.

"Obviously not. I just want you to consider your alternatives."

"Like what? What are my other options?"

"Things like guided imagery, sunshine, essential oil massage, acupuncture. There are others, too, but you're not ready for those."

She might as well have slapped me. What could I possibly not be ready for? I had a mind to get up and call Dr. Hill right then. Or Shane. Maybe, I thought, I should just go home. "Well, it sounds like you think I should be at a spa," I said. "Which would be fine with me, as long as you're paying. But I know neither my husband nor my insurance company will spring for that sort of luxury."

I didn't know what got into me. I loved it there at the cabin. I loved being with Leila. She was only trying to help.

She cleared her plate, wrapping up her uneaten fish and setting it in the fridge. "I'm sorry if I upset you. I was just offering some ideas to consider. I would hate to see you get addicted to that medicine."

"I'm an athlete. I'm not going to get addicted to anything."

We spent only a short while in the living room that evening, each of us reading separately from books of poetry we'd selected from Emily's collection. Later, as I crawled into bed, I told Leila I was sorry. "I'm not usually like this. I'm normally a lot nicer than I was tonight."

"No worries. It's probably the pain talking. And I know it's hard to be the one being taken care of, rather than the one who gives the care. I'd be the same way."

I couldn't imagine her being as snippy to me as I'd been to her, and I told her as much.

The next morning, before I'd even had my first sip of coffee, she said she'd been thinking about our conversation from the previous night. Here goes, I thought. If she were anything like Shane, she'd let me have it for having been so rude and childish.

"I was really intrigued by what you said about your son," Leila said. I breathed a sigh of relief. No lectures about pain meds? No accusations about my behavior? "And now I'd like to hear about your daughter."

Like most mothers, I normally loved being given the opportunity to talk about my kids. But things had been so tenuous with Delaney that it was painful to admit our relationship was so sour. Embarrassing, too.

"When will I be able to ask about *your* personal life?" I said. "And when are you going to tell me about Maggie and Emily?"

"Soon."

As she whipped up a batter for crepes for breakfast, I tried to think up something to say about Delaney. I could easily have started whining about how she wouldn't speak to me, but I didn't want to go there. I didn't want to sound pathetic.

"Well, if you want to know about Delaney's spirit animal guide, I have no idea what to say. Delaney's really smart. And independent. A bit of a tomboy. And stubborn."

"Does she get that from you?"

I couldn't tell if she was joking or not. "I'm not sure. But one thing she did get from me is my hair."

"You should be in a shampoo commercial," Leila said. "I've been wanting to ask if it's natural."

"Yep, it's all me."

"We don't have many redheads in my family," Leila said.

I hadn't given any thought to what Leila's family might look like, but since she and J.P. both had dark features, I wasn't surprised that her genes would be ginger-free.

"Your daughter must be beautiful," she said. "If she looks anything like you."

I blushed. "*I* think she's beautiful, but not because of what I look like." I wanted to tell Leila that she was beautiful, too, but I couldn't figure out how to say it without it sounding like obligatory reciprocity.

She asked a variety of questions about Delaney: what her interests were, her dreams, her vulnerabilities. Then Leila asked if Delaney had a boyfriend.

Delaney hated that question, as if relationship status was the most important thing that defined a person. *Facebook isn't real life*, she often used to say.

"I don't think so," I said. "She's not that into boys. I mean, she *had* a boyfriend a while back, but I don't know what happened."

Whenever I'd tried to process with Delaney what might have happened, and why the relationship with her boyfriend didn't work out, Delaney clammed up. It was actually the last time she spoke to me—out loud like a normal daughter talks to her mom—when she said I couldn't possibly understand. *Not given the way you let Dad treat you. You don't have a clue about how relationships are supposed to work. As far as I'm concerned, you and I don't have anything to talk about. Like ever again.*

Those words were probably the most painful ones I'd ever heard, and losing a relationship with my daughter was certainly the greatest loss I'd endured. I wanted to share my feelings and experiences with Leila but didn't know where to begin—or where my sharing might lead. I certainly didn't want to divulge *all* the trash I'd accumulated in my garbage-truck life. Or how badly I'd fucked up with my daughter. So I decided to keep it to a minimum.

"Delaney's not talking to me right now." Could Leila, or anyone, possibly understand why a daughter wouldn't speak to her own mother? What did that say about me? "But that's okay. Everyone says she'll come around. Besides, I think she's mostly focused on her music for the time being. That's what she's studying at school. First year away from home."

"College?" She set a plate in front of me with two crepes drizzled with strawberry puree. "Here's some powdered sugar, if you'd like."

Leila had a way of making me feel like I was already at a spa. I sprinkled some sugar over the crepes, then took a bite. Leila, seated across from me, grinned.

"These are incredible," I said. "Are you going to tell me you figured this recipe out instinctively, too?"

"Sorry, but yes," she said.

"You should run a restaurant." I devoured the rest of my food. When I was finished, Leila reminded me we had been talking about my daughter.

"Oh, yeah. So Delaney decided to go to Indiana University in part because of her devotion to her brother and in part because the school has an excellent music program. At least that's what she told me back when she was talking to me."

"So now, with no communication from her, you have no idea how she's getting along in her first weeks at college? Does she even know about your accident?"

"Not a peep so far, except for a few emojis now and then. Carson has sent a few texts, asking me questions and wishing me well. He did forward a text from Delaney to him, in which she asked him how I was doing. So she knows, probably through Shane. But the only thing I get directly from her right now is emoji-speak."

"That must be hard for you."

When she started to clear my dishes, I made a lame attempt to stand and help. She motioned for me to stay seated. I was not yet addicted to any medications, but I was quickly becoming addicted to her nurturing ways.

"Sometimes I think she doesn't need me anymore," I said, wiping up the crumbs on the table with my napkin. "That's what Shane says, anyway."

"Nonsense," Leila said. "We all need help from one another. And especially we women. We need to take care of each other. That's part of our society's problem—we're expected to take care of others, but we think we're weak if we need help ourselves. That must have been incredibly hurtful when your husband said your own daughter didn't need you."

I held my hand to my heart. "It hurt like hell. Especially because she also implied, before she stopped talking to me, that the breakup with her boyfriend was somehow my fault, and now I can't seem to make things right."

One afternoon, as I watched Leila sort through her grandmother's belongings, I started to ask about Emily. She'd been born in the cabin, Leila told me. Emily's mother had also been born there, way back in 1878.

"I had no idea this place is so old," I said. "It's really charming."

"It's been rebuilt a few times, and added onto, over the years. But, yes, it's rather ancient."

Leila removed each of Emily's blouses from the closet, then carefully laid them out on the bed as if they were valuable antiques about to disintegrate. They probably were; some looked like they were from back in the mid-twentieth century. Leila buried her face into the folds of the fabric, and I tried to imagine what Emily might have smelled like. Onions and garlic? Foundation makeup? Or the outdoors: pine, roses, sunshine? As Leila carefully folded an ivory blouse with professional dry cleaner skills, I asked if her own mother had also been born in that cabin.

She set the blouse down and sighed.

"You've been sharing some of your story with me. I guess it's about time I share some of my story with you. No, my mother wasn't born here. And Emily is not my real grandmother. When my mother was a young teen, she was orphaned, and she spent the next few years bouncing around the foster care system. Eventually she ran away. No one knows many details about her childhood; there are various stories, none of them good."

Leila's mother had met up with a trucker passing through the Dakotas when she was living on the streets. He took her in, and together they traveled across the country. It started as quite the adventure, and Leila looked almost wistful as she recounted her mother's past.

"But then she got pregnant with me."

I guess I gave her a sympathetic look because she held up her hand. "Don't be sorry. It's all in the past. I'm just telling you this so you understand how Emily came into my life. One day, while my mother was in a little market in Lapwai, Idaho—just a week before I was born—the asshole trucker drove off. Left her with five dollars, a bag of groceries, and me in her belly. That's when Emily came along."

Emily regularly went to the market, and that day she'd bought a couple of cans of cat food for the feral cats living nearby. "As she told the story," Leila said, her eyes bright, "my mother looked more hungry and scared than any wild cats Emily had ever seen, and she took her home to the Nez Perce reservation."

"But I thought Emily lived here, outside of Yellowstone. Not on a reservation."

Leila was now pressing wrinkles from a violet blouse with her hand.

"Why don't you keep that one?" I said. "That color's incredible against your skin."

She held it up and looked in the mirror. "Maybe I will." She put it back on the coat hanger. "You're right, Emily lived here. But she went to Lapwai frequently to visit relatives. That's another story for another day. Anyway, Emily essentially adopted my mother and brought her back here."

"So you were born here."

Leila nodded.

She said nothing further, and I was dying to ask more about her mother. But I didn't want to pry. "So you were close to Emily all your life?"

Again she nodded.

"I bet Emily really appreciated having you here during her last few months. What a special time for the two of you."

"It was mutual." Leila brought a kelly green shirtdress out of the closet, folded it, and put it in the giveaway pile. Then she closed her eyes as she pulled her shiny black hair back from her face, and it seemed as if she was suddenly transported a million miles away. "I'm ready to call it quits for today," she said, letting her hair drop around her shoulders. She, too, could have been in a shampoo commercial, except that today she looked tired, and I couldn't tell whether it was from sorting through clothes or memories.

Later that week, we moved into the living room after dinner, as had become our habit. It was barely eight o'clock, and I was too tired to read, talk, or think. Leila, who was quiet throughout dinner, had already stretched out on the sofa and closed her eyes.

"I think I'll go to my room," I said, "and leave the rest of the evening to you in peace." By now I had graduated out of my wheelchair but still wasn't quite accustomed to crutches. I'd never known how much your armpits can hurt on those things, and it took some wincing effort to shuffle out of the room. When I got to the guest room doorway, Leila called out to me, and I was grateful for a reason to stop.

"Maybe you should have told her everything, including all those fears that made you stay with Shane."

I turned around. She was still on the sofa, eyes closed. "Excuse me?"

"I'm talking about Delaney," she said, opening her eyes and affixing her gaze on me. "About that conversation we never really had a few days ago. Maybe admittance of your vulnerability would have helped. Maybe it would have shown your internal independence. Maybe having your daughter on your side would have given you the oomph you needed to stand up to your husband. I realize it's easy for me to say that here, from the safety of this vantage point."

I was shocked and didn't know what to say. Flattered that she'd been thinking about me, but also curious how she knew, or intuited, so much. I'd shared very little with her. I also wasn't sure whether or not to be incensed that she would suggest I could have handled my relationship with Delaney—and even my own husband—differently. But Leila was probably right.

"Maybe," I said.

"Why *did* you stay with him? I can see in your eyes, every time his name comes up, that you're not happy."

I shrugged, leaning against the wall, unsure if I wanted to get into this, and unsure if she had a right to ask. But when someone shows sincere interest in you, it's hard to turn them away.

"I don't know. Because we had taken marriage vows. Because it was the right thing to do. Because he never hurt me." That old conversation with Linda threatened to bubble up again. "He was good-looking and successful. Funny, charming. Everyone loved Shane. I did, too. I still do."

"But he's changed. Or you've changed," Leila said. "People do that, you know. Sometimes, in a partnership, they stay on a parallel track. Sometimes they grow closer. But sometimes they grow apart." She moved her hands in and out to illustrate what she was saying.

Everything Leila said sounded so wise. Who made her so smart?

"After the kids came along, the trouble started," I said.

Leila sat up and patted the sofa, inviting me to come into the room and sit with her. I did.

"We had different ideas about parenting. I used to joke that people who love each other shouldn't have children together, that kids are bad for marriages. And later on, when I started to see what was happening, I was stuck. It's not easy to leave a husband when you have kids, when you've been out of the work force and only have a small business that barely pays its own bills. Or when your husband has convinced you that he's smarter than you, that he's always right and you're always wrong. I know that makes me sound pathetic, but it's the truth. He's very persuasive in a loving sort of way."

I stopped. I was lost. I had no idea where to go from there. Leila made me a cup of chamomile and ginger tea.

"I've known women who left their husbands and it didn't work out so well for them, or for their kids," Leila said. "I ask you these questions, but I do understand."

"I've known those women, too," I said. "Happy at first, then lonely and depressed. And some of them got ripped to shreds in court. Shane's an attorney, and he's also a shrewd man who doesn't like it when he doesn't get his way."

"Nobody does."

"Right. But I never wanted to face him in court. I'd have lost everything, including the kids."

"So facing him in the bedroom was better?"

"At least I knew the kids were safe and cared for." I stopped to reflect. I saw myself adjusting my silk nightgown after we'd make love, turning off the lamp on the nightstand, and turning away from him to fall asleep night after night.

"So you stayed with him for the sake of the children."

The warm mug comforted me. "It was for my sake, too. Better to put up with a little emotional trouble than to have all my weaknesses laid bare for the world to see."

Leila lay back on the sofa again and threw an arm over her eyes. "Tomorrow we're going to start having you do more for yourself."

"What? My physical therapy doesn't start yet for another week. I'm supposed to rest."

"Just a little more independence, that's all."

"So my confession of vulnerability marks the end of all your TLC? Is that it?"

She pulled her arm from her face. "Strength begins with vulnerability, my friend." She pointed to a wooden plaque above the front door. *From where the sun now rises, we will fight forever*. "My mother made that. And now it will be your motto."

It sounded so rebellious, so harsh. I could understand why a confused, teenaged mother who was dumped by a good-for-nothing man would adopt a sentiment like that. But it didn't represent me in the slightest.

TEN

Anne

I AWOKE WITH renewed hope and energy, refreshed with the promise of new life much as I had been the morning after Thomas and I were married. But this morning was even finer: no soreness between my legs, no recollection of his weight and belly pressing on my slight frame, no private man-part arising to greet me like a cobra awakening to a snake charmer's flute. Above all else was the foreign sensation of freedom I now felt; although I had done little to assure our survival over the past twenty-four hours, the truth was that we had survived, my new friend and I, without a man.

I sat up and stretched, feeling remarkably rested despite the substandard sleeping arrangements—especially the horribly hard ground, and after taking care of my morning activities, which was distasteful without the appropriate necessities but still better without a man watching or questioning what could possibly be taking so long, I pulled myself together as best I could. With a horse blanket wrapped around me for warmth, I made my way toward the lake and a tantalizing aroma.

I found the girl squatting by a camp-fire, nibbling from a twig and studying my sketches. She reminded me of a schoolgirl struggling to understand an arithmetic lesson.

"Good morning," I said. "I thought we might get this day started on a better foot." Laughing at my own joke, I wiggled my injured foot, which felt almost good as new. But she did not laugh or even acknowledge my presence with a greeting or meeting of the eyes. This irritated me, until I recalled how Thomas had accused me, on more than one occasion, of being too full of chatter in the morning. Without disengaging from my sketch—this one being the image I had drawn of her horse, the girl reached up with the twig from which she had been eating. I assumed she meant it for me. Fluffy dough surrounded its tip, and while I normally would refuse to eat from the same utensil as another, let alone that of a stranger, I dared not decline her gesture. Especially not after insulting her the day before. And not given how hungry I was, or how enticing the treat. I took the twig and bit off a small morsel. Still warm from the fire, it hinted of sugar and cinnamon. I took a larger bite, and then another, ultimately devouring every last bit as though I were the savage—one with no manners whatsoever.

"Delicious," I said, placing my hand upon my belly and licking my lips. When she still didn't look up at me, I cast another joke and asked for her recipe, knowing full well she couldn't possibly know what I meant.

The girl finally squinted up at me, tendrils of black hair, which had come loose from her braids overnight, blowing across her face in the breeze. I handed the twig back to her.

"Thank you," I said, again placing my hand upon my belly. I wanted to apologize for being so gluttonous but assumed she would not comprehend my meaning anyway. I lowered myself clumsily to the ground beside her and extended my hand. "My name is Anne. Anne Blakemore."

She stared at my hand as though it were a foreign object. She did not offer me hers in exchange, but she was so young; she was probably not married. It had scarce been two years since it became proper for me to offer my hand in greeting. Now I brought it to my bosom and laid it against my heart.

"Anne," I tried again. "My name is Anne." I gestured toward her, speaking slowly to help her understand. "What-is-your-name?" I had so many questions. Where was she from? Why was she alone? How old was she? Was she friend or foe? I was still alive at that moment, but this certainly did not mean I would remain so for long.

She turned back toward the fire, where she'd placed a tightly woven basket atop a pile of rocks. In the basket was another batch of dough. I tossed a pair of small pine-cones into the fire; they popped in the heat as I still waited for some semblance of response. She twirled the twig over the fire and, once that dough had turned golden brown, she waved the stick back and forth like a flag to let it cool. She took a bite, then handed it to me. This time she watched me as I nibbled. It was stickier than the last one, but still good. I nodded.

"I am not a savage," she said, her gaze hard as rock, her fingers tapping the hollow beneath her neck.

The wind blew again, and she squinted into the breeze. I endeavored to chew and swallow the dough as quickly as humanly possible, then held my hand in front of my mouth and ran my tongue across my teeth for any remains of the sticky dough. Satisfied that I could now offer a proper smile, I did just that, hopeful it conveyed the warmth I intended.

"Of course you are not a savage."

"You called me a savage the day before. Even as I helped you." She pointed at my foot.

"I am sorry," I said. "I am so sorry. And stupid, too."

The corners of her lips twitched, and she extended her arm toward me, palm facing up. "Stupid. Anne. You are Stupid Anne."

I laughed. "Yes, quite right. I am Stupid Anne. And you?"

She lifted her chin almost imperceptibly—just enough to convey what I deemed to be either confidence or pride. "I call myself Maggie."

"Maggie?" Yet another surprise. An Indian girl in the great Far West who wore animal skin for clothing but spoke English and had such an ordinary English name! I had expected Girl-With-Braids or something of the like, and began to wonder what other truths I might discover about her. "Maggie. What a lovely name."

That same day, Maggie hunted for more rabbit, then fashioned a pair of moccasins for me from the hides, lined with fur. They were more luxurious than any pair of slippers I'd ever owned. I could not comprehend why she would be so kind to me, when I had little to offer in exchange and indeed had insulted her so deeply. Watching her work brought to mind a novel I had recently read in which an admirable character named Jo is boyishly industrious but also heartwarmingly nurturing. Maggie was my very own Jo.

"It is time to move," Maggie said shortly after she finished the moccasins. "We will follow the buffalo south."

I asked why south. Her people and my husband had gone east. Also, Thomas had told me the Indians were afraid of evil spirits inhabiting the land of the geysers, south of here.

"You were told many untrue things about my people," she said. "If we go east, we will encounter your army. White men who cannot be trusted. Also, unfriendly tribes. West is where I came from. It is not an option. We will go south for now."

We traveled south over the next few days. Maggie walked most of the way and let me ride the horse, although at times we rode together. We edged along the forest's border when possible, avoiding open grassland. We kept our focus on the distant horizon, where strange clouds in the sky mingled with bursts of steam from geysers. Along the way, we made our camps within the safety of the forests, and Maggie hunted birds and other small animals for our meals. By the third afternoon, I grew tired from the tedium of nomadic wandering. We were both walking, side by side, to give the poor horse a rest. I began to sing a song for her.

> Buffalo gal, won't you come out tonight
> Come out tonight, come out tonight?
> Buffalo gal, won't you come out tonight
> And dance by the light of the moon?

She stopped abruptly, taking hold of my arm to bring me to a halt as well. I asked if something were wrong.

"Quiet!" she said, her voice low and angry. "You know nothing about how to move about these lands safely."

"And you know nothing about how to have fun."

She narrowed her eyes at me.

"Might we stop and rest awhile?" I asked.

Her eyes softened, a bit, and she took a blanket down from the horse. I helped her spread it on the ground, then waited for her to be seated before doing so myself. She wrapped her arms around her legs and faced south, away from me. I lay on my back and interlaced my fingers behind my head—a most unladylike pose, I was well aware. Thomas would have been appalled. But the position afforded a stretch for my aching muscles, an airing out of other personal parts, and a comprehensive view of the sky. It also gave me a taste of what it might be like to live somewhere beyond civilization's ridiculous demands of etiquette.

"I do know how to have fun," Maggie said, as I was nearly falling asleep. "And I know when we must keep moving." Although my eyes were still closed, I sensed that she was pulling herself upright. I then felt the gentle toe of her moccasin in my side. "You are the one who knows nothing. Remember? You are Stupid Anne. Now get up."

The one thing Thomas loathed more than my morning chatter was my tendency to dawdle in bed. As I tried to will my eyes to open and my body to rise, I heard her swiftly mount the horse. Before I sat up, she galloped off.

I waited. And waited. It was nearly dark by the time I decided she was not going to return. The wind howled. A wolf called. I shivered. I had nothing for protection, warmth, or sustenance aside from the blanket on which I had lain, now wrapped tightly around me. I began walking in an approximate southerly direction, where the sky still held a glimmer of light, and before long a silhouetted horse approached with what appeared to be a headless horseman on its back, bringing to mind that Washington Irving story I had read. I shivered again.

The horse stopped directly in front of me. Maggie sat in the saddle, a blanket wrapped around her head and shoulders. Neither she nor I said anything. The horse snorted, as though it were laughing at me.

Finally I apologized for my most recent insult. "I meant no harm," I said.

My preference would have been that she accept the apology and offer forgiveness, but she did not. "Come," was all that she said.

I rode on the horse behind her, my arms wrapped tightly around her waist, and we hurried to the camp-site she had already scouted before the sun completely set. It was situated alongside a river, and I so desired a delicious fillet, grilled to perfection. Another serving of rabbit was unfathomable.

"Do your people eat fish?" I asked.

She tossed the horse's heavy blankets to me. "*Nimi'ipuu* eat plenty of fish."

"*Nimi'ipuu?*"

"That is what we call ourselves."

"I have not heard of a *Nimi'ipuu* tribe."

"Your people call us Nez Perce."

I remembered little of the French I had studied as a girl, but I recalled enough to know what this meant. Maggie, however, did not have a pierced nose.

"We eat salmon," Maggie said, distracting me from my inappropriate study of her nostrils.

"Salmon? Oh my goodness! We have salmon where I hail from as well!" To think a little fish could be a common denominator between our two cultures! I was elated, as though we had just discovered we each had two eyes. I did not much care for the salmon that had recently been introduced to Lake Michigan—lake perch was my preference. Still, I would gladly have accepted grilled salmon over a camp-fire that evening, or fish of any kind. "Can we fish for our supper in this river?"

"No," she said, deflating my hopes. "These fish are no good. But wait." She reached into her saddlebag and produced a small morsel, a brownish-purple clump no larger than my nose. "*Ton-nut,*" she said. "Dried salmon with huckleberry. I brought it from my homeland."

I took it with some hesitation. It looked to be tough as leather. But as usual, Maggie produced another surprise. This was a delicacy, with a rich salty-sweet flavor. And the chewy texture was remarkably satisfying here in the open wilds.

We did not have fish for supper, but Maggie's grilled hawk was quite good. After we ate, I sat beside the fire, contemplating my fate. We had seen neither hide nor hair of another human being, and I was beginning to doubt whether I would ever be rescued. Moreover, I felt like an insect in a giant's kitchen, with the vast array of geysers and other bubbling pots of mud surrounding our camp-site. It was eerie and magical and tremendously frightening, knowing that one wrong step in the dark could scald me alive.

Maggie walked down to the edge of the river and began to untie her braids. She removed her dress and leggings. She folded them on the ground. Completely naked, she waded into the water.

"Maggie! Be careful!"

She had explained that the fish were no good because of the scalding water that poured into the river from the geysers. I worried now that she herself would be scalded—cooked alive, like a lobster from the East Coast. Along our journey, Thomas had regaled me with stories of unfortunate travelers who, unaware the geysers spilled out into the river, had suffered tremendous burns. Yet Maggie stood where the water line reached her hips unfazed.

I watched her silhouette as she dipped her hands into the water, then lifted them skyward. She did this over and over beneath the winking stars. I tried to look away, believing she was praying to a native spirit and deserved privacy. But I could not resist the beauty of her figure, the grace of her movements, the notion of spiritual purification in the grandeur of this landscape. When she scooped her long hair into one hand and lowered herself completely beneath the water's black surface, I knew what I had to do.

I searched for my sketch-book in the dark, intent on making at least a rough outline of her figure, which I could finish in the light of day. I rustled through our blankets. I scavenged through our other minimal belongings. Worry stabbed me that it had been lost, but only for a moment, because I soon became distracted by something as precious to her as my sketches were to me. Her pouch.

She had untied it from her waist and left it behind.

Without thinking—yes, one of my worst flaws as Thomas continually reminded me—I reached for it, and I had only just untied the rawhide straps when a silvery blur flashed before my eyes.

Maggie's knife. With Maggie's hand clenching it tightly.

"Give it to me," she said.

Naked, she dripped river water. I could not see her eyes, but I heard her panting. I handed the pouch to her.

"Never again," she said. "Stupid Anne."

We did not speak for two days. I made some unsuccessful attempts to prepare her sticky dough recipe and also to skin a squirrel—by the time I was done destroying the carcass, there was scarcely enough meat to feed the squirrel's cousin—but I spent most of those silent hours sketching. Maggie, meanwhile, worked tirelessly some distance inland on a small tipi constructed with branches from young lodgepole pine trees. As the second long day drew to a close and night enveloped us, she sat beside me at the fire. I had been quietly whistling *Buffalo Gal*. I stopped.

"You are amazing," I said, only then noticing how her dress was layered in dirt and sap from all her toil, and numerous leaves were caught up in her braids. I gently picked them out, one by one, hoping she had forgiven me. When I had finished, she took my hand.

"Come and see," she said as she stood.

I had never seen a tipi before. I stepped inside the dome of sapling trunks and marveled at its design, how symmetrically each tree leaned upward and inward toward the center, like arms reaching for the fountainhead of heaven. The ground was covered with twigs and grasses, on top of which a blanket had been spread. I sat down. I lay down, my eyes drawing up to the dome, and beyond to the deepening sky. Maggie lay down beside me, untied the pouch from her waist, and unsheathed her knife, setting it atop the pouch.

"Do not worry," I said. "I will not try to look at it again."

"I believe you," she said. "And someday I may reveal what is inside. But not yet."

We talked. Or I should say, I talked, and she listened as we lay together, face to face. I told her about Thomas, but only the happy times; I did not want to think of my feelings, nor of *him*, at this moment. Rather, I described our home in Chicago: our feather bed, my piano, my Persian rugs. I explained where Persia was.

I surprised myself as I regaled her with my stories, becoming aware of a gloomy fondness inside, the sort of warm melancholy one feels about an old pet who died long ago. I missed the city, with its multi-story buildings where men worked in offices. The railroad yards where trains were loaded with steel and building supplies. The wondrous stockyards, despite the stench. I told her about The Great Fire and the many parks along the lakefront. I described the artistic performances Thomas endured at my behest: the dramatic readings at the Academy of Music, *Horseshoe Robinson* at the Chicago Museum, and *The Huguenots* at Crosby's Opera House.

"What a horrible tragedy that was, the massacre of all those Protestants by their Catholic neighbors," I said when telling her the story of the Huguenots. "Hard to imagine such a thing among civilized, God-fearing men." Slow idiot that I was, I continued to prattle, further demonstrating my stupidity by talking about an extravagant performance I'd seen about life on the prairie. "There were live Indians on the stage! None were anything like you, however. They did not speak English or seemingly any language at all. They simply grunted and used hand signals and behaved not unlike wild animals."

Maggie harrumphed, rolled onto her back, and crossed her arms. "I see why you were afraid of me. Did it not occur to you that perhaps those Indians behaved as their white captors demanded? That they would have in fact had a language among their people but chose not to share it with white men? That they were not wild animals?"

My insensitivity astounded me at times. I apologized for not anticipating how upsetting my stories would be. And for so readily becoming distracted from the masterpiece she had just created. Thinking I could make up for my error with a little song, I quietly began to sing the hymn *Onward Christian Soldiers*. I was clearly still of dim mind.

"Please stop," Maggie said.

I asked what was wrong with a little church song. "Is it the mention of soldiers and war? It is just a metaphor."

I began to explain the concept of metaphor.

"I understand the intention, but I do not accept it. I do not agree with forced conversion of spiritual belief."

Maggie had attended a school run by missionaries, she explained. There, she had been forced to speak English, dress like American girls, and worship Jesus Christ. "I no longer wear those distasteful garments. Or worship your gods."

I asked her to tell me more.

"When I was young, my mother believed what the government told her, that it would be good for me to dress and learn as the white girls did. She believed in the treaties. But in time we discovered the true intention of your missionaries, and your government. To take everything from us. To take away our land, our freedom, our heritage. We were not permitted to wear our traditional clothing, not even in our own homes. Or speak our own tongues. Or practice our own traditions and spiritual ceremonies."

I had read about the missionaries and their schools for Indians. I had believed what I read: the schools and churches served the best interests of the savages. They civilized them.

"Before the last snow," she said, "my father gave my hand to a warrior from a different band of the *Nimi'ipuu*. The Wallowa people had not accepted the white teachings. By becoming this warrior's wife, I was able to return to our old ways. This made my father and mother very happy."

An animal cried—a wolf or coyote pup, perhaps. Or a bird. I knew so little of this place, I could not tell one animal sound from another. I moved closer to Maggie.

"My husband and I were happy," Maggie continued. "Until your army came along to move us to the reservation. My husband and some of our other warriors refused. Instead, we quickly gathered all of our possessions and abandoned our homeland."

I recalled the wagons and horses laden with so many things. The boys delighting in my belongings. The girl with the rifle.

She said no more. I endeavored to comprehend what she had said, what it must be like to move away from all you have ever known. After I was sure she had fallen asleep, I tried to doze off as well, but my mind was like a water pump that continued to drip. Every time I thought of Maggie and her people having to move their children and horses and dogs and clothing and Onondaga salt and *ton-nut*—and guns—from the homeland they loved, the only home they knew, my stomach roiled. Knowing it was my people who'd chased them away made it worse. Perhaps it was right that the Indians had retaliated by stealing my Thomas, and every worldly possession I had brought with me.

Just as sleep began to embrace me, Maggie sat up and threw off the blanket. I asked whatever might be the matter.

"There is no sleep for me," she said.

After tying her pouch around her waist, she went to the river. I followed, as did Maggie's obedient horse. There was barely enough light in the sky to see the way. As she walked, she told how her people had made camp in a wide basin near a river. They had been traveling for days and were exhausted, needed rest.

"In the middle of the night, your army attacked."

Dozens of her people were killed that night, including her husband's mother and sister. She started to say something else but stopped suddenly, as though frightened by a snake. Or something worse. I bumped into her. The horse drew up beside us.

"My husband told me to run. He would stay and fight. I grabbed the *tekash*. I called for my horse." She reached up and ran her hand along the horse's strong neck. When she stopped, it lowered its head to grab a tuft of grass. "I ran for the river," she said. And now she began to run from me. I hesitated, confused, but then followed, straining to hear her words.

"We entered the river and went upstream, away from camp," she said, now sidestepping down the steep riverbank. "Away from our tipis and my husband and dying friends." Her voice had changed, risen in pitch. It sounded as though she was crying.

"What are you doing?" I asked from the precipice of the bank. "What are you saying?"

"I did what he told me to do." By now she was at the river's edge, and she waded into the water, fully clothed.

"Maggie!" I could not see the ground beneath my feet, in the shadowy twilight, and I stumbled down the bank, trying to keep one eye out for Maggie. The river churned. Spray from the rapids spat at me when I reached the bottom.

"I carried the *tekash* into the water with me. I held it high above my head. My horse followed."

She raised her arms above her head. She whistled for her horse. It approached the riverbank but stood beside me rather than following her into the water.

"A gun fired. My horse was spooked. She tore out of the water and ran off into the woods. She left me alone." She whistled for the horse again. It pawed at the ground.

"And then came the sound of another gun. I ducked down into the water, but still held the *tekash* aloft. There was nothing else I could do."

I stood at the river's edge, wary of the rocks and pebbles at my feet. I peered through the dark to see Maggie lowering herself down into the torrent of water. Her head disappeared beneath its surface. Only her uplifted arms and hands remained in view. I held my breath.

When she finally surfaced, water spilled all around her.

"Do you see? I held the *tekash* aloft so she would not drown. And in so doing, it was she who took the third bullet, not me."

"She? Who?" I called. By now, I was quite frantic. The rapids looked deadly. I considered climbing onto the horse, if that were even possible without a ladder or stirrup, and going out into the water for Maggie. But fear held me captive. I called out, but she lowered herself again into the water. "Who took the bullet, Maggie? Who?"

She was now submerged completely. I swatted the horse, pushed at its rump. Surely the damn animal would save her. It would not budge. "Maggie!" I called. "Maggie!"

Even in the thickening night, I could see her lying prostrate in the river, her braids flowing downstream like twin snakes. Any moment, she would be swept away.

"Maggie!"

I splashed into the river and fought to right myself, slipping on the rocks, falling not once but twice and taking in mouthfuls of water. When I reached her, I wrapped my arms around her waist and lifted her up, even as my feet slid from under me yet again. Now we were both faltering, flailing, gasping for life. Somehow, with our collective and perhaps involuntary wills for survival, we regained our footing, and we sputtered to the bank. The horse lazily glanced our way.

Once on flat, dry ground, we collapsed, our arms still around each other, and now—with the air so much cooler than the water—we shivered. Back at camp, we began to undress.

"No, no, no!" She searched around her feet in a frenzy.

I asked what was wrong.

"My pouch! My pouch! It is gone!"

We raced back to the riverbank. She waded in, and I feared I would lose her forever this time. She dove under the water over and over like a bird fishing for dinner. I scanned the river's surface.

Downstream, a fallen log jetted out over the water. I ran along the riverbank toward it and ascertained that my suspicion was accurate. The silhouette of her pouch dangled from one of the branches. Without thinking, I trounced out into the river to retrieve it, keeping my hand on the log for guidance. Shortly before reaching the pouch, however, my feet slipped out from under me, and the current whisked my body under the log. Instinctively, I shot one arm out of the water, and then the other, and took hold of the log as I lifted a leg up and around it. There I hung like a sloth, wondering how, when, or by whom I would be rescued. All the while I heard Thomas's voice. *My dear, what on earth have you gone and done now?*

ELEVEN

Brooke

AFTER WE FINISHED our breakfast of buckwheat pancakes and huckleberry jam the next day, Leila said she was going into town to a donation center, where she would deliver the giveaway boxes we'd accumulated so far. She asked if I'd like to ride along.

"You must be going crazy with cabin fever. And you need to start practicing with those crutches outside of this cabin. Rehab starts next week."

"Actually, that ranger—Palmer—called last night and said he wanted to stop by today. Said he wants to ask more questions about the bear incident."

Leila had been loading plates into the dishwasher. She stopped and straightened, her shoulders drawn back. It was as if a Canadian cold front whirred through the kitchen.

"I'm sorry, I should have asked you if it was all right if he came over, since this is your house. I just assumed you wouldn't mind."

I followed her gaze out the back window of the kitchen toward that mysterious cabin. As usual, the cat was sprawled out in the sunshine on the porch.

"No, it's all right. Just keep him outside."

I wondered about this, as if Palmer were a dog with muddy paws, but promised to do as she requested. After she left, I waited for him on the cabin's front porch in one of Emily's rockers. Finally, a dusty Jeep Wrangler bounced along the gravel driveway, its canvas top down, and when Palmer waved up at me, my heart surprisingly pinged. I didn't particularly like the man's personality—he was arrogant and odd. He was also kind of old, at least seventy. Guilt wagged its finger at me whenever I found another man attractive, as if I were cheating on Shane. But it wasn't like I wanted Palmer as a lover. He simply had movie-star magnetism, with his handsome rogue face, precious gem eyes, fit physique, and contagious smile. Then again, Palmer wasn't the only one who'd awakened a guilty pleasure; Dr. Hill was equally attractive, although younger and far more humble. Maybe it was some sort of hero worship I was feeling for both of them. Whatever it was, something inside me had been triggered—a longing I hadn't felt for an eternity, it seemed—and I tried to convince myself to honor the feeling rather than squelch it.

When he climbed out of the Jeep, a massive black dog bounded out as well. It followed him up to the cabin, then leaped onto the porch in front of him with neither invitation nor reservation.

"Who's this?" I asked as the dog assertively nuzzled its wet nose into my palm.

"Sorry, she's a bit forward. Her name's Row. Short for Arrowhead. My daughter named her."

Daughter. Given his age, I figured she must be around my age.

"She's huge. Must be a handful."

"Part Lab, part Newfoundland. Strong as an ox but tender as a lamb. Good girl, Row," he said. He hesitated before stepping onto the porch, leaning back to take in the view of the cabin as if searching for something. Eventually, he sat in the rocker next to mine. We reached for the dog's head at the same time, brushing our fingers together. I pulled my hand back.

"How's the leg?" He pointed at my ugly therapy boot.

"Getting better day by day, I hope."

"And the bite and claw marks?"

"Healing, slowly. No sign of infection."

"Good, good." He nodded, and I nodded, and we rocked in our chairs, like a couple of old geezers. After an uncomfortable lull, during which we both watched the dog settle herself into a lazy recline, we started to chat about the weather, and then the news, and then the smoke in the air from a distant wildfire. Safe topics.

"Tourist season's almost done," he said. "Thank goodness. Next week, after Labor Day weekend, things will all begin to shut down. Looking forward to that." Another lull came along, and this time instead of watching Row, we stole glances at each other. My heart did another little dance.

"You said you had some things you wanted to discuss?" I said.

"Yes." He slowed his rocker to a stop. "I'm still working on my report from the 24th. You know, the day of the bear attack. And I just wanted to go over what happened with you one more time, now that you're a little more…with it. If you feel up to it, that is."

"Sure, that's fine."

"Are *you* sure? I mean, it was a pretty nasty scene."

"I am absolutely positive."

At his prompting, I described everything I could remember, and then he told me his version.

"Mystic Falls is one of my favorite short, accessible trails in the park," he said. "I lead that hike once a week all summer long. Just two and a half miles round trip, give or take, but you see a lot of varied scenery there. And wildlife."

"I can vouch for the wildlife part."

He laughed, nodded, and resumed rocking, faster this time. "Yes, you certainly can. Anyway, there are about thirty tourists in my group on this particular day, and a couple of children are skipping ahead of us, even though I'd asked the parents to please keep them back under control." He stopped rocking, shook his head. "Parents nowadays, they let their kids run wild. 'Course as a ranger, I'm the one responsible for their safety." He resumed rocking again. "So these two little buggers run ahead, and I shout out to them to get back here right now, to the mother's dismay—apparently it's not socially acceptable to scold a child that's not your own. The next thing we know, the little girl is screaming—a blood-curdling, high-pitched scream—and now the entire group stampedes up the trail, pushing at one another, and all the while I'm trying my best to stay in the lead, figuring they must have come upon a deer carcass or something grisly like that."

By now, Palmer's chair was rocking so fast, I worried he might tip it right off the porch.

"When we catch up to the kids," he continued, "the girl is sobbing—her shoulders heaving up and down, tears spilling down her cheeks. The little guy is standing still as a robot with his arms hanging by his side, looking down at something off the trail." Again, the rocker stopped abruptly, and his eyes glazed over as he studied something just off the end of the porch, something I couldn't see.

"Looking down at me?"

"Yes, indeed, looking at you. And all your blood." He began to rock once again, at a frenzied pace. "'Course I quickly get the situation under control, moving the crowd back, assigning tasks to some of the tourists." His tone pitched higher, his pace of speech accelerated. "I have them apply pressure on your wounds, fetch medical supplies, stand guard on the lookout for the creature responsible for the mess, which I assume to be a bear but can't be sure just yet. The key is keeping everyone corralled, giving them responsibility so they don't stand there gawking and groaning, and so they won't wander off, either. Yes, it's all about crowd control. You never know how tourists are going to react at a time like this. You can't have half of them go running back down the trail and the other half go off looking for a bear."

If his demeanor was as frenetic then as it was just now, it's a wonder any of the tourists stuck around at all. I was worn out just listening to him tell his version of the story, the way I used to feel when Carson and Delaney were young and they'd race through a narrative about something exciting that had happened at school, intoxicated with their stories. *Calm down*, I used to tell them. I wanted to say the same thing to Palmer now. Instead I took a long, deep breath. Like magic, his rocker slowed.

"Meanwhile I'm lying on the ground dying?"

"Well, yes, as a matter of fact, you are." Now the rocker stopped mid-swing and he leaned in, as if to impart a secret. "When you're the person in charge, you also need to quickly assess the victim's situation, like whether she's dead or alive." He winked at me. "You aren't dead yet. So I radio for help. The worst part is those poor children."

I was still envisioning me on the ground and him calling for help. It took me an instant to realize what he'd just said about me not being dead, *yet*. And then his comment that the worst part was *the children*?

"Terrible for them to see something like that," he continued. "Absolutely terrible. I tell those parents to take their children straight for counseling when they get home. You never know what impact this trauma could have for them down the road."

His magnanimous worry about the children and his attention to crowd control were honorable, but I found myself feeling uncharacteristically bitter that I was a lower priority in his retelling of the event. Row lifted her big body off the porch floor and ambled over to me as if she sensed my hurt feelings. I scratched behind her velvety ears.

"Do you remember any of this?" he asked.

"Not much." In truth, flashes of memory had been returning day by day, but it was easier to just say no.

He studied the bandaged side of my face, and then my eyes. I looked for compassion in his.

"All the while, I knew you were all right," he said, appeasing my bruised ego. He looked out toward the sea of lodgepole pines between Emily's cabin and the road. "It was a strange feeling that came over me that day on the trail. It was apparent, somehow—when I touched your beautiful mane of hair—that you would survive. Whether you were sending some energy vibes to me, or it was the power of my touch on you, I wasn't sure."

Woo-woo new age, Shane would have said if he were here. *Crystals and magic potions and faith healers, oh my.* I couldn't help but feel a bit cynical, too. How could this park ranger know by touching my hair that I'd survive? On the other hand, I *had* survived. And his version of the story—at least the factual parts—matched the snippets of memory that had been coming back to me.

"Row, my girl," he said. The dog lifted her head. He scratched underneath her chin. She closed her eyes in bliss. "It certainly was a wild day. Intense. I'm just so thankful I was there. Right place, right time."

As I tried to decide how to respond, the dog noticed something through the cabin's front window. Her eyebrows and ears both lifted, and she hefted her giant body to a standing pose, as if coming to attention. I followed her gaze and thought I saw a face peering out from behind the living room blinds. But then the face disappeared, and soon afterward a door slammed at the back of the cabin.

"That's weird," I said. "I think I just saw someone inside. Right there in that window behind you. But Leila's gone; she went into town before you got here. Nobody else is home."

The gray tabby shot out from a patch of tall grass just then and nearly flew past us. I practically jumped out of my seat. Palmer quickly rose from his chair. Row took off after the cat.

"I'll investigate," he said, stepping off the porch and walking stealthily to the side of the building.

"There's an old woman out back," he said excitedly when he returned. "I saw her going into a smaller cabin, just beyond the fire pit. I called out, tried to introduce myself, but she was too quick for me. Too quick. Seemed she was avoiding me." He stood at the porch step, leaning on the railing and tapping his fingers against a post.

Row came back, panting but cat-less. Palmer jogged to the Jeep and came back with a large metal bowl, which he filled with water from the hose bib. Then he began to pace.

"You know, I haven't been able to sleep much since that day," he said. "I know, I know. That sounds crazy. I wasn't the one attacked. But still. The whole thing's been bothering me something fierce, something fierce."

I hadn't noticed his tendency to repeat words until just now. A nervous tic, I assumed.

"My mind keeps racing. Buzzing thoughts, buzzing all the time like angry bees trapped in a jar. So much paperwork to do. The boss breathing down my neck. The public relations office. And the media, the media. Everyone wants to know what happened. And then there's the question of what to do about the bear. And what to do about you."

"What to do about me?"

He stopped pacing, tilting his head as if listening for something—or receiving a message from an alien mother ship. Weird.

"Would you like to go into town? Grab a bite to eat?" he asked. "It would do you some good to see different scenery."

"That's pretty much what Leila said."

"Come on, then. Let's go have a glass of wine."

Wine, without Leila watching over me. Why not?

We drove into town after several awkward attempts to squeeze me into the Jeep. My leg didn't feel right in any position, and I figured I'd catch hell from my physical therapist next week, but I forgot my discomfort when we drove past the motel where I'd initially been staying. My stupid Chevy Corvette was still there, its cherry red body now caked in high desert dust. Darn it; a part of me wished it had been stolen.

When we got to the Blind Bear Bistro, Palmer helped me out of the Jeep. I hobbled with two crutches and zero grace to the small outdoor seating area. I knew there wouldn't be many warm days left in the season so decided to take advantage of this opportunity to sit outside. While he parked the car, I popped a dose of oxycodone. A minute later, Palmer hopped the fence surrounding the patio, and Row did the same. An elderly couple at a nearby table was clearly offended by such inappropriate action—the woman actually pressed her hand to her breast—and I also thought his behavior was irresponsible and childish. But also rather charming.

Palmer popped some of his own pills from a medicine vial, an action the elderly woman didn't miss. He then ordered a bottle of Chardonnay. I knew what Leila would say, which was all the more reason I wanted to have a small, rebellious glass.

In the bright daylight, I realized that Palmer seemed thinner than just days earlier when I'd seen him at the hospital. I also noticed purple half-circles beneath his eyes, which I hadn't detected on Emily's shady porch.

He guzzled his first glass of wine.

"My daughter once had a bad accident," he said when his glass was empty. "I hadn't thought about it for years—it was a memory I'd shoved into a locked box for safekeeping. And then this thing happened with you, and the horror from her accident came back. It's been tormenting me."

Before I could ask, he answered.

"Hit by a motorcycle, right before my eyes."

My heart lurched. "Oh, Palmer." I extended my hand on the table toward him.

"Total jerk speeding along a residential street." He ignored my hand. "Hit a pothole, lost control. Taylor had been standing at the side of the street, ready to cross under my supervision. I was too far back to save her. I didn't protect my baby."

All the judgments I'd felt about this strange, seemingly self-absorbed man dissipated. I searched for something meaningful to say but came up empty, as one often does at times like these. "Oh, I'm so sorry, Palmer. So terribly sorry."

"Look, here she is." He pulled out his phone and showed me a picture. She was a teenager in the photo, maybe a couple of years younger than Delaney was now. I asked how long ago the photo had been taken, assuming it was decades ago.

"Just last spring. Isn't she a beauty?"

Last spring? *Isn't*, rather than *wasn't*? He had a teenaged daughter and she was still alive? I laughed out loud at my assumption that his daughter should have been my age and that this accident must have occurred long ago. He straightened, pulling back from the table, his brows pinched. I had hurt him.

"I'm sorry, I didn't mean to offend you. I was laughing at myself for…oh, never mind. So she's okay?"

It seemed only now that he noticed my hand on the table. He took hold of it and squeezed, hard.

"She nearly died. And it would have been all my fault. But those doctors…they performed miracles. Even so, my life spun out of control after that. And I've been feeling the same way this week, after that bear attacked you." He poured himself another glass of wine with his free hand. The one that lay atop mine felt strong and warm, but nevertheless I pulled my hand out from his.

"It certainly wasn't your fault the bear attacked me. You're the one who saved me. So it's all good, right?"

Palmer's knee started to jiggle up and down, and he began to look around over each shoulder, like a fugitive on the lam. I looked around, too, unsure what or who I was looking for.

"Maybe we should head back to Leila's," I said when he drained that second glass. I hadn't been out in the full sun for more than a week, and I didn't really want to leave. Especially knowing what a struggle it was going to be getting back into the Jeep. But I felt like a storm was coming—this man was not stable, and he'd already had plenty of wine.

"Good idea," he said. He stood up and walked away.

Dumbfounded, I called out to him. "Hold on a minute." By then he'd already exited through the cute little garden gate. "We need to pay. And you can't just leave me here with your dog. I need a little help."

His expression made it clear that his thoughts had also left the premises, but then he sort of came back to consciousness. He threw a twenty-dollar bill on the table, slapped his leg for the dog to come, and served as my spotter as I made my way back to the Jeep. I worried about him driving, and rightfully so. It seemed we were going at Indy 500 speed once we were beyond the town's limits. Whether he was thinking about me on the trail, or his daughter's accident, or something altogether different was the first of several Palmer mysteries I'll never solve, but it was clear he wasn't focused on the road. When I asked him to slow down, it seemed my mere presence in the vehicle startled him.

Gravel flew wildly when he turned off the main highway and, as he headed up the long driveway, I saw something I hadn't noticed when Ruth first brought me there, several dark evenings earlier.

"Wait! Stop!" I said.

He slammed on the brakes. It's a wonder Row didn't wind up in my lap.

"What's that?" I said, pointing at a bizarre scarecrow-ish thing. Standing roughly fifteen feet tall, its head was a grotesque and terrifying face carved out of wood, and it wore a tattered shirt stained with what appeared to be blood. "Has that always been there?"

Palmer shivered aloud, dramatically. "That thing gives me the creeps. This whole place does."

"But what is it?"

He shifted into first and continued up the hill toward the cabin, now at a more civilized pace. "I'm not the right one to ask."

When we pulled up, Leila came running out.

"Where have you been? Is everything all right?"

"I'm fine," I said. "No worries. Palmer just wanted me to join him in town for a short while. I didn't mean to worry you."

"Oh," Leila said to Palmer, giving him the once over. "So *you're* the knight in shining armor."

"That's me." He sat behind the wheel, grinning but making no move to help me out of the Jeep.

"Well, thanks," I said to Palmer through the open passenger window after Leila helped me climb out. I was tired and ready for him to leave, although I knew a strong cup of caffeinated coffee should be in order before he drove anywhere. As it turned out, my failure to invite him in didn't matter. As Leila helped me up to the porch, the car's engine shut off. The next thing I knew, Palmer and Row were at my side.

"It's okay, Palmer," I said. "We're good here."

"That's no way to show your gratitude," he said, handing Leila the more-than-half-drunk bottle of wine.

"Were you drinking?" she asked me, in the same tone I used to ask the same question of both Delaney and Carson when they were in high school.

"Only a small amount." I sounded as guilty as they had. Lucky for me, Leila's intention to scold was interrupted by Palmer talking into his phone.

"Note to self. Call Monique. Warn of threats, threats. Set up bear management meeting."

Leila shot me a quizzical look.

I shrugged. "Threats?" I asked him.

"Just little reminders," he said. "Nothing for you to fret about. I need to meet with the boss tomorrow. Tomorrow." He fixed his eyes on Leila. "May I use your restroom before I go?"

She hesitated, then acquiesced and went inside with him, directing him to the only bathroom in the cabin. I took a seat on the porch rocker and scratched Row's head. While Palmer took care of his business, Leila talked to me through the screen door, arms folded across her chest.

"Something's not right about him."

"You're telling me," I said. "He's really freaked out about what happened with the bear."

"But he's a ranger, right? He's trained on stuff like this? He's freaking *me* out. Which is pretty hard to do. He needs to leave."

"I think he could use a friend."

When he came back outside, Leila disappeared into the cabin. He reached out to me, as if inviting me to join him for a dance. I'd noticed at the restaurant how clean and manicured his hands were. But they were also experienced, outdoorsy, skilled. I liked hands like that—hands that had known the stab of a splinter from rough-hewn pieces of wood or the scorch from a campfire or the blister from gripping oars too tightly in a wild patch of water. Hands that had known life.

I let him help me out of the chair and into the house. We awkwardly stood there on either side of the threshold, me resting on my crutches and him holding the screen door open. A housefly flew through the doorway, and I waved at it too slowly. It winged its way inside. I knew Palmer was waiting for something, but I wasn't sure what.

"Do you want to come in for some coffee?" I asked. Only after I spoke did I recall Leila's admonishment that he remain outside. But now he stepped into the cabin, and the door squeaked shut, and there we stood. I couldn't renege on my offer now.

Row whined from the other side of the door.

He followed me into the kitchen. Leila had already started a pot brewing, although she was nowhere in sight. When I turned to get some cups down from the cupboard—all the while trying to balance the crutches in my armpits and making sure not to place any weight on my right leg—Palmer closed in behind me. With his arms reaching up to the cupboard, one on either side of me, and his belt buckle grazing against my lower back, I was trapped.

"I debated about coming over today," he whispered. "I didn't want to bother you. But I had to. And I knew you'd want to see me again." The light stubble of his beard brushed against my left, uninjured cheek. His warm breath tickled my ear. "Tell me I did the right thing, Brooke. Tell me you wanted to see me."

What I wanted was to shout out for Leila.

The coffee pot gurgled as the last of the water made it through the filter and into the carafe. The hinges on the kitchen door creaked.

"What are you doing?" Leila said, a demand more than a question.

"I was just leaving," Palmer said.

TWELVE

Brooke

EMILY'S ESTATE BECAME our primary focus over the next week. When I told Shane I was helping Leila settle the estate—using it as one of my many excuses for why I wasn't yet ready to come home—he asked what could possibly take so long.

"Hire 1-800-JUNK," he said. That's what he did when he, as appointed executor, handled his own grandmother's estate.

What Shane didn't, and couldn't, understand—which I was only beginning to appreciate—was the history that still lived and breathed inside Emily's historic cabin. One afternoon, we pulled down her old cookbooks and laughed at the notes she'd written in the margins: *add a walnut-sized turd of butter, shave a fly's wing of salt from the recommended amount, cook this outside or else the stench will drive everyone away.* I especially loved the notes that mentioned her friends: *Willis sure enjoyed the boiled dry corn* and *this is Harry's favorite.* Each note had been dated, the oldest going back to 1941. The venison and elk, which was *delivered by George*—whoever he was—*had to be the tastiest and most tender meat ever.* Her venison ragout with mushroom recipe, which called for steaming the concoction in a foil packet buried in the ground, earned five pencil-drawn stars.

Leila attested to how delicious Emily's fry bread was. "Let's make it tonight," she said. The basic recipe was simple enough: water, salt, sugar, baking powder, flour, and oil. But Emily had also written in the margin *two shakes of secret sauce.*

"Do you know what her secret sauce was?" I asked Leila.

She laughed. "Emily said every woman's born with a zillion secrets, and every time she reveals one, she grows another gray hair. Do you know she didn't start turning gray until she was eighty?" Leila dramatically ran her fingers through her own thick hair. "I think I inherited that gene from her, even if we aren't biologically related." In other words, no secret sauce recipe for me.

Leila and I also read Emily's books during the evenings. It was a diverse collection, with plenty of poetry by Aiken, Alexie, Dickinson, Hughes, Midge, Oliver, and Woody. There were also dozens of novels, including dusty old tomes by the likes of Shelley, Eliot, and Melville. We took turns reading to one another, sometimes repeating lines over and over because we loved the sounds of the words and their rhythms, or because we couldn't quite discern, or agree upon, the meaning behind phrases like *tallied compulsion* and *the hour of lead*. One evening, we sat on the front porch long after sunset, wrapped in blankets and reading by candlelight. Another evening we settled on the sofa, my legs propped on Leila's lap and a plumeria-scented candle burning on the side table. We laughed when an owl hooted from a tree outside the door right after I'd asked Leila who wrote the sonnet she'd just read. "Who-who-who wrote that sonnet?"

The best find in Emily's cabin was her old trunk. It was a veritable museum. In it, along with raggedy scrapbooks and photo albums and embroidered handkerchiefs, we found her traditional American Indian attire and accessories. Like a little girl, I wanted to dress up in costume, but I didn't dare tamper with such beautiful and ancient artifacts.

"That buckskin dress must date back at least a hundred years," Leila said as I petted it like fur on an old cat. She found a handwritten note her grandmother had tucked into the garment, one of many little notes Emily had left behind in the trunk and throughout the cabin. "No, I was wrong. This goes back to 1875. This belonged to Emily's grandmother, Maggie."

"Of Maggie's Place?"

"That's the one."

I was tempted to ask her again to please tell me about Maggie, but I didn't want to pester her. So instead I asked what she was going to do with the dress.

"Probably deliver it, along with most of this stuff, to the reservation in Lapwai if they want it. Or give it to a museum if I can find one that will take it. If not, I don't know. Goodwill?"

"No! You have to keep it," I said. "This dress, and all this stuff—these are precious mementos. They're artifacts of history. You can't give them away."

"Maybe. But they're from Emily's history, not mine. As attached as I was to her, I don't feel particularly attached to her material possessions, except for a few things I'll bring home with me. Like this pouch." She dug into the trunk and gingerly pulled out a pouch the size of a slice of bread. The hide was dry and cracked, and the leather strap ripped in several places. But the embroidery was exquisite, and the colorful glass beads that ornamented the flap were still intact.

"Is there a story behind it?" I asked.

"There's a story behind everything."

I reached out for it, but unlike the other things Leila had been sorting through, she didn't pass it over to me. The pouch, like the secret sauce, was off limits.

After she set it and the buckskin dress aside, Leila pulled more mementos out of the trunk. As she did, I thought back to all the memorabilia my mother had saved for me, and all the preschool artwork and participation trophies I'd set aside for my own kids. Our closets, garage, and even our yard were stuffed with clothes, gadgets, and electronics—along with a tangle of cords and wires. Candlesticks and coasters, picture frames and crystal figurines. Stuffed animals galore. Baseball bats, tennis racquets. Decorations for every holiday. And the biggest monstrosity: a life-sized bronze statue of a golfer that Shane had once won in a golf tournament and which now watched over our backyard lawn like a god of the greens. When I contrasted Emily's few precious things to all the crap we had amassed, I wondered how Leila *couldn't* feel attached to these select objects. Not to mention wondering how my kids would one day feel about all our stuff after I was gone.

"Do you have any sentimental things that belonged to your mom?" I asked.

"A few, back home. She wasn't much for saving stuff either."

Later, while Leila was making an abbreviated version of Emily's venison ragout, with tofu instead of deer meat and without the underground baking method, I decided to pose what could be a dangerous question.

"So, without sounding judgmental—which I'm not, I'm just curious—if things don't matter to you, then what *does* matter?"

Leila stared into the stew. "What matters is home—but not in the material sense. Rather, the *place* of home, not the building or its contents. And family—which can be loosely defined, too; family can mean community. And land. Home, family, land. The things my mother didn't have until Emily brought her in. These are the things that matter." Only then did she lift her face and turn to me. I wanted to peer into the pot to see what other magic wisdom was bubbling in there.

"So if land and home are so important to you, why are you selling this cabin?"

"Good question," she said, tasting the ragout from a wooden spoon. "I've been wondering the same thing for the last few days. The problem is that my family's out in California. I can't manage two properties so far from one another."

Leila was holding onto something—a memory, a heritage, a truth. A dilemma of some sort. I knew there were layers and layers of complexity beneath her surface that I had yet to discover. She was like a *New York Times* crossword puzzle: intriguing and unsolvable.

After dinner, she spread a map out on the table and pointed to a spot near Yellowstone National Park's northern border. "Here, I'm going to show you something next week to help you see what I'm talking about, where family and place and land intersect, where you can feel your heart beating right through the soles of your feet."

We both looked down at the boot on my bad foot and laughed.

"Or at least through the sole of one foot," I said.

Our archeological excavations through Emily's history were put on hold the next day because it was time to return to Idaho Falls for my follow-up appointment with the surgeon and an initial physical therapy appointment. Afterward, Leila and I met up with Dr. Hill for an early dinner.

I'd assumed we'd meet at a casual café or roadhouse, but instead he picked what was most likely the nicest restaurant in town. White tablecloths, fine wines, and a tuxedoed maître d' were not what I'd been hoping for after being poked by doctors and pushed by therapists all day. Whatever makeup I'd put on before leaving the cabin that morning had long since worn—or perspired—off, and I seriously doubted the restaurant appreciated my athletic attire. Worse, it would have been easier for Leila to lead a clumsy herd of bison through Macy's crystal figurine department than to guide me, on crutches, along a zigzagging journey past cozy two-tops to the back of the restaurant where her cousin patiently waited. When I finally plopped down in my chair, grateful I hadn't knocked over a single wine glass along my journey, he offered a glass of bubbly to me.

"To a full recovery," he said.

I reached for it, but Leila took it from him and set it back on the table. "She's still on oxy, you know. No wine for Brooke." She winked at me.

His handsome hand caught in the proverbial candy jar, he told me not to be bothered by Leila's comment. "The bossier she is, the more she likes you. She used to push me around constantly when we were kids."

"I did not," Leila said.

"Did so."

"Leila thinks I should stop taking pain meds altogether," I said. "But everything still hurts."

He nodded. "She's probably right. How long has it been—two weeks? By now you should be able to handle the pain with just an NSAID. Or maybe a combination of ibuprofen and Tylenol."

I told him I'd tried to go without the oxy, but felt worse, not better.

"She's a bitch when the meds wear off," Leila said. Although I'd been a little cranky a few times, I hadn't thought I was that bad. Our conversation could have spiraled down into an argument, especially given that my current dosage was indeed wearing off, if a server hadn't, thankfully, interrupted us with a tray of appetizers.

"I took the liberty of ordering some munchies before you bulldozed your way through the restaurant," Dr. Hill said. "I hope you like roasted figs, escargots, and asparagus with crispy quail eggs."

Three credits for Shane. First, he taught me to be a foodie, to notice every detail about food—whether related to appearance or flavor or nutrition, whether the attribute was positive or not. I'd never anticipated his lessons would help me get through this trauma, but they did, along with Emily's recipes and Leila's culinary skills. Now I practically salivated as the server set the plates down on our table and the garlic wafted up at me. Second, Shane always insisted on impeccable manners, and accordingly I waited for my host, and for Leila, to lift their forks and take the first bites. J.P. went for the asparagus; she chose the snails.

Third, Shane taught me all about aphrodisiacs, and it did not escape my notice that the good doctor had loaded up on these.

I had been developing a girl-crush on Leila these past two weeks and at times thought she was flirting with me. I had also suspected that Dr. Hill had been flirting with me before I was discharged, and he was now sending me similar vibes. We were a seductive little triangle—with the cousin connection serving as hypotenuse. It struck me then how much Leila and J.P. looked like each other. I knew they weren't related, given that her mother had been a street kid taken in by Emily. But in addition to their dark hair and eyes, they shared the same complexion: skin the color of dried figs but smooth as ancient river stones.

Leila picked up a snail shell with a set of delicate tongs, dug into the shell with a tiny fork to extract the meat, and lifted the fork to her lips. She slipped the meat into her mouth and closed her eyes. The corners of her pink lips rose. She sighed through her nostrils. I could have sworn she shuddered.

I reached for a fig, but unable—or unwilling—to copy Leila's coquettish flair, I stuffed it into my mouth. I hadn't eaten much that day, and I chewed only once or twice before gulping the thing down.

"I hear your exams went well today," J.P. said, pouring another glass of champagne for himself. "Sure you don't want any? I'll let you have a little bit if you promise to stop the oxycodone."

"As much as I'd like to taste it, I'd better hold off. I'm not ready to give up the meds, Doc."

I told him about the exams, and Leila added that we'd found a good clinic in West Yellowstone for my PT.

"At least for as long as I'll be around," I said. I held my breath, waiting for their replies, hoping they'd each insist I stay a lot longer. I took a drink of boring water; he took yet another nip of wine. I caught a glance between J.P. and Leila, unsure what it meant.

"So what are your plans?" he asked me, although the question would have been equally relevant for Leila.

"I don't know. That depends on how long you're going to stick around," I said to her.

"And how long is that going to be?" he asked her before winking at me.

"I don't know," she said, slicing off an asparagus tip. "I had planned to be home by now, but I've still got a lot of work ahead of me." She nodded in my direction and said she'd been distracted. Her smirk assured me I was a welcome distraction.

When they both turned to me, I felt like I was under an investigator's spotlight, but I couldn't think what to say. I let the moment pass.

"What about Cody and the kids?" J.P. asked Leila. "How are they managing without you?"

"They're good," she said. "But they miss me terribly. And obviously I miss them."

I didn't doubt what she said was true. I wished I could say the same about Carson and Delaney missing me. But more than that, I ached knowing that soon I'd be missing her, too, when she returned to California and I went home—or wherever I might wind up going.

Over the next few days, as we busied ourselves with trips to my physical therapist and more work around the cabin, I stuffed any thoughts about our inevitable separation way back into a dark corner of my mind. Sometimes I could be the queen of denial.

But I was also distracted by the increasingly frequent texts from the kids, and the emails, too, although there wasn't Internet at Emily's place, so I was only able to access them when we went into town. I'll never know why the pace of their interest in my existence and well-being accelerated—if I believed in things like telepathy, I could say I willed their behavior to change—but nevertheless I was overjoyed that it did, even if the messages were sometimes silly. Carson's were filled with stupid memes about grizzly bears, links to articles citing examples of unintended injuries from physical therapy, and warnings about recent UFO sightings in Montana. Delaney sent me daily emojis, pictures, and links. One morning, her text included a picture of an adorable joey hanging onto its mother, arms clasped tightly around the mama's neck. Some days she sent selfies: one in front of her dorm, one in a playground, and one in a coffee shop with a venti Starbucks latte—a froufrou drink I would have gladly committed a felony to get my hands on. My favorite was a picture of a little girl looking up at her mother with a dandelion in her hand, followed by tearful emojis. I missed Delaney so much, but wasn't sure how much love she'd be willing to receive, and I didn't want to do the wrong thing and turn her away, so I kept my texts short, newsy, and upbeat.

The therapy was far more grueling than I'd expected, and Leila sat through the early sessions as my cheerleader. Who knew how out of shape you could get in just a couple of weeks? Or how even the uninjured parts of your body could hurt after moderate exercise? Who knew how hard it could be for a runner to lift her leg after two weeks of inactivity, let alone put on a sock? The lacerations were healing, but they were still decisively ugly: dark and scabby, like the skin of a prehistoric creature come back to life. I made Leila turn away whenever the PT wanted to check the wounds, and eventually I fired Leila as my wound-care nurse. I didn't want her to see my body that way anymore. I didn't want her to remember me like that.

One day, while Leila was running errands, I waited for her in a coffee shop and got caught up on my email. The coffee was unremarkable, and so were most of the messages that had accumulated in my inbox. It had always been one of Shane's pet peeves that I didn't check my email often enough—by his estimation—or that I didn't take care of them efficiently. *Your inbox is so cluttered, I don't know how you can think straight,* he'd say. To which I'd reply that half of it was junk, and furthermore I couldn't recall ever receiving an email so important that the world would have ended if I'd ignored it indefinitely. *Even so,* he'd say with his signature judgmental sigh and furrowed brow.

But of course I did need to periodically scan the inbox for messages from my clients, which was what I'd had in mind in the coffee shop that day. As it turned out, there was an email from Shane. It had been sitting unopened for a couple of days.

Brooke,

I've had some conversation with the kids lately. They don't understand why you won't come home to recuperate. You know we have excellent physicians and therapists here, and neither the kids nor I think it's wise for you to stay there any longer. Also, it doesn't look right in the public's eye. You know we need to tread lightly from here on out until the election. Besides, we have something special, you and I, which quite frankly doesn't work when you're not here with me.

So, I've made a unilateral decision to bring you home. Your first appointment with a local surgeon will be next Monday, the 18th. I've made it clear this is just a check-in for him to take a look at the work those cowboys did. I've also got you lined up with a top-notch physical therapist and a psychologist, too. You can't be too careful when it comes to PTSD.

You'll be pleased to know I've chartered a flight for you to fly directly out of West Yellowstone this Friday, the 15th. That will be so much smoother for you than trying to get to Denver, even if it is pricey—see below. (I trust you can find a way to get to the airport. They do have taxicabs there, I presume?) I've also arranged for a courier to pick up the Corvette on Friday morning, before your flight, and drive it back to Portland for you. You'll need to send me the address where you're staying so I'll know where to tell him to go.

By the way, this escapade of yours has come with an intolerable price tag. I've started checking in with our insurance reps and it doesn't look good. When you get home, we'll have to talk about cutting back on household expenditures until your hospital bills are settled.

Having said all that, I want you to know I'm very concerned about you, and we all want you back here, the kids, too. I can tell your little game of silence with Delaney is starting to weigh on her, and I don't want it to impact her studies. You'll need to make reconciliation with her top priority. As for you and me, I know we've had a rough go of it lately, and I'll do my best to make things easier for you. We're a team, which means we need to work together, and it also means we need each other.

Yours in love,
Shane

I hit delete before I'd digested all he'd written. His sentiments may have been sincere, but the audacity that he would make a decision to bring me home, without conferring with me, struck me hard. Friday the fifteenth was four short days away. I was also taken aback with how he'd conspired with the kids behind my back to corral them into his corner of our marital boxing ring, and how he seemed to blame me for the chasm between Delaney and me, as if that whole situation hadn't been breaking my heart. He knew nothing about what it was like to be a rejected mother. His comment about medical expenses irked but did not surprise me. And the suggestion that he needed me? Of course I wanted to feel needed by him; need is an important part of any solid relationship. But the more I reflected on how I'd left things back home, the more it seemed his needs were directly tied to his political events, when he required a smiling wife, and to our bed, for his frequent booty calls.

I laughed, though, when I thought about the car. If only he knew that little baby wasn't even in my line of sight. I hated that thing almost as much as I hated how he'd surprised me with it. There it had sat, in my Subaru's spot in the garage, when we came home from delivering the kids to college that fateful day. He'd arranged to have a friend handle the details, including tucking a note that read *Happy Empty Nesting, Babe* beneath one of the windshield wipers. I knew he'd meant it to be a generous gift, but a car like that wasn't the least bit my style. I loved my Subaru.

And now I didn't want the Corvette hauled back to Portland. I wanted it hauled to the dump.

When Leila came to get me at the coffee shop, I didn't tell her about Shane's email. I no longer wanted to burden her, or our relationship, with my shit, given the short time we had left together. She noticed my crabby demeanor, which was also probably due to the reduction in my oxy dosage, and we were both silent on the drive back to Emily's. I feigned a headache when we got there and snuggled under the covers in my room, staring at the wall in the quickly fading afternoon light while trying to wrangle my thoughts. Maybe Shane was right. Maybe I did need to go home. Maybe it was time to stop living in some fantasy world of grizzly bears and Indian lore and handsome doctors and park rangers. Maybe I needed to stop living in Leila's world. I had lulled myself into thinking I was on some new path to self-discovery when in fact I was more likely on the road to nowhere. The two weeks I'd initially planned to spend away from home had come and gone. It was time for me to grow up and rejoin my pathetic reality.

As I lay there, the phone in the kitchen rang, and my eyes drifted to the framed sketches on the wall as I listened to Leila's soft voice, a sound that could cure any ailment. I wasn't trying to eavesdrop, but I did hear certain words—*girls, symptoms, trauma*. I made up stories in my head about who these girls-in-trauma might be.

I'm not sure when I started to focus on that old artwork. By now Leila had gone through most of Emily's things, but she hadn't taken these pictures down. Maybe she was waiting for me to leave, not wanting to dismantle my room while I was still there. Maybe I was overstaying my welcome.

Each of the sketches was drawn on what was probably once white paper that had become seriously yellowed over time. They reminded me of history projects Delaney had done, for which we'd scorched edges of paper for an antiqued look. Because they were so faded, the images were a bit difficult to make out. I hoisted myself closer.

One of the sketches portrayed a lovely little lake, another a gently flowing river. The third sketch was of a horse in a forest, an Indian blanket across its back. The fourth depicted an Indian girl with two long, black braids, kneeling on that same horse blanket beside a campfire, her hands warming over small flames. And the last one, which was unfinished, showed the same girl, I presumed, bending over a strange little structure that looked like an igloo made out of tree branches.

In the lower left hand corner of each sketch was miniscule handwriting. One read *Little Firehole River, 1870*-something; I couldn't read the last digit in the year. Another read *Mary Lake, 1877* and was signed by Anne somebody. The two finished Indian girl drawings were marked *Maggie, 1877*.

Maggie? So the girl at the campfire was Emily's grandmother? But I could not see her in the sketch with the horse, even though it was also entitled *Maggie, 1877*. I switched on the flashlight of my phone, and that was when I spotted two legs, dressed in buckskin trousers, extending down from the horse's belly. Maggie had been hiding behind the horse.

I wondered if the sketches held other secrets, like those puzzles in children's magazines with hidden objects. But then Leila knocked on the door, and when she did, warmth flooded over me. I had been angry with Shane and taken it out on Leila by sequestering myself.

She came in with two steaming mugs. "Here's some acorn squash soup. I thought you might be hungry."

She handed me the mug with a bear's face and kept the moose's face for herself. The soup was hot, rich, and delicious.

"Cayenne?" I asked.

"Too much?"

"Nope. The spicier the better." I didn't admit the heat of the soup was warming me up so much that my scabs, especially the one on my face, were starting to itch badly again. I needed boxing gloves to keep from scratching—the trick we once used when Carson got into poison oak. I suspected, though, that Leila didn't have a pair handy.

When she sat down on the bed beside me, she didn't have her normal joie de vivre. "I might need to leave for a few days."

"Is it something I did? Or said? Am I in your way? I can go home, Leila. In fact, that's what Shane wants me to do. He sent me an email asking me—no, commanding me—to go home later this week. Back to Portland. On Friday."

She raised one eyebrow, the one with the silver scar. I wanted to reach over and touch it.

"Commanding you? That's not right."

"Yes, it was a command. But sorry, I didn't mean to interrupt you. You were saying?" I recalled overhearing about girls in trauma.

"My husband needs my help. For a few days."

At last she acknowledged that she even had a husband.

"Is everything okay?" I asked.

"Yes, as a matter of fact, everything is fine. Good, actually. I know I haven't told you much about my personal life."

"You're right. You haven't."

"I'm sorry. This isn't the first time I've been accused of being too private. I wasn't intentionally withholding from you; I don't have any secrets."

"Other than a secret sauce," I said.

"You've got me on that. Anyway, Cody's a disabled vet. He's got it rough, and has been dealing with a lot of pain—and other issues—for a long time. The pain's been worse lately. But he's hanging in there as best as he can, and he just found out he was accepted into an experimental treatment program that may require him to go out of town every few weeks. The first session is this weekend, and our babysitter can't take care of the girls. So I'll have to go home, just from Friday to Sunday."

I took a big gulp of soup and burned the roof of my mouth. She hurried out of the room and came back with a glass of ice water.

"Maybe it's for the best that I go home this weekend, since you'll be leaving on Friday anyway," she said. "I've become accustomed to having you here, Brooke. It'll be odd being here all alone, without you."

I wanted to fling my arms around her and kiss her. But my fear of ruining things between us kept me from doing so. Besides, I had that hot mug of soup in my hands.

"I never said I was leaving on Friday. I only said that Shane told me to go home."

"So you're not going?"

"I'll stay until you kick me out," I said. I blew into my mug. She took a drink from hers. We shared a long, authentic, silent moment of kindred connection and soup.

"You know, it was a godsend when J.P. asked if you could stay with me for a while," she said. "The girls, Annie and Maggie, had spent the summer here with me—and with Emily, while she was still living—and had only recently returned home for school. You kept me from falling apart after they left. But I've felt guilty, too, about being away from Cody so long."

She explained that, as a Gulf War veteran, her husband had been experiencing something called Gulf War Illness for years: pain, memory and other cognitive problems, and severe mood swings. I told her I was sorry she had to deal with all of that. And that I was there to listen, whenever she needed an ear.

She shrugged. "We've learned to adapt. Most of the time it's okay. But once in a while it flares up. What's even worse is how hard it is to work with all the government bureaucracy. You have no idea. If that's not enough to worsen your PTSD, I don't know what is."

I made a mental note to talk to Shane about this. If he won the election and got to Washington, maybe he could help.

"It's great Cody got into the program, but now childcare is the issue," she said. "After this weekend, I'll come back to the cabin to wrap things up once and for all, but I won't be able to stay long."

Just when our friendship was strengthening.

Leila pulled her phone out of her back pocket and showed me a picture of the girls. The one missing her two front teeth was Maggie. "She's named after Emily's grandmother."

"And what about Annie? Does her name have anything to do with those sketches?" I pointed to the wall.

Leila laughed. "Oh, yeah, it does. I'd forgotten about those—they've been on that wall forever. I need to figure out what to do with them, too. Anne was Maggie's dear friend. Emily was so happy when I named my girls after those women."

She removed one of the sketches from its nail. Even in the dim light, I could see how much the wall paint had faded around the picture.

"Here, look," Leila said, sitting beside me.

I switched the flashlight of my phone on and directed it toward the artwork.

"See that, right there?" Her index finger lay on the smudged glass, pointing at Maggie's waist.

I squinted, not sure what I was searching for, and then I found it. The very same pouch we'd found in Emily's trunk. In the sketch, it hung from a leather strap tied around Maggie's waist.

"Wow," I said, immediately recognizing that my vocabulary didn't contain any words that could capture what I felt at that moment: the reality that I'd witnessed in person the precious, historic pouch; my confusion about how Leila—a woman who understood so deeply the meaning of family and place—could part with Emily's artifacts, their provenance so pure; the grief I already felt from losing her even as she sat beside me. All these thoughts or feelings or emotions muddled together and raced through my veins, creating a powerful fervor—an awareness of something that could not be named.

We finished our soup. She took my mug and kissed me on the forehead. I lay in bed for hours, my mind both full and empty at the same time.

I woke the next morning to the sound of Leila's voice on the phone. I could tell she was making plans to go somewhere, and my stomach cramped as I remembered she'd be leaving on Friday. Then I heard the front door open and close and wondered where in the world she might be going—without me—and for how long. An hour or two? An entire day? Not that she didn't have the right to have her own life. As it was, I had probably already become a nuisance, a needy leech. I hoisted myself out of bed and, using my crutches, hobbled to the living room's picture window. Emily's pickup truck was gone.

The aroma of coffee called me back to the kitchen. I settled down at the table and stared out the rear window, waiting for my mind and body to fully wake up and anticipating how I'd spend the day without Leila. I needed to get back to my clients; they probably wondered if I'd fallen off the edges of the earth. I missed the online chats we regularly had about their latest projects, or a new gallery opening, or a website I might have discovered for them to sell their work. One of my newest clients, a steampunk jewelry artist, had just been written up in *The Oregonian*, and I began to compose, in my mind, what I should say in a congratulatory note.

My thoughts were interrupted when the gray tabby came into view. I watched it chase fluttering insects, leaping and pawing into the air, oblivious to me as its observer. And then I discovered that I had also been oblivious; there, coming into focus, was the ghost woman's face, peering out through the little cabin's window, her gaze focused my way.

I waved. Her face disappeared.

I must have sat there for nearly an hour in my pajamas, composing and re-composing a message to my client, while wondering who that woman was and what her secret might be. Finally I heard the truck's wheels crunching the gravel out front.

"Have I got a surprise for you," Leila said, standing in the kitchen doorway. She set a bag of groceries down on the counter. A long baguette protruded above its rim.

"Mmm. Fresh bread," I said.

"Yes, but even better. Hold on, and no peeking." She left me alone with the baguette and its bag. I peeked.

"I couldn't help it," I said when she returned. "The baguette made me do it."

She set a backpack down on the table and began transferring food from the bag to the pack.

"So...what's the surprise?" I asked.

I tried to read Leila's face. She was unquestionably happy. Delaney, when she was little, used to check out my clothes first thing in the morning to figure out what was in store; if I was wearing my workout clothes when I got her out of bed, she knew she was going to be imprisoned in the health club daycare for a couple of hours. If I wore jeans and an ordinary top, she knew we were heading for fun. And if I was dressed up, she keenly suspected Mommy was going somewhere Mommy didn't want to go and would invariably come home in a rotten mood. Leila was in her standard attire: tank top, bike shorts, flip flops, sunglasses on top of her head. Today's tank top was bright turquoise. Nothing out of the ordinary. Nothing to give away her little secret.

"Do you trust me?" she asked.

"Is that a trick question?"

"Don't be stupid."

But I'm so good at that, I thought.

"Yes, I trust you."

"Then get dressed," she said.

"Are we going somewhere?"

"Yep."

"So how should I dress? Formalwear?"

She gave me the once-over. "No. But also not pajamas. Jeans are fine."

"I've only got one pair that fits over my boot. And they're dirty."

"Dirty's even better. Where are they? I'll get them."

I couldn't imagine where dirty jeans would be okay. I made my way into the guest room. Leila brought the jeans to me from the laundry closet, then left me to fend for myself, which had become *de rigueur*. As I dressed, I tried to figure out what she possibly could have planned. A short while later, she helped me out to the truck, where the baguette backpack, two other backpacks, and a small cooler sat waiting, along with a giant pad of some sort—like those wrestling mats you see in high school gyms.

We headed into Yellowstone National Park and followed the Madison River east, passing several herds of elk grazing at the water's edge.

"You're not taking me back to Mystic Falls, are you? Where the bear got me?"

"Give me some credit," Leila said. "Remember the map I showed you last week?"

"Where you feel the heart of the land through the soles of your feet."

"Right," she said, downshifting. "Look. Up ahead. Bison jam."

I was tempted to make a smartass remark about preferring huckleberry jam to bison, but decided against it. We slowed to a stop, behind dozens of other cars and trucks, all of which were blocked by a throng of bison standing on and near the road. Passengers and drivers hung out their windows, snapping pictures of the beasts. A scrawny calf wandered toward us, and an older gentleman in the car in front of us got out of his Ford sedan. He approached the calf with a 35-mm camera held up to his eye.

"That's trouble," Leila said. "One sudden move by that guy and the whole herd heads this way."

"And we get squished?"

"Pretty much."

"Great," I said. "The bear didn't kill me, so now the bison will. Shane will love this."

"What an idiot," Leila said. "Not Shane. That old guy. Hasn't he read the signs about staying an appropriate distance away from wildlife? Twenty-five yards from all animals, except bears." She looked over at me. "You're supposed to stay a hundred yards away from bears."

"Now you tell me."

A horn honked. "Someone else figured out his stupidity, too," I said.

"Except honking a horn isn't exactly going to calm down the bison. We're getting out of here." She maneuvered the truck out of the line of traffic with a few forward and reverse shifts, then headed forward in the lane designated for oncoming cars—which was now empty thanks to the hairy creatures.

"What are you doing?" I asked. "Now are *you* trying to get me killed?"

"Quite the contrary. No one's coming from the other direction. Don't worry, I know what I'm doing."

She carefully, but not exactly slowly, proceeded in the wrong lane for a couple hundred yards while my fingers tightened around the door handle. When she came to a barricade comprised of several fully grown, very large bison, she slowed but showed no intention of coming to a full stop.

"You're going to hit them!" I said, pressing on the invisible passenger brake. "Stop!"

She gave me the same sort of look Delaney had perfected when I was teaching her how to drive. When the nose of the truck was only inches from the largest bison's enormous head, Leila stopped the truck fully. The damn beast stood there, literally staring us down. I held my breath. Lazily, and on no specific time schedule, the bison finally decided to turn away from us, which was an ordeal in itself. First, the huge head. Then, with great effort, the giant body. Finally it plodded to the side of the road, reminding me of the downtrodden Eeyore character in Winnie the Pooh's world. In what seemed like perpetual slow motion, the rest of the bison in the road eventually followed.

"How did you know he was the leader?"

She winked at me and tapped her index finger against her temple.

"Palmer would have you locked up if he knew you pulled a stunt like that."

"Palmer. What a work of art. Well, no one needs to tell him I did." When the last bison tail was barely off the road, Leila darted back into the correct lane in front of the car at the front of the traffic jam, and we were on our way again.

We headed north toward Mammoth Hot Springs, then veered toward Tower-Roosevelt and the Lamar Valley. I'd read there were lots of grizzlies in that part of Yellowstone. I asked if she was planning another bear encounter for me.

"You said you trusted me."

"I'm reconsidering."

Finally, she screeched off the road onto a path of sorts—a beaten down swath of grassland just wide enough for the truck. We bumped along, and it took a few minutes before I realized how all this jostling didn't hurt the way the rides in Ruth or Palmer's cars had. I was, indeed, healing.

"If this isn't the middle of nowhere, I don't know what is," I said.

At last, we came to a clearing where several cars were parked, as well as a camper van with a horse trailer. Two horses were saddled and tied to a nearby tree.

"Wait here," Leila said. She left the engine running and scrambled out her door. Another woman got out of the camper van. They embraced. I opened the passenger window once the dust from our arrival had settled.

"Come on, Brooke!" Leila called. "We're going horseback riding today!"

"Very funny," I called back. "I can't even walk."

She and the other woman came toward me.

"Exactly," Leila said. "You won't need to walk. That's what the horses are for."

"I haven't ridden a horse since Shane and I first dated, and that was an experience I've tried hard to forget. Shane's saddle slipped sideways and the horse threw him. To this day, he blames his chiropractic bills on what he calls those two man-hating dykes who owned the ranch."

Leila's eyebrows reprimanded me.

"I'm sorry. I shouldn't have said that. Neither should Shane. Trust me, he's softened his stance on LGBTQ matters in recent years. My point is that I haven't ridden in forever and I can't possibly do it today. Come on, you know that, Leila."

"You'll be fine," she said. The other woman, whose expression had soured after my idiotic remark, patted a chestnut mare on the neck and said she was the gentlest ride in the county. The mare eyed me and snorted.

Leila had gone to a lot of trouble to plan this day. We only had a few days left. I certainly didn't want to upset her, so I decided to be a good sport. If I wound up back in the hospital by day's end, well, so be it. At least I'd get to see J.P. again.

Leila unpacked my crutches and her gear from the truck and strapped it all to the horses. She and the other woman then somehow got me up onto the mare. I felt the skin on my right leg stretch like a dry, old rubber band. So much for healing.

The horses fell into an uncomfortable trot, and I cursed Leila under my breath, until we made our way into the forest and were surrounded by pine trees, chittering ground creatures, and jumbles of rock. Here I was able to relax. The ride became smoother, too. This was the solitude that I'd been looking for when I first came to Yellowstone.

"What about bears?" I called up to Leila.

"What about them?"

"Are there any around here?"

"This is Yellowstone, Brooke. Yes, there are bears here. Grizzly and black." She patted her hip, upon which hung a holster with a can of bear spray. "But lightning doesn't usually strike twice in these parts."

It wasn't long, maybe thirty minutes, until we came to a clearing by a creek, where I was happy to discover we weren't completely alone after all. A couple of anglers waded upstream. Downstream, two swans paddled in a circular eddy. Leila slid down from her horse, tied it to a tree, and spread out a blanket on which she set the backpacks. She then untied my crutches and helped me down from my horse.

"So. Here we are." She unpacked the food from one of the packs and arranged it on the blanket. I tried to figure out what to do.

"Just relax," she said. "Lie back and feel the earth beneath you. Remember? That's one of the reasons I brought you here. Sacred land. Today you're going to ground yourself on sacred land."

I lay down on her blanket. "Aren't you going to join me?"

"Actually, I'm going to do a little rock climbing. That's what I do when I need to unwind. I climb."

I evaluated my options for how to respond.

"I know what you're thinking," she said. "I don't mean that I need to unwind *from you*. You've actually been a treat to have around." She gave me a coy look.

"A treat. Like a piece of candy."

"You know what I mean. I just thought you'd like it here, that's all."

"I do. I already love it here." It was just that I didn't want to sit on the blanket by myself. Partly because I was skittish about being in bear country. Partly because I wanted her company. But I didn't want to seem clingy, so I said nothing.

She collected her climbing gear and left me with the food and bear spray. I watched her head for a giant wall of rock, maybe seventy yards away or so. I should have been able to gauge exactly how far away she was, given how many hours of my life I'd spent at swim meets watching Carson. Once there, she met up with two other women. I scanned my surroundings for bear. And then I found the binoculars she'd packed and trained them on Leila.

She pressed the toe of her tiny left climbing shoe into the rock wall, her arms extended overhead, her fingers gripping for purchase. She lifted herself off the ground. Her right foot searched for a hold, and then she reached up with her right hand, and then her left, and alternated with her arms and feet as she climbed higher and higher, as gracefully as a ballet dancer. She seemed to belong to the wall, and it belonged to her, and now I understood. She was feeling the land's heartbeat through her soles.

She came to an overhang and studied it for only a few seconds before swinging her right side to the wall and lifting her left leg up as high as her head—a contortion I couldn't imagine ever being able to do, even in my healthiest of days. She hooked her heel onto the ledge of the overhang, like a coat hanger over a rod, and when she released her left hand, I nearly gasped. She hung like a monkey, shaking out her free arm the way I shake my fingers when running in hot weather.

The other two women climbed toward Leila as she hung there, and I saw how they all chatted with one another while dangling fifteen or twenty feet above the ground the way most friends chat over coffee. None of them was roped to the wall or to each other. I was frightened for Leila, and envious of those women, being so close to her, sharing her passion.

One of the horses stamped the ground, drawing my attention back to where I sat. Two hikers came along. Stopping when they came upon me, they said hello and asked if I was new in these parts. I said I was just visiting.

"Well, you picked the right place to visit," one of them said.

I told them it was Leila's idea, and when I mentioned her name, they both smiled.

"She's here?" one of them said. "Fantastic!" They wished me a good day and continued toward the climbing wall.

Lying around on a blanket can really trigger an appetite. I broke off a large piece of baguette and nibbled on some Brie cheese while mentally composing the letter I needed to send to my clients about my situation. I recalled that one of them lived in Wyoming—Jackson, maybe. Her paintings were dark, sometimes gruesome, but critically praised. It would be fun to visit her studio someday. Then I lay back and dozed off. I awoke to someone tapping against my good leg. It was Leila. Her golden, muscular legs were at my eye level. I looked up at her, shading my eyes from the sun. Perspiration ran down the front of her tank top between her breasts.

"It's as bad as the hospital here," I said, sitting up as she sat down. "You can't get a moment of rest." When she didn't laugh, I explained that I was joking. "Actually it's cool how everyone's so friendly around here." I told her about the hikers whose faces lit up when they heard her name, and others who had come and gone while she was climbing.

"That's what I mean about community as family," she said. "Sometimes in life you come across a magical place where everything works out right and everyone cares about one another. This is one of those places. I'd trust my life, and the lives of my children, with anyone here."

"Even the bears."

"I'm telling you, I've climbed here a lot, and I don't think I've ever seen one here. That's not to say they aren't around. I know they are. Maybe that's just part of the magic of the place."

"So you believe in magic?"

"I believe in life."

Leila spread some olive tapenade on a chunk of baguette, took a dainty bite, and offered the rest of it to me. Then she asked if I'd mind if she climbed a while longer. The women she was climbing with, Lynn and Frankie, had been living in the area for the summer. Like Leila, they'd be leaving soon, and Leila wanted to spend as much time with them that day as possible. I knew the feeling. I told myself not to feel jealous and gave her a thumbs-up. As she jogged back to her non-invalid friends, I couldn't help but notice how her calf muscles flexed with each step, how her tight bike shorts accentuated her round buttocks. Women notice these things about each other—sometimes with envy, sometimes with admiration. I was also vaguely jealous I couldn't have been jogging alongside her, training for my marathon. I wondered how long it would be before I ran again.

I lifted the binoculars to my eyes. Leila tied a purple bandana around her head, pirate style. One of the other climbers reached up to adjust it for her. I wished that could have been me. There was no question about it: I had a major crush on her.

The jagged cliff loomed over Leila, casting a shadow on her. As I watched, the hikers who had passed earlier returned. One of them asked if I was staying with Leila at Maggie's Place.

"Shhh," the other hiker said. "You're not supposed to mention it by name. Remember?"

"As a matter of fact, I *am* staying there," I said. "So your secret's safe with me."

They asked how Emily was faring and were saddened when I told them about her passing. "Leila's in the process of settling Emily's affairs. And about to sell the property," I said.

"She can't do that. We need Maggie's Place, now more than ever," one of the women said.

"It's too bad more women don't know about it," the other said. "But then again, that's the whole point, I suppose."

The first one asked if I was going to the upcoming longhouse celebration. When I said I knew nothing about it, the second hiker chastised the first for revealing another secret and said they needed to be moving along.

"Well, if you ever have a chance," the apparent blabbermouth said, "be sure you attend one. It'll change your life." The two started down the trail, and then the talkative one turned back toward me and asked if Phoebe was still living there. "Now *she's* a special gal."

Longhouse? Phoebe? Sometimes my kids would mention a new TV series or phone app that I'd never heard of, and they'd roll their eyes, and I'd feel like crawling under a rock in embarrassment and ignorance. Obviously there was so much more to Leila and Emily than I'd been privy to, and I had that same feeling of shame now. I should know more. Why had Leila kept so much from me?

THIRTEEN

Anne

MY ARMS WEAKENED to the point of convulsion. I could no longer maintain a grasp on the overhanging branch, and despite Maggie's efforts to rescue me—bless her heart—the current claimed me as its own and whisked me away from her. Every inch of my person became subjected to scrapes and bruises, and I feared that come to-morrow—if there were a to-morrow—I would resemble the tattooed men in those magnificent circus events that periodically came to town.

When the current deposited me onto a rocky beach like unnecessary debris, I lay there gasping for air and clinging to the ground. Maggie appeared momentarily and gently pulled me away from the river's edge lest the water change its mind and reclaim me. I lay face down, trying to catch my breath, as she took note of my wounds, murmuring soft sounds. When, after a while, the rhythm of my breath matched hers, I feebly rolled onto my back. Only then did she realize what was entwined in my fingers.

She untied the leather strap, took the soggy object from me, and collapsed beside me, uttering words in a language I did not know. She hugged the pouch to her face, her tears and words mingling with wet leather. I had my doubts whether I would ever be able to stand or walk again after that turbulent river ride, but whatever damage had been done was worth it once I saw how much that pouch meant to her.

"This is all that remains," Maggie said, her voice nasal between sobs.

I struggled to comprehend how such a small item could represent the remains of something so dearly beloved. Was it possible Maggie mourned for a creature so small it fit inside this parcel smaller than her hand—a butterfly, perhaps? A hummingbird? Or was it symbolic of the place she left behind? She stroked the pouch with the smallest finger on her right hand.

"My daughter," she said. "This is my daughter."

I was perplexed. Was it possible, I wondered, that she had held her head so long under the water that she had lost her faculties? Whatever that pouch contained, it was not a human being. But this was not important; what mattered was that Maggie had been distraught over its loss and was now delirious with gratitude that it had been found. I shifted toward her and tentatively placed one arm around her shoulders. She leaned into me, and when I sensed her warm tears trickling off her chin and down my neck, my eyes began to water as well.

Later—so much later, her tears stopped. She wiped her face dry with her hands, then turned to me.

"I will never be able to thank you for saving this," she said. "And for saving me from the river. I do not want to die. But at that moment, I did."

So my suspicion had been true, that Maggie had indeed been trying to drown herself. A shiver raced down my spine as I recalled how she held her hands aloft as she lowered her head beneath the water's surface. "Why, Maggie? Why would you want to do this?"

"Because I do not deserve to live."

"Of course you do. You saved me." I did not, in fact, believe the worth of her life had anything to do with me. I had only been attempting to lift her spirit with humor.

"I may have saved you, white woman," she said. "But I was unable to save my daughter."

I glanced at the pouch. "Your daughter is in there?"

"Stupid Anne. No, she is not in here. She was strapped to the *tekash*. The cradleboard. When my horse left us in the river, we were alone. There was no place to hide. By lowering myself below the water, my hope was that we would not be seen by your army."

Now it all began to make sense. The Indians running from the army. The battle where she lost her friends. The way she raised her hands above the river when she tried to drown herself. I started to feel heavy, as though a weight of iron were descending upon me. I did not want her to continue.

"But they saw the *tekash*, even if they could not see me. They saw an infant on a board in the middle of the river. And they fired their guns. Three shots."

I closed my eyes. I had a strong desire to crawl back into the water and let it rush over my head and around my ears. I did not want to face the horror of her truth. Or hear any more of her words.

"My daughter died as I held her above the water's surface," she said. "My attempt to save her led to her death."

"Oh, Maggie!" I said, flinging my arms around her and burying my face into her neck. There is nothing one can say when a mother discloses this most unimaginable grief. All one can do is stay by her side and share her sorrow. It was my turn, then, to let the sobs flow, which reignited her grief, and together we wept and keened for her daughter until the sun rose.

I stayed close by Maggie over the next several days, helping her in whatever way I could and hoping Stupid Anne's wilderness inexperience might distract her from her pain. I did not ask her to satisfy my curiosity about the pouch—I still had no idea how it represented her daughter. But I also refrained from making any complaints about my husband or the scabs and scars I had been given by the river or my fears about the future. I willed her survival lessons to distract me from my own pangs of torment as well.

We stretched her few buffalo hides across the tipi's frame and stitched them together with sinew. We built a small fire pit in the center of the tipi, and I learned how to manage the opening in the top as a flue. I inquired how to identify the best wood for making fire and encouraged her to train me in the art of proper kitchen organization with her baskets and rawhide bowls. I also requested instruction on weaving platters from long, dried grasses, and to my surprise, mastered this craft quickly. Reluctantly, I allowed Maggie to show me how to use a bow and arrow, although I would never grow comfortable with such an instrument of death. And because I had discovered that I could indeed survive a body of water larger than my kitchen washtub back home, I permitted her to indoctrinate me in the sport of swimming.

Had Thomas seen me then, how proud he would have been!

Maggie worked tirelessly. Perhaps this was her approach to handling grief. I could not match the energy she possessed, and by mid-day I was usually exhausted and found respite with my sketching work. There was a large boulder not far from our tipi, positioned for maximum sunlight, which was a perfect spot to sit and summon my creativity. It was also a perfect location for keeping one eye out for possible rescue.

One afternoon, Maggie was about to set out with her bow and arrow and offered to teach me how to hunt large animals. For a moment I imagined returning home to Thomas with a trophy for him—an elk head perhaps. But I was reluctant to leave my watch post, just in case this was to be our lucky day.

"Will you be needing Thomas's pistol?" I asked, holding the gun out to her, after she vaulted onto her horse's back with both grace and ease.

Her hand rose to the hollow of her neck. "No. It will not do me any good."

"Why do you do that?" I inquired. "Why do you touch that area just beneath your neck at times?"

She did it again. "I do not know. It is…what do you call it? A habit. When I am about to reply with a no, my hand flies up to my neck and chest. My mother used that gesture as well. There is no reason. Does it bother you?"

"Not at all. I assumed it was a signal of a sort." I shook the gun at her. "Are you certain you do not want this? You never know when it might be helpful."

"Yes, I do know. Your gun is empty. Without bullets, it is useless."

"No bullets?" I opened the chamber, never having thought to do so until now. She was correct; it was empty. "You could still use it to hit someone," I said. "It is not completely worthless."

"X'axa c, maybe?"

I asked her to translate.

"Grizzly bear."

"I cannot imagine hitting a grizzly bear with a gun." I laughed.

"I cannot imagine using a gun for anything. Ever," she said. Her eyes locked with mine, like two friends clasping hands.

"I will be back as soon as possible." She patted the horse's neck. "Do not do anything stupid, Anne."

As I watched her horse run off, my imagination ran as well, causing me to wonder what I would do if she did not return. I retreated into the tipi with a rawhide sack of dried rabbit that Maggie had prepared a couple of days earlier and crawled under the blanket for warmth. No, I would never survive without Maggie, my new-found friend. I would be lost.

Last winter, I became lost without Thomas at my side. I endeavored to see the strange ice formations he had spoken about after a recent blizzard, so I bundled up and walked to the lake-front. It was a frigid day, and the winds were brutal, and before long my ears and nose were numb and my fingertips stinging. My mind seemed to be frozen as well, because when it came time to return home, I turned the wrong way.

Many hours later, a gang of orphans found me shivering in an alley between two decrepit buildings. They led me to a kind police officer, who escorted me home and delivered me into Thomas's arms. I had assumed my worried husband would rejoice to see me again, but instead he was angry. By becoming lost and thus not returning home in a timely fashion, I had inadvertently let the stove go out. Also, there was no supper waiting for him upon his arrival home from work.

All this to say I was tempted to stay inside the tipi until Maggie's return, to avoid becoming lost, but I did not want to upset her with my idleness. So I tended our fire and prepared a berry compote—which was dreadfully bland without proper sugar—and once satisfied I had earned my keep for the day, I set out with the intention of sketching at my watch post. Once there, however, I determined it was still a long way from the main trail that led to Old Faithful, and if I had any serious thought about being rescued before winter came rolling along, I needed to be much closer to it. I ventured past a collection of angry, devilish geysers toward the trail with my sketch-book and Thomas's good-for-nothing pistol in hand, cleverly dropping a trail of pine-cones along the way so I would find my way back again.

A fallen log promised to be a most suitable place to settle, and I proceeded to work on the river sketch I had begun of Maggie. This particular drawing caused me great distress, however, as every time I attended to it, it became worse. By now it looked as though a young child had made the attempt. It seemed Maggie's beauty was too magical—with her long braids, her high cheekbones, her native dress—to be documented, in the same way that images of ghosts cannot be captured by camera. The more I drew, the more objectionable the illustration became. I cursed aloud.

I pondered why this portrayal of Maggie was so important, why I could not cast off my desire to produce her likeness. There was so much splendor in this uninhabited wonderland, and my sketches were meant only to be approximations, to help me better recall the scene when I returned home and brought out my paints and brushes. Why could I not simply sketch a geyser? Or the tipi in the forest? Or the stage-coach that brought Thomas and me to this place—a remarkable mode of transportation despite its creaking wheels—bumping through the prairies? I had not been trained in the art of portraiture, and I had no intention, really, of painting Maggie.

But the truth was thus: soon, I would be rescued. I would return to Chicago. A sketch of my Maggie could very well be the only remembrance I would have of her. I did not want her to become a long-forgotten ghost of my past.

I set my pencil down. The sketch-book as well. I lay lengthwise along the log and closed my eyes, letting the sunshine warm my face. As I rested, I saw far more than the red lining of my eyelids. My mind became a wild horse racing through the forest, kicking up dust and darting around obstacles, determined to avoid capture. And then my eyes sprang open of their own volition, and I sat upright.

What had I been thinking? I could not return to Chicago with only a sketch of Maggie to remember her by. I would bring her with me, of course! I pictured Thomas safely back in Chicago, greeting me at the threshold of our modest home, his strong arms open to receive me in his embrace. And then I envisioned introducing him to Maggie, standing at my side. He would open his arms to her as well—

No, *that* he would not do.

In his eyes, Maggie would be a member of the savage tribe that had captured him, no better than a tag-along dog that had followed me home. He would send her away without a moment's hesitation.

And then what? If I had to choose between Thomas and Maggie…whom would I choose?

I leaned back on my log, trying to sort through this dilemma, until the pounding of hooves—yet again—startled me from my reverie. I expected to find Maggie and her horse when I opened my eyes, but instead found two horses and two riders approaching. They came to an abrupt halt upon reaching my log. Dust swirled.

"Ma'am," one of the two men said, touching the brim of his hat as his mount danced in place. I coughed from the dust and shielded my eyes from the afternoon sun behind him. I dared not look up at him on his horse; a proper lady would never let an unknown gentleman gaze into her eyes. Then again, a proper gentleman would not attempt to converse with a lady without first dismounting.

"Hello," I said, stealing only a quick glimpse before looking away. A recollection of the military men who came through our camp that first day, after Thomas had been taken, chilled me.

These men were neatly dressed, however, in matching brown shirts and pants, and seemed far less menacing. But, alas, they were men.

The shorter of the two spoke first, introducing himself as Ranger Biesen and his companion as Ranger Newman. "Of the National Park," he said.

A rush of heat coursed through me. Rangers? Rescue at last?

I detected Ranger Biesen's eyes scanning my entire countenance. "Pardon my bluntness, but are you out here all alone?"

His inquiry made me quite uncomfortable. In the warm sun, I had removed the horse blanket I had previously used as a cloak, and I still wore nothing underneath my frock, which was by now filthy and ripped. I crossed my arms.

"No, I am not alone. I am…traveling with a friend."

Now the other rider, Ranger Newman, surveyed the terrain as he wiped his face with a bandana, no doubt looking for said companion. Thomas's useless gun lay on the ground at my feet.

"I wonder," I said, "have you heard about a recent encounter with Indians at Mary Lake? My husband was captured by them and I am worried about his well-being."

"An encounter at Mary Lake?" Ranger Biesen said, removing his hat and scratching his head. I wondered whether his mother had taught him any manners.

"Yes, an encounter with the Indians. He was taken as their prisoner."

I caught the two of them looking at one another in puzzlement.

"How long ago did this happen?" Ranger Newman asked.

"Eleven days, to be precise."

The two rangers appeared to turn over my news, each in his own mind perhaps puzzling that neither he nor his partner had heard of this abduction.

"May I ask your husband's name?" the taller one asked.

"My husband was...is...Thomas Blakemore."

Ranger Newman shook his head. "I don't know the name. I heard about the Cowans. And of course the Helena party. Were you with either of those groups, ma'am?"

I explained that it had been only Thomas and I, but that I had seen two white women with the Indians when they took Thomas. "A woman and a girl."

"I'm betting that was the Cowan party," he said, nodding. "Chances are your husband was released when those women were. We don't know his whereabouts now. But one thing is certain, it's not safe for you to be here. The Nez Perce are still in the area, and there could be more Indians from other tribes. Not to mention transients and wild animals.

"And winter is going to fall here any day now," Ranger Newman continued. "And when it falls on Yellowstone, it lands hard. How about if we escort you—and your friend—to Old Faithful? We're heading that direction anyway, and once there, you can make arrangements to safely leave the park and return home."

His offer was as tempting as ice-cream on a hot day. But then he suggested I lead him to our camp, where the two of them could help us break it down. The suggestion did not sit well with me. Maggie had taken great care to ensure our camp-site was well hidden. And I had yet to determine how to reconcile my desire for rescue with Maggie's desires—whatever those might be.

"We are camped inland a short distance," I said. "First I will have to confer with my companion."

It was not every day, to be sure, that those rangers came upon a lone, bedraggled woman who demurred at the opportunity of rescue. But I realized at that precise moment how attached I was becoming to Maggie, my personal Sacagawea.

"All right, then," Ranger Biesen said. "You go ahead and *confer*. We'll return to-morrow at the same time for you."

He jerked his reins and spun his horse around; the other ranger followed suit. As they rode off, déjà vu and Thomas's voice both scolded me. *Foolhardy soul!* I worried whether the rangers would indeed return. I also worried that Maggie might think me stupid for letting them go.

I returned to the camp-site without becoming lost, but feeling as forlorn as ever. By then, the sun had dipped behind the tree line and a wind had kicked up. I crawled into the tipi and lit a small fire to warm up and dry out. Once the fire was steady—I had become quite proficient at fire-building by now—I curled up beneath an unfinished quilt of rabbit and squirrel pelts, and I dozed off. A while later, I thought I heard a violent crashing of trees and brush. I told myself it was surely a dream.

FOURTEEN

Anne

I NEARLY DIED of fright when the tipi flaps opened.

Maggie charged in, her hair matted, her dress ripped—and her smile broad enough to cover the entire Wyoming Territory.

"You are back!" I exclaimed.

"I have good news. My hunt was a success."

"Rabbits again?"

Her hand positioned itself just below her neck. "No, much bigger."

"Lynx?"

"No." She rarely showed her teeth when she smiled, but this time she did. "Buffalo."

"You caught a buffalo?"

"Anne. You do not *catch* buffalo. You kill buffalo. Come, I need your help. It will be dark soon."

I had no time to contemplate the breadth of what it meant to take the life of such a huge beast. Instead, I assisted Maggie in gathering sharp implements and all our rope. As we climbed onto her horse, I was giddy with the news of the day—impending rescue and a most extraordinary opportunity to participate in a buffalo feast. I whistled *Buffalo Gal* again as we galloped afield together; Maggie had by now become willing to listen to the cheerful melody, and when the final line of the chorus came along, she hummed along as well. But when we came to the site of the kill, my glee gave way to horror. A buffalo lay in a pool of blood with multiple arrows protruding from its giant head and chest. I dismounted but was unable to take a single step farther.

"What is it, Anne? Are you unwell?"

I dropped to the ground. I held my head between my knees. Trying as it was to cope with my bloodied foot on that first day, or the rabbit carcass she'd brought to camp, or the poor squirrel I'd butchered—the latter experience had brought me to gagging several times—this was worse. This was carnage.

"It is the sight of blood," I said. "And death."

"Do you think I enjoy killing?" she asked. A vein in her forehead thrust beneath her skin. Her nostrils flared. "Do you think I do not understand the meaning of this? Winter is coming, Anne. We are going to run out of food. And we need hide for clothing and blankets. This is what I had to do. And you must help me. This is one task I cannot do alone."

The implication stung, even if true. I had not sufficiently contributed to our survival, and now it was clear that Maggie was disturbed by this fact. I endeavored to muster the strength to help when suddenly I recalled the rangers' visit earlier in the day.

"But Maggie! We do not need to worry any longer. We are about to be rescued!"

If this were true, then Maggie had slaughtered the poor beast for naught. She, however, did not inquire as to the meaning of my announcement. Instead, she rushed to the corpse, dropped to her knees, and closed her eyes with her head bowed. Even Stupid Anne understood she was offering a prayer.

"The buffalo is dead and its spirit has moved on," she said. "We must carry on with our work."

I pressed the matter no further. With the help of her horse, a clever pulley system Maggie had designed, and two strong branches on a great pine tree, we were able to hoist the carcass into a vertical position, hanging from the branches with its nose barely touching the ground. I turned away just as she began to slit it open with her knife, but my ears could neither muffle the sound of the ripping hide nor my nose escape the stench of the dying innards. Soon after, I heard her footsteps brushing through the grass. She set something heavy beside me, which I spied from the corner of one eye. Chunks of moist, bloody meat.

"Here is your job," she said.

"What am I to do with that? Were we in Chicago, with a stove at the ready, I could make stew. But we are not."

"Roll it up in bundles. Tie the bundles with rope."

I reached for the first chunk. I felt its warmth, and my imagination detected the animal's pulse throbbing through the skin of my palms. I dropped the meat.

"Anne. Please help me."

I had no choice and did as she asked. She continued to slice more meat and bring it to me, faster than I could work. A swarm of voracious flies found us, and I had to fight them all the while I rolled and tied. Before I was halfway through the pile, Maggie set another clump of unrecognizable body parts beside me, then proceeded to identify each one.

"Tongue and liver, good to eat raw. Ears, good for seasoning. Brain—we keep this for tanning the hide."

The slime was more than I could bear.

"I cannot do this, Maggie. I am sorry to be so troublesome." Maybe now, I thought, was as good a time as any to explain my previous exclamation. "I met some rangers today. Park rangers."

She flicked her eyes to the carcass. "I would like to hear about your adventure of the day." Her voice dripped of sarcasm as her hands did of blood. "But now we must work. We will talk later."

Again, I dropped the matter, but as I bundled, I prepared the speech I would later give to her. Before telling her more about the rangers, I would suggest we talk about our plans. We had done little of that, and when she mentioned winter, it struck me that she was planning to stay here, or somewhere nearby, for a long while. She was not planning to return home, and she clearly did not think I would either. Yet before I could even broach the business of our plans, I must tell her how much I cared about her. Start always with love.

Then I would ask about *her* plans. We would discuss our alternative choices. And only then would I tell her about the rangers, how they could help both of us leave the park safely, and that I planned to take her home to Chicago with me. I would not let Thomas factor in to our decision. Or discussion.

A fly landed on the tip of my nose, but my hands were soaked in blood. I blew at it. I shook my head. All that did was to cause my hair to slip down from the twine I had used to tie it back. Meanwhile, the fly remained perfectly happy where it was.

After a while, Maggie came to sit beside me and picked up the raw liver. She sunk her teeth into it and tore off a chunk. As she chewed what was obviously a tough piece of meat, she closed her eyes and relaxed her face. A smile appeared. She offered the liver to me. In the interest of friendship, I accepted it.

"With a little salt," I said, "this would not be bad."

Maggie was proud. I took her blood-stained hands in mine.

"I love you," I said. My words sounded simple, and I wondered how her people expressed love. What words? What gestures? I brought our entwined hands to my heart. "You are like a sister to me, Maggie. Not just because you saved me, for which I will forever be grateful, but also because of what you have taught me. And who you are."

"You have learned a great deal."

"Yes, and not only about how to survive. I have learned about friendship, and the earth, and—"

"Tell me about your rescue. Please do not try to…what is the word? Yes, *sugarcoat*. I am not a child."

I was surprised she knew that word, and I wondered who might have taught it to her, it being such a modern addition to our vernacular. Surely it was not a word the missionaries had incorporated in her school lessons. Then again, so much about Maggie had surprised me, whereas it seemed nothing I did or said astonished her. Even the mention of park rangers failed to disconcert her.

"The rangers are coming back to-morrow," I said, careful to exhibit only joy—and hide any hint of doubt. "For us. For both of us. We are going to be rescued, Maggie! You will come to Chicago with me!"

Maggie shook her hands free from mine and picked up another organ.

"This is the tongue. I am going to hang this from a branch for now. We will save the buffalo's voice for later."

She returned to the carcass as though I had not spoken a word. I watched, dumbfounded, as she walked, until it occurred to me that I had not inquired after Maggie's desires, as had been my intention. I had not demonstrated any consideration for her feelings or her grief. Stupid Anne! And yet I knew I could not continue on in Yellowstone through the winter. I could not live in a tipi forever. I decided to remain quiet for the remainder of the night, help with rolling the meat, as well as the hides, and let her celebrate her victory. To-morrow, after the sun awakened, we would discuss the matter and reach a resolution.

By now it had become quite dark. I could not see what I was doing, and I could barely see Maggie. I suggested we return to camp.

"No. We have much more work to do."

"In the dark?" As though on the cue of a stage director, a wolf howled. "It no longer feels safe to me."

"Then build some fires. There." She pointed. "And there. And there. They will give us light and keep animals away. And sing your stupid song if you want."

I built several fires with kindling and dried grass, which I collected with immense difficulty in the dark. But Maggie was correct; my fires cast a great deal of light and offered much needed heat, too. The next time I heard a howl, and a buffalo's sorrowful bellow, I felt safer. Under her direction, I cooked small bits of meat over the open fires, which we devoured before the food had even cooled to the touch, my hunger overruling the queasiness I still felt after participating in the butchery.

It must have been well past midnight when we began to haul the meat and hides, bundle by bundle, to the trees to hang them out of reach from the many animals that might find our bounty interesting. I was so exhausted, I stumbled and fell several times on rocks hidden in the shadows. Finally, she gave me permission to extinguish our fires, but only after I fashioned two torches from branches and grass. They illuminated our way back to camp.

Maggie stopped her horse along the river. I complained that I was too tired to bathe or swim.

"Your fatigue is not my concern. What concerns me is the likelihood we will not live to see the next sun if we do not go into the river. What do you think we both smell like?"

Now I understood. "Delicious, raw meat," I said. "Speaking of which, I believe we had a visitor in our camp earlier today. While I was in the tipi, and you were out hunting, I heard a great deal of rustling amongst the trees."

"Ah," she said. "Perhaps you earned a visit from x'axa c."

She waded into the water fully clothed. "Come."

Although she had taught me how to float, and I had become much more courageous around the water during daylight hours, and although the river was wide here and the current calm, I was reluctant, now that night had come, to go in.

"Come, Anne. I am here. You will be fine."

Our torches were dying quickly, and the moon was in its waning phase. I carefully stepped into the water, took a breath, and pinched my nose shut at the nostrils. I lowered myself, and as my head slipped below the surface, she combed her fingers through my hair. I surfaced for air.

"Good. Now three more times. And then we will scrub our clothing."

That night, as our dresses hung outside the tipi, Maggie slept easily. But my thoughts kept slumber away like guards at a castle's gate. To-morrow, I would be leaving for home, and in so doing I would either be taking Maggie as my own hostage and forcing her into a foreign world, or I would be saying farewell to her—abandoning her—forever.

As I lay beside her, I replayed the last several days in my mind, from the morning her people had first ridden into the Mary Lake camp-site, to the discovery of Maggie's legs behind the horse, to our travels alongside the Firehole River and her declaration that this site would become our new, albeit temporary, home. I recalled her knife gleaming at me when I was about to open her pouch, and I relived the terror of clinging to the tree branch over the rapids to save her little treasure. I could not shake off the macabre scene of her buffalo slaughter, the stench of which still remained within my nostrils. No matter which image I dwelt upon, I experienced an immense swelling in my heart. Certainly, it was love for Maggie. But it was also pride, knowing that we had survived without a man, even in the roughest of conditions and under intense emotional distress. In fact, we survived rather happily.

I concluded, therefore, that neither Maggie nor I needed a man. Had this thought crossed my mind even a month ago, I would have thought myself mad.

The wind rattled the tipi's hides throughout the night, the way my thoughts rattled the inner workings of my mind. As the hours passed ever so slowly, I became increasingly determined to bring Maggie to Chicago with me. It would not matter what Thomas said, or what exasperation he might feel. Indeed, I was prepared for—perhaps even anxious for—an altercation with him. I began to envision how the three of us would rearrange furniture to make room for Maggie and what Thomas would think of her kitchen skills. I delighted at the idea of introducing her to some of the great artists; she would certainly appreciate John James Audubon's work. And the library! I could scarcely wait to escort her to the new library at the water tower, or to the outposts around the city. I would introduce Maggie to the great writers of our time: Susan Cooper, George Eliot. Even Melville; I suspected Maggie had never even heard of a whale.

Finally, as dawn approached, Maggie stirred. I brushed her hair from her face with my littlest finger, pulled our blanket higher up over our shoulders, and wrapped my arm tightly over her. Only then, in that firm embrace, was I finally able to sleep.

I awoke, however, with a cough. When I poked my head out of the tipi, I found her pouring boiling water into a small basket lined with leaves that miraculously did not leak. She had already put on her buckskin dress. I hurried over to my dilapidated, threadbare frock; it was still damp and cold, but it was the only garment in my current possession. I pulled it over my head and shivered.

She handed the basket to me. "Mountain tea. This will be good for you and your cough. I am sorry you did not sleep well."

Her hair hung long and free that morning.

"Maggie, we need to talk."

"Talk now, while I make our food. After we eat, there is more work to do." She set a slab of buffalo meat on a rack she had made of twigs, which she now placed over the fire.

"Your energy makes me weary," I said. "Can you please stop working for a moment? For goodness sake."

She sat on the other side of the fire, facing me. I scooted over to sit beside her, then reached for her hand.

"Maggie. I cannot begin to tell you how much you mean to me. You were the only reason I survived. I am not sure I will ever be able to repay you."

"Helping you was the honorable thing to do. I do not expect payment."

She ran her fingers through her hair to detangle it and began to weave her braids. As with everything else, she was efficient and skilled, and within moments, she had finished. I waited for her to complete the task by tying each of them with thin rawhide strips. But before I had turned my thoughts over sufficiently to speak, she said she knew what I was going to say.

"You are leaving me." She poked the fire with a branch. "I knew this would happen just as I have known it would soon snow."

"And how do you know it will soon snow?"

"I can tell from the call of the birds."

"I suppose they also warned you of my plans?"

"No. The birds cannot understand you as well as I can."

"I do not know what the birds understand. Or what you understand for that matter. What I do know is that the rangers will return today to escort us to Old Faithful and help us find our way to home. To my home in Chicago."

"Your home."

She looked out toward the edge of the forest, toward the main trail. I sipped the tea. It was fruity and minty and grassy all at once, as complex as medicinal wine. As complex as Maggie. I followed her gaze and tried to implant the vista in my memory.

"We cannot live here, in Yellowstone, forever," I said. "We are not prepared for winter. We cannot live in hiding from others forever, either."

"We have the buffalo. We will survive."

"No, Maggie. That is not…acceptable. You must come and live with me. It is my turn to take care of you."

She poked at the roasting meat; fatty juices oozed from the slab and flames licked at the buffalo like hungry tongues.

"Keep an eye out for *x'axa c*," she said. "It will follow this scent directly into our camp."

I glanced around. "If I bring you with me, we could have a delightful life together. We could talk and laugh and gossip and play. We could brush one another's hair. I could teach you how to play the piano or dance the polka. We would be like sisters."

She sprinkled salt over the cooking meat. Her salt bag was nearly empty.

"I cannot go to Chicago," she said, tripping over the pronunciation of my city's name and leaving truncated space between syllables.

"Why ever not?"

"It is your people's rule. Remember? Indians must live on reservations."

Stupid Anne had forgotten this important detail. I took a moment to think. "All right. Then here is my plan. I will go to the trail. You will stay here and cook our buffalo meat. When the rangers come, I will talk with them. I will talk about this Indian reservation dilemma. They will surely know how to assist us."

"Two rangers cannot overturn a treaty. It is a government order. Also, what about all this buffalo meat? And the hides?"

"We will bring it with us."

"Do you think I am stupid, Anne? There is too much here to travel with. If you need to leave, then you should. Go to the trail. Go home."

To hurt someone you love is unbearable. To be hurt by them is as much agony.

"I am sorry, Maggie," I said. "Truly sorry. For everything."

With two twigs, she deftly skewered the meat and flipped it over. Once again, fatty juices dripped onto the fire and flames jumped.

"But I will not leave you here! It is not safe for you. If the winter does not kill you, something—or someone else—will."

"It will be your people who kill me," she said. "You have not known what a comfort it has been, for me, to have a white woman beside me."

I had never thought of myself as a guardian for her, but this idea had some merit.

"All the more reason you must come with me."

"I do not want to live with your people."

"Do you want to live on a reservation?"

She added yet more salt to the meat. "The rangers will be arriving soon. You had better go. There is nothing more either of us should say."

It was quite possible she could hear the rangers' horses better than I could. Maggie was like that—like an animal with senses far superior to mine. Flummoxed, I quickly gathered up my sketch-book and Thomas's gun and wrapped them together in a remnant of hide.

"I will be out at the trail if you need me," I said. "Or if you change your mind." I refused to say goodbye.

She nodded as she added another bundle of meat to the fire, but she did not look up at me.

I started to walk away, and then stopped. What had I been thinking? I had just asserted how I could not leave her in the forest alone. And surely not while cooking meat. What if a bear did come along? Or a pack of wolves?

Or a mad man? But, of course, Maggie had proven all along to be a skilled hunter and a smart, confident young woman. If anyone was at risk, it was I.

The sky now laden with clouds, I proceeded toward my destination, downtrodden as though I were going to my own funeral. Chipmunks scolded me along my path; an elk bugled its fury in the distance. The wind blew colder. My pathetic dress did little to keep me warm.

After settling on my log where I resolved to wait, I began to work on an old sketch, but my mind refused to cooperate with my hands. I could not stop dwelling on the idea that Maggie and I were about to separate from one another, forever. I scanned the southern panorama, whence the rangers would likely come. Steam rose from geysers but no riders headed my way.

I turned to a fresh page, intent on creating an image of Maggie that conveyed the affection I felt for her. I tried to recall how other portrait artists depicted love on canvas. A teacher had once said it was in the eyes. I recalled that first moment when I knew something special was forming between Maggie and me; it was the first night we had lain together in her makeshift lean-to at Mary Lake. We had not yet shared our names with one another; we had not yet learned to trust one another. But I had seen in her eyes something deep and surprising, desperate and exquisite. This was what I needed to express with my pencil.

I worked furiously as the wind buffeted my back. When I took a short break to shake out my fingers, I noticed the clouds had further thickened. And darkened. A small herd of elk had wandered near; in the distance a black shape roamed through the grasses. A week ago, I would have fainted at the mere suggestion of a bear in the vicinity. But not any longer. I felt quite at ease now. My only fear was that the rangers had forsaken me.

I added pencil strokes here and there, drawing the rapids as they coursed around Maggie, like life itself trying to skirt its way around obstacles. I sketched trees in the background. I filled out Maggie's form, shading in the muscular curve of her uplifted arms at that moment before she submerged herself entirely.

Thomas's voice suddenly came to me like an intruder. *Do you honestly call this art, my dear?*

"Go away," I said aloud. "Go away!" I had never been able to say such a thing to him without risk of repercussion. How odd that I felt safer here in the wilderness than in my own home.

A gust of wind picked up behind me and flapped the edge of my page. I slammed the book shut and hugged it tightly, wondering how long I would have to wait and whether I should continue to sit here. Soon, the wolves would be howling in unison and the bats flying, and dusk would lower itself over me yet again in this vast, enchanted land.

FIFTEEN

Brooke

DESPITE SHANE'S EARLIER insistence that I return home at the end of the week, I stayed in West Yellowstone, and my life began to find solid ground. My physical therapy sessions, three times a week, were going well, even if they were grueling. I reconnected with my clients once I figured out where I could get reliable Wi-Fi in town, and most of them wrote back with both sympathy and awe about my story. The one who lived in Jackson—the artist whose work often involved bloody images—asked to hear more about the bear attack. I also reached out to a couple of new artists, asking if I might send them a marketing proposal, and I connected another one with a CPA I knew who could help with tax planning. It felt refreshing to be back in my online art business saddle.

My relationship with Leila also found a rhythm—albeit a pendulous one, fluctuating from hot to cold, from laughter to tears, from conversation to silence. It wasn't that her moods were swinging, I decided; Leila was just one of those types who would indulge others with all her love and energy, without judgment or limitation, and then she'd hit a wall and retreat to recharge. I learned not to take it personally and, if anything, I loved her more for this complexity.

I was building other relationships, too. J.P. called me every few days to *check in*. Whether his interest was platonic, romantic, or professional, I wasn't sure, but I enjoyed our telephone chats. He had a sparkling personality—and he'd extended my oxycodone prescription, and even offered something for the resultant constipation before I had to ask. I also checked out one of those Internet dating sites. Who knows what got into me; although Shane and I had been having rough times, I hadn't really been giving the big D any thought. Still, it was exciting to learn about a whole new world out there.

Meanwhile, Shane hadn't taken it well when I informed him I wasn't going home as he'd demanded—and arranged. Now he'd cut off almost all communication with me. Although part of me appreciated this break from him, another part felt wounded. And curious about whatever it was he might have been doing. I left voicemails for him. I sent emails and texts. I rarely heard back. I tried carefully to inquire of Carson whether he'd talked to his dad lately, without letting on there was a drought developing in his parents' marital landscape, but I couldn't get anything out of him—boys will be boys. Discussing the matter through emojis with Delaney was impossible.

Shane's biting cold shoulder wasn't all that unusual. Whenever I'd refused in the past to give in to him, he'd been a sore loser. Like the time I agreed to chaperone Delaney's choir to a prestigious competition, which happened to take place on his birthday. You'd think a grown man could handle celebrating his birthday on a different date than the actual anniversary of his birth, especially for an event as important as this was to our daughter. But not Shane. He didn't speak to me for three days after the competition—which her choir won.

I even searched the news for headlines about him; the only thing I found was an article describing how he'd fired an assistant but hired a campaign manager. Nothing out of the ordinary to worry about. But we couldn't go on like this forever, so in the interest of trying to heal my marriage, and also to satisfy the kids' curiosities about how ravaged I really was after the bear mauling, it was my turn to make an executive decision: I arranged for everyone to fly to Yellowstone during the university's fall break. When the airplane confirmations and invoices hit Shane's inbox, I got a reaction. Surprisingly, a favorable one.

He looked exhausted, however, when I opened Leila's front door that Thursday afternoon, exactly three weeks after I was supposed to go home per Shane's earlier commandments. Now, he looked as if he were the one traumatized. I'd never seen him like that before: pale, purple circles under his eyes, his hair uncharacteristically mussed. If I hadn't known better, I'd have thought he actually missed me.

It had always been me who was the fatigued one. All those years of schlepping kids around, fighting about homework, maintaining a perfect household, and defending my entire world to my husband—from why I used semisweet morsels instead of bittersweet in the cookies to why I let Carson get away with only a B+ on his latest history essay. I had always been the one who had greeted Shane at the door with worn-off mascara, stains on my blouse, and a sallow complexion from too much coffee and wine, too little exercise, and a heavy monthly bout of PMS. In the early years, whenever I'd needed to fall into someone's arms at the end of a long day, Shane was there. But once the kids were older—his career demands greater, each of us taking the other for granted—he wasn't. He was either holed up in his man-cave, at the office, or out entertaining clients. On the occasional evenings when we did connect, he was frequently at the ready with list in hand, asking why I hadn't made it to the dry cleaner's, or wasn't it about time I clean out the refrigerator before someone got sick from spoiled food? As if we were the only family on the planet that let food spoil now and then.

Now, on this day of his arrival in West Yellowstone, the table had turned.

I had worried how he might react to my bandages, and especially to the developing scar on my right cheek, given he had always been so concerned with appearance in general, mine in particular. But he made no mention of how I looked and instead gave me a tentative hug and a peck on my good cheek. Carson stepped forward and let me wrap my arms around him as tightly as I could. When I released him, I studied his face, trying to figure out what was different from how he'd looked just seven weeks ago. His hair was unkempt. He was dressed in a loose T-shirt and ripped jeans. And his eyes, like his father's, looked tired. Either senior year was wearing hard on him, or my trauma had impacted him more than I'd ever imagined possible.

Delaney, however, looked as marvelous as ever. No one could have guessed she'd been traveling for hours to get here. Dressed fashionably in a red leather bellboy jacket, tight jeans, and black boots with red stitching—perfectly drawn eyeliner and lash extensions, too—she was more beautiful than ever. My Delaney. I wanted to grab hold of her, squeeze her dangerously tight, and never let her go. But I was unsure what our relationship was and, knowing that kids are always in charge whether or not you like it, I decided to play it cool. I stood face to face with her and waited for her to make the first move.

Her face twitched as she worked hard to hold every facial muscle in check. I took one step forward, and so did she—awkwardly bumping the pointed toe of her fashion footwear into the toe of my walking boot. She leaned in to hug me the way you would a distant relative, then quickly let go.

"We'll talk?" I said, holding each of her wrists in my hands, hoping that she would indulge me with conversation soon. I couldn't imagine an entire weekend with only emojis. "But first," I turned to Shane, "let's get settled at the hotel."

"We're going to a hotel?" Shane asked. "How much is that going to set us back?"

"Well, we can't stay here."

By now, Carson had meandered to the side of the cabin but was still within earshot. "Why not?" he asked. "This place is awesome. It's so…rustic. And we've been traveling for hours."

"Yes," Shane said, surveying Emily's cabin, the weeds in the garden beds, the entire landscape. His voice dripped with arrogance. "Rustic is certainly one word you could use."

"Dad, you sound like Professor Snape," Delaney said.

"I'll take that as a compliment," he said, lovingly flicking his fingers against her shoulder. I didn't think she'd meant it as one.

"Hey! There are a bunch of cabins out back," Carson said. "We could each have our own. Come on, Mom. We're tired. Can't we just stay here?"

"No. It's complicated," I said. "And it simply isn't an option. So I've booked us a suite at the Lake Hotel. Very historic, very proper. This is the final weekend of the season. And this is a special occasion for us, being all together like this. You'll enjoy it, Shane. I promise."

"I hope so."

After checking into the suite, my old codependent self showed up, and I soon found myself attending to Shane's needs. I helped him unpack, rubbed his sore shoulders, and fixed him a drink from the hotel suite's minibar. In one sense, it felt comforting to be with someone who knew me through and through, like going back to visit an old childhood home, even if you had deplored the place when you lived there and have no intention of staying for more than five minutes now. It also felt good to be the giver, after all those weeks of Leila giving to me. On the other hand, it would've been nice if he'd offered a little TLC to me, particular given what I'd gone through, the obstacles I'd overcome. A bear mauling. A major surgery. Physical therapy. All on my own, far from home. I was proud of how well I'd done and, although I was no longer looking for sympathy, I was hoping for a teensy-weensy acknowledgement, a pat on the back, kudos for a job well done.

As soon as Delaney and Carson went off to explore the grounds—after we'd told them to meet us in the hotel dining room at six o'clock for dinner—Shane locked our bedroom door and began to unzip my hoodie. In no time he had unbuttoned and removed his shirt and my various layers, and we were pressed against one another, skin to skin, exchanging body heat and sweat and smells for the first time in months. Sex wasn't what I'd had in mind, and we were initially awkward coming together, but this was the TLC he knew how to deliver best so I went along with him. He held my face gently and kissed me softly at first, with his eyes closed and shoulders lifted, the way he used to when we'd first met. This was a ghost from the past, whispering how much he'd missed me. Then his kisses came harder, and more passionate, his fervor escalating. We moved to the bed, and once he'd finished with his agenda, he turned his attention to me and awakened desires I'd forgotten I had.

The late afternoon sun bore down on us through the windows, making it impossible to linger on the bed even if we'd wanted to. After showering and getting dressed in silence, we went downstairs to the hotel lobby, where a humming din permeated the air, with perhaps twenty different conversations underway throughout the grand area. Thoughts darted around the inside of my mind in all directions, like spilled marbles, as I tried to make sense of what had just happened between Shane and me upstairs. Was it possible we still loved each other?

"Let's get a cocktail before going into the restaurant," he said, heading to the lobby bar.

"Let's not," I said, taking hold of his shirtsleeve. I was impressed with this strange authoritative voice that came from inside me. With my arm hooked in his, I steered him toward the dining room. "We're already late for our reservation, and the kids are waiting."

At the maître d's desk, I pointed to the corner of the dining room, where Carson and Delaney were seated at a large, rectangular table, and I questioned the maître d' why such a large table had been reserved for a party of four.

"Oh, no, madam," he said. "There must be some mistake. There will be quite a few guests joining you."

I beamed up at Shane, thinking he had planned some sort of surprise for me. But the intensity of his scowl proved me wrong. He started to protest about the restaurant's apparent incompetence. Surely they had confused us with another party. The maître d' insisted that no error had been made, so I took Shane's arm and suggested we go with the flow—whatever it was and wherever it went. It wasn't often we got our family of four together, and if the restaurant wound up seating some strangers with us, so be it. People were friendly around here. It would be a new adventure.

I began to guide my crutches around tables and chairs through the dining room—much more gracefully than I'd done back in Idaho a few weeks earlier—while at the same time feeling the gaze of other diners upon my scarred face and wondering how many of them had heard or read about the incident. Was I a celebrity of sorts in these parts? When I felt a hand on my back, I turned, but instead of the hand belonging to Shane, I saw that it was Leila's.

"What are you doing here?" I asked.

She hugged me, a one-way hug since I couldn't very well wrap my crutches around her.

"Surprise! We decided to make this a special night," she said. "So that your family could meet your new friends. And so we could meet them." She extended her hand to Shane, exuberantly, and he took it into his with equal, and unexpected, enthusiasm. The immediate chemistry between them jolted me.

"Leila's my host here," I said. "She's the woman who's been taking care of me."

"The one who lives in the cabin with the odd totem pole," he said. "How charming." There was that arrogant Professor Snape again.

"It's a historical artifact," she said.

"What artifact?" A familiar voice from behind drew our attention, and when I turned I found Ruth and J.P. standing behind me. They each hugged Leila first, then me. She introduced them to Shane.

This simple little evening was becoming increasingly complicated by the minute. I half expected to see the ghost of Emily and my grizzly bear amble in next. But it was almost as much of a surprise when a woman I didn't recognize approached Leila, along with a much younger woman who was the spitting image of Palmer.

We situated ourselves at the table, which in itself was no small feat as everyone had a different opinion about who should sit where. Leila took charge, directing me to the middle of the table as the guest of honor, next to Carson, who reeked of so much pot I thought we'd all get high just sitting at the table with him—or thrown in jail. Meanwhile, Shane pulled out the chair on my right, and when Leila gestured for him to sit at the head of the table instead, I held my breath. He never liked it when other people made decisions for him—especially women—and everything about this day had been designed without his input. Now he wasn't even allowed to sit next to his wife, the woman to whom he'd just made fierce love. But being offered the head of the table, in his mind, was the true seat of honor while also laden with responsibility. Which he took on with flourish, wasting no time to browse the wine list and order what turned out to be the most expensive wine on the menu.

Ruth sat at the end of the table next to Carson, and J.P. took the seat to my right. He smelled of lemon-lime, which I hoped would counteract Carson's aroma. J.P. handed me a small piece of paper and whispered to me.

"This is the last one."

This was not the time or place to discuss whether I was ready to get off my painkillers. I discreetly tucked the prescription, along with my irritation, into my purse as Leila positioned herself between him and Shane. The two women I didn't know introduced themselves as Jolene and Taylor, Palmer's ex-wife and daughter.

"It was so kind for you to include us in your celebration," Jolene said to me as she offered me her hand. She was blonde, tan, and at least thirty years younger than Palmer. Her daughter looked to be around Delaney's age. Before I had the chance to explain that I had nothing to do with their invitation—or even Palmer's—she explained that Palmer had told her all about my ordeal. "And what a coincidence that we happened to be visiting him this weekend. Look, our daughters are already becoming friends."

Delaney and Taylor were in fact already sitting next to each other and laughing about something; if nothing else came of the evening, seeing a smile on my daughter's face would make it worthwhile, even if it had nothing directly to do with me.

The seat across from me, reserved for Palmer, remained vacant.

After the flurry of handshakes and scraping chairs subsided, a server took our beverage order. Taylor and Delaney ordered sodas.

"Delaney, you know you shouldn't have that," Shane said loudly. "That stuff is poison."

Delaney acted as if she hadn't heard him, but poor Taylor's ears and cheeks reddened. She, too, had ordered Coke. I couldn't very well kick Shane under the table, so I held my hand midair toward him and pantomimed lowering it, with the hope he'd understand the message I was trying to send.

"Don't worry about him," Carson said to Taylor. "He's a control freak."

"Carson," I said. "Don't start."

Shane's jaw tightened, and when the sommelier—distracted by Carson—accidentally dripped sparkling wine on Shane's sleeve, he snapped at the poor guy. "Hey, watch what you're doing. That's expensive wine. And a designer shirt."

Taylor giggled and whispered to Delaney that the two of them shared something in common.

"What's that?" Delaney asked.

"Weird dads. You'll see."

Thankfully Shane didn't hear what Taylor had said, still too busy wiping his sleeve. The next several minutes went smoothly; we studied our menus, and Shane announced his plan to pick up the tab. This didn't surprise me, even after all his whining about money. Whenever he could make himself appear magnanimous, he did. Already I saw that his charm was working down at his end of the table. Although Leila had heard a few of my various complaints about him over the past several weeks, she now sat with her chin on her hand, leaning in to him as though listening to God himself.

I elbowed J.P. "She's not falling under his spell, is she? Tell me it's just a hospitable act."

He rubbed his chin as he pretended to look out the window behind Shane, the better to get a look at Leila's face.

"Can't tell for sure," he said. "I'm giving it fifty-fifty."

A few minutes later, it was evident to me that Leila was past the fifty-fifty stage and was becoming entrapped in Shane's sticky web of charm. She fiddled with the leather choker around her neck. His eyes twinkled at her. They laughed together. And their conversation was just quiet enough, amidst the cacophony all around us, that I couldn't hear a word either of them said to the other. I stood up and fumbled with my crutches, excusing myself—to anyone who cared—to go to the restroom. Ruth said she'd go with me. But I didn't need to use the toilet. What I needed was fresh air.

"Something wrong, honey?" Ruth asked as I hobbled out the hotel lobby door.

"Everything's wrong. This isn't how the evening was supposed to go. I know Leila meant well, but this was supposed to be a night for family."

We sat on a bench on the veranda.

"Really? Your face sure lit up when you saw J.P."

My hand rushed to my cheek. "There are so many dynamics going on in there. And our family is fragile right now. I know this sounds insensitive and ungrateful, but I wish I could politely ask everyone to go home."

"What dynamics are concerning you?" she asked.

"Don't tell me you haven't noticed. There's my daughter who refuses to speak to me. And then there's whatever's going on between Shane and Leila." I looked out at the choppy lake, the heather gray sky overhead. "Storm's coming."

"Are you saying that metaphorically?"

"No. Look. Those clouds don't look too friendly. I had hoped to take the kids out on the lake this weekend." Trail running hadn't been my only goal while in Yellowstone. I'd also wanted to reconnect with my younger self, a woman who once loved kayaking and canoeing. Once the bear got to me, all athletic endeavors had been put on hold. But just maybe, I'd thought, I could maneuver into a boat with the kids. Now, with Shane flirting around and bad weather on the horizon, those plans were about to disintegrate.

"It'll pass," Ruth said.

"Are *you* speaking in metaphor?"

"Take it as you'd like. What I see more than anything is a woman and her own inner storm. It feels to me that you're fighting something within yourself." She stood and extended her hand to help me get back up. "Something to think about."

I kept Ruth's wise words in mind throughout dinner. Afterward, Carson escorted me through the vast lobby, where a dozen upholstered chairs had been arranged around the baby grand. We'd been the last to leave the table, and by now J.P. was sitting at the piano, playing an old Billy Joel song. I had no idea he was musically inclined beyond his famous iPod routines in the hospital. Taylor and Delaney were sitting in a couple of chairs nearby, Shane was over at the bar, and Leila was nowhere in sight.

When J.P. spotted me, he began to play and sing a different song that, by the refrain, I could only assume was called *Boogie Bear*. A flame ignited somewhere inside me—or better yet, a switch was flipped. Now that neither Shane nor Leila was with me—and seemingly not with each other—I wanted to stay. I sat down next to Delaney, ever hopeful, but she shifted and turned her back to me. I decided I wouldn't let her ruin my evening. Then Taylor asked Delaney if she had a boyfriend.

"God! Why does everyone keep asking me that? I'm so sick and tired of people thinking you have to be in a relationship to be happy. To be normal."

"I was just making conversation," Taylor said.

"Well, make conversation about something else."

I was about to snap at Delaney for her rudeness, but I knew I would suffer the backlash, and others would see the strain in our relationship. I didn't need it to be any more obvious to everyone else than it already was. As I mulled over my options, Shane came along and let out an exaggerated yawn.

"Time to turn in, Brooke?"

That was another of his irritating habits: leave the party before it dwindles so you're never caught in the doldrums with the normal people. Go out when you're on top, that sort of thing. Also, he had shared me with the world long enough for one night. It didn't matter that this was *my* night. I knew his desire to go upstairs didn't mean he wanted to actually spend time with me; we'd already made love, or fucked, or whatever it was. Chances were good he'd go upstairs and check his email or clip his toenails. He just didn't want others enjoying my company, or vice versa.

My first instinct was to argue, or to plead with him to let us stay a while longer, like a child begging her father for more cake. But I didn't want to ruin the evening with conflict, and the truth was that Shane had been a trouper, especially given how much he was out of his comfort zone here. So I let him help me up, and we said our goodnights.

As we waited for the elevator, he analyzed the dinner. Although the wild rice was overcooked and bland, his trout was sweet and succulent. "And the roasted vegetable chili that Leila ordered, with that jalapeno-roasted paprika combination, was *espléndido*." He kissed his fingertips, then waved them away. "You should try to make that sometime."

My attempt to reply was interrupted by a commotion at the hotel's main doors. Palmer stumbled in, his face bruised around one eye, his clothing striped with gashes. His lips were swollen and bloodied. He headed toward the restaurant.

"Palmer!" Forgetting about my crutches, I made an instinctive move for him. My good knee buckled, and I went down. Several people came to the rescue—both mine and his. After several unidentified arms helped me stand up and Palmer sit down, I asked what happened.

"I had an accident. Accident." He shook his head back and forth as if trying to shake out a memory, his agitated hands waving about. His eyes were glassy, his gaze unfocused.

"Who's this?" Shane asked, taking a step back the way he might if approached by a disheveled homeless person.

"This is Palmer. The ranger who saved me. Taylor's father. Jolene's ex." I noted the surprise in Shane's scowl before returning my attention to poor Palmer and placing a hand on his shoulder. "What kind of accident, Palmer?"

"This was the no-show at dinner," Shane said, his voice overruling Palmer's. I thought I heard Palmer say something about a bear but couldn't be sure. Two ears should afford you the ability to listen to two people at once, but they don't.

"Is Taylor here?" Palmer asked, looking around the lobby and ignoring Shane's sneer. "Taylor here?"

"Yes," I said. "Just stay put while I go find her. And get some help for you."

"I think I'll leave you two alone," Shane said, missing this golden opportunity to help his disabled wife and the man who saved her. Yep, he was pissed off. I had allowed Palmer to derail Shane's plans, so now he was going to go off and sulk, leaving me on my own. So be it, I thought. I would manage, as I always did.

Once I found J.P., he masterfully tended to Palmer's wounds, his hands competent but gentle, his manner compassionate. He was not thrown off by Palmer's bizarre rants or nonsensical explanation about vigilantes assaulting him on a trail. Quite the contrary, J.P. seemed to calm Palmer down like a horse whisperer with a wild mustang.

Jolene and Taylor listened to J.P.'s instructions about caring for Palmer's wounds, which thankfully were superficial, and they escorted Palmer up to their room. By then, J.P. and I were the last ones of our group down in the hotel lobby. As we waited for the next elevator, I hoped I wasn't just imagining the heat waves emanating between our bodies. I wanted so badly to go to his room rather than mine. I wanted to be with J.P. that night, not with Shane. I wanted his hands on my body. When the elevator car doors opened, I held my breath, unsure what I would say if he extended an invitation. But instead he asked which floor we were on, and he pressed the button, and moments later we were saying goodnight to each other even as I wondered what type of lover he was.

It must have been the wine. Or maybe I was high on the excitement of the evening—or the residual fumes from Carson's marijuana. At any rate, I'd agreed, at the dinner, to take the family out to Lewis and Shoshone Lakes. Taylor had gone canoeing out there years earlier with her father and said she was certain he'd loan us some canoes or kayaks. Carson and Delaney knew that, in my former life, I'd been a river guide, and they'd frequently asked me to take them out on the water. But I never did because, well, that's the way life goes. Best intentions are forgotten. Or bowled over. Now, two days after the party, we were going, and I was giddy with anticipation, and also with hope that maybe this was what Shane and I needed more than anything else. We'd been living our lives largely on his terms before I came to Yellowstone, and maybe if we could squeeze a few more things into it that I liked to do, like outdoorsy things, whatever fissures had formed between us might mend.

We met Palmer and Taylor at the Lewis Lake boat launch. He was bandaged but otherwise appeared to be in much better shape—physically and psychologically—than he had been at the hotel. When I asked how he was feeling, he said fine. Questions about what had really happened to Palmer still lingered on my mind, but I decided it wasn't the best time to ask for more details.

"I was wondering if Taylor could go with you," he said. "I've got work to do, and she's been after me to take her on an adventure. She sure enjoyed being with you folks. 'Course if it's an inconvenience, then by all means say so."

Delaney had to be the decision maker. You don't shove two teenage girls into the same kayak unless they like each other. After the way she'd snapped at Taylor about the boyfriend comment, I wasn't sure where Delaney stood.

"Delaney? Is it all right with you?" I asked.

As expected, she didn't acknowledge my existence, but the smile on her face and the high five she gave Taylor told us what we needed to know.

I clambered into the stern of Palmer's fiberglass canoe. He helped the kids put on their lifejackets and climb into their kayaks, and he gave everyone a few lessons on paddle strokes. The kids practiced paddling just off the end of the dock, and Shane—still on the dock—fiddled with his keys, wallet, and phone—double-checking to be sure they were sufficiently waterproofed in nested Ziploc bags. He'd never liked being on, or in, the water, and I felt a bit guilty that I was making him do something so completely out of his comfort zone. I lay back in the canoe and listened to water gently lapping against the side.

The sun reddened the inside of my eyelids, and I felt so at home here on the water, even after all the years since I'd been out on a boat. To be floating—with my family—in the oldest national park in the country, which one of our country's forefathers wisely recognized well over a hundred years ago as a special place, was beyond anything I had hoped for.

"I should've brought fishing gear," Shane said, interrupting my reverie. His comment also shattered whatever guilt I'd been feeling about forcing him to do something against his will. It brought to my mind the luxuriously outfitted fishing trips he'd taken on the Deschutes River over the last couple of years. He would be fine.

And I was glad he wasn't going to be fishing. When I saw the anglers out on the lake when we'd first arrived, something jumped in my stomach, a frantic little fish-self inside me. I'd never supported fishing or hunting, and since coming to Yellowstone, my convictions only strengthened, especially when I'd read in a park brochure that the native cutthroat species of fish were dying out because some bright idiot years ago introduced non-native species like rainbow and brown trout to this area. All for the entertainment of city boys with long poles trying to prove themselves macho to one another.

And now that humankind had successfully screwed up Yellowstone's water ecosystem, we were messing with land animals. Carson had done more than send funny memes to me. He'd also been doing some research about grizzly bears and learned that, because their population in the Lower Forty-Eight was on the rise again after near decimation, they were no longer endangered or threatened—which meant that, at least in some states, they could legally be hunted again. I instinctively scanned the shoreline for hunters and bears.

"Want some sunscreen?" Shane asked. I squinted one eye open and took the tube from him. After smearing some lotion on my face and shoulders, I tossed the tube across the water to Carson, and we all watched its arc, holding our breath and waiting to see if my toss would be adequate or if our hopes to avoid sunburn would splash down short of his reach. Miraculously, it made it all the way into his hand.

"After you kids put on some sunscreen," I said, "we'd better get going. We've got a lot of paddling to do today. And Palmer says the winds pick up in the afternoon."

We began by paddling along the western shoreline of the lake, northward toward the Lewis River channel.

Carson asked if we couldn't take a more direct route across the lake. "This lake is shaped a lot like Africa, if you add in the Saudi Arabia peninsula," he said. "The boat launch is down at the southern tip near where Cape Town would be. If we take a direct path toward the channel, it would be like paddling directly to Algeria on the Mediterranean, bypassing Liberia and Sierra Leone and all those other countries along the west coast."

Delaney splashed water at him with her paddle. "You're such a nerd."

"Given how smooth the water is," I said, "it's all right with me if we go straight to Algeria. If it were choppier, I'd recommend the West Africa route. You always want to stay by the shoreline when the weather's bad."

We corrected course. Listening to all the paddles was like listening to music, and with each dip of the paddle and subsequent pull through the water, I felt like I was making progress not only across the lake but also through life. Maybe I'd been land-bound for too many years. And city-bound. Maybe I just needed more of the great outdoors for everything to be okay.

Delaney and Taylor's double kayak bumped into our canoe from behind.

"Don't do that!" Shane yelled from the bow as he reached for the canoe's rim for stability. "These aren't bumper boats."

I gave the girls one of those *it's okay but don't do that again* looks.

"Brooke? Can bears swim?" Taylor asked me from the stern of their kayak.

"Why? Did you see one?"

"God, stop being so paranoid," Delaney said, looking over her shoulder toward Taylor and away from me. She blew her bangs out of her face.

"It's wise to be on the lookout," I said, trying to catch Delaney's eyes. "But you probably just saw a log. Or another boat." I smiled at Taylor, trying to ease her fears, and when she returned a friendly look to me, I couldn't help but wish Delaney would give me a fraction of the same warmth. Instead, Delaney's attention swung in an arc from her father to the distant horizon to Taylor in the back of the kayak—carefully choreographed to avoid any glimpse of me. I was growing tired of the charade and wondered if she could really maintain this disdain toward me for the entire weekend. I also couldn't help but wonder why she bothered to come for this visit at all.

"Maybe we should have hired a real guide."

Shane's zinger ripped my attention away from my daughter and stung like a hornet. So much for a harmonious day. I should have known our peace wouldn't last. I nodded at the girls to paddle on and tried to match my stroke with Shane's, but he was erratically switching from side to side. I struggled to get in sync with him. The result: an unintentional but unavoidable tacking back and forth. We fell farther and farther behind the kids, who had by now entered into a race with one another.

Finally Shane and I found our rhythm, and I switched my J-stroke into autopilot. I imagined what it might be like if the kids could stay longer than just this weekend, how we could go on all sorts of excursions in the Yellowstone area. And then another thought burst into my head, an unwanted but intriguing one: how lovely it would be to spend more time here *without* the kids. And without Shane. As grateful as I was for his agreeing to this excursion, I was finding his uneasiness on the boat irksome. What would my life look like if I did decide to stay on in this area for longer? Maybe not in West Yellowstone; it was such a small town, and Leila would soon be going home. No, if I were to stay on, maybe it would be better to try somewhere else. I could already see a cute little house with an herb garden within walking distance of a quaint Western town. A coffee shop in the heart of downtown where everyone would know my name, just like in *Cheers*. I could get a job in the winter as a lift line operator and in the summer as a river raft guide. A middle-aged raft guide.

"Well?" Shane said, interrupting my thoughts. "Are you going to answer me?"

"Pardon me? Did you say something?"

"Never mind. You never listen."

"It wasn't a case of not listening, Shane. I didn't hear you. It's hard to hear when your mouth is facing away from me, and your words are coming at me through the back of your skull." Your *thick* skull, I thought. "Especially now that the breeze is picking up."

He said no more, and I once again felt guilty—a near constant feeling when around my husband. It had been wrong of me to think that condescending thought about him. But was it wrong to fantasize about pursuing my own interests in this next phase of my life? I tried to picture what life would be like back in Portland, and it was like watching a tired old movie for the umpteenth time. If I went back with Shane, I'd slip into my old role, pretending I was the perfect wife, mother, housewife, and politician's wife, too. A terrifying thought. I didn't want to attend a bunch of glamorous dinners or stand on a dais behind my husband. I didn't want to plaster a smile on my face. I wasn't *The Good Wife*.

I looked up ahead, past Shane's dark mane of hair, to the shoreline. The last time I'd seen Carson, he was several boat lengths ahead of Delaney, but now, although I saw the girls' red kayak and Delaney's long red hair, I couldn't see Carson anywhere. We were finally approaching the channel's mouth, and I assumed he'd wait for us, but apparently he hadn't. Worry assaulted me. All sorts of thoughts crammed into my mind, but the one that kept bullying its way to the top of the heap was the image of a swimming bear and an overturned kayak.

"Have you seen Carson?" I called up to Shane.

He shook his head.

"Let's pick up the pace."

"I'm sure he's fine. He probably just went into the channel ahead of us. No need to worry."

That was Shane. Always telling me when it was or wasn't appropriate to worry. When it came to our son, it was almost never appropriate, because he was a boy—or now a man. *Men and boys can handle themselves.* Oh, how that attitude got under my skin.

In addition, Shane's thoughts and opinions had a habit of tacking back and forth like our canoe. Sometimes he was calm and expected me to mirror his demeanor; sometimes his anger ramped up without warning. One minute he'd be telling the kids what they couldn't do—and making it clear he expected me to side with him—and the next minute he'd change his mind and acquiesce, usually after I'd put up a good fight to support him. Whenever I called him on these turnabouts, he'd just say surprise was the key to a good marriage.

Today, he was nervous about the boat and water at first, but now he was remarkably calm and laid back. Carson used to call Shane bipolar when he flipped his stance on things. I'd never thought Shane was mentally ill, but I did sometimes wonder if he could use a little counseling to learn the art of consistency for the sake of those around him. Although, to listen to his coworkers, they never had a problem with him. They loved him.

We caught up to Delaney and Taylor, and I asked them if they'd seen Carson. They shook their heads.

"Do you think he went into the channel?" I asked.

They shrugged. You'd think at a time like this, with her brother missing, Delaney could stop being so bullheaded and actually speak to me.

I didn't want to paddle all the way up the channel to Shoshone Lake only to find that Carson had never made it that far. If it turned out he was in danger here, it would be hours before we'd get back. On the other hand, I searched the shoreline and saw nothing to indicate that anything bad had happened, or that he was even anywhere around here. He knew our itinerary, and there really wasn't anywhere else he could have gone with his kayak. Even if he'd capsized, the craft would likely have been floating.

Delaney tried to call him on her phone but got nowhere. We all checked our phones; none of us had service.

"Well, what are we going to do now?" Shane asked. "Sit here all day and wait for him to come back, or stick with our plans and paddle up to Shoshone?" He didn't give me time to think about it or to answer. "I'll tell you what we're going to do. We're going to enjoy ourselves just as we said we would. We'll go up the channel, have our picnic on the shores of Shoshone, and then turn around and head back to the launch. We're not going to let Carson ruin this. And we're not going to sit around and wait all day for him, either. I don't want to be getting back to the hotel at midnight. We've got early flights tomorrow morning. You too, Brooke."

I was sure I hadn't heard him correctly.

"What?" Delaney asked. She glanced first at her father, then at me.

"Did you say I'm flying back with you tomorrow?" I asked.

"Yes, I did. And why not? We've had a lovely weekend, for the most part anyway. And now it's time, Brooke. That's all. Time for you to come home." His tone was no different than a father telling a child that playtime was over.

I had no intention of going through this all over again with him. "We'll talk about it later," I said. "Right now, I've got a son to find."

A mother doesn't ignore her missing offspring, no matter how old he is or what curveballs her husband pitches at her. Even though Carson was a competitive swimmer, I wasn't convinced he was all right. Something was amiss. And I couldn't ignore the notion that, just as this was the Lake Hotel's last open weekend of the season, this was one of the last good weekends for the bears to gorge themselves before going off to hibernate. Continuing up the channel did seem the best course of action, although I really didn't want Shane to think I was deferring to him.

"Let's keep going," I said. "And keep a good pace. Stay close behind us, girls."

I thought I heard Shane say something about coming to see things his way, but because he was facing forward I wasn't sure. Better to let it all go, I decided. We took the lead, and I kept glancing back to check on the girls, who were continuously peering into the forest on each side of the channel, which narrowed with each stroke. We were all on the lookout for Carson. And for mule deer, elk, fox, or large cats. At one point, Taylor cried out, and I turned around to see a bald eagle swooping overhead, like a plane coming in for a landing. It snatched a fish out of the water not more than twenty feet ahead of Shane and soared up into the forest's canopy, landing with its lunch on an overhanging bough.

We paddled on. Once again I fell under the spell of the rhythmic strokes, the orderliness of our collective motion. The clinks of the paddles against the rims of the boats, the voices of the girls behind us. And the muscles flexing in Shane's strong back. He had always been physically fit, and handsome, and sometimes I found him sexier from behind—when I couldn't see the criticism on his face. But eventually, as the channel became even narrower, it also became shallower, and the spell was broken as we bumped into rocks and scraped the bottom.

Then Shane and I got stuck on top of a rock.

"Shane, the person in the bow has to be the lookout person. When you see a big rock coming up in the water, you've got to tell me to steer right or left. I can't always see what's in front of you."

He spun around, his middle finger scratching the side of his nose and his lips grinning. "Sorry," he said.

I tried to figure out what to say in response to that gesture, one that should have no place in a marriage unless it's clearly done in humor. Clearly this wasn't. Instead I maneuvered us off the rock. As we pushed out into the water, I told him we were lucky that time. "Sometimes you have to get out of the boat to manually get unstuck, and there's no way I can do that with my bad leg. If this happens again, you'll be the one getting out into the current. Or else we could be stuck forever."

"Stop being so melodramatic," he said. He splashed water at me with his paddle. Was he angry? Or being playful? I couldn't tell.

"Okay. Maybe we wouldn't have been stuck there until the end of time. But we certainly could run aground again and again." A perfect metaphor for our marriage.

Finally we made it to Shoshone Lake, the girls directly behind us. Immediately upon leaving the protection of the channel, the wind blasted our faces. Clouds organized like storm troopers in the western sky. The water in front of us bulged as waves thrust up from the surface. There was still no sight of Carson or his orange kayak.

"What's the deal with all this weather?" Shane asked, his long hair blowing around his face. I'd always loved his hair, until now, when I saw it for the tangled mess it was. He struggled to get it pulled back into a ponytail.

"I know," Taylor said. "It's like we went through the back of the wardrobe and came out into another world."

I explained what Palmer had told me, that the wind and weather always worsen in the afternoon here. "We were just sheltered in the channel. We didn't see the change coming. Let's take a quick break here and figure out what to do next."

Delaney and Taylor beached their kayak and went off to find a private place to pee. Shane climbed out of our canoe and unzipped his pants at the nearest pine tree. I decided I'd hold off for now; getting in and out of the canoe wasn't easy for me, and going off into the woods would be impossible. I checked my phone for service. Still none.

As we snacked on energy bars and tangerines, Taylor thought she saw something out on the lake. A boat. Shoshone was even bigger than Lewis Lake; if that was Carson way out there, it would take an hour or two to reach him, especially in this wind, assuming he didn't paddle farther away from us. If he were with us right now, I'd say we needed to turn around and head back before the weather got any worse. If the average paddler traveled three miles per hour, we had two to three hours of paddling ahead of us as it was. Even with the downstream current in the channel helping.

After watching the lone boat on the lake for a few minutes, I told everyone to pack it up.

"We're not even sure that's Carson," Shane said. "But given the paucity of food choices for this so-called picnic, I'm ready to move on. Maybe the girls should stay back here, though. That water looks awfully choppy."

"We'll be fine if we stay by the shoreline," I said. "I don't want to leave them here alone. Safety in numbers, and all that."

He looked at me, his eyes now dark. He was becoming frightened.

"We're not going to leave Carson out there," I said. "Get in the boat, Shane. And you girls, put on your life vests and make sure they're nice and tight."

As we paddled along the western shore, black clouds rose up over the tree line, now reminding me of a squadron of fighter jets. "We need to pick up the pace, team. This is going to be a kicker of a storm, mark my words. Let's go."

Shane drilled his paddle into the water, each stroke expressing his newfound conviction. Whether it was fear—or anger that I'd arranged this excursion in the first place—I couldn't know. As long as he kept the paddle going at that pace, I didn't care. I'd lost track of that boat we thought was Carson's, but now I saw it again, pulled up on the shoreline ahead.

"There he is," I called up to Shane, hoping my voice could force its way through the wind. "He's up there."

I turned back toward the girls and motioned for them to pull up beside us. When they did, I shouted over the wind to them. "Head over to that inlet, over there. Carson's on the shore. See? Just stay close to land. We'll meet you there."

When we got to his kayak, Shane and the girls hauled our canoe as far as they could onto the shore with me still in it, and I managed to climb out onto the shore. Carson's backpack was in the cockpit of his kayak.

"God damn it," Shane said. "Where is that kid?"

"Maybe he's peeing," Delaney said to him. She had yet to speak to me, and the weekend was nearly over.

"Well, we can't just stand around here. Let's spread out and look for him," Shane said.

"Not a good idea," I said. "Trust me. You three need to stay together. This is bear country." I spotted what looked like a deer trail into the woods and suggested they start there. "I'll stay here. You go on ahead."

"What if a bear comes along here? You'll be all by yourself," Taylor said. Interesting that neither my husband nor my daughter thought of this.

"Someone told me lightning never strikes the same place twice around here," I said. No one laughed. "Anyway, if it does, I'll be in one of those boats faster than a shotgun shell."

"I think she means a speeding bullet," Delaney said to Taylor. "She always gets her idioms mixed up."

I scooted onto a boulder, trying not to think about being alone on that rock as they went off to search for Carson, but the spotty memory of the bear attack kept surfacing. My adrenaline rushing, each sound startled me. Was that Carson's voice? Was there a bird in the brush? Did I just hear a bear's huff? The wind murmured eerily through the trees. I tried to imagine how I'd fight off a bear using only a crutch. I tried not to think about what we'd do if we couldn't find Carson. Or perhaps worse, if we found him in the same condition Palmer had found me. There was no cell service here. The anglers on Lewis Lake would surely have packed up and gone home by the time we got back there. We were miles from any ranger station or visitor center. And at this time of year, it was unlikely we'd run across other tourists. The only saving grace was that Palmer knew where we were and would be waiting for us at the boat launch in another couple of hours. Provided he was lucid.

Finally, after a long fifteen minutes or so, they returned—with Carson. Shane was scowling, the girls smirking.

"Thank God," I said, sliding down from the boulder. I wanted to run out and hug him but couldn't, so I held out my arms for him to come to me. But even from where I stood I could tell he once again reeked of marijuana, and instead of gracing me with an embrace, he shuffled in place and studied the ground.

"As if we didn't already have enough problems," Shane said. "He's high."

"I don't know what the big deal is, Pops," Carson said.

"Don't call me Pops."

They began to bicker, and Delaney started in on Carson, too.

"Okay, everyone, calm down," I said. "The good news is that you're all right, Carson. We were worried about you."

"You worry way too much," he said.

"Okay, maybe I do. That's what moms are for. If we didn't worry about our offspring, the human race wouldn't survive. At any rate, we've got a situation we all need to worry, or at least be mindful, about." I pointed at the sky. "See that? Not good."

At that precise moment, a large raindrop hit me on the forehead. Right on cue. Drops fell on Carson and the others, too, and plopped on the fiberglass kayaks and canoe.

"Sounds like popcorn," Carson said. "Cool."

"Let's go," I said. Everyone seemed frozen for a minute, listening to the popping corn as I scooted back to the canoe. Once seated in the stern, I kept an eye on Carson as he climbed into his kayak; he seemed steady enough, albeit slow. Shane and the girls, all now looking like drowned lake rats, pushed the three boats off the beach before climbing in.

We paddled along the shoreline back toward the channel, the tailwind helping us along as lightning cracked at our backs. The girls led the way and we brought up the rear; I wanted to make sure Carson could handle the kayak in his condition. I also wanted to monitor how the kids positioned their boats in relation to the wind and waves. So far, so good. In an hour, we made it back into the channel, where we got a slight reprieve from the gusts.

The girls kept pushing forward, the current now helping them, and picked their way among the large boulders that threatened to block us. But Carson set his paddle across his lap and drifted slowly, laughing as he bounced from one rock to another like a pinball, his mouth open wide to collect raindrops. Shane shouted his signature command to *get with the program*, but Carson didn't hear—or ignored—his father. I tried to slow our canoe so we wouldn't pass him by, but Shane kept paddling up front, and I wasn't strong enough to counteract his force.

"Stop paddling," I said, two or three times. But he kept on going. Soon we left our son behind and caught up with Taylor and Delaney, who had discovered the art of paddling in place within a little eddy. We pulled up alongside them.

"Carson! Get moving!" Shane yelled back upstream, but a boom of thunder drowned out his voice.

This was so unlike Carson. Whereas Delaney had always given us a challenge, from her toddler days when she'd escape from her crib during the night, Carson had been the easy child.

"Delaney, do you know what's going on with him?" Shane asked.

"Not really. We don't talk much. I think he's just scared about growing up and graduating and all that."

"Scared? What's there to be frightened about?" he asked. "When I was his age, I couldn't wait to get out there and conquer the world."

"Times are different now," I said.

"Come on, Taylor. Let's go," Delaney said, as if in direct response to my existence, or as if she hadn't even heard me at all, or as if she wanted to paddle away not just to get back to our starting point but to escape from me. She started paddling hard.

"Wait!" I called. "We should all stay together." But Delaney defied me—no surprise—and kept going, soon disappearing into the thick wall of rain. I looked upstream, hoping I'd see the orange kayak appear, but so far no luck. The channel current kept trying to pull our boat out from the eddy, and I was getting tired from fighting it. From fighting, period.

I called Carson's name upstream one more time but had trouble projecting my voice over the elements. Shane called his name next. Finally, our son came drifting along, seemingly unconcerned with pretty much anything. I glanced up at Shane and saw his clenched jaws. He was going to tear into Carson again if I didn't do something about it.

"Let it go," I said. "For now. Later, you can rip him. And me, too, for getting us into this predicament, which I'm sure is what you're thinking right about now. Our first priority at this moment should be getting back safely. So, please, let it all go for now."

He hesitated, his jaws flexing and releasing, then nodded. He was scared. If he hadn't been, he wouldn't have abided my plea. But this time he did.

When Carson's kayak finally approached our canoe, I let our bow drift back out into the channel and steered it next to him, grabbing the side of his boat. I told him to give me one end of his paddle and to hold onto the other end across his lap so we could make a sort of catamaran. But Carson was even more out of it than I had thought. I'd heard about how today's marijuana was so much stronger than the pot of the past, and the vacant look in Carson's eyes seemed to be the proof. Before we had his paddle in position, he let go. I barely caught it before it hit the water. But in so doing, I let go of his kayak, and the current swept him away.

Another streak of lightning, this time slashing the sky directly overhead with a simultaneous roar of thunder. Carson stared up at the clouds, unaware that he was literally up a creek without a paddle. I maneuvered our canoe back to him. Handing him the paddle, I gestured toward the shoreline.

"Pull over there!" I shouted to Carson and Shane. Both gave me a bewildered look. "There's no way Carson can get his kayak across Lewis

Lake to the boat launch by himself." I spoke to Shane as if Carson wasn't even there because, essentially, he wasn't. "Not in his current state of mind."

"Or lack thereof," Shane said. Carson was so out of it, he didn't even try to defend himself.

We made it over to a shallow landing just before the channel's mouth. I hobbled out of the canoe and over to the kayak. Under my direction, Carson clambered out of the kayak and into the front of the canoe, and Shane moved to the back, clinging to the sides with each step. It was what we used to improperly call a Chinese fire drill. Sweat, mixed with rain, poured down from the top of my head.

I couldn't squeeze my bad leg into the kayak's cockpit, so instead I had to rest it on top of the front deck. It was a horribly uncomfortable position, and I knew my lower back might never forgive me, but I really had no choice. And the fact that my boot was already saturated and probably unsalvageable didn't change anything.

"Ready?" I asked.

Shane's eyebrows were raised, his forehead creased. I knew he was sick with worry. This was the first day in such a long time that he wasn't arguing with me or otherwise pulling rank. We were living in a parallel universe that, despite the hazards all around, felt refreshing.

"You can do this," I said to whoever might be listening. Neither of them knew much about guiding a canoe—or working as a team—and now Shane, in the stern, was in the driver's seat. "Stay close to the shoreline and perpendicular to the waves. You'll both have to paddle hard to stay on course. But stay out of the reeds and logs along the shore. And by all means don't let yourself drift out into the lake."

"Mom?" Carson seemed to finally join the land of the living. His voice was hesitant, even tender—it was his little boy's voice from a decade ago.

"I'll be right beside you," I said. "Let's do it."

They pushed out and I stayed close behind, trying to stay balanced in that awkward position as I decided what my best strategy might be. I kept the nose of my kayak right on their tail, so I could nudge the canoe to help Shane steer if I needed to. But the winds were stronger than I was. And my kayak didn't have the stability their canoe did. On top of all that, my muscles couldn't match Shane and Carson's collective strength. I backed off. My top priority, I decided, was to keep my kayak afloat. Rolling was not an option.

The wind toyed with us as we paddled, and for a good hour we were batted around like field mice in the paws of a mountain lion. Shane rose to the occasion without a single complaint, and Carson, with his strong swimmer's back and shoulders, came through too as he hauled ass in the bow of the canoe. Even though I had more paddling experience and a lighter craft, I had a hard time keeping up with them once they found their rhythm. Along the way, I kept searching for Taylor and Delaney, hoping they'd make their way to the boat launch safely.

It wasn't until we were back in the narrower southern part of Carson's Africa that I finally spotted the girls, and it wasn't good. They were too far out from shore, and I could tell the wind was pushing them even farther toward the center of the lake. They were on a course that would completely miss the boat launch. Worse, the waves out there had to be at least a foot high, judging by how the crest matched the rim of their kayak. If they tried to adjust their direction, they could easily capsize.

"Shane, we've got a problem," I called out. "Hold on!"

When I caught up to the canoe, I pointed toward the girls. "They're too far out. I'm going to need to help them."

"How do you propose to do that?" Shane asked.

"You'll see."

"What about us?" Carson asked. "You're not leaving us, are you?"

Most of the time you're proud when your kids grow up and no longer need you. You're grateful when they get to that stage in life where you know they'll be able to survive. Even so, a mother's heart naturally pings when her grown children reveal their vulnerabilities and that innate need for their mother—a need that really never dissipates completely. Her heart also aches anytime she must choose between her two kids.

Our boats now side by side, I reached over to Carson and placed my hand on his arm. "You and Dad are doing great. Just keep working together and you'll be back at the boat launch in no time. Right now, it's Delaney who needs me the most."

"We'll come with you," Carson said.

"Absolutely not. Now get going." I adjusted my course toward the girls and didn't look back.

The wind came at me from a northwesterly direction, so when I turned eastward, it immediately rattled the kayak. I shifted in my seat as much as possible—which wasn't much—and I had to continuously adjust my steering to stay upright. Meanwhile, with my bad leg propped in that unnatural position, the lower right side of my back screamed with each stroke. Rain pounded my face, dragging my hair down across my eyes. This rain was cold, colder than it had been so far this season, warning of winter. I shivered even as I perspired. My shoulders and arms ached, too, and my wet tank felt abrasive against my healing wounds. I was a complete mess. But my daughter needed me.

After losing sight of them in the poor visibility, I finally saw something red in the water up ahead. I powered forward. Digging into the lake with my paddle felt like stirring cement with a toothpick, all while balancing on a tightrope.

Then I realized what I had seen. Their kayak had overturned.

I grunted with each hellish pull. Something tore on my side—skin, a wound, my tank top: I couldn't tell. I didn't care. I also couldn't see; the rain and my tears and perspiration conspired with one another.

"Delaney! Taylor! Delaney!"

Delaney's head popped above the surface, and a sound emitted from her mouth. A sob, a gulp. "Mom! Mom!"

She let go of her kayak's grab handle and tried to swim toward me.

"No!" I shouted. "Go back!" Again, that damn lightning flashed across the sky. It illuminated the fear on Delaney's face as she bobbed in the water.

"Where's Taylor?" I yelled.

"She's under the kayak!"

"What do you mean?"

An image of Taylor caught in the kayak's cockpit, and held under water, burst in front of my eyes. I had taken someone else's daughter out on the water and now she had drowned. I hadn't taught them how to roll. But she hadn't been wearing a kayak skirt. How could she be trapped under there? My heart was racing too fast to think.

"Mom! You're bleeding!" Delaney pointed at me.

"Delaney! Swim under the boat. Get Taylor out! I'll be right here!"

Waves jostled my kayak as I tried to get as close as possible. She dove under, then resurfaced.

"Mom! Help!"

I knew exactly what I needed to do. With my bad leg already resting atop the deck—at least it wasn't stuck in the cockpit—I leaned over, spilling into the water. The cold stung. I flailed, gulping for air. Then I dove.

Delaney was under the boat with Taylor, whose eyes were open wide. I pulled at her shoulders, but one of her legs was stuck. I reached into the cockpit; her shoe had become caught on one of the foot braces. I released it. She gave such a hard kick that her foot barely missed my face. But at least she was alive.

Delaney and I swam her to the surface and positioned her arms across the bottom of the overturned kayak. We rested on either side of her, all of us gasping and coughing as we struggled to keep a grasp on the slippery bottom of the boat. When the lightning blazed across the sky, I saw how white Taylor's face and lips were.

"We need to get the boat upright," I said.

"Mom, where's your life jacket?"

I hadn't even realized I wasn't wearing one. In the course of trading places with Carson and making sure he and Shane had on their life jackets, I'd forgotten about putting one on myself. Shit. Now my muscles began to cramp.

"Taylor, Delaney. Listen to me." I could barely hear myself in the wind and rain and waves. I tried to think and steady the kayak and speak, all the while ignoring the burning in my leg and my side. At least my back wasn't in pain at that moment. "We're going to flip this kayak over. And then you're going to climb in and paddle over to the boat launch. Okay?"

Their lips trembled as they nodded. I instructed them on next steps. With Delaney and me at each end of the kayak, treading water, and Taylor in the middle—barely treading—we were able to right the boat relatively easily. It took a few tries to get them into the kayak without it rolling over again, and each time it threatened to roll, Taylor screamed, but finally, we did it.

"Now you're going to paddle directly to the shoreline and then work your way back to the launch. Do not go over any more open water than necessary to get to shore, got it?"

"Mom, what about you?"

My overturned kayak had drifted ten or fifteen feet away, the paddle slightly farther. I wasn't sure I could make it that far. My boot felt like it weighed a hundred pounds, and every kick just to tread water was getting more and more difficult. I didn't know how many kicks I had left in me. My arms and shoulders were completely wrecked, too, after all that paddling. The headline of a drowned kayak guide from earlier in the summer flashed before my eyes. It was hypothermia, the article had said.

"Don't worry about me," I said. "You and Taylor need to get to shore and warm up."

"We'll get your kayak and paddle, and bring it to you," Delaney said.

"No! Forget about me! Get going!"

The rebel took off her life vest and tossed it toward me. I watched her fingertips let go of the orange fabric. I followed its arc in the air. I saw it jog left as a current of wind snatched it, but then released it as if it had nothing to offer. It dropped into the water just out of my reach.

"Hang on, Mommy. We'll be right back."

As my legs and arms thrashed toward the life vest, my mind tried to make sense of all that had happened. A family outing. My son under the influence. Shane and I paddling harmoniously. The girls, their overturned kayak. Taylor underwater. My daughter's voice. The name she hadn't called me in over a decade. Mommy. Splashing water; paddles clinking against the rim of a boat.

"Put it on, Mommy! Put the life vest on!"

Her frantic voice brought me back to the real world. They had trailed my kayak back to me. I slipped my arms through the armholes of the vest and described how we were going to do a T-rescue to flip my kayak over and get me, or at least part of me, back inside. The maneuver worked. Once out of the water, I saw how badly the girls were shivering. And I felt my last ounces of strength preparing to drain away.

"Thank you," I said.

There was so much—so much—more I wanted to say, but my mind had gone blank. I couldn't find a single word to express the love, the guilt, the regret—and the fear—swelling up inside me. And the gratitude I felt for Delaney, the little girl who had grown up to be such a strong young woman, the daughter who was now speaking to me again.

"Get going!" I said as the girls sat in their kayak staring at me as if I were an alien from outer space. "Hustle!"

A small crowd had gathered at the dock: Carson, Shane, Palmer, and a group of anglers. Shane helped the girls out of their kayak, and Palmer grabbed hold of Taylor so tightly with a blanket I was afraid he'd suffocate her. Carson and an angler helped me out of my boat, and an itchy army-style blanket was tossed around my shoulders. Someone said an ambulance was on its way. Several people were sobbing, including Delaney and Taylor—and then even Carson joined in. I wanted to comfort the kids—that's a mother's job, isn't it?—but I had nothing more to give. I couldn't even cry.

I sat down on the dock, shivering beneath the blanket. A thermos of lukewarm, stale coffee was handed to me. I was grateful when I saw, out of the corner of my eye, Carson rubbing his hands up and down Delaney's arms, trying to warm her up. More blankets were distributed. What a change this was from all my years of suburban ennui.

Shane sat down beside me. When he didn't bother to wrap an arm around my shoulders, I braced for criticism. He would ask something like how I could possibly get myself into not one, but two, life-threatening situations in a matter of months. But he didn't do that either.

"You did great today," I said. "I know this wasn't your thing. But I appreciate your willingness to go along with me. I'm sorry for all that happened. And I'm proud of you, for pulling through and doing your part in a dicey situation. I know you were scared. We all were." What I didn't add was that fear, I now saw, can have a profound power to inspire change. For some insane reason, I thought that just maybe this experience might bring us back together.

"Scared?" he said. "That's what you call it? Scared?"

"What would you call it?"

"It was sheer terror. We were all traumatized, thanks to you, Brooke, and this stupid outing you planned. You, and your great outdoors, nearly killed us all."

"Dad!" Delaney's voice came from behind. "Shut the fuck up."

She lowered herself to the dock and squeezed into the space between Shane and me. Taking hold of one end of my blanket, she wrapped the two of us in it, drenched and shivering, laughing and now crying, our cheeks pressed one to the other so that our tears became mingled, mother and daughter, together again.

SIXTEEN

Anne

I WEATHERED THE next three days alongside the dusty trail. On the first two days, I worked on my sketch. On the third day, it snowed. At my urging, Maggie took a reprieve from her work and joined me as I awaited the rangers' arrival. We built a fire, huddled beneath blankets, and watched the elk and buffalo migrate south, deeper into geyserland, where they would find warmer ground for the winter.

I tried to make conversation, but a rift had developed between us. And why would it not? When a rosebud is pruned too soon, it will not blossom. If a berry is plucked before it is ripe, one may never know how sweet it might have been.

She stirred the fire with a long stick. Sparks shot out at me. "Tell me more about this husband of yours," she said. Her interest, if that is what it was, astounded me. I told her I would, if she would first tell me about hers.

She set the stick down and looked into the breeze, her eyes narrow. "*Sahkonteic*—White Eagle—was a good husband. He was my father's friend. I knew him since I was young; our families gathered each year for the Winter Spirit Dance. He was always very kind to me. That is all."

I waited for her to continue. Her eyes were now closed, her smile pleasant. It seemed she was remembering him with fondness, and I dared not interrupt; Maggie would go on when she was ready. But many minutes passed until she opened her eyes and repeated herself. "That is all. Now tell me about your Thomas."

Now I picked up the stick and poked at the fire as I attempted to solve the puzzle of who this man, who had been my husband, truly was. "I believe Thomas thought himself a good man, and I fancied him from the very beginning. He was quite handsome and ambitious. He courted me with grace. But after we married, he changed." I was unsure what to reveal next, or how best to put it. I attempted to wear a pleasant smile as Maggie had when conjuring her memory of White Eagle, but a smile on my lips felt as wrong as a right boot on my left foot. "Once we married, Thomas began to mock me, for example. He ridiculed my artwork, my housekeeping skills, and even my hair when it became hard to manage on humid days."

"A good husband does not mock his wife," Maggie said. Her voice stern, I was uncertain whether she was disappointed with me or with Thomas. Either way, I was compelled to come to our defense.

"He meant well. We were both young, and his parents were far away. He had no one to show him how to behave with a wife. My mother died before our wedding, so likewise I had no one to turn to for advice." I absent-mindedly began to rub my elbow.

"There is more," Maggie said, as though she possessed those skills of clairvoyance about which I had recently read. "There is more you have not said."

"Yes." I released my elbow and rubbed my hands together over the fire. "It was not with malice or intent that he injured me. Thomas had the misfortune of being plagued with a volatile temperament. He always apologized afterward and promised it would never happen again. Men like Thomas must be made to feel important. And they must have their other needs attended to, as well. It was my job, as his wife, to do these things."

"But he hurt you."

"Yes, occasionally. One evening, Thomas came home from an arduous day of work. I was preoccupied with a new recipe for stew and failed to greet him as a wife should. He grabbed my arm roughly, and spun me around, and in the midst of this little skirmish I fell back against the stove."

I showed her the scar on my elbow. When she cringed, I reined in my voice, refusing to let the memory of his anger run wild, refusing to let her see the monster he could sometimes be. "He was overwhelmed by his job—the boss was an unlikeable fellow."

I stood, threw off the blanket, and walked away from our log. Maggie hurried behind me, reaching out for the elbow with the scar. Reluctant to let her see my tears, I squeezed my eyes shut.

"You are holding back, Anne, and you are in pain. Whatever it is that you are burying in your heart, you must set it free before it destroys you. I am your friend. Your story is safe with me."

How could I share my secret with her—with a woman who had the perfect man? The anger and self-pity I had been experiencing was quickly becoming replaced with humiliation.

"If you cannot speak the words, then sketch them," Maggie said. She led me back to the log and handed my book to me. "Let your artwork take you back to this day you recall."

I wiped my tears with the back of my hand and attempted to follow her suggestion. Instead of drawing the stove, I found myself drawing a can of lard as it sailed across the room.

"The skin beneath my elbow is singed. I reach for a can of lard, to smear it onto the burn. But Thomas swats the entire can away."

She wrapped the blanket around my shoulders. I drew a doorway next, and through the doorway, the outline of our marriage bed. Maggie urged me to continue.

"He drags me into our bedroom by the locks of my hair. He frightens me as never before. He takes hold of my dress by the neckline and rips it apart. As I stand trembling, he strips me of my clothing. He pushes me down and mounts me, my fresh burn rubbing raw on the quilt. I plead for him to stop, or at least to slow down." I adjusted the tone of my voice to approximate the feral snarl he then whispered into my ear. "'A husband should not have to wait for his wife,' he says."

I set my pencil down and stroked my jaw, unsure if I could utter the final words that longed for release. I took one of Maggie's hands in mine and squeezed.

"His knuckles swing into my jaw so hard I am sure it is broken. When I cry out, his fist strikes again."

I wiped my nose against the sleeve of my dress. My legs involuntarily squeezed together. "You can imagine the rest," I said. "I suspect I do not need to spell it out for you."

We sat together, listening to the echo of my story.

Her hands slipped out from mine and reached up to either side of my face. "A good husband does not injure or force himself upon his wife, Anne. I do not understand why you want to go home to him."

I hung my head low and shivered as tears streamed down my cheeks. She would never understand because she had not walked in my shoes. The snow had begun to accumulate all around us, even on our moccasins. Maggie stood, removed the blanket from my shoulders, and flapped it wide so that she could wrap it around both of us. When she sat down beside me again, I discovered snowflakes on her thick eyelashes.

"Look." She pointed to a herd of buffalo. Snow had coated them, too; their hairy humps looked like powdered sugar on chocolate cup-cakes. She asked me to sing *Buffalo Gal*, and when I did, she sang along as well, failing miserably to match my pitch. We laughed, but afterward she became somber. To my surprise, and relief, she did not mention Thomas.

"There were once twenty million buffalo roaming this land," she said. "My father remembers those times. Now there are no more than a million, perhaps fewer."

"The meat is good," I said.

"Most have not been killed for meat. White man sells the hides."

"The hides are warm."

She shook her head. "You do not understand. Many animals have been sacrificed for white man money."

"I am sorry," I said. I thought about that poor buffalo she had killed for us. "I am sorry about the buffaloes. And about all of white man's sins."

"And I am sorry about Thomas."

When a gust of wind blew across the prairie, the herd repositioned itself so that each and every animal faced the same direction. If only human beings could see the world so simply.

"What do you think happened to White Eagle?" I asked. "Do you think he is still alive?" I had a sudden desire to meet him.

"As each day passes, I become more certain that he is not. But I am not ready to give up hope yet. Hope is the fire that keeps you warm. You must tend to it, and try to keep the embers alive, until the snow becomes too deep."

Because of the thick snow-clouds, dusk had come early. The temperature plummeted. We returned to camp.

I awoke in the middle of the night to the sound of the horse stamping its feet. It was then I felt something between my legs. I had begun my flow. I quickly gathered some cloths that Maggie and I had set aside for this occasion and proceeded to leave the tipi. It was black as coal outside now; there was not much moon, but the clouds had drifted away so there was a small amount of light from the stars as well as from the embers that remained in our camp-fire.

I felt my way cautiously in the dark, and tended to my needs several yards from the tipi. After using snow to clean myself, I buried the cloths in the snow-clad dirt, intending to wash them in the morning light. Turning back toward the camp, I heard branches rattling and peered through the trees. Indeed, despite the deficit in the lighting, I was certain something huge stood at the tipi's opening, presumably studying Maggie. I crept closer and detected a hideous odor of musk and rot, not unlike the stench of Maggie's dead buffalo. I froze in place just in time to see it lift its snout, as though sniffing the air. The extraordinary beast turned its head in my direction and locked its eyes on mine. My heart stopped.

"Go on! Get out of here!" I yelled, thinking not of my own well-being but of my dear Maggie's. The bear and I each shared a moment of hesitation before it clumsily turned itself around and ambled away. A saner woman would have stood quietly, shivering, until the animal had disappeared completely. Or she might have fainted, aghast. But as Thomas had so often declared, sanity was not my greatest strength. I picked up a fistful of rocks from the ground and ran after the bear, pelting it with my feeble weapons and my anger. It picked up its pace, and so did I, chasing the horrible, lethal, beautiful monster out of the forest and all the way down to the bubbling geysers and pools.

SEVENTEEN

Anne

MAGGIE WAS FURIOUS after my escapade with the grizzly.

"You could have been killed," she said as we lay side by side the following morning.

"You told me they are more afraid of us than we are of them."

"That does not mean they will not kill you, Stupid Anne. Fear can be reason enough to kill."

Her stomach rumbled, and she looked to be in pain as she pressed her hands to her sides.

"And so can ill health," I said. We had consumed as much buffalo meat as humanly possible since the slaughter, and we had dried and cured the rest. But our diets were not balanced, and Maggie and I both began to suffer from periodic queasiness and other symptoms one does not openly discuss. Likewise, I did not reveal why I had been out of the tent in the middle of the night.

"Perhaps we should leave the park on our own, without waiting for rangers," I said.

"Soon the bear will hibernate," she said. "We will be safer then."

"It is not only the grizzly that worries me. We do not have all the necessary provisions, and medications, to help us through the winter." The water at the river's edge had begun to freeze, and the air hinted at more snow. Shivering had become my latest pastime.

"I need to find more berries and grains," Maggie said.

As much as the fine art of winter survival intrigued me, I did not believe we would be able to find and store much more than a chipmunk's cache.

"Also," she said, "it is too soon to leave. The rangers may not return for us, but White Eagle still might."

This was the first time she had acknowledged actively waiting for her husband to rescue her.

"I know how to survive winter," she continued. "We will be all right until he comes for me. You have to trust me."

Her stomach rumbled again. She coughed, then rolled to her side. I felt the goosebumps on her arms and the heat on her forehead.

"You are ill, Maggie. Let us make our way to Old Faithful. We can find a doctor for you."

"I am safer here. You know what will happen if I am discovered. Your doctors will not treat me. They will ship me to the reservation."

"Perhaps Thomas will come for me. He knows important people. He will help."

"You do not even know if he is alive. And from what you have told me about him, I have doubts about whether he will help an Indian girl like me."

In all likelihood, she was correct about him. Since revealing to her what he had done to me, I had come to believe that rekindling our marriage would be impossible.

I tried to imagine where he was now and whether he had safely escaped from Maggie's people. Whether he was back home in Chicago. Whether he was trying to establish a posse of his associates to search for me. Or whether he was feeling the same about me as I was about him: rather grateful that fate had pulled us apart. I tried to envision what he looked like, and whether by now he had shaved his beard, and I was startled to realize I could not remember his eyes.

"Would you change your mind if I told you I have nearly run out of pages in my sketch-book? Then would you come to Chicago with me?"

She coughed. "We surely cannot survive without more pages for your sketch-book. Let us travel beyond the horizon, through vast stretches of dangerous territory, and risk our lives so that you can procure more paper."

The eloquence of her words struck me nearly as much as the sarcasm burned. She lay still for so long that I assumed she had fallen asleep again, until she pulled her arm from beneath the buffalo hide and ran her fingers through her flowing hair. She had released the braids the night before; watching her do this, for me, was like watching a wild animal released from its zoo cage.

"I will not go to the reservation, even though my mother and father are there. I will find a way to live here, and I will bring them to me someday. I am sorry, Anne, but going to *civilization* is not an option for me any more than having tea with *x'axa c* is an option for you. How I wish you could understand."

I reached across and ran my own fingers through her hair. She pushed my hand away, sat up, and began to dress. I giggled at the image of a bear sipping tea. And then I told her I did understand: I simply did not want to accept it as the truth.

The next night, I awoke to find Maggie's face directly above mine. I felt her slightly sour breath against my cheeks, and my first thought was that her illness had become more grave. But then I felt the firm pressure of her hand across my mouth.

"Listen," she whispered.

By now my vision had adjusted to the dark. I saw her concern in the whites of her eyes. I nodded. She removed her hand from my face. We lay still, listening to branches breaking. Strangely, I imagined the grizzly bear returning for tea, although I clearly knew this to be impossible. Then we heard Maggie's horse squeal.

A flash of light drew my attention to the eastern side of the tipi, then another to the west. Soon I smelled smoke and heard fire crackling. She threw back the buffalo hide blanket and grabbed her knife. I picked up the useless pistol. We tore outside.

Flames shot up around our tipi.

"Maggie!"

We heard a man's voice call *ya!,* a tinkle of breaking glass, and the clip-clop of galloping hooves. New snowflakes floated down from the sky.

I ran after the intruders, shouting at them to stop, then cursing at them when I stepped on a shard of glass. I picked it up and in the dim light ascertained it to be from a whiskey bottle. I yanked the glass from my sole, then ran back to Maggie, now beating at the tipi with our blanket, flapping it wildly. The flames ignored her and rose higher than she could reach. I dove inside for our dresses and then raced back out again to beat them against the tipi as well. We scooped dirt with our hands and threw it onto the stretched hide. We flung what little water we had left in our baskets. But still the fire burned hotter. It raced around the circumference of the tipi, as though stretching its arms around and embracing it. Now Maggie lunged into the tipi, quickly emerging with an armful of belongings and sparks in her hair. I threw her to the ground and wrestled her until the sparks surrendered to my wrath.

The fire jumped from the tipi to the trees. The forest grew orange. With a few meager supplies in our arms, we retreated from our camp-site, all the while watching the inferno destroy not only our home but also the home of all the little critters that had shared their hospitality with us.

Maggie had believed we could survive winter, but neither she nor I had anticipated a calamity like this.

"I cannot fathom who would do this," I said. The snow had turned to sleet, and Maggie coughed profusely now. "You'll catch your death if we do not find new shelter soon."

"Shelter is not my primary concern. This was an act of hatred," she said.

The newspapers had run stories about people in the South who committed horrible acts against Negro men: arson, murder, and so on. But I found it difficult to believe anyone would intentionally harm two women, even if one of us was Indian.

"We must stay and fight," she said, a notion uncharacteristically unsound for her.

"With only a knife and an empty pistol?"

Her jaw jutted forward. "And with our hearts."

By late afternoon, the sleet had killed the fire, except for several smoldering embers. We inspected the scorched remains of the tipi. It smelled to high heavens of burnt hide and kerosene, and offered little protection from the weather. After all of Maggie's hard work.

I built a small camp-fire while Maggie retrieved our dried buffalo meat, which had survived the blaze because of where Maggie had cached it. We ate in silence. When I wiped a smudge of ash from her face with my thumb, tears welled in her eyes. I tried to offer words of comfort and hope.

She shook her head. "It is not just the fire. It is the dream I was having before we woke to the flames. White Eagle came to me and said we must not let this defeat us."

"White Eagle knew about the fire before you did?"

"Yes."

I did not understand how that could be but let her assertion go unquestioned.

"The good news is that he came to you in a dream, right? Does this not bring you joy? I should think a dream about your husband would make you happy."

She turned away from me, biting her lip. "When he appears in a dream like that, it means he is dead."

Thomas always dismissed my dreams as nonsense. But I was beginning to learn not to question Maggie's wisdom or beliefs. I only wished she were not still afraid to show me her sorrow, now that I had shown her mine.

"Do not be afraid to cry, dear friend," I said. "I once read there is a sacredness in tears. They are not a mark of weakness, but of power. They are the messengers of overwhelming grief and of unspeakable love. Let me share your sorrow. That is what friends do."

"I appreciate you, friend," she said. "You believe you have offered little to me during our time together, but you are incorrect. You have given me the comfort I needed in this time of loss and grief."

She leaned on my shoulder for a while, and then scrambled to our pile of rescued belongings, as if a thought had suddenly come to her. With one swift movement, she sliced off one of her braids with her knife.

"What are you doing?" I asked.

She proceeded with slicing off the other braid and tossed both of them into the fire. Her face was orange in the glow, her dark eyes more resolute than ever.

With White Eagle presumably dead and our supplies decimated, we needed to consider what to do next. It was a cold night, and we stoked the fire repeatedly to keep it going strong. Maggie fell asleep first, shivering beneath our scorched blanket and undoubtedly exhausted from both her sorrow and her illness. I watched the rise and fall of her frame with each breath. The flutter of her lashes. Her curled fists.

I missed her flowing hair.

My desire was to stay awake all night to guard her. But I could not manage to keep my eyes open nor my thoughts active. Now it was my turn to dream: the grizzly bear returned to our camp, and when its wet nose touched mine, I startled awake.

Instead of the bear, a man lay on top of me, pinning me down with his arms on either side of my shoulders. He stank of stale drink and tobacco. I kicked and shoved as best I could while trying to scream. He covered his hand over my mouth. It was only when I bit it that he reared back. I then lifted my knee, catching him in his groin. He let out a pitiful moan and rolled off of me, his hand cupping his private area. I hustled to my feet and reached for Maggie. She was not there.

"Maggie? Maggie!" The ground was bare where she had lain only hours earlier, when I had vowed to stay awake to protect her. I knew she would not choose to leave me alone and vulnerable. Something was terribly amiss.

My assailant grasped my ankle, and I lunged for a long branch protruding from the camp-fire's remains. I swung the smoldering torch back at him, making contact with his head. He staggered. I hit him again. He dropped to his knees. I hit him with my makeshift weapon yet one more time. Now he was flat on the ground, and I stomped on his back and kicked him between his legs. He let out another wail and curled into a ball.

"Maggie!" I called out again.

I scanned in every direction for her while holding my torch beyond arm's length of my opponent. Once I was satisfied he was unconscious, I ran toward our now-worn path that led back to the main trail. Along the way, I stepped on something. In the waning light of my torch, I saw it was Maggie's pouch. I picked it up, clenched it in my free hand, and called for her over and over before returning to the man who had attacked me.

He began to stir.

"Where is she?" I asked, kicking him in the side. "Tell me where she is!"

When he rolled over, onto his back, I spotted his holster. Quickly, I snatched his gun. Now that Maggie had taught me how to check whether a gun was loaded, I did so. This one was. As tempted as I was to shoot him then and there, I refrained and only kicked him in the head. Then I ran back toward the trail. Although the moon was but a sliver, I had learned how to see in the dark. I had become an animal in the wilds. And now I was a predator.

I stopped to listen for her. There, a whisper of wind. To my right, the flapping of our tipi's remnants. And behind me, my assailant's curses. No sound from Maggie. But then I heard the unmistakable stamp of a horse's hoof. Cautiously, I made my way into the trees, where I found two horses saddled and loosely tethered to a tree. Neither was Maggie's horse.

Brushing the first one's face gently, and then the other's, I collected my thoughts. First, determine whether there are any guns or useful supplies on these horses. Second, use one of the horses as a shield, just as Maggie had done when we first met. How much I had learned from her! Indeed, the second horse had a rifle butt protruding from its saddlebag; I removed the gun and hid it under a nearby shrub along with Maggie's pouch. Then I untied the first horse and walked alongside it, whispering to the animal as I went, as Maggie had done.

"Tikkatukka. Tikkatukka."

In a few minutes, I heard a reply.

EIGHTEEN

Brooke

SHANE WAS SILENT on our way back to the hotel from the near-fatal outing. Once back in the living area of our suite, he ordered us all to start packing. Carson, lying spread eagle on the floor, said he was starving.

"We'll get some food soon," I said. "But first I need to get some medical help for these wounds that ripped open. I don't need some sort of flesh-eating bacteria in my body right now." What a grim thought. "Leave it to me to die from a bacterial infection instead of a grizzly bear mauling or hypothermia." To which Delaney responded with a story about a woman in the news recently who died not from flesh-eating bacteria but from a brain-eating amoeba found in lake water. To which starving Carson said how cool that would be.

"Just take a shower," Shane said. "But be gentle with your face—I'm worried about all that scarring. I'll help you put on fresh bandages. By this time tomorrow, you'll be back home in Portland in the hands of a doctor who knows what he's doing. At last."

"Seriously?" Delaney said, her question directed at me. How delightful, I mused—despite the subject matter—that she was finally speaking to me again. She flopped on the sofa and began to comb out her tangles. "You're really going home, Mom? But why?"

Heavy silence fell as if someone had muted us.

"I mean, you love it here," she said. "That's obvious. We need to have a talk. You...and me...and all of us women. We have to stop doing things we don't want to just because some guy tells us to."

"Oh boy," Carson said, heaving his body up from the floor. "On that note I think I'll leave. And if you know what's good for you, sister, you'll stop right there and come with me."

She heaved a sigh and followed Carson into their room. I followed Shane into ours. Delaney's words followed me.

Shane turned on the shower. "You can go first," he said, his voice more gentle than I would have expected after Delaney's comments and his certain knowledge that a conflict was brewing.

I stepped in and cranked the water to hot. The shower immediately filled up with steam. Just as I began to relax, Shane started in. His voice found its way over the glass shower door like wisps of steam going the wrong way.

"You're not going to argue this point anymore, I assume. You need better medical care—those wounds are nasty. It would be less of a drain on our finances. And my manager says it would look a lot better to my constituents. Sympathy for your condition, in fact, might even draw in a few new voters. Did I tell you the neighbors have been asking about you?"

I was a captive audience in the shower—nowhere to hide. I leaned my head back and let the water cascade over my hair, my scalp, and my ears, while trying to keep the heavy stream from bombarding my torn skin and scabs.

"Have you given any thought to what your antics are teaching the kids?" Shane continued. "You heard what Delaney said. Made me sick to my stomach."

Really? As a matter of fact, I'd been thinking about my impact on the kids now more than ever. They both needed to know that a woman has options, and I'd done a poor job of modeling that to them by being a stay-at-home mom who catered to her husband's needs and desires all those years. He said something else, which I couldn't hear while I shampooed and rinsed. Probably a good thing. He could go on and on—without needing any sort of response from me. That's the way Shane was: always speaking from his pulpit, assuming anyone within sound's reach would be grateful to hear whatever he had to say.

When I finally dragged my prune-like body out of the shower, he held a towel open, then wrapped it around my body and carefully twirled me as if we were dancing, open wounds and all. He held me tight, the two of us looking at each other in the steamy mirror. I couldn't remember the last time he held me like that. It almost worked.

Then, hunching down, he rested his chin on my shoulder. "You're being one hundred percent selfish," he said.

I slid out from his embrace, grabbed another fresh towel, and began to dry my hair with it.

"Either that or you've lost your mind," he went on. "Those are the only explanations I can come up with for why you keep on insisting that this whole adventure was necessary and right, or why you even remotely think you should stay on here. And the more I think about it, you're not just being a poor example to Delaney. You're brainwashing her."

I stopped towel-drying my hair and stepped away, with half a mind to swat the towel at him. But not playfully. To hurt him, to retaliate for how much that accusation about Delaney stung me. If there had been any part of me that still loved Shane, that still wanted to make our marriage work, it had been washed down the shower drain, like dead skin sloughed off, moments earlier. My outdoorsy, feminist self—the one who wanted to pursue her own path—was finally clean, refreshed, and anxious to step out and make it on her own. Which is why I didn't dare turn to look at him or even acknowledge his reflection in the mirror. I squirted some body lotion into my hands.

"Why should I pay for you to live way out here when we have a perfectly good home back in Portland?"

"You should pay for me to live here because I don't have any money to pay for myself," I said. I was fully aware that my business didn't earn enough to support my pinky finger, but in that moment I didn't care. Financial concerns were something to worry about another day. All I could focus on then, as I navigated the lotion around my freshly opened gashes, was the exhilaration of impending emancipation and the itchiness that began to develop all over my skin—a combination of the dry Yellowstone air, the hot shower, and my agitated scabs. When I started to scratch, he grabbed ahold of my arm.

"Don't," he said.

I twisted out of his grasp. "You should support me because we decided long ago I should be a stay-at-home mom without a sustaining career. Because it's time for me to get to do some things that I want to do...because now that the kids are grown, it's my turn." And also because this wasn't the 1970s, and we'd been married long enough, and I knew enough about Oregon law to know the courts would tell him to give me money if we were to divorce. Little beads of blood surfaced where I'd scratched, and he noticed.

"Babe, what you're saying here is that we should have our own little welfare system within our family."

I used to love Shane's affectionate name for me, but not anymore. It made me cringe. And when he pulled a box of bandages out from my overnight bag, I winced. Even that felt like an invasion of privacy and personal space.

"I do the work, then hand over my earnings to you so you can play? Do you know how many women are doing just that—essentially raping our economic system by choosing to stay single, or by becoming single once again? But they can't support themselves or their families, so someone else has to pay for them. Their ex-husbands. Or their parents. Or taxpayers." He picked up my container of floss, pulled out a strand, and began to work on his molars. Whatever he'd squirreled away in the back of his mouth now splattered the mirror.

I wanted to roar. Or worse. I wanted to pummel him with my fists. I wanted to pick up the hair dryer and bonk him on the head with it. I wanted to go stomping out of the room, naked if necessary, and proclaim his idiocy to the world. Instead, I tossed my hair towel at him, turned off the fan, and glared at that man facing me in the mirror with disgusting floss dangling from his mouth. Who the hell was he?

"Do you hear yourself?" I asked. "How dare you, first of all, suggest that I would be hijacking your precious earnings? I have worked just as hard as you all these years, raising the kids and keeping our home up to your perfect standards. And you know it takes a while for new ventures to make money; eventually my business will. Furthermore, for you to suggest that women who choose to remain single are hurting our society is one of the most ridiculous things I've ever heard you say. It doesn't begin to compare to the things men have done to ruin our world. Think war, rape, fossil fuels. Did you ever think about the fact that some women don't *choose* singlehood? Or that some do because they want their *freedom*? They don't want obnoxious, controlling men micromanaging their lives, financially and otherwise. Whoever decided that women shouldn't or couldn't be single was a moronic pig."

Shane now took my cuticle scissors from my cosmetic bag and began to trim his nose hairs. I grabbed them from him, ran them under hot water, and tucked them back in with my other belongings; his non-reaction irked me more than his assumption that he could use them in the first place.

"Until men figure out how to treat women like equals—which you, as a collective gender, still aren't—this is what happens." I zipped the cosmetic bag shut, fully aware of the symbolism of that action as well as the fact that I was now going on without waiting for his reply, just as he had done with me, and I figured it was an appropriate demonstration of equal soapbox time even though he likely wouldn't get the subtextual meaning of any of this. "You've heard of Susan B. Anthony, right? Way back in the 1800s or so, she predicted this would happen, that more and more women would need to remain single before men figured out what they'd done wrong and what they needed to do to fix things. And you're right, sometimes we can't support our families well, but that's often because we've been held back in education, and in equal pay, and in so many other opportunities. Or we've been taking care of the family and not furthering our career skills. Not to mention we've been put down by sexual and verbal assault. Even in these so-called socially aware times in our own society. Don't get me started."

"Get you started?" he said, crossing his arms across his chest and his right leg in front of his left. He leaned against the bathroom wall. He was smug, but I knew him well enough to see a hint of surprise behind his arrogant smirk. He wasn't accustomed to me disagreeing with his worldviews—or with much of anything he said or thought. He was curious—or at the very least amused. I'd made it this far so, emboldened, I went on.

"And then there are all the underprivileged women elsewhere in the world." I dabbed some face cream onto my neck and cheeks, then began to spread it in gentle upward and outward motions. "We've got a long, long way to go. *Babe*."

A click near our bedroom door drew our attention away from the mirror, ourselves, and each other. Delaney had popped her head into the room and now, as she leaned in on one tentative foot, her hand still on the doorknob, she cleared her throat. I adjusted the towel still wrapped around me, wondering if she'd been listening to us from the suite, outside the bedroom door, for a while. Wondering how much she'd heard.

"Sorry. I knocked," she said. "I guess you didn't hear me. Um…did I hear someone say something about equal pay?"

"Not now, Delaney," Shane said. I agreed with him, quite possibly for the last time.

"I just wanted to find out what we're doing for dinner." She gave me a once-over in my towel. "I guess I need to give you guys a little more time." She started out the door, then stopped and leaned back in over the threshold. "Oh, and I thought you might want to know that Carson's smoking more weed."

"Order room service," Shane said. Had he not heard what she said about Carson?

"He's smoking in our suite?" I asked.

"Yeah. I didn't think you'd go for that," she said, shooting an arch smile at me, like we were in on something together. She turned to Shane. "But thanks for the room service. There's a great vegan pasta dish on the menu."

As she began to leave for the second time, I called after her. "Tell Carson we'll deal with him and his marijuana later." Thinking about his new drug habit awakened a little voice inside my own head. It reminded me it was time for more oxy. Delaney nodded and closed the door, more firmly than I expected.

"Okay," Shane said, missing not a beat after the door closed, "let's not get any deeper into this whole women-in-society thing. Let's talk about you. And me." Dismissal was one of his favorite methods for dealing with loss, and he had clearly been losing the women-in-society battle against me. "Bottom line: if you're going to abandon me, I'm not going to support you, at least in the manner to which you've obviously become accustomed."

The towel slipped as I rubbed lotion on my legs. I couldn't catch it in time.

"I didn't say I'm going to abandon you." I turned to him, fully naked. "I didn't say I'm *never* coming home. Come to think of it, I never really said what I was going to do because I'm not even sure myself. I thought we were just having a discussion. But your attitude might very well be helping me make up my mind." I don't know why I came off sounding so wishy-washy just then. Was I wavering in my commitment to independence, to self? Or was I just a chicken when it came to saying those very hard words to Shane? His eyes grazed over my body. My conviction strengthened in my veins. I felt more certain now than ever about what I needed to do, and what I needed to not do. I needed to not go home.

I saw his cognitive wheels spinning as he tried to figure out his next move. I slipped into one of the hotel's terry robes and sat down at the pretty little writing desk. A big, cheesy bison burger and a plate of homemade steak fries had been on my mind for the last hour, so I called room service.

"You have no idea what sort of mistake you're making," Shane said.

"The burger and fries?"

"You know what I'm talking about." He pulled his T-shirt off. I watched his pectoral muscles flex.

"Is that a threat?" I said.

He slipped off his shoes and unbuckled his belt. "I think it's time you come clean and call a spade a spade, Brooke."

I was lost. I'd just become quite clean in the shower and had been daydreaming about that first bite into a juicy burger. "What are you talking about?"

"Have you given a moment's thought to what everyone will think when they hear that you've taken up with a woman?"

"What? Taken up?" I laughed. "You think Leila and I are...a couple?"

"Aren't you?"

"Obviously not, given how she flirted with *you* the other night."

"Look at you. You're jealous," he said. I felt my cheeks flush and hoped he hadn't noticed. "Which confirms—"

"It confirms nothing," I said. Shit. He *had* noticed. "Leila and I are just friends, and that's that."

"I guess I'll take my own shower now," he said. He unzipped his jeans and let them fall to the floor. I watched the jeans drop, and then my eyes slowly floated upward from his jeans back to his face. His eyebrows were scrunched, his forehead creased. He scratched at his hairline with one hand. "But I don't believe it's just a friendship. I saw the way her eyes lit up when she spoke about you. What I'm having a hard time accepting is the idea—"

Her eyes lit up? When she spoke about me?

"—the idea that I've been married to a *lesbian* all these years and didn't know it." He hit his head with the heel of his hand as if shaking a thought loose. "You won't even look at me anymore."

I hadn't realized it. But it was true. I wasn't surveying his naked body the way I once would have. Sure, I noticed his pecs—anyone would—but it wasn't the same, and now I'd been scanning the room service dessert menu.

"I'm sorry. I got distracted by the warm huckleberry cobbler."

We stared at each other. I had hurt him, and I hadn't meant to. And as fond as I was of Leila, I didn't believe I had actually become a lesbian. I stood, untied my robe, and walked across the room to him with the robe's belt in one hand. I pushed him down on the bed. When I saw his puzzled expression, I felt even more empowered. He'd thrown out a challenge and I'd accepted it, and now I would have him on my terms as he'd had me so many times on his. I straddled him carefully, mindful of my wounded skin and, to some extent, his wounded ego.

"You know how I like it," I said. "Get busy."

"So, you do still want me," he said when it was over. "Now are you ready to come home?" He reached out and traced a finger down the good side of my torso. "To be my wife? I promise I'll change, however you want me to. I love you. You mean the world to me."

It had felt more like break-up sex than make-up sex to me, but I couldn't hurt him any more than I already had. Not today. I rolled off him, took his hand in mine, and squeezed hard. "Right now I'm getting back in the shower. You can have it when I'm done."

Ruth drove me from the hotel to West Yellowstone the next day, after Shane and the kids left for Portland. The drive was quiet for the most part; I spent much of it ruminating about what a disaster the weekend had been. Yes, Delaney was finally talking to me again, and I was thrilled about that. But the rest of my world was falling, or had already fallen, apart. And like the punchline of a cruel joke, thousands of runners had crossed the finish line of the Portland Marathon—a race that I was supposed to run—before Ruth and I had even pulled out of the hotel parking lot.

When we got back to West Yellowstone, Ruth said she had a hankering for pasta and parked in front of one of the few restaurants still open now that tourist season had ended. After we ordered our food, a server delivered a wedge of almost-wilted iceberg lettuce, with a sad little slice of tomato, to each of us. The salad looked the way I felt. I asked Ruth if I could tell her something in confidence.

"Of course. Anything."

"I thought Leila and I were becoming really close, but then she was flirting with Shane the other night at the dinner. And then she left abruptly. It really hurt my feelings. It's been troubling me all weekend." I neglected to mention what Shane had said about her eyes lighting up. I just couldn't see that as a realistic possibility.

Ruth shook her head slowly, closed her eyes, smiled.

"Leila cares about you a great deal. More than you'll probably ever know."

It was at this point I wanted to ask if Shane was right. If Leila was gay.

"In fact," Ruth went on, "she asked me to stay back at the hotel to be there for you after the party because she couldn't."

"What do you mean she couldn't? I don't get why she had to leave so abruptly after going to the trouble of planning the dinner party for me in the first place."

The server placed Ruth's spaghetti Bolognese in front of me, and my fettuccini Alfredo in front of Ruth. After we exchanged plates, I burned the roof of my mouth with my first voracious bite. She twirled noodles around her fork.

"The short story goes like this," Ruth said. "Soon after Chief Joseph allegedly made his historic surrender speech in 1877, a Nez Perce woman, the one that founded what came to be called Maggie's Place, made a similar speech. Only her sentiment was a bit different. What she said was something like 'from where the sun now rises we will fight forever.'"

"Wow. Leila pointed out a plaque with that quote in Emily's cabin, but I hadn't really given it much thought. I thought her mother made it. Instead, it was an Indian woman who wanted to fight?"

Ruth laughed. "You have so much to learn. Yes, it was Leila's mother who made the plaque. And it was an Indian woman, too."

I quickly swallowed a clump of noodles. "Wait a minute. Leila's mother was Indian?"

"Yes. Lakota. Anyway, it was she who made the plaque, but it was actually a Nez Perce woman who came up with that saying, long before. That woman had wanted to fight for women—whatever it took. Long before women's lib or even the first major suffrage movement. And that cabin was the beginning. Ever since then, women have been welcome there for nurturing and support. Whatever they need."

"That's where Emily took Leila's mom when she sort of adopted her."

"That's right."

"And men were not welcome."

"Right again," Ruth said.

It struck then me how, having spent some time in Emily's cabin, and having seen that plaque every day if only subconsciously, I had begun to learn to stand up for myself—even to fight for myself.

Ruth continued. "And on the first full weekend of October, we gather there in celebration of Maggie's sentiment. Of Maggie's Place."

"You mean this past weekend? Leila hosted a celebration for women this weekend, at the very place I've been calling my home for the last several weeks, and I wasn't invited?" My stomach started crawling up my throat. "I don't get it. I would have been the perfect poster child there: Woman takes sabbatical from controlling husband, gets mauled by bear, comes to Maggie's Place to recuperate. I feel like the little girl who doesn't get the birthday party invitation when everyone else does. Was it because I'm not Indian?"

She set her fork down and smiled. "Of course not. A woman's background is irrelevant at Maggie's Place. And you're right about being the perfect modern-day example of the type of woman who's welcome there. I understand how it must hurt that you didn't get to go to the celebration."

As she took a bite of spaghetti, I realized she hadn't been able to attend because of me.

"Thank you," I said. "For being here for me."

She nodded and waved her hand in the air. "It was a tough decision for Leila. You know, Emily and I used to talk about this sort of thing every year. Who to invite to the event. Whether to let the public meet the women living there, or even whether to let the women meet one another. Legally, there's little Leila can do to assure confidentiality, but confidentiality—and safety—was of prime importance to Maggie. Haven't you appreciated being incognito? Wasn't it a comfort to know Shane didn't know where you were and couldn't readily find you even if he'd wanted to?"

I may have been wrong to feel that way, but it was true. Being off most everyone's grid had allowed me to focus entirely on myself to the point of feeling selfish.

"But there *were* people who knew where I was," I said. "Like you and J.P. And Palmer. And Leila let me give directions to Shane when he and the kids came to visit."

"Of course it's impossible to keep it a hundred percent secret. We try to use our best judgment, for the safety of everyone. And trust me, those people you just named wouldn't dare step foot on that land without permission."

"Why?"

She laughed as she slurped more noodles into her mouth. "Local folklore says the place is haunted. It's not, of course. But some folks have a tendency to braid fact and fiction together."

I couldn't imagine an intelligent, educated doctor like J.P. being afraid of legend.

"But back to the celebration," she said. "This was the first one since Emily's passing, and it was up to Leila to deal with this dilemma."

"So. I was a dilemma. This gets better and better. Maybe I should have gone back to Portland. I wouldn't be such a burden here, then."

"Please don't take it that way. You aren't a burden. In fact, I've never seen Leila so happy, especially given that Emily's gone and Leila's daughters are so far away. She just takes everything in life very seriously, including her friendship with you, and she wants everything to turn out right. She wants the whole world to be happy, and as you know it's impossible to be all things to all people all the time. She's especially hard on herself when someone is disappointed in her. Arranging your dinner party and this celebration, while keeping her family satisfied from a long distance, has been especially trying for her."

"But keeping me in the dark, or thinking of me as a burden, or hiding me from the public or other women who live there...that's not going to solve anything. Tell me this, then. What's the story with the ghost woman? Was she allowed to be at this celebration and I wasn't?"

"Ghost woman?"

"That's what I call her. I've seen her. She's pale and thin and has a grumpy cat. And she's always spying on me from behind her curtains."

Someone at the restaurant suddenly turned on the sound system, and music from the 1980s blared through speakers right overhead. Pat Benatar: *Hit Me With Your Best Shot.*

"I couldn't acknowledge if someone else is living there, even if I knew," Ruth said. "Normally, Emily left it up to the residents to introduce themselves to one another. This woman will meet you when she's ready. The bottom line is that this is a women's sanctuary, and all the secrecy is for the protection of the women."

"So what makes the place so safe? If you ask me, it looks more like a target than a fortress, sitting out there all by itself. Surely the whole idea that it's haunted doesn't keep everyone away."

"As a matter of fact, that legend holds tremendous power around here."

"Because?"

"Because a long time ago, some men came looking for a woman there, and they didn't fare so well. As the story goes, only one man was allowed to step foot on the property from that point on. A freed slave who actually owned the land and gave it to Maggie."

"What about Palmer? He went inside one night."

"Was he invited in?" Ruth asked.

"Not by Leila. I let him in."

"And he did subsequently experience some mysterious misfortune afterward, didn't he? Think of when he showed up at the hotel with those injuries."

"I refuse to believe in superstition," I said. "Palmer's clearly got some issues. My guess is that he got in a fight."

She nodded. "You're probably right. I'm not sure I believe in the legend either. That's one of the many issues that Leila needs to work out as she settles Emily's affairs. She needs to decide if the operation will continue as is and, if so, how the power of that legend will be passed along."

"If it will continue? I thought it was decided she'd sell the property."

Ruth shrugged. "Leila inherited it from Emily, so it's up to her to decide what to do. It's not an easy decision."

Later, as we pulled up to the cabin, I asked Ruth how she knew so much about Leila and Maggie's Place, given that she lived in Idaho Falls.

She turned off the engine. "You mean nobody has told you how I fit into this family jigsaw puzzle?"

"Nope."

She laughed heartily. "You might feel like an unappreciated dilemma, but I feel like an unappreciated convenience. I'm Leila's aunt."

"You're kidding," I said. "You're her aunt? And what about J.P.?"

"He's my son."

"I can't believe I hadn't put all this together. So Emily was your mother?"

She nodded.

"And Maggie?"

"My great-grandmother."

Leila and I avoided the herd of elephants in the room over the next several days. We didn't discuss her performance with Shane at the party, or the omission of my name from Maggie's celebratory invitation list, or what happened to the boxes of Emily's belongings that had been stacked at the back door, or what exactly our relationship was, or what her future plans were for Maggie's Place, or when she was going to kick me out, or who in truth the ghost woman was. We actually didn't talk about much at all, and I couldn't tell if we were having a friendship version of a lover's spat, or if we were both conflict avoiders. Even though Ruth tried to convince me that I wasn't a burden, I couldn't help but feel like one. Maybe Leila had just had enough of me, with all the cooking and chauffeuring and whatnot. I had been so wrapped up in my own drama that I really hadn't given enough thought to what an intrusion I'd been for her. Or to even wonder why she'd gone out of her way for me, not just with the party but with everything.

We were both also very busy those next few days. I had four physical therapy sessions that week, and I learned more about my pathetic body in those four sessions than I had in the last four decades. Like what poor range of motion I had, on my good side as well as the bad. And how inferior my balance was for someone my age. How my gait had probably been off for years, too, which was why I had that big bunion on my left foot. The good news, my therapist said, was that because of my bear incident we'd be fixing most of those problems. The bad news: it seems that everything's connected to the ankle bone, including emotions, and after citing an obscure study that claimed wounds heal faster if you write about your trauma, she insisted I write for fifteen minutes every day about what happened to me.

I had a difficult time staying focused when sitting with my journal. Leila and Delaney kept sliding into my thoughts and words. Sneaky little devils. Delaney also kept sliding into my phone, texting me every morning and night and occasionally calling in between. I heard from her more over the next few days than I had for several months. Not that I complained; on the contrary, each call or text rocketed me straight to cloud nine, even when the subject was difficult. Even when she called past midnight—well past my bedtime.

"Dad's an ass," Delaney said on one late-night call. Stifling a yawn, I asked what was wrong. She explained that she and Shane had gotten into a big fight about what major field of study she should declare in addition to music.

"Dad's always interrogating me, like he always does. He keeps asking about my math and science classes, and harping on me about how I have to do well in those because that's the ticket to my future. So I told him that I was thinking about a double major with music and something in the social sciences. Possibly social work. Obviously I'm only a freshman and have no clue what I really want to do, but I know I have zero interest in those stupid STEM classes. And I told him so." I told her it was perfectly fine for her to follow her own path and not to let Shane bother her—advice I myself should have heeded years earlier.

On another phone call, she complained about the boys on campus and how so many were hounding her to study with them or go to parties with them or get drunk with them. I assured her she should follow her heart and good sensibilities and that there was nothing wrong with her just because she didn't want to behave as wildly as the boys wished she would. Afterward, she sent me a text with an emoji that reminded me of the person in Edvard Munch's artwork, *The Scream.*

All this correspondence with Delaney made me feel ten pounds lighter. I shared some of it with Leila, and she laughed about how grateful she was that her children were still far too young to worry about those young adult matters. By talking about Delaney's reentry into my life, Leila and I were able to avoid talking about whatever was, or wasn't, going on between us.

Later in the week, on the eve of another trip for Leila back home to Tahoe, I asked if she could yet again drive me to my appointments in Idaho Falls the following Thursday.

"Hopefully this will be my last trip there," I said. "As long as my orthopedic surgeon isn't too upset about the boating accident. And as long as the PT there gives me the green light to get rid of this damn boot and lets me start walking in real shoes again."

Leila had been making dinner when I brought up the drive back to Idaho, sautéing a vegan dish with silken tofu, Tuscan kale, and a spicy peanut sauce she whipped up on the spot.

I said her husband was lucky to have her, given what a good cook she was. I believed that; Shane—the self-proclaimed foodie—had commented on numerous occasions throughout our marriage about my less-than-stellar culinary prowess. But I was also fishing for something about Leila's relationship with Cody, about whom she'd spoken so little. My selfish heart half-wished she'd be able to stay here with me forever. Instead of reacting to my comment, however, she simply said it would work out fine to take me to the appointment in Idaho Falls. She had some legal matters to attend to, and that was where Emily's attorney was located.

That weekend, while she was back home in Tahoe, I went on a little reconnaissance mission. Everything Ruth had told me had been gnawing at my curiosity. Besides, my local PT wanted me to start putting a little more weight on my foot. So I headed out the back door, water bottle in one hand and a can of bear spray in the other. Emily's binoculars hung around my neck, and I had my phone in my back pocket. I wasn't sure what I might encounter, but I wanted to be prepared.

My first obstacle was the ghost woman's gray tabby, which hissed at me as I walked past her cabin porch. A lesser person would have aimed the pepper spray at the thing. Instead, I hissed back. From there I wandered out toward the woods and, once among the pines, I glimpsed a building farther back. It was well camouflaged; certainly anyone arriving at the front of the property would never see it, and no road led back there. But I spotted a path ten yards or so to my right that zigzagged through the underbrush.

The building looked to be as long as a twenty-five-meter swimming pool and was built entirely of beautiful logs stacked one atop the other with interlocking joints. An enormous rectangle of Lincoln Logs, with a vaulted roof of timber and a large rock chimney rising near its center. Each of the four exterior walls was lined with transom windows too high off the ground to peer through. A heavy wooden door was adorned with a handle fashioned from forged iron.

My curiosity got the best of me, and I built an unstable pile of branches and football-sized rocks beneath the lowest branches of a nearby pine tree. It was foolish to think I could readily climb up to the windows, but then again I'd survived a grizzly attack and a kayaking incident. I could handle this.

I shimmied my way up into the branches, scraping my arms as I went, and just as I'd hoped, I was able to see pretty well through one of the windows. This was no ordinary barn or lodge. This was a freaking spa.

The overall décor was traditional western lodge, with timber beams and beautiful cedar walls throughout. A circular stone fire pit served as the centerpiece, surrounded by tree stumps as seats. Through the binoculars, I saw a wooden altar, with unlit candles, at the far end, as well as comfortable seating for ten or twelve women arranged in a circle. And a bar! Cartons of china and glassware were stacked along one wall; a tub of wilted flowers sat beside it. Gorgeous rugs, woven with intricate geometric designs, were aesthetically scattered around the entire lodge, as well as large, colorful floor pillows and numerous life-sized, bronzed animal statues.

I couldn't see what was along the wall beneath me, not from this angle; I'd have to climb another tree for that. But I'd seen enough to know this was no haunted house. This was a hidden paradise, a fabulous setting for a celebration.

As I started down the tree, clinging to the trunk with every muscular molecule in my arms and legs to avoid a fall, I heard rustling. I considered climbing back up, but by then all four of my limbs were quivering like pine needles in a windstorm—from both fear and fatigue. My fingers dug like claws into the bark, so when the bark tore away from the trunk, I lost my grip entirely. I crashed into the underbrush and rocks I'd piled below.

Instinctively, I climbed out of the woodland debris before I even knew if I was alive, or injured, and looked around as one does in such times with the hope nobody had seen what just happened. And that it hadn't been another bear in my midst.

The ghost woman scowled from a distance, arms across her chest. She was so skinny she could blow away in a breeze, but I had the feeling she could also kick my ass. I started toward her, mulling over what I might say. But she pivoted and circled back to her cabin.

That evening I called Shane, although I wasn't sure why. Maybe I was lonely. Or maybe it was because I couldn't get the ghost woman and her strange appearance in the woods out of my mind and I just needed to hear a familiar voice. As usual, he started the conversation by talking about himself: he'd found a permanent campaign office downtown on Yamhill; the final tally for the fund-raiser dinner was nearly twice what he expected; he'd gotten a massage that afternoon and never felt better. Yada yada yada. I flopped down on the sofa where Leila usually sat in the evenings and recalled how I'd spent more than two decades listening to him talk about himself. Nothing had changed. He probably thought Carly Simon's song was about him.

Finally, he turned his attention to me. "Do you have any idea how many insurance statements are coming in the mail these days? Or what the medical costs are adding up to for your little Yellowstone fiasco?"

I said to scan and email the statements to me.

"I'll do no such thing."

"Why not?"

"Look, I'm going to say this for the last time, and I mean it," he said. "You. Are. Coming. Home. It's time you stop playing the poor little girl who runs away to find herself. You've had your adventure and the party's over, literally. If you aren't home by the end of next week, then—"

"Then what?"

"You're trying my patience," he said.

I glanced up to Emily's plaque above the door. "The feeling's mutual."

So much for his promise to change—but, oddly, I wasn't upset. After a long pause, I checked the phone to see if I still had service and battery power. It wasn't the phone. "Shane?"

"What you have never realized is that I've done it all for you, Brooke. The hard work, the long hours at the office, the big fancy house. I gave you two beautiful children who we sent long distance to your alma mater when we could have saved a lot of money by sending them to the U. of O. I gave you your freedom with that little Internet hobby of yours. I did it all for you. And this...this obstinacy...is the thanks I get."

"*My little hobby?*" Now he hit where it hurt. "I'm helping people, Shane—artists who need help getting their work out into the world. Art is important—contrary to what you and your STEM friends believe. Art and music and literature, and flowers for that matter, are what make us human. So I'm not just helping the artists; I'm helping our world see their work. You're right, I'm not raking in millions, but my business has been in the black every year I've had it. It might be a small black dot, but nevertheless it's black."

"Maybe, but like everything else, it's taken you away from me. Sometimes I think you care about others more than me."

His line of discourse was heating up my blood, but at the same time I couldn't help but wonder if what he said was true. I got up and looked out the window at the solitary night. *Did* I care about the rest of the world more than I cared about him? And if I did, was that so wrong? Didn't his immersion in politics suggest he, too, was focused on the world more than our relationship?

I also wondered if he was telling the truth when he said he'd done this all out of his overwhelming love for me. If I could have—*should* have—been a better wife. And yet, I also knew that, for now, I needed to stay the course. Now was not the time to wobble. I'd done enough wobbling on that tree for one day.

"I hear what you're saying," I said. "But I wasn't put on this earth just for you. Last time I checked, I was a free-standing person with a brain and a will of her own. What you don't, and maybe have never, appreciated about me is that I also have needs and desires. And lately I've found the courage to look at them. It took me a long time to develop that courage, but now that I've found it, it's getting stronger every day."

"Sometimes I think you've lost your mind."

I thought about my old friend Linda and whether she'd say a comment like that was abusive. She'd once said that love doesn't belittle. Love lifts up. As naive—or foolish—as I was, I hadn't really understood what she meant. But now I did.

"Maybe I *have* lost it," I said. "Or maybe I've finally found it, after it's been MIA for years. The case of the missing mind, solved at last."

Again a long silence. A chilly breeze blew through the open window. I lowered the sash. Winter would come soon in this part of the world.

"So where does this leave us?" Shane asked.

"I don't know."

"Well, I think I do. It sounds to me like your mind is made up."

He was correct. I had made up my mind, but I still hadn't figured out how to accept the decision. Now, my courage hit the skids the way it sometimes did back in the old days on the river, right before hitting a Class IV rapid, when you want to start back-paddling furiously like a cartoon character even though you know there's no going back. Shane was going to do it. He was about to break off our marriage for me.

"I'll give you one more week," he said. I breathed a sigh of relief only because, sometimes, procrastination can be more medicinal than wine or oxycodone. "But just one. I don't care how you define the week's end. Hell, I'll give you till next Sunday, a week from tomorrow. A bonus day. If you're not home by 11:59 on the 22nd, we're heading for Splitsville."

Splitsville? I couldn't believe he really said that. "Ultimatums don't belong in marriages," I said to the dial tone.

NINETEEN

Anne

I FOUND MAGGIE, panting, just off the path in a stand of pines. A man lay on the ground at her feet, her knife impaled in his back. I patted the horse and tossed its reins over a tree limb.

"Is he dead?" I asked.

"Not yet." She held one fist inside her other hand, her stance at the ready, her gaze firmly on him.

"Did he...hurt you?"

She did not reply, but I knew the answer by her silence and her refusal to look at me. I kicked him between his legs, twice. He barely winced. The knife remained implanted in his back, and now I smelled the iron of blood. I knew what had to be done.

I knelt beside him and leaned in. With his face turned to one side, it was easy for me to ascertain that his breathing was labored, and he had only moments to live. My heart made no attempt at compassion but rather pumped as violently as the heart of a fiend must, and then, without warning, my fist grabbed hold of the knife as though it had a mind of its own. It pulled the weapon from the dying body, inch by inch, and I turned away as blood spurted out. The villain moaned hideously for the last moment of his miserable life.

Once the knife was free and dripping blood, a troubling image crossed before my eyes. I saw myself grabbing his long, filthy hair and slicing a quick, circular motion around the top of his head. I saw his filthy scalp dangling from one hand.

Of course, I did not really do it.

I handed the knife to Maggie, stood, and kicked the corpse once more. Now that the sky was lightening sufficiently, I saw the man's long hair was bloody and matted—and orange as a carrot. I also observed the stains on Maggie's dress, my suspicion now fully confirmed. I would need to find a watering hole for her soon.

The enemy wore a gold band on his left finger. I took the ring, and then we gathered our limited rations, along with the marauders' extra rifle and horses. Before leaving our camp for good, we tied the living man to a tree.

This time I felt my arm rising, Maggie's knife in my hand. It hung for a moment midair, high above the miscreant. Just before my arm swung down toward his flesh, Maggie caught it and shook her head.

"Leave him. He will die here; *x'axa c* will see to that. And you will retain your honor."

We were now two bandits, Maggie and I. A pair of galloping shadows with an extra horse in tow. The morning sky hung low; the clouds were thick and Wedgwood blue. More snow would be upon us soon. We skirted the forest's edge whenever possible while trying to keep our pace strong. I still had not learned how to ride a horse properly, and I could barely keep up with her. Before long, every part of my body ached. The only thing that kept me going was a fantastical hope that soon we would come upon a quaint little hotel with a bed and proper accommodations for washing.

We rested for a short while that night before Maggie mercilessly roused me from a dream in which I had been sipping fine tea and nibbling finger sandwiches. I was ravenous when I awoke, and the three horses must have been as well. But she insisted we move on. Despite their hunger, the horses were nimble dashing through the woods and seemed to be as delighted with their own escape as we were with ours.

We rode them hard until sometime the next afternoon, when we came upon a small shack and barn, both badly weathered. Smoke curling up from a crooked chimney confirmed that somebody was home. Maggie hid in the trees with her horse, its painted appearance well camouflaged amidst the brush. I tied my horse and its companion to a fencepost and approached the windowless door.

A woman with a washed-out complexion and a double-barreled shotgun answered my knock. Gaunt and frowning, she looked like a witch. But as I had not seen a mirror in weeks nor eaten much besides buffalo for several days, I decided I might look equally dreadful.

"Hello," I said. Her eyes, dark circles beneath them, were devoid of welcome. "I wonder if you could spare me some water for my horses. And perhaps a chunk of bread for myself?"

I was tempted to turn away when she did not speak. Clearly, she was as destitute as we were and would not dream of sharing any meager goods with a perfect stranger. But when she coughed, I thought of Maggie, who was still unwell. The old woman studied me out of her left eye. The other eye seemed to roam off in another direction of its own volition.

"I've been traveling for many days and have run into a great deal of misfortune," I said.

She took note of my two horses and asked if I was alone. I abhor deceit, but thought it in everyone's best interests if, for the time being, I offered a small fib as my reply.

"Come on in," she said, her tone insinuating I was a great bother.

The hinges creaked as I stepped inside, where I immediately took stock of the surroundings. It was a simple, one-room structure, which contained a narrow bed with a filthy quilt, a rickety table constructed of knotty wood, a single chair with a dilapidated cane seat, and a soot-covered potbellied stove. A charred and dented pot rested on top of it. The old woman had a slight coughing fit, then offered some coffee to me. I told her I would be most grateful for that.

She gestured for me to sit in the single chair, and I prayed it would refrain from collapsing. For ten minutes or more she watched me attempt to drink the coffee, which was so strong and bitter, I was sure hair would quickly grow in places unbecoming to a lady. Finally, she asked me my name and where my travels were taking me.

I gave her an abbreviated tale of woes, omitting the part about Maggie.

"Yep," the woman said, her eyes now coming to life. "I heard word about some o' them Indians taking people captive. Emily Cowan, that was her name I do believe. Or, no, lemme think. Emma Cowan. Emma Carpenter Cowan. Poor young thing. Some folks say she was on her honeymoon. Terrible shame."

I asked if she had heard any news about a man named Thomas Blakemore.

"No, can't say that I have. News don't travel too fast around these parts, however."

As I asked her name and whether she was there alone, the questions from those mysterious riders on that first day at Mary Lake—and later the voices of the rangers—echoed in my memory. "I am sorry. That was impolite of me to ask such a delicate and personal question."

She waved her hand midair. "Oh, nothing to worry about on my account. I'm as open as a barn door."

Clara did reside alone, her husband having died several months earlier. They were homesteaders from Missouri and had lived in the area for a number of years. She rambled on about how they had lost so many loved ones in the War, and they'd aimed to start their lives over when they moved out west. Now the government went and set up a national park practically in their backyard.

"And then my dear Jonathan up and died. He's buried out back. I can show ye his grave if ye like."

The last thing I desired was a visit to a recently dug gravesite. Furthermore, I had difficulty concentrating on the woman's story knowing Maggie was out there hungry and thirsty and distressed, waiting for me. As impolite as it may have been, I interrupted Clara and asked if there might be a way I could water the horses now.

"Oh, where are my manners? Ye sit right there and rest. I'll see to the animals." She started for the door but stopped to retrieve her shotgun from beside the bed. I poured myself another mug of the nasty coffee and waited for her return.

In a few minutes, the door opened and Maggie walked in, the tip of Clara's shotgun digging into my friend's back.

"Look what I found out yonder," Clara said, coughing so hard I worried the gun might fire inadvertently. "This little Indian was fixing to steal yer horses."

Maggie shrugged as though she had, indeed, been caught in the act of theft, and I laughed. I then explained our story to Clara. She lowered the gun, cocked her head as she listened.

"Ye had me believin' ye were travelin' alone. And now this. I'll forgive ye yer little lie if only on account of yer bravery and otherwise fine manners." She adjusted her hold on the weapon, now aiming it directly at my heart. "But don't lie to me again. Or else."

A smile slowly grew on her face, and a nervous giggle issued forth from my lips.

"As a matter of fact, I believe this calls fer celebration. What do ye say we each have a little drink, and then I'll fix us some of my special venison stew?" She set out a bowl of water for us to wash up, then withdrew a bottle of whiskey from beneath her bed. Given how evident it was that Clara was not well, we both declined her offer of liquor, but she took a drink—two actually—and after a while she said she needed to lie down. "Ye girls can do the cooking."

It took scarcely a minute or two to discover that Clara had scant quantities of potatoes or deer meat, and I wondered if she was ill for lack of nutrition. While the pot bubbled like the geysers in Yellowstone, we made up a place to sleep in her barn. Over the next several days, we endeavored to be of little burden to Clara so that she could convalesce. Maggie tried to resurrect the garden, pulling out weeds and tilling the soil to prepare it for spring planting. She also foraged for wild herbs to help with her own cough, and Clara's, too. I cleaned and aired out the cabin from floor to ceiling and took over Clara's job of traipsing to the south fork of the Madison River each day for water. But we knew this was not a permanent solution for either of us. One matter of great importance was the visibility of Clara's place; every traveler who came through these parts stopped in for water and rest, she said. It was no wonder she had come down with an illness, being exposed to every unsavory, lice-ridden vagabond who happened by. And although Maggie and I did not know what we planned to do in the long term, we did know that we needed to stay out of public view.

One day, as we rounded a bend on our approach from the river, we spotted a wagon parked directly in front of the shack. A droopy old horse stood in front of it. Maggie set down her buckets and ran to hide in the barn. I set my buckets down as well, but I ran for the cabin. For Clara's sake.

To my surprise, I found yet another woman inside when I arrived. Her back faced the door when I came in, so my attention snagged on the colorful scarf that was wrapped around her head and trailed down her back. Reds, blues, oranges, yellows—I'd never seen the likes of such fabric. And when she turned, I was astounded to see her obsidian-black skin.

"This here is my friend Evalene," Clara said as she added wood to the stove. "And she's brought us some news."

A cloth had been spread across the table and covered with numerous small bowls, cups, and vials. Some were empty; some were filled with powders and liquids of varying colors. On the stove, a large pot of water boiled, from which a minty scent wafted.

"Come on, Miss Clara," Evalene said, and Clara followed orders and sat down at the table.

"First, I'm going to give you some herbs to swallow in a cup of tea with vinegar." Evalene mashed something in a stone mortar with a pestle. "Lots of garlic, some licorice root, pepper, and dried celery. Dried marigold, too. It won't taste so good, but never you mind that. Then we're going to do some blood cupping, and finally a steam treatment. Are you ready?"

I watched Evalene administer the medicines with the proficiency of a skilled nurse, and she accompanied her work with what seemed to be an incantation. Her voice was as beautiful as a songbird's. I waited, impatiently, for her to complete the spell and then asked about the possibility of infection.

"She's already got the infection," Evalene said. "Probably can't get much worse. But this garlic potion will help a good deal."

When she was all but done with her procedures, she spread a greasy salve over the places where she'd cupped Clara, and then another minty salve on Clara's décolletage.

"Saved the best part for last," Evalene said as she brought the steaming pot to the table. She set it in front of Clara, instructing the old woman to lean over it, and then she draped a floral cloth over Clara's head and shoulders. "Now you just sit in there and breathe for ten minutes or so, Miss Clara."

A face appeared in the little window beside the table, startling me. It was Maggie's. I opened the front door, called her into the cabin, and introduced her to Evalene. The black woman looked Maggie up and down.

"Hmm." She put her mysterious concoctions away in a purple sack. "Now I know why I've been hearing about there being Indians here at Miss Clara's. It's the truth. You all have got to go. There's talk around here that you'd best be on your way before the lynch mob shows up. Wouldn't want to cause no trouble for Miss Clara, now, would you?"

"We have no place to go," I said. "We have already been attacked inside the park. They burned our tipi, stole our things—"

Maggie slowly shook her head, a movement so slight I nearly missed her message. She did not want me to reveal what had happened to her, what those men had stolen from her. However, as I thought about what they'd done, indignity rose inside me the way steam rose from Clara's pot.

"Maggie is not just an Indian girl. She is my friend," I said. "She helped me in my greatest hour of need. And something horrific happened to her in the park. I had hoped we would come upon a town where we could settle for a while—with townspeople, especially some kind ladies, who would accept her. Accept both of us. I had thought people out here would be accommodating. In addition to Clara's fine hospitality, that is."

Evalene held her hands on each of Maggie's cheeks. She inspected her eyes, ears, and tongue, and listened to her breath.

"You need some of this here medicine, too," Evalene said, seeming to care not a jot about what I'd just said. Maggie sat down and waited for Evalene to mix some potions.

"Probably some miners that accosted you in the park. Or maybe some of them military volunteers who did what they did. Breaks my heart. No telling what gets into the minds of men like that, why they think they have a right to treat us that way." After giving Maggie a cup of special tea, Evalene took her into her arms and began to rock back and forth like a mother with her baby. Surprisingly, Maggie melted into the embrace. "I'm also sorry to tell you you've come to the wrong place if you're looking for an understanding kind of folk."

"Will we at least be able to locate a dry goods merchant for supplies?" I asked. "We have nothing. And what about one of those new telegraph stations?" I had promised Maggie I would send a telegram to my sister as soon as we found civilization. "And what about Clara?"

"Oh, I'll be all right," Clara said from the steam treatment. "Y'all've got enough to worry about."

"I think Miss Annie is right," Evalene said to Clara. I liked the way she called me Annie. "I don't like it when you're all alone and under the weather, and I can only come around here now and again. Besides, you know everyone in these parts. Looks to me like you all might be able to help one another." She let out a big, bosomy sigh. Maggie sat up.

Clara removed the steam cloth and asked how in the Sam Hill she would be able to help us. "As it is, my wood pile's nearly gone." At that moment, a burst of wind blew the door open, sending a scrap of Evalene's cheesecloth sailing across the room.

"One good windstorm and this entire residence might blow away," I said. I had not considered taking Clara with us, but the idea was worthy of some deliberation. "We three have a few things in common. It might not be a bad idea to set up a place where we could take care of one another. And who knows? Perhaps we will find another lady or two who needs our assistance. We could set up a safe place, a sanctuary." The vision of frilly linens and gardens lined with rose bushes came to mind.

"Sanctuaries are for churches," Maggie said. "No more churches."

"No churches," I said.

"They have places like what yer talkin' about back east," Clara said. "Places fer women. They're called asylums."

"I am not referring to asylums or churches," I said. "I am envisioning a place where ladies come of their own free will and worship or study or dress or otherwise behave as they wish. Places where ladies come to be nurtured and loved. Or to rest from all their hard, thankless work. And where they come to think for themselves."

Evalene laughed heartily and asked where she could sign up. Clara said we would be the laughing-stock of everyone for miles around and possibly labeled as witches.

"Put your head back under that steam cloth if you want to live long enough to see this dream come true," Evalene said.

That evening, after we had a light supper of broth, and after Evalene left and Clara fell asleep, Maggie and I retreated to our straw beds in the barn. Something hung about her, and I asked why she was so sullen given the day of nurturing camaraderie we had had.

"I am not sullen," she said, completely without conviction.

"Yes you are. Talk to me."

"You are going to think I am silly."

"No, I will not. That would be impossible."

She confessed her worry about our friendship. "If we do undertake this enterprise you speak about, you will find happiness with others."

It took me a minute or two to comprehend the source of her worry. "Oh, Maggie." She was lying on her stomach. I sat up and straddled her to rub her neck and shoulders. "You are too special to me. No one will ever replace you. It is you, in fact, who has inspired me. You cared for me when I was lost and injured and alone. What could be more perfect for you than a sacred place where you could offer your nurturing gift to others?"

Only now did I realize what had happened. White Eagle had died, we had fled the park, and—in so doing—she had yet again traveled to an unknown place. Moreover, I had tossed out a vision of our future together like a pitcher tossing out a ball at one of those baseball games Thomas had read about to me from the *Chicago Daily Tribune*. Maggie had become accustomed to the idea that she and I would stay together, just the two of us, for the long term.

She rolled over beneath me. I immediately climbed off, aware how unseemly it was for one woman to sit atop another one like that, but as I did, she reached for my hand.

"It will be dangerous for us. Thomas might still come for you. Other husbands will come looking for their wives. And white men will come looking for me when they learn of my whereabouts. The risk would be great for all of us."

It was too dark for me to see her expression, but I cradled her face and noted her eyes and cheeks were dry. I blinked to gain control of my own tears. What if Thomas came looking for me now? What would I do?

"You worry too much," I said. "You are right, there will be risk. But risk will accompany us wherever we go. Why not surround ourselves with people who love us and whom we love? This is an opportunity to build a new home, a new life…in a new world."

A colony of bats flapped down from the rafters and out into the sky. I lay down beside Maggie, nuzzled my face into her neck—knowing full well this intimate gesture would be frowned upon by the *civilized* world—and wept as my hope for our future endeavored to conquer the memories and fears from our past.

TWENTY

Brooke

WHEN LEILA CAME back from California, she was bubbling like Old Faithful right before it erupts. There had been much I wanted to talk about with her, but she was clearly, and rightfully, preoccupied with her own life. The first round of results from her husband's treatment already looked promising. His pain was lessening, his mood improving.

Sitting on the sofa, I rubbed my good foot. As much as I wanted to be excited for her, and for Cody, I found I felt sorry for myself. My theory of the universe surfaced yet again: one family breaks apart, another family heals. I stretched out and invited her to tell me more.

"I haven't seen Cody this upbeat since forever. This will be so good for him. For all of us."

"I'm happy for you." My sentiment came out flat as wood.

"He's supposed to report back at the end of the month, and the program will go all the way till Christmas. Which means I've got to head home and get back on full-time mommy duty. God, I can't wait. I've missed them all so much. You have no idea how hard it was to leave them this morning."

She lifted my legs, slid underneath them to sit on the sofa, and rested them back on her lap. Normally this act of intimacy would ping my heartstrings, but everything had changed all of a sudden, now that Cody was in the picture again. He belonged there, but still I resented him for coming back into Leila's life.

"Here's more good news!" she said. "I told J.P. we're coming to town this week for your final appointment, and for my meeting with the attorney, and he asked if we'd like to spend the weekend at his cabin afterward. It's between Idaho Falls and Jackson, near Grand Targhee. It's a simple little cabin…oh, Brooke. It's beautiful up there. He said they've already had a dusting of snow. What do you say? Girls' weekend away?"

"He won't be with us?"

"God, no. That would ruin everything. Come on, let's do it. Just the two of us. One last fling."

It turned out to be a threesome. Palmer had called and asked me to take care of his dog for a few days. We hadn't spoken for a while, and I couldn't imagine why he needed me to dog sit—or why he trusted me to do so, as I had no experience with dogs and had nearly drowned his daughter. But I felt sorry for him. Whatever was going on with his mental or emotional state, it was clearly weighing on him. I checked with Leila and J.P. They both said it would be all right to bring Row, so Palmer dropped the dog off at Leila's on his way out of town.

At my appointment on Thursday, my orthopedic surgeon said she was pleased with my progress and discharged me from her care with one last reluctant prescription for oxycodone—the one J.P. had given me at the hotel had just run out. She also gave me a stern lecture that I needed to get off those meds. God, everyone was so worried about me and the pain meds. It wasn't like I was going to go down that opioid addiction path that was always in the news.

Even though the surgeon and I had only seen each other on a few occasions, it was a bittersweet discharge, as my stay at the hospital turned out to be such a life-changing event. The physical therapist discharged me, too, saying I should keep doing whatever I had been doing. It would also be fine, I was told, to begin to wean myself from the boot and to occasionally wear a shoe instead—but only for short periods of time and only if I wore a shoe that had a low heel. A cowboy boot's heel.

"I need to buy a pair of cowboy boots!" I told Leila when we met up later in the afternoon, after she'd had her appointment with the attorney. "My PT said so."

"You're joking."

"Only a little." This was cowboy country, and I wanted to have a souvenir beyond the titanium in my leg. "I'll need a good pair of snow boots, too, if there's snow at the cabin."

Leila rolled her eyes, but she also found a western wear store at the edge of town. That's one of the things I loved about her, the way she always accommodated my needs and wants. She took Row for a sniff-and-stroll while I impulsively bought on-sale snow boots, a pair of brown leather cowboy boots with silver and turquoise inlay designs, and a brown Stetson hat with a silver band. Yee-hah.

We stopped at a pharmacy, and Leila begrudgingly ran in to fill my prescription. Soon after that we were on the road.

"So what did you think about the longhouse?" Leila asked after we'd gone a few miles.

I tried to play dumb, without success.

"I heard you climbed up in a tree last weekend. You're lucky you didn't break your other leg."

So the ghost woman could talk after all. "I'm not sure if I should feel more sheepish about spying or about being so reckless," I said. "But I'll tell you one thing: if I had to run away to a shelter, I'd definitely want to come to Maggie's Place. In fact, if more women knew about it, more women would run away from home. Did you know your aunt filled me in on Maggie's Place and the celebration I missed?"

Leila tightened her grip on the wheel.

"I enjoyed hearing about it. Except that the person I really wanted to hear it from was you." It still hurt that, after being with Leila for nearly two months, she'd told me almost nothing about the women's sanctuary, and nothing about the annual celebration.

Row poked her wet nose between our two seats. "Look. The dog wants to hear about it, too."

Leila reached back and scratched between the dog's brows, then glanced at the clock on the dashboard.

"I guess now is as good of a time as any. Mind you, it's as much legend as fact," she said. "Everything I know was passed down from my grandmother, who heard it from her mother, who heard it from Maggie. But what has come to be known as fact is that Emily's cabin was originally built in 1877 by Maggie and her friend."

"Anne. Of the sketches."

"You know?"

I tapped my head. "Two and two. I'm smarter than I look."

"Well, you're right," Leila said. "Maggie was a Nez Perce woman who had become separated from her tribe during the 1877 tragedy. You've probably heard about Chief Joseph."

"A little. He made a famous speech when he surrendered to the military."

"Right. He was a member of the Nez Perce tribe. He, and many others, didn't want to be rounded up on a reservation in Idaho."

"Understandably."

"Right again. So they left their homeland and tried to settle with other tribes, like the Crows. But things didn't go according to plan, and all this time the United States military was chasing after them."

"I've heard and read some about the Indian Wars over the years, and seen some plaques about the Nez Perce in Yellowstone. But our history books don't seem to tell much of the story." I yanked off my new cowboy boots. They had started to pinch my toes.

"As is the case for a lot of history the government doesn't want us to know about. Anyway, Maggie was a product of those times."

According to Leila, there were several hundred Nez Perce who came from Eastern Oregon and Idaho across the Bitterroot Mountains into Montana with all their worldly possessions. Maggie was part of that band. Their trail took them right into Yellowstone, which was a brand new national park then. From there, they eventually headed north, trying to get to Canada.

"But they didn't make it?" I asked. Damn, those boots were tight. I'd only worn them for maybe an hour tops.

"No. They surrendered just short of the border. Already too many had been killed, and Chief Joseph didn't want to see any more die. Sadly, many who surrendered were shipped off by train to Oklahoma, of all places, and some of them died on the way there; their bodies were just shoved off the train."

We drove for a while in silence, imagining the horror. "So the captured ones weren't even allowed to go to back to the Idaho reservation after all that?"

"You'd think, right? Let them be closer to their homeland? But no, they weren't allowed to do that. Instead they were forced to abandon their clothing and customs and try to act like white people—so-called civilized people—in the middle of nowhere."

"It's heartbreaking," I said. "Makes no sense."

"Neither did those boots you bought." She caught me rubbing my feet. "Anyway, the way Emily told it, not much the military did back then made sense. Then again, they're not much different than some of the politicians today."

Ouch. It was hard to hear her say that, given Shane's political ambitions. I tried to remember if I'd told Leila my husband was a politician. Regardless, I knew she was right.

"This ongoing belief system we have, thinking some people are better, and more worthy, than others, even more human than others…it's hard to believe so many people still subscribe to it. Look at the LGBT struggles. Civil rights. Immigration issues."

"Women's rights, still, after all these years," I said.

"Right."

"And Native rights, like with all the pipeline problems and whatnot."

"The list goes on and on," she said.

"So how did Maggie wind up here, and not on the reservation or in Oklahoma?" I asked.

"During the Nez Perce journey, there were a number of skirmishes. Many of her people were killed. Maggie—"

"Emily's grandmother?"

"Right. Emily's grandmother lost her one and only child at that time in a battle that became known as Big Hole. We're not sure what happened after that, but somehow she was separated from the rest of her people."

"I can't imagine. Being a woman all alone out here. No cell phone, no Internet. No car."

"Especially with all the white soldiers, and enemy Indians, and sleazebag trappers and miners wandering about."

"Not to mention grizzly bears."

She checked the rear view mirror and adjusted the air conditioning before reaching over and squeezing the back of my neck gently. I leaned into her fingers. She carefully reached around my face to the scarred side.

"Your face is healing nicely, by the way," she said. "I don't think I've mentioned that."

"Thanks."

"You know that pouch in Emily's trunk?" Leila said.

"The same one that's in the sketch? The one you didn't want me to touch?"

"Yes, that's the one. I guess I can tell you what it was if you promise not to think it's odd."

"Promise."

She described the Nez Perce custom—which was also a custom of many other cultures, apparently—for mothers to keep their children's umbilical cords. Maggie had lost her baby, but the pouch with her infant's umbilical cord had previously been tied around her waist, and she survived the battle with it. "It was all she had left of her baby."

It sounded macabre, but then again, we white Americans had some customs that others might find bizarre. Like viewing open caskets at memorial services. Or performing autopsies. Or eating copious amounts of tuna casserole, delivered by ostensibly well-meaning neighbors, after the death of a loved one.

"I see now why you were so protective of the pouch when I was pawing through Emily's trunk. Thank you for sharing the truth with me."

I was about to ask Leila to tell me more about the origin of Maggie's Place when a text came in from Delaney. *Call right away.* I tried, but we had such poor service that I couldn't get a call to go out.

"Shit," I said. "Why do texts work in zones with poor service but phone calls don't?" Row had been lying in the back seat but now sat up and rested her chin on my shoulder. "The dog's wondering the same thing."

"I don't know, but I'm sure she's fine," Leila said. "She seems like a responsible young woman."

"Deep down, she's got a good heart. I'm just not sure she's got her head screwed on tightly. And she's been upset a lot lately about some arguments she's been having with her father."

"We all went through that at her age. Remember?"

"I don't. Early onset of senility, maybe."

"Emily always said that was why storytelling is so important," Leila said. "When you speak out loud about your past, it strengthens your memories, and it also makes sure the next generations learn from you before you forget or get around to writing it down. And when you say it aloud, the listeners can also feel your emotions."

I made a mental note to tell Delaney more stories, if she'd be willing to listen, although I wasn't sure what those stories would be. I tried another call to her. No luck. "So tell me more stories," I said. "About Maggie."

"Like I said, there were a lot of skirmishes," Leila said. "There were more Nez Perce killed than whites, but there were also several instances when white people were either held hostage or killed by the Nez Perce in retaliation. Maggie encountered a white woman whose husband had been captured by her people."

"Anne of the sketches again?"

"Yes. Anne had injured herself, and Maggie—who was just a teenager, we think, even though she had been the wife of a chief—nursed Anne's wounds. Can you imagine if you were all alone in Yellowstone, scared out of your mind, and I came along, equally scared, and all we knew about one another was bad stuff?"

"Anne had probably heard that all Indians were savages," I said. Leila snapped a glance at me. "I mean...that was what the whites thought back then. I'm not saying it was true."

"Some white people still think that. At any rate, Maggie had heard the same about the American military, and how they raped and murdered tribal women. So Maggie and Anne were enemies, but they needed each other. Maggie helped Anne survive in the wilderness; Anne served as the interface between Maggie and white people. Maggie eventually determined that her husband had been killed by the American soldiers. Anne revealed how abusive her husband had been to her. They formed an unexpected bond."

"So Maggie was on the run from the army, and Anne was on the run from her husband. And the two women teamed up," I said. "Wow. What a story."

"I know, right? And together they started to build a life, and a sanctuary for women, too."

"Maggie's Place. Someone should turn that into a Lifetime movie."

"God, no!" she said. "That would ruin it."

I laughed. "You're right. Sorry."

The horizon ahead of us was still distant but had grown shadowy. I pulled my hoodie tighter around my shoulders.

"Here I am worried we won't get to J.P.'s cabin before nightfall. Those two women must have been scared shitless every night. Not just about grizzly bears. They must have been worried about starvation, or freezing to death, or bad guys around every turn," I said.

"And worried about being found. If Maggie had been found, she would have been sent to the reservation...or killed."

"And Anne would have been returned to her husband to get beaten up or sent off to an asylum." I recalled how Shane had suggested, on numerous occasions when I didn't see things his way, that I should see a therapist. "Men get away with so much shit."

"Which was exactly what Maggie and Anne probably thought. The other thing Emily always said was that they realized that women behave so much differently when men aren't around. They're more authentic. More down to earth. I have friends in California that put on makeup before they go to the health club, but when we all get together for a hike in the woods—where it's unlikely we'll run into members of the male species—they wear nothing on their faces except sunscreen and ChapStick."

It wasn't long ago that Shane and I were heading out to a political event. When I came downstairs, he gave me the once-over, then gawked at my face as if I'd broken out with an alien rash of green spots. When I asked what was wrong, he suggested I put on a little more eyeliner and another layer of mascara. *And maybe that Spanx thing. You need to look stunning tonight,* he'd said. *This is a fund-raiser, after all.* As I thought back on his comment, chills crawled up my spine. He'd been pimping me—figuratively speaking—for campaign donations.

"I've never once felt uncomfortable in your presence without makeup or body-shaping underwear," I said. "And I'm grateful to you for that, Leila."

We rode for a while, each of us thinking our own private thoughts about whatever. Eventually I asked if we were almost there.

She tapped the steering wheel. "Not too much farther. We'll get to the parking place before dark. But not the cabin. We'll have a bit of a trek."

"A what?"

"A trek."

"Leila! There's no way I can trek anywhere. I just got permission today to *begin* to wean myself from this boot. Did you, by any chance, bring a horse?"

She threw her head back toward Row, then patted my leg. "You'll be fine. You trusted me with the horseback ride, didn't you? And look how that turned out. I won't let anything happen to you."

That horseback ride was already a lifetime ago. Now I envisioned hobbling through the snow in a strange forest at night. Which reminded me about Maggie's Place being haunted. Then, Leila pulled into an isolated gas station—the kind where only one person works inside and you know he's an axe murderer. I checked my phone: still no service. I hoped Leila was right about Delaney's well-being.

It took forever to fill the tank, and the sky kept darkening with each tenth of a gallon of gas. Finally, she got back in the truck, and I immediately hit the button to lock my door. As she pulled back out on the highway, I asked what she thought about Maggie's Place being haunted.

Leila sighed. "This is the sort of story that gets embellished over the generations. For now let's just say it has to do with the legend of a scalped posse."

"Okay, fine. Then what's the deal with the ghost woman? The one with the mean cat who lives in the middle cabin? Is she like in witness protection or something? And are there any other ghosts there?"

"I can't tell you anything about the residents. It's the rule."

"Ruth said the same thing. Come on, Leila."

"What I can tell you is that Phoebe's not a ghost."

"Phoebe."

She cringed. "Okay, yes, you got me. Her name is Phoebe." Little did she know that I already knew the ghost woman's name, thanks to those women on the horse trail. "And no, she's not in witness protection. She's been here forever, since I was a little girl. And it's definitely time you get to know her."

My phone vibrated; another text had come in from Delaney asking why I hadn't called her back and telling me it was urgent. Several frantic emoji faces were lined up in a row. Still, I only had one bar and I couldn't get a call to go through. I texted to let her know I'd been trying and was in a bad service zone. The text could not be delivered. What could be so urgent? When the kids were young and I needed my privacy, I insisted they leave me alone except in the case of vomit, blood, or fire. Was she sick? Had there been an accident? Did the dorm burn down? I hit my phone, as if doing so would improve service.

"This is driving me crazy," I told Leila.

"Do you want to turn back?"

I asked if there would be cell service or Wi-Fi at the cabin.

"I'm not sure."

A cattle truck passed us, its draft shaking Leila's truck and its stench clogging the air vents. Row, who had resumed her napping position on the rear seat, lifted her head and looked out the side window. The prairie on either side of the road had turned into vast stretches of shadow, interrupted only momentarily by small ranch houses or clusters of buildings and the occasional sign suggesting an actual town. Now and then I spotted an antelope bounding in the distance; up ahead, the horizon had become jagged. We were finally heading into the mountains.

"No, let's keep on going," I said. To turn back would have meant at least a couple more hours without service anyway. "I'm sure she's all right." If I'd been the religious type, I would have said a prayer.

There was more than a dusting of fresh snow at the trailhead; there must have been three or four inches on the ground. But at least Leila had been wise, and kind, enough to pack a sled in the back of the truck, along with a tarp. Once we parked the truck, she lashed our gear onto the sled with rawhide ties and covered it with the tarp. Then she donned a pair of snowshoes and offered to help me put on my new snow boots.

"I don't think these are going to fit over my walking boot. And I don't think this is the type of walking my PT had in mind when she said I could try to go without it."

Leila helped me put a snow boot on my good foot and threw the extra boot back into the truck. She fitted a plastic bag over my walking boot, tied it on with some extra shoelaces, and led off. Row followed her, lugging the sled behind. I checked my phone one more time for service before bringing up the rear.

Although Leila said it was only a mile, it felt like at least three miles of trudging through heavy snow. But it was heavenly out there, despite the darkness and the effort. Like hiking through a forest dusted with powdered sugar. I loved the idea of being hidden away, but at the same time, I couldn't help but worry about Delaney, or our own safety, especially after my still-recent bear attack and with all my just-now-healing injuries. Except for J.P., no one knew we were here, and the deeper into the forest we went, the darker it got, as in a fairy tale in which a wicked witch and a hot oven waited for us at a candy-covered cabin. If something jumped out from the forest and grabbed me—the one in the rear—neither Leila nor Row would know the difference.

And Delaney would think I'd run off and abandoned her forever. Now certain I was the world's worst mother, I asked Leila again if there would be service at the cabin. Again, she said she wasn't sure. Then I asked if the bears had gone into hibernation yet.

"Probably not. But soon."

"Did you at least bring Emily's secret sauce?"

"Of course I did," she said. "A fresh batch."

"But you forgot the snowmobile."

She assured me we were almost there.

When the trail finally took a sharp curve around a small hill, I saw a cabin up ahead. There were no gumdrops or candy canes adorning it, but it definitely fit the image of a fairy tale cabin, dressed head to toe in snow, which glistened in the beams from Leila's headlamp. Spindly fir seedlings on either side of the door waved to us in the breeze, and triangles of snow had begun to accumulate in the corners of the four-pane windows. A small stack of firewood had been piled up, itching to be thrown into a fire. When Leila unlocked the door and we stepped inside, dust motes flittered everywhere in her headlamp's light.

My back ached. My sides stung. Even after all my therapy, my right leg hurt so badly I wasn't sure if I'd ever be able to walk again. I collapsed onto the bed, even though I could barely see anything around me—for all I knew, Goldilocks was already sleeping there. Row jumped up beside me. Leila grabbed a crocheted afghan from the back of a rocking chair, flapped it wide into the air, and spread it over Row and me.

I wanted to take my meds, but I was too tired to get up and look for them in all our gear. The dog and I lay there like bumps on a sleeping log as Leila hauled in our gear and an armful of wood for the stove. Soon a fire was crackling, perfectly timed as the heat from exertion had by then left my body. Ah. The smell of burning pine. Leila asked how I felt, and I told her I had actually died but that it was A-OK. "This is the afterlife as it's meant to be." She scruffed my hair as if I were another dog.

"I'm going out to chop wood."

I offered to help. She laughed.

Cell service had improved, oddly enough, so I called Delaney from my cozy little nest. No answer, of course; kids nowadays didn't wait till Friday to have parties, and Delaney had historically been known to be overdramatic. I had probably spent hours worrying for nothing. Now, when her voicemail greeting answered, I wasn't sure whether it was better to leave a message or send a text. I was fully aware that voicemail was obsolete for her generation, but I didn't want her to forget what my voice sounded like any more than I wanted to forget hers. The good thing about being indecisive, however, was that I tended to cover all my bases. I left a voice mail and a text for her, and I Facebooked her as well, telling her I had gone off for a girls' weekend with Leila, that we were in a primitive cabin with no electricity or running water, and that my phone battery was about to die. I Snapchatted a picture of the cabin's interior, too. Then, I dozed off.

It was pitch black when I awoke, other than the orange glow through the window of the woodstove door. I got up, went to the window, and pressed my forehead to the glass. The expression *cold as ice* surfaced, along with the melody from that old Foreigner song. Snow still fell outside, and Leila was still out there chopping wood, her hair and eyelashes flecked with snow. She had a red bandana tied around her neck but had draped her parka over a snowy tree branch. I watched as she wielded the ax with such ease and grace. She was stunning. And Cody was such a lucky man. As if she'd heard my thought, Leila looked up at me, there in the window, and smiled.

I searched through the gear for my meds, and also to see what Leila had packed. Not much, considering we were out in the woods for a weekend. A small cooler containing two little packages of cheese, a couple of apples, and some hummus. A Rubbermaid box with crackers, a Tetra Pak of broth, two boxes of herbal tea. Four jugs of spring water. And that was it. Either she'd forgotten an awful lot of stuff or we each had different ideas about what a girls' weekend out would be. I couldn't even find any wine.

Or my oxycodone.

"Do you know where my meds are?" I called out the door to Leila. She held up one finger and said she'd be in soon.

I grumpily set a kettle on the woodstove. My leg really hurt. I frantically scavenged through the cupboards in search of at least some Advil, but all I found were plates and cups, a roll of paper towels, a book of matches, an ugly spider, and a partially used eucalyptus candle. I caught the spider and set it outside the door, then lit the candle.

As I waited for Leila to finish outside and for the water to boil inside, I sat on the floor and moped. My back was killing me, and there was nothing to make the pain go away. Also, Leila seemed more interested in chopping enough wood for a lifetime than spending time with me. Delaney wasn't answering my communication attempts, either. Even Row was unavailable to me, snoring through her little doggy dreams. I tried to sort through my feelings, not just of the here and now but from the past several weeks. And my worries about what was next to come: what Delaney was up to, and why she'd been so urgently trying to reach me. Not to mention whatever the hell was going on with Carson and his current obsession with marijuana; all the articles I'd read about the dangers of massive levels of THC came flooding back to me while I sat there in the dark. But most of all, more than everything and everyone else, I worried about how it would be to separate myself from Leila for good.

I still didn't understand our relationship. It had been platonic this entire time, but it had also seemed to have an undercurrent of something else from that first night she'd kissed me. The truth was that I didn't know what I wanted from her. I'd never felt this way about a woman before. Leila had wedged herself into my heart the way a wildflower wedges its roots into a jumble of rocks.

When she came into the cabin, I got up from the floor and took her wet jacket. After handing her a dry towel, I poured our chamomile tea.

"Any idea where my meds are?" I asked.

"No idea," she said. "Maybe you left them back in the truck."

"Shit." There was no way I could make a round trip to and from the road. And no way I'd ask her to do it. She didn't offer to get the meds, either.

Leila gently nudged Row off the bed, lay down on her side, and propped her head on her hand, lifting one mysterious brow. Uncertain what to do, I lay on my back beside her, resting my hands beneath my head. Leila tucked my hair behind my ear.

I'm pretty sure I gasped at her gentle touch, Hollywood romance style.

"It's okay to breathe," she said. "You don't need to be afraid. This is all good."

"I don't know what *this* is," I said, trembling like a young teen on her first date.

"It's just you and me. Just here and now. No right, no wrong. No should or could."

I took a risk. Sitting halfway up, I pulled her mouth to mine.

She didn't resist.

We kissed. Her lips were moist and soft, reminding me of vanilla ice cream, even though her breath was warm as tea. We kissed, released, kissed, released. Tender, unhurried. No ultimate objective. After a while, we stopped. It was a good stop. Not rushed. Not one-sided. Not something that had to be analyzed or explained. We just stopped, as if all that had just transpired was perfectly natural and that was that. As if we were never meant to take it any further. And maybe as if it would never happen again.

"I have something for you," Leila said as I thirstily gulped my tea. I hoped she was going to produce my missing meds. Instead, she removed a wooden box the size of a child's shoebox from her backpack—the one place I hadn't searched because I hadn't wanted to invade her space. She handed the box to me. "Open carefully."

I did as instructed and peered inside, where a stack of envelopes had been tied together with what had once been a ribbon but which now could only be called a ragged clump of thread. The envelopes looked equally old and fragile. I asked what they were.

"Maggie and Anne's correspondence," she said.

I stopped breathing. Never had anyone given me something so significant, so rare. So personal.

I started to open one of the envelopes. It was so fragile, I was afraid it would rip.

"You don't need to read them right now," Leila said. "They're my gift to you."

"But why? Why are you giving them to me? Why are you doing any of this for me?"

"You'll figure it out, in due time."

TWENTY-ONE

Brooke

I COULDN'T SLEEP.

What had happened between Leila and me? What had it meant? Was Shane right—was I a lesbian? Was she? Were we bisexual or sexually fluid or whatever the current correct label would cast us as? Was what happened perfectly normal, and I'd just led such a sheltered life that I hadn't known that women went around making out with one another? I knew Shane got a thrill from movie scenes when women kissed each other, but that sort of thing had never turned me on. Even now, I wasn't so much turned on as exhilarated by the gentle touch of Leila's lips—but I was also ashamed and stunned and satisfied all at once. I felt remarkably loved, but also more leery than ever about the future. And guilty. I'd cheated on Shane—we were still married, after all.

Needing to find grounding, I grabbed my phone from the nightstand and called Delaney. Not that I would share any of this with my daughter. Maybe just hearing her voice would help.

"Mom? Are you all right? I've been trying to reach you for like hours."

I searched for the right words, my thoughts battling one another about what they wanted to confess versus what they knew was right. I settled on a simple apology for having gone AWOL. Even though my responsibility to be available 24/7 to my daughter could have theoretically ended on her eighteenth birthday, it hadn't—and I was thankful that was the case. I explained where Leila and I were, all the while unable to shake the memory of our make-out session and hoping my voice didn't reveal my secret. I then asked Delaney why she'd been trying so hard to reach me.

"I quit, Mom. I quit school. And Dad's gonna kill me."

This jolted me right out of my Leila reverie.

"You're right," I said. "He is going to kill you."

Despite the late hour for both of us, she tore into a litany about how she had been failing her math class and hating her other classes, and had tried to talk to Shane calmly about her difficulties, but he wouldn't listen and simply told her to get a tutor and try harder. "And he said to stop chasing boys, which pisses me off because they are the furthest thing from my mind. That's what I wanted to talk to you about."

So quitting school wasn't a big enough bomb? And then I saw: my daughter was going to come out. On the same night I'd kissed a woman for the first, and probably last, time. "You're gay?"

"What? No, I'm not gay. Not that it matters. I'm just not interested in dating anyone. Or even hooking up. Or partying. And that's all *everyone* wants to do here: party and hook up."

The last time she'd said words to this effect, I hadn't asked, despite my temptation to do so, how it was that all 20,000 boys on campus wanted to get in her pants. Now I wanted to ask whether it was really true that all 40,000 or so students on the Indiana University Bloomington campus—male, female, whatever—were there solely to hook up and party.

"Mom. It's all too much pressure. I can't do it. Any of it. I'm not like everyone else. Maybe there's something wrong with me, but I just don't think I can do this. So I went to the dean and quit."

My poor baby: the only thing wrong with her was that she was wise, too wise, for her years. Pride immediately washed over—and nearly drowned—me, and before I had a chance to say anything, she changed the topic and asked me what all this business was about hiking into a cabin in the woods.

"Mom, you need to take better care of yourself than that. You're lucky you even have a leg to walk on, and you've been doing way too many crazy things when you're supposed to just be recuperating. Horseback riding, kayaking, now trekking through snow? You're going to wind up old and crippled if you're not careful."

I didn't even tell her about climbing a tree. Instead I swung Leila's parka over my shoulders and slipped into her snow boots—even though they were at least two sizes smaller than my feet. I went out into the night. The snow had finally stopped, and as I breathed in the crackly dry air and listened to Delaney breathing on the other end of the phone, the whole episode with the bear rushed back to me. My eyes suddenly teared up and my hands hunted for Kleenex in Leila's parka pockets, but I came up empty.

I woke in the morning to the sound of Row, hastily slurping her dog food, and when I blinked away those last cobwebs of dream that always threaten to keep me from rejoining reality, I saw—in the dim light of dawn—that our gear had been neatly repacked by the door. Also, the fire in the woodstove had almost died out.

My heart quickened. "What's going on?"

Leila's face was so tight you could bounce a buffalo nickel off it. "I think we're done here. We've said and done everything we needed to."

"Are you angry with me?" Talk about déjà vu. I'd spent the last several years wondering what I'd done wrong to make Shane mad at me.

But her face softened and she placed her hand gently on my cheek. "No, silly. Not at all. I was just thinking. Here, let me help you sit up."

She adjusted the pillows behind me, just as she'd done nearly every morning and evening since I'd come to stay with her.

"I knew this would be a difficult weekend, for both of us," she said. "I have feelings for you just as you do for me, but we both belong elsewhere and with other people. You've got Delaney, I've got Cody. Really, staying here any longer doesn't make sense. Besides, we've got some things to take care of back at Emily's place."

"Maggie's Place."

"Right," she said. She opened the door and snow blew in. The swirls it made in the draft mirrored my frantic and aimless thoughts just then. "The sun will be out in all its glory soon. Shall we have one cup of tea before we go? There might be just enough heat in the stove to warm some water."

"I'd rather have a full breakfast of eggs, potatoes, and fruit," I said. When she didn't laugh, I said I'd meant it as a joke. The kettle took forever to heat the water. Finally, when it did, Leila placed a stick of intertwined leaves into each cup and served a mug to me.

I sniffed the tea water. It had a weird fragrance. Grassy.

She nodded. "It's good for you. And speaking of what's good for you, we need to have a talk."

Those six words no one wants to hear. "We do?"

"Yes, we do. It's about your meds."

I groaned.

Leila took a deep breath. "You know we all care about you, right? And none of us wants you to suffer. But the thing is, you've been on oxy longer than you should have been. Way longer. You should have switched to NSAIDs weeks ago."

"But J.P. kept prescribing the oxy for me. He's the doctor, not you."

"Yeah, you're right. But he was being too soft on you. He was hoping that you'd wean yourself off, that the last prescription he gave you would have been the end of it. When you had me fill a new one, written by your surgeon, I knew something needed to be done. In fact, we had already discussed what the plan would be if indeed you found another source for the oxy."

"What, you and J.P. had some sort of intervention…without me? Are you two addiction experts now? Because if that's what you think I am—addicted—then you're way off base. Me, a drug addict? Tell me you're joking."

I had questioned Leila's loyalty to me after the Lake Hotel fiasco, but that was minor compared to this. How dare she accuse me of being an addict, especially after what had happened the night before. Had that just been an act? And how dare she discuss it with others! Hating her at that moment, and hiding behind denial, I took a long sip of the tea—and immediately spit it back into the cup. "What the hell is this stuff? Are you trying to poison me?"

"It's kuding. In Chinese medicine they say it's good for wind-heat. But I say it's just good for overall health."

"It's gross." I tried to hand my mug back to her, but she motioned for me to try again.

"Take it in small sips. You've got to acquire a taste for it."

"No thanks."

"You may not realize this, but J.P. and I have both been procrastinating on this whole intervention thing. It's hard to talk about."

No shit. I had meant to have a conversation with Carson about his weed-smoking the weekend he'd come to visit, but I kept avoiding the confrontation, knowing it would be a nightmare and he'd blow up at me, and the whole family would be fighting. Knowing, too, that it's hard to tell someone to stop using drugs when you yourself are using drugs. Maybe this was my punishment for not following through with Carson.

"So, what, you bring me way out here in the middle of nowhere and somehow make sure I forget my pills in the car? And then you seduce me and poison me with whatever this tea is? Suddenly I feel like your hostage. I don't even know if I can make the trek out of here, I'm in so much agony. This pain is like Tolstoy's white bear: the more I try not to think about it, the more everything hurts."

"I thought it was Dostoyevsky's paradox."

"Whatever. It doesn't matter. The point is that you and J.P. can't just unilaterally decide what I should do. You don't own me. When I get back to the car, the first thing I'm going to do is find that oxy and swallow it. Maybe even a double dose."

"I was worried that's what you'd say. That's why we also consulted with Phoebe."

"You mean ghost woman? You shared my problem—a problem I don't even have—with some weirdo with a mean cat who goes around spying on me?" The mug of that kuding concoction desperately wanted to be flung across the room.

"I'm breaking Maggie and Emily's rules now, Brooke. But here's the story: Phoebe came to Maggie's Place a long time ago, when I was just a little girl, five or six. It wasn't long before my mom died. Phoebe was a cocaine addict, and she was a frightening skeleton of a woman. Emily told me to leave her alone, but I couldn't help it—her suspicious nature was magnetic to me."

"So the truth comes out," I said. "Maggie's Place is for addicts." I forced myself to swallow a sip of the nasty tea. It gave me something to do besides scream. Ironic that after all the cups Leila and I had shared over the past eight weeks, this—our last one—would be so bitter. "What I don't get is why J.P. and Ruth sent me there before I'd even had a chance to become one."

"Maggie's Place isn't just for addicts. It's not for anyone in particular, except women. We've certainly never had any counselors or nurses there. It's just a place for people to get away from whatever, or whoever, is torturing them. All we do is provide them food and shelter, privacy, and acceptance. If they want to talk, we listen. If not, that's okay, too. Sometimes we bring in speakers who help with personal growth or spirituality. But mostly it's about letting women be true to themselves, and have a quiet place to heal from whatever ails them, and—if they so desire—settle in a place where connectedness comes naturally without the false pressures of society. And of course there's the lodge."

"Oh, yeah, the other secret you kept from me."

She apologized for withholding so much from me but said disclosure would go against the grain of their mission. Suddenly I felt more like a client than a friend. Or lover. My heart felt as if it was being sucked right out of me and spiraling down a drain.

"So what was it that made me qualify for acceptance there, since I wasn't an addict at the beginning? Or could you and the ghost woman somehow foresee that I'd become one?"

"It wasn't the drugs. And it wasn't Phoebe. There was something about you that Ruth saw. We don't need to assign a particular name or diagnosis to take you in. We've had refugees here. Domestic violence survivors. Women who are depressed or anxious or healing from an accident. We've had several women who were dealing with self-esteem issues and who Emily believed had been subjected to psychological abuse."

Again I thought of my old friend Linda. I wondered where she was right now. If only I'd realized how wise she was all those years ago.

"Women with cancer," Leila continued. "Widowed women. And just lonely women who needed a friend."

"So now I'm a pathetic loner." At least Row, who had finished her breakfast and come to the bedside with her disgusting dog food breath, loved me. Unless she was in on the whole intervention conspiracy, too.

"There are no admittance criteria at Maggie's Place," Leila said. "But we only have the five cabins, counting Phoebe's."

"And somehow I rated top priority and got to share Emily's cabin with you? Or was that so you could keep an eye on my so-called addiction?"

"Stop it. You know that's not the case. Ruth brought you to Emily's cabin because you needed help with everyday activities at first. If you were going to stay long-term, we'd probably move you to one of the smaller cabins, into your own cabin."

Ouch. So even after practically falling in love with Leila, I would've been demoted, shipped out among the addicts and other lowlifes and misfits. I was fully aware that a major pity party was starting up, and I didn't want it to stop.

"So you agree I'm nothing like Phoebe."

"Of course you're not. When she first arrived, she could barely feed or bathe herself. Emily's goal was to support Phoebe however she could so that Phoebe could get clean, because that's what Phoebe wanted. And she did. But it took a long time. I remember peeking into her window sometimes, in those first few weeks she was here, worried not so much that my grandmother would be angry with me but that Phoebe would find me spying. I thought she was a witch, especially when I'd see her stirring brews on her little stove. Her hair was prematurely gray, and always a mess. Sometimes her hands would shake. Sometimes she'd be curled up on the floor in the fetal position. Sometimes she'd walk in circles, talking to herself and crying."

"Phoebe doesn't look much different now, near as I can tell, from what you just described. She still looks like a crazy witch."

Leila scratched Row's head and laughed. "Phoebe is the most gentle person I know. And she would do anything to help you get off the oxy."

I tried the poison tea again. This time it was almost tolerable. "She doesn't even know me."

"That's exactly how I felt when she brought me to the mountains on my spiritual quest, when I was only twelve."

Before I could ask about that news flash, Leila took my mug from me. End of discussion. "We'd better move on out," she said.

"Wait. You say the women at Maggie's Place are encouraged to be true to themselves, but then you micromanage them, or at least me. How do you explain that?"

"I'm not micromanaging you. I'm just trying to help you. I'm doing it from a place of love. Pure love."

Sometimes a person only needs to look at you—not speak a word or even touch you—and you feel her love wrapping itself all around. You feel warm and safe and full of hope. That's how it was with Leila. Even as I wrapped myself up in defense mechanisms, I couldn't fight off her love.

But soon she'd leave me, and all the oxy in the world wouldn't subdue that pain.

TWENTY-TWO

Brooke

I MOPED THE rest of the weekend away. As expected, the pills were "missing" when we got back to the truck, and although I knew I was pouting like a child, my self-pity was comforting. Leila was also withdrawn, whether because she was focused on finishing her business with Maggie's Place and packing to go home, or because she had fallen into her own melancholic vortex, I didn't know. So when Emily's landline rang late Sunday afternoon, neither of us exactly raced to answer it.

"It's for you," Leila said, rolling her eyes.

I put down the stupid journal I was supposed to be writing in. I'd described the beauty of the cabin but had yet to muster the courage to write about the important parts: the kisses, the fight. The missing oxy. When I took the phone from her, I tried to figure out what that eye roll had meant. "Hello?"

"I thought you'd like to know what's about to go down—*go down*." It had been so long since I'd talked to Palmer that I'd nearly forgotten about him. And I'd certainly forgotten about that verbal tic. He sounded more agitated than ever. "I'm heading up to meet with the head of the bear management program and other park authorities on Monday. It's time for your bear to be destroyed." He lowered his voice to a whisper. "Unfortunately, the boss doesn't agree with me."

I wasn't so sure I agreed either. Yellowstone was wild country. The bears were there first. I had foolishly ignored recommendations against being alone in the backcountry. I was at least partly culpable.

"What the boss doesn't seem to understand is how serious the threats are that we've been receiving. If we don't put the bear down soon, we'll be back in the Wild West. People will start taking matters into their own hands. And who knows who, or what, will get caught in the crossfire."

"But nobody's going to shoot a bear in the park, right? Aren't they protected there?"

"Theoretically. 'Course the bears don't abide by park boundaries. And we're right smack in the middle of hunting season."

Leila went into the kitchen to fry bread, and I followed her, half-hoping to finally discover the secret in the secret sauce. While listening to Palmer, I was entertained by how she stretched and pressed the dough by hand, rather than using a rolling pin. Once she placed the first piece of dough into the sizzling pan, I found my attention vacillating between worry over the bears' future and my hungry stomach—which by then felt about as empty as Carson's wallet.

"You're on board with this, aren't you?" Palmer asked. "It would be in everyone's best interests if we simply euthanize the bear, announce it through the media, and keep the public calm and happy."

I knew nothing about bear management policy. But I didn't like the idea that some poor bear was about to get killed—perhaps even a mother bear that had been protecting her young. I wasn't the type to get involved in political matters, which irked Shane, but I didn't like the way this smelled. The scent of fry bread was far more appealing.

"I'll come to the meeting with you," I said. Leila gave me a thumbs-up and handed me a plate. Palmer said he'd pick me up first thing in the morning.

There's nothing more emotionally satisfying than a fresh batch of fry bread with melted butter, local honey, and ground cinnamon. I dipped a chunk of bread into the condiments and shoved it into my mouth. She asked if it was all right.

"You had me at the first dip." I knew it was corny. I couldn't resist.

On Monday morning, I struggled to shake away the dissonant memory of Shane's call, which had come in right after Palmer's the night before. He'd reminded me that his ultimatum was expiring. And I'd reminded him that I wasn't coming home, that I had important business to take care of in Yellowstone.

As expected, he asked what *important business* I could possibly have. I explained that I'd been invited to testify to the national park authorities about what had happened when the bear attacked me. It could have an impact on policy, I told him, thinking he'd latch onto words like *testify* and *policy*. No such luck. Instead of latching on, he'd lashed out, and our communication ended abruptly.

Even though I remained committed to my decision to not go home, Shane still had a way of undermining my self-esteem. So I was gloomy as I got ready for the bear meeting. I stared into the closet, trying to decide what to wear, unable to see or focus on anything. Leila walked in, noticed my paralysis, and advised to just be myself. I laid out jeans and a sweatshirt.

"Not that self." She replaced the hoodie with a nice sweater. "And put on a dab of makeup."

She sounded like Shane. "You want me to get dressed up for a bear?"

Maybe it was the oxy withdrawal, but my compassion for the bear kept mounting, especially now that it might be facing execution. It wasn't a murderer; it had just been doing whatever bears do when they feel threatened. It had been true to itself—something we humans strive for and fail at far too often. I almost felt grateful to the bear, although I'd never admit that aloud. If it hadn't attacked me, I wouldn't still be in Yellowstone. I wouldn't have met Leila. Delaney wouldn't be talking to me. And whatever was going on with Shane would've been different than it now was. Most likely I would have returned home to my normal, frustrating life after my sabbatical. But thanks to the bear, I was feeling stronger now than I had for a long time.

After I showered, Leila combed the tangles out of my hair and asked if I wanted it braided, even though she had to catch a flight soon. That was Leila, always thinking about others. I declined her offer, saying I wasn't a braid kind of woman.

"But," I went on, "I was wondering if you happen to know who the head of the bear management program is. Palmer made him sound like a bigwig."

"I do know him a little. Hamlin Gerhardt. Great guy, super nice. Emily loved him. And he knows his stuff."

She left for the airport before I left for the bear meeting, promising to return the next weekend for our final goodbye. I counted to ten, just in case she came back for something forgotten, then dug out the oxy I'd stashed away weeks ago. I'd survived the last few days without it, but it hadn't been easy, and now that I was facing an entire day with Palmer and a mixing with people I'd never met, I needed something to help me along. There wasn't much left so I'd need to dole it out carefully throughout the day. I then rifled through her cupboards, looking for a snack to take along in my bag. Leila had plenty of apples, carrots, and gluten-free granola bars, but my irritable mood demanded decadence. I searched everywhere I could think of, and was about to take a second dose of meds when I had a hunch that something could be lurking in the baking ingredient cupboard. Sure enough, I found premium organic chocolate chips. I shoved them into my bag.

When we arrived at the meeting, Palmer introduced me to the others: Hamlin, Palmer's supervisor Monique, and Andy, the head of the bear program at Grand Teton National Park. Although Palmer's bruises had nearly disappeared, and his other cuts and scrapes healed for the most part, I noticed that Monique and Hamlin seemed to be studying him closely.

"Let's cut to the chase, shall we?" Palmer said, as if he were the one in charge when he was, in fact, the lowest rung on the totem pole. He spoke rapidly while thumbing through a stack of papers on the table like a kid playing with a picture flipbook. "I've got all the research and statistics here, but the bottom line is that we all know what happened on the Mystic Falls Trail on August 24th. And we all know about the other bear attacks in our parks over the past couple of years, some of which have involved fatalities. Our policy for managing bears has been mostly hands-off. So long as the bear doesn't consume a human, we let it go. But that's not working. Not working."

He stood and began to pace back and forth. Everyone watched. Then he stopped and looked out the window, where tree branches swayed in the wind. Abruptly, he turned and pointed a bully finger directly at Hamlin. "I've argued till I've been blue in the face that Glacier had it right all along, hazing bears to keep them away from heavy human traffic areas. And Mystic Falls would have qualified as a heavy human traffic area if we'd followed their way of doing things. We wouldn't be sitting here today if we had done that. But *nooo*." He narrowed his eyes. "No, you, Gerhardt, have been insisting that our situation is different from Glacier's. And you've also insisted that hazing doesn't work because the bears just become familiar with the park employees and learn to stay away from them. Well, what do you say now—*say now*?"

He opened his arm toward me like a magician introducing his assistant. "On August 24th we had yet another victim who nearly lost her life because of your goddamn namby-pamby policy."

I appreciated Palmer's commitment to me and the passion of his argument, and his points seemed valid, even though I had no idea what hazing of bears meant in this context. It sounded to me like a fraternity stunt. But I felt sorry for the way he spoke to Hamlin, who seemed to be the likeable guy Leila said he was. And I noticed that Monique squirmed in her chair when Palmer directed his attack at Hamlin.

"'Course I'm not just here to say I told you so, Gerhardt. You see, I've received phone calls—anonymous calls—threatening that someone is going to go out there and start hunting those grizzlies. And soon. Take out those menaces once and for all. They make it sound like it's an all-out war."

Monique lifted her eyebrows as she made a note on a yellow legal pad. I glanced at the pad. Something about security.

I couldn't help but think it odd that a national park ranger would be so anti-animal. Weren't rangers supposed to serve as stewards of the natural resources in the park? Palmer had told me he'd been working there for years; why would someone who hated wild animals work in a place like Yellowstone?

"So as I see it, we have two matters on the table to consider. The first is what to do with Brooke's bear—*Brooke's* bear—and that's an easy one. Kill the sucker." He gestured a knife-edge maneuver across his neck. "That will calm down the public for now. The second matter is more difficult but more necessary, and I recommend a multipronged approach. First: round up as many bears as you can and relocate them to a remote area. Probably the Lamar Valley. And fence them in. Make it a wildlife preserve, if you will. As more bears are discovered outside the designated wildlife viewing area, trap and transfer them, too. It may take a few seasons to get them under control, but it can be done."

"So you want to build a wall around Lamar Valley," Andy said.

"Yes, I suppose you could put it that way. And the second prong: control the damn tourists."

His pause was long enough for me to feel the intended unease: I was the problem tourist this time. Monique tossed a compassionate glance my way.

"What, are you going to round them up, too?" Andy asked.

Palmer ignored the Grand Teton manager's snide comment. "And here's how we do that." He held up his thumb. "Number one: restrict backcountry access. If we move the bears to Lamar, then we restrict the number of hikers in that area. We require registration permits and so forth for all hikers, even daily ones. We can also open up more ranger-led hikes." Next, he held up his index finger. "Number two: require all backcountry hikers to attend a park orientation or to hike with certified outfitters. Like climbers on Denali."

"Our situation is entirely different than Denali," Hamlin said. "And it's not like they don't have any casualties, either."

Palmer ignored him and raised a third finger—the middle finger. "We also need to search all backcountry hikers—maybe all tourists—for firearms or other weapons that might be used against bears. That will eliminate the possibility of the Wild West vigilantes I've been warning you about." And now the ring finger. "And, this is a biggie, but it has *got* be done. Restrict the number of tourists coming into the park on any given day. One way you could do this is by restricting where cars can go, and offer buses into parts of the park, like they also do at Denali. Or just close down the gates when we've achieved our quota. Whatever. We've gotten way out of control here, especially with all the foreigners coming to Yellowstone. Come on, people. Four million visitors and roughly four hundred miles of roads. What is that? Ten thousand tourists per mile?"

"Palmer," Monique said. "You know that doesn't even make sense. The tourists are not all here at the same time, and they're not all on the roads at the same time. You're exaggerating the situation."

"I hear what you're saying, though," Hamlin said, cracking his knuckles. "We are getting increasingly crowded, and mathematically speaking, more tourists could mean more animal encounters. Thank you for your thoughts, Palmer."

It was as if Palmer had been ranting in his sleep and now woke up. Somehow Monique and Hamlin's interruptions had interfered with Palmer's train of thought. He appeared disoriented and sat down.

"How about we hear from Brooke?" Hamlin said. "She came a long way to give us her thoughts."

His invitation to speak caught me off guard. I realized, too late, that I should have been thinking more about the bear over the past couple of months. Or at least since Palmer called and told me about this meeting. I told Shane I would *testify*, but I hadn't actually believed that I would. Now I realized I should have gathered my thoughts, made some notes. All eyes were on me.

"Well, I've just been thinking about this one bear as it pertains to my situation," I started. I cleared my throat before going on. Although I hadn't given the bear much thought at all over the past few weeks, it had found its way into my dreams now and then, and now recollections of those dreams came to my rescue. "I can't help but wonder: who are we to decide if a bear lives or dies? I'm not the religious type, but it feels like we're playing God here. And as for the idea of rounding up all the bears, it seems to me that we humans have already taken over too much land from the natural environment. And rounded up too many animals in zoos. Look at what happened to the orcas in captivity. At SeaWorld and so forth."

"I'm not talking about putting them in a zoo," Palmer said.

"Right, but you're talking about moving them all together. I'm no expert but I imagine they wouldn't like sharing such close quarters with one another. Also, I read on the Internet that we've reduced the grizzly bear habitat by ninety-eight percent over the last two hundred years, so restricting it further doesn't seem right."

"You can't believe everything you read on the Internet," he said.

"Let her talk," Monique said. "Besides, that statistic sounds about right."

"Close enough," Hamlin said.

"I've been staying in West Yellowstone with a woman who lost her grandmother recently. Maybe some of you knew Emily. Anyway, she had treasures dating back to the 1800s, when the American Indians were rounded up to reservations, and I can't help but think this recommendation to round up the bears, and force them to live in an arbitrarily designated space, sounds awfully similar to the way we rounded up the Native people back then. Or the Japanese during World War II."

"You can't compare bears to people," Palmer said.

"You're right," I said. "But your vigilantes who want to come in and eradicate the bears aren't all that different from white people who have wanted to destroy Indian or other populations."

Hamlin held up his hands. "Okay, I think we're going down a path we don't need to take right now. But your points are well taken. Anything else you want to say, Brooke?"

Yet again I was about to be shushed. Was it just me? Or did all men want to shush all women? I wanted to say more about the environment, about climate change, about all the federal government's policies that worked against environmental efforts to save the planet and the species on it—all those problems that have been flooding the Internet lately—but I couldn't collect my thoughts fast enough. An awkward lull ensued, during which I tried to piece together something coherent. Thankfully, it was interrupted when the conference room door opened. A scraggly old woman in faded overalls walked in. She wore a necklace of bear claws, much like the one hanging in Emily's room.

"Can I help you?" Hamlin asked.

"This is Max," Palmer said. "I asked her to join us. She's also a bear expert."

"Sorry I'm late," Max said. She sat in an empty chair next to me. Her fingernails were long and dirty, and she smelled like the forest. Hamlin, Andy, and Monique exchanged skeptical glances.

"Wait," I said with courage that shot out of nowhere. "I do have one more question for you. If you were to euthanize the bear, how would you be sure you got the right bear? The one who attacked me?"

Hamlin explained that some of the bears were tagged and that the rangers generally knew a lot of the bears by their unique characteristics, where they tended to live, and which ones had young versus sub-adult cubs.

They had narrowed down their choices, regarding which bear attacked me, to one of two likely sows. Both had dark brown fur and a blond dished face. "And based on your wounds, we're guessing five-inch claws, especially long for a female. We've been trying to track both suspects," he said. "And if we can, we'll get a DNA sample to see if it matches the DNA taken from you and your belongings at the hospital. But no decision has been made to euthanize. So no need to worry, yet."

He typed something into his laptop, then turned it toward me. His screen showed two side-by-side images. "These are the two bears we're looking for. Look familiar?"

I studied the pictures. The bears were enormous. And beautiful. I felt like a victim observing a lineup and not wanting to finger anyone.

"I can't say. I never got a good look at the bear. But it still doesn't feel right. I did exactly the wrong thing. I went out to a backcountry trail alone and I didn't have my bear spray handy. It wasn't the bear's fault."

I felt Max shift in her chair but didn't want to let her distract me.

"What I don't understand," Monique said, "is why we're even considering taking any action that violates our policy just because of some alleged phone call threats. It's akin to negotiating with terrorists."

Andy agreed, then circled back to the topic of better managing tourists.

"Hold on. Tourists aren't the major problem," Hamlin said. "The ranchers and developers selling land to wealthy big city types are the ones who cause the most disruption to the ecosystem. You know, Hollywood actors and all. They build their luxury vacation homes in the midst of wildlife habitat and actually *set out food* for the animals. Those are the people the bears are becoming habituated by, not park tourists. Then, when the bears come back into the park, they expect similar hospitality. I'd say, if you want to really bring about change, you need to call your congressmen to stop all these land sales. And revisit the status of grizzlies as threatened."

Another political matter to discuss with Shane. If he won the election. If I ever went home.

"If I may," the old woman interjected, her voice so gravelly it hurt to hear. "I've been around these parts a long time. In fact, some folks used to know me as Grizzly Max. I've killed me a number of bears in my lifetime. I even stabbed one with a fishin' knife one time as it went after my trout. I used to have bearskins all over the floors and walls of my cabin. I used to serve bear meat to my guests.

"I was asked to come to this hearing by Palmer, here," she said, pointing her thumb toward him. It was wrinkled and arthritic. "He said y'all might need to kill one of these big gals and that he'd like me to get the job done.

And you know, I could. There ain't no one around who's got more experience than me when it comes to killin' bears."

Palmer nodded in affirmation, seemingly proud of his forethought to bring Max to the meeting.

"But I want to tell y'all a little story before you go any further with this witch hunt. And that's what it is, you know. Just a witch hunt."

Now Palmer shot a quizzical look back toward Max, who held her index finger up in the air.

"A few years back, when I lived out on a ranch in Eastern Idaho, there was this sow that came nosin' around my land. It was late summer. She had a couple of cubs in tow. And she apparently had a hankerin' for my dog. One mornin', she lumbered right up the driveway toward Ol' Shep. I was in the kitchen fixin' some eggs when I saw her comin', and I knew the dog was out on the porch snoozin' up a storm."

It was near lunchtime, and all I'd eaten that day so far was a handful of Leila's chocolate chips. The mention of eggs made my stomach growl, so I squeezed my abs tight.

"I went for my shotgun, took aim, and fired," Max said. "Hit her right between the eyes. She dropped dead right there in front of my house—which was an awful place to have to deal with such a large carcass—let me tell you it's not easy to dispose of such a thing. But that's not the point. The point is that all of a sudden those cubs had no mama. No way to make it in the world. They came up to her and sniffed and pawed at her the way Ol' Shep paws at me in the morning to get out of bed and get him his breakfast. No more breakfast for those young'uns. After they moseyed off, I went out to the bear. Her cold eye stared up at me. It gave me a chill, as if—even though her body was dead—her soul was still there, questioning me. It brought me to tears."

We all waited for her to go on.

"I'm sorry, Palmer. I don't hunt bear no more."

Palmer slapped a hand down on the table. "What the hell do you think you're doing, Max? I thought we had an agreement."

"Our agreement, Palmer, was that I'd come and talk to this group about killin' bears. And that's what I've done. You all are decidin' the fate of one of the most beautiful creatures on earth, quite possibly a sow at that who may or may not have done the only thing she knew to protect her kin."

Now she zeroed in on me. "I'm sorry about what happened to you, Miss, but it looks like you're gonna be all right. In fact, I predict you're goin' to be better than you ever were before. When I orphaned those cubs, my life changed. That bear carcass, lyin' in front of my own home, was like a gift that made me stop and think about life, and death, in ways I'd never done before.

I'm thinkin' this bear attack might turn out to be a gift for you, too. Sure, you might wind up with a scar or two, but how many other people can say they've been so close to such a magnificent creature that they could smell its breath or feel the scrape of its claw? So close they could look it in the eye?"

As she spoke, the attack flashed back into my mind. I now recalled seeing her eyes after she dropped me, as I rolled into a ball, shortly before I passed out. Dark brown. Expressive. Alive.

"I'll tell you, when you look a creature like that in the eye, you realize it's not just a four-legged life form amblin' about," Max said. "There's a soul inside. You make eye contact, your souls connect. You kill the animal, you kill a little bit of *your* soul, too."

She removed her string of bear claws, slid each claw off the rawhide strand, and distributed them among us.

"I'm givin' these claws to you as a reminder about the sanctity of life. About the soul inside each creature. Whether they help you make decisions about how to manage your bears here in these parts or how to relate to your own kin, makes no difference to me. They're yours to keep."

My bear claw lay on the table in front of me, waiting. Brown at the base, its shade darkened to black at the sharp tip. Shaped like a scythe, it seemed to speak more of power than soul. I didn't know quite what to make of it, which was probably Max's intent. I picked it up, ran my fingers along its smooth surface, then pricked the palm of one hand with the point.

"I am truly sorry if I let you down, Palmer," Max said.

Palmer stood up so abruptly that his chair fell backward, the metal legs clanking onto the floor. "You're all in it together, I see that now." He glared first at Max and then systematically at each of us. "One big conspiracy." Sweat beaded on his upper lip and brow. He shook his bear claw at Hamlin. "There's going to be trouble. You just wait and see. And then you'll be sorry. Mark my words."

He stormed out. The conference room door slammed. Everyone else sat there, stunned, in the reverberating vacuum of his departure.

"He was my ride," I said.

TWENTY-THREE

Anne

SQUEAKY WHEELS WOKE me the following morning. I peered out the barn door; the sky was barely pink, and silvery dew covered the ground like complicated spider-webs.

"Time to go, Miss Annie." Evalene motioned to me from her wagon's seat, where a wool blanket draped over her lap and another wrapped around her shoulders. She wore a different colorful scarf than the day before.

"I got word there's a group of outlaws looking for you," she called. I ran out to greet her in my thin, tattered dress.

"Some say you stole their horses." Her eyes, twinkling despite the chill, said *good for you*. She said we had to skedaddle, bothering only with our horses. She and Miss Clara would come along soon with our supplies.

"But I have no idea where we shall go!"

Evalene informed me about a place five or six miles up yonder. "When the highway—what you call a trail—bends to the south, you'll see a narrow path—a deer path—to the north. Head up that slope into the woods. It's a bit farther from the river than I would have liked, but other than that it's a fine setting. We'll meet you there. But first, you've got to cover up those paint spots on the Indian horse with a blanket." She handed an army-fashion blanket to me. "That was Sam's, from the War. It's ugly but it'll do the job. And here's an old coat of his for you. Wouldn't want you to freeze to death."

She reached back into the wagon and pulled out a leather jacket, well-worn but warm.

"Now get going; word travels fast about Indians 'round here."

Clara found an old jacket for Maggie as well. We took one of the stolen horses, and Maggie's, and we raced along the dusty highway. The terrain was flat and open, dotted with only a handful of lodge-poles here and there, and low-lying scrub brush. If someone were looking for us, they would find us. Accordingly, we ran the horses hard. We passed a couple of shacks and a good-looking ranch house with smoke billowing from a chimney, then circumvented a small collection of buildings that seemingly wanted to call itself a town. I longed to stop and search for a general store, curious what sort of wares it might have to offer, but I knew we dared not dawdle.

We found what we assumed to be the deer path Evalene described, and wound our way up the hill into a stand of trees, wishing upon our arrival we had some water for the horses. We waited for at least two hours, and given that we did not know Evalene or Clara well at all, I began to worry we had been set up for an ambush—another concept I had heard about but had never thought to be a true possibility, at least not for me. Indeed, we had been ushered out of Clara's place so quickly that we had neglected to bring our firearms. Thomas's voice, accusing me yet again of being a fool, tried desperately to make itself heard.

Maggie sat on the ground beside her horse and leaned against a tree, closing her eyes and crossing her arms. My heart jumped into my throat when I realized I did not see her pouch. But when I inquired, she nodded and patted her side. She now wore it beneath her dress.

"Do you have your sketch-book?" she asked.

I shook my head. "Stupid Anne left it behind."

Finally, we heard those squeaky wheels, and I nearly cried. We next heard huffing and puffing; it was Evalene, making her way up the hill. When she found us, she stopped and patted the perspiration from her face with her colorful scarf. Poor dear.

"The wagon can't make it up here," she said as she tried to catch her breath. "Too narrow, too steep. And I don't want Miss Clara hiking up here just yet. Let me have one of your horses to haul up some supplies."

We brought both horses down to the wagon, which, to our surprise, was loaded down with an abundance of provisions. Clara had brought her old mattress, her kitchen supplies, an axe, four water buckets, a lantern, two shovels, and a variety of other useful items. Evalene had provided sacks of flour and coffee and a can of lard. Our meager belongings were there, too, including our charred buffalo hide, our guns, and my sketch-book. After we made several trips with the horses to bring everything up to the spot that Evalene dictated as the safest and most scenic spot to settle, she prepared to leave.

"Will you stay with us tonight?" I asked. "You have done so much for us. Let us at least make you supper, sorry as it might be."

She laughed. "First of all, Miss Annie, I've got a man waiting for me. And more importantly, I've got a bed. Don't you worry one whit about our helping you. If it weren't for the help we received from some kind folks along our journey, I wouldn't be standing here talking to you. I'm just doing what the Good Lord wants me to do. So you just get yourselves a good rest and keep up your spirits. Sam and I'll be coming up here every day. We want to help you build your dream. Such a beautiful dream. We might even be able to get our two sons to help out. And who knows? Perhaps one day, if the Lord takes Sam before me, I'll be moving in with you."

When four women share a dream, nothing can stop them from bringing it to life. By the time Evalene showed up the next day, we had already staked out several buildings on the land with twigs and Maggie's rope. We planned for a main cabin, several smaller cabins, including one that could serve as my artist studio, and a community building—or what Maggie wanted to call a longhouse.

The three of us—Maggie, Clara, and I—would live in the main cabin initially. In my estimation, it would serve not only as our home but also as a gathering place for meals, sewing circles, baking parties, and important discussions. It would also be the place we would congregate if ever there were a safety issue. Once that was complete, we would build a separate cabin for Clara to live on her own, as that was her preference.

Evalene's role, in addition to providing us with a section of land that she and Sam owned together, was procuring supplies. She brought lumber salvaged from Clara's old cabin and barn, along with Clara's old ladder and stove. Sam generously provided the timber he had already felled for his own use, saying there was plenty more where that came from and he was in no hurry. He also brought hammers, nails, hinges, and the like. Evalene rounded up some fresh blankets, a bolt of cotton, sewing needles, and thread. Their gifts were much appreciated, but we lacked both construction expertise and money. I gave her the gold band I had stolen from Maggie's attacker, but there was so much more we still needed, and we could not expect Sam and Evalene to continue to fund our necessities forever.

Maggie and Clara were busy clearing land one afternoon. Evalene was due to arrive any minute. "It is time for me to find Thomas," I said to myself aloud. Sometimes when you talk to yourself, your thoughts make more sense. I did not know that Maggie had stopped working.

"What did you say?" she asked, throwing her axe to the ground. She held her hand to that endearing spot beneath her neck. "No. You cannot contact Thomas. You know what will happen if you do."

"I should at least try to find out if he is alive. We need money."

"My people survived for hundreds of years without money."

"I will grant you that truth. But we are not a tribe of Indians. Our dream is to live among...among white people. Or among all people, I should say. Which means we will have to pay for goods."

"So yer plan is to write to yer husband and ask fer money?" Clara could see that Maggie and I were having a disagreement and was on her way over to us. "And ye believe he will just hand some gold coins over to ye, no questions asked? From what ye've said about him, that doesn't sound too likely."

"I had some money before we were married. I will ask him for that."

Clara rubbed her eyes while shaking her head. I had the distinct recollection of being a small child, admonished for being silly. "Ye do realize that your property became yer husband's property when ye exchanged weddin' vows? That money is no longer yers."

I quickly felt heavy with fatigue and dropped to the ground.

"So now what do ye think yer husband will do?" Clara asked, standing over me. "A better idea might be to sell one of them horses. That would hold us over fer a while. Particularly that Indian horse; I hear they fetch a pretty penny."

"We are not selling Maggie's horse. We can sell one of the other ones if we have to. But I would rather not. If there are three of us living here, we should have three horses."

"What about feed?" Clara asked. "That'll cost ye somethin'."

"There is one other option," I said. "I can write to my sister Mary. She will know what to do." Mary and I had not been close, and she would undoubtedly side with Thomas about my being a fool, if she were asked. But that did not mean she would reveal my whereabouts to him. We were family, she and I. She could be trusted.

While waiting for my letter to reach Mary, and for her reply, we worked as hard as the squirrels and chipmunks readying for winter. In only two weeks, with help from Sam, Evalene, their sons, and a couple of their neighbors, we had the first cabin's walls erected and a roof laid. One wall turned up taller than the others, so that the roof looked somewhat intoxicated, but the building was functional, if not handsome. Evalene brought us a locking mechanism for Clara's old door, and for the first time in a long while, I felt safe—even without glass panes in the window openings.

Sam and Evalene came over for supper one evening, bringing along a roast chicken, potatoes, and beer. We sat on the floor, picnic style, and gorged ourselves as Sam explained how he—a freed slave—had acquired rights to three hundred acres under the Homestead Act. He also told us about the new Desert Land Act, under which he was in the process of applying for additional, adjacent land, which would double his holdings.

"I'd like to deed a little bit of this land over to you, Miss Annie," he said. "If it's all right with you." He winked at Evalene.

She tilted her head to the side, held one hand to her heart, and reached across the table to him with her other hand. "Oh, Sam, I knew there was a good reason for loving you."

My cheeks flushed. I tried to say something but kept tripping over my words.

"I think Miss Annie is trying to say thank you," Evalene said.

Sam handed me an old tin cup half-filled with beer. "Here, have some of this. It'll clear your head up right away."

I took a sip, then gulped the beer. I so wished Thomas could see me now. When the cup was empty, I leaned over to Sam on my right, and embraced him tightly while thanking him a thousand times over. I may have overdone it; when I finally released him, his forehead was damp with perspiration.

"But there are some complications," he said, wiping his forehead. "As I understand the law, single women can own property, but not married women. So as long as you're married, Miss Annie, I can't."

For the second time in as many weeks, I was dismayed to learn how women were no better off than slaves, or perhaps even worse, when it came to financial matters.

"But Maggie is a widow. You can deed it to her," I said.

He let out a long, drawn-out sigh. "I'm afraid we're a ways off from that. As it is, it might be illegal for me to even let an Indian live here, seeing as she's supposed to be on a reservation."

The image of Maggie being captured and hauled away gave me a frightful chill.

Clara excused herself to fix a pot of coffee.

"But I'm not too worried about all the details," Sam said. "I've got a lawyer helping me with all this. For now, Evalene and I are tickled to have you here working the land. So long as you promise to look after her if ever something should happen to me, then I will gladly sign this piece of land over to Maggie, or you, just as soon as I am able. Whether through deed or inheritance or whatever."

That evening, after Sam and Evalene left, we sat outside beneath the stars. Maggie positioned herself in front of me the way I used to sit in front of Thomas on a sled. I wrapped my arms around her, and my legs too. I inhaled her woodsy aroma, and felt the muscles in her back against my breasts. Bewitched by the soft curves of her hips between my legs, I burrowed my face into her hair.

I had never felt this way toward another woman, nor had I so readily displayed my affection for any other human being when in the presence of others. Clara, bless her heart, tolerated the unusual friendship between Maggie and me, and I regretted any discomfort she may have felt, especially late at night or in the morning when she would see Maggie and me sleeping beneath the same blanket.

Were she to inquire as to what sort of relationship Maggie and I indeed had, I would have been at a loss to describe it. We loved each other deeply; we were the best of friends; we were sisters. But there was something deeper, something unspeakable, not for lack of propriety but for lack of vocabulary. I was attracted to her beauty as an eagle is to the sky.

One afternoon, while Clara was whittling bits and pieces of wood cast off from her cabin logs, and Maggie was embroidering the neckline of the cotton dress I had made for her—which she called the ugly, *civilized* dress—I embroidered a handkerchief I had stitched together from fabric scraps. We had all been working hard, and I insisted we enjoy a well-deserved respite on such a fine afternoon. The sky was the hue of a robin's egg; the breeze was unseasonably warm. Back home, we called this Indian Summer.

I had just tied the knot in my embroidery thread when I heard Evalene's wagon wheels. Despite her age and girth, she nearly flew up the hill to the cabin, waving a small pink envelope in the air.

It was from my sister, Mary.

> My dearest Anne,
>
> You have no idea how relieved I was to finally receive word from you. I have been sick with worry for months now, ever since you informed me of your plans to travel into Indian Territory with Thomas. You may recall I begged you not to go. And then, when newspapers began to print horrendous reports of tourists being taken hostage by the red devils, and some of them being killed, I could not sleep for many a night.
>
> It was only when Edgar received a letter from Thomas that I knew there was hope. I have no idea if you have been in contact with your husband by now; you neglected to even

mention his name in your letter to me, which I thought rather odd. At any rate, his letter described your horrible ordeal. He was taken by those savages almost all the way to the Canadian border, and only when the Indian chief wisely surrendered, at last, was Thomas rescued.

He, too, has been sick with worry about your safety and whereabouts, which was why he wrote to us at all. Edgar replied, advising Thomas that we have heard nothing and prayed that no news was good news. Alas, now we can advise him that you are alive. I am sure he will send for you shortly.

I dropped the letter at once as though it were cursed. I bent over and retched. Evalene immediately went for water.

"Is it Thomas? Is he dead?" Maggie asked.

"No," I said, instinctively touching my décolletage the way Maggie did when answering with a *no*. "Thomas is quite alive—and evidently worried about me. Worse, my dear sister has contacted him about me."

She wove her embroidery needle into the fabric and set it down. "Did you not ask her to keep your letter a secret from him?"

The wave of nausea passed as quickly as it had come upon me. Evalene handed a ladle of water to me. I sipped at it, then spit it out. "That idea never occurred to me."

I picked up the letter to finish reading.

Edgar has granted your request for interim funding, until Thomas reimburses him. Accordingly he has transferred $100 via Western Union to you. It will be up to you to figure out, on your end, how to access those monies as you did not specify exactly where you are.

Fondly and with much relief that you are alive and well,
Mary

TWENTY-FOUR

Anne

WE DID NOT hear from Sam and Evalene for the next three days. We debated whether it was because they had to go a long distance to the nearest Western Union station to claim my sister's funds, or whether they were busy procuring more supplies for us, or whether they had met with misfortune. I chose to believe they were taking some time for their own business matters, and it aggrieved me because I was so anxious for Mary's money and what it could provide: a feather bed, cotton towels, durable china, crinoline I had seen in the new Ward's catalog that Evalene had brought along one day. Clara had also been anticipating additional supplies for her cabin, which I had offered to fund. And my poor Maggie was now hungry all the time. When I questioned the reason for this change in her appetite, she claimed she needed meat for her blood.

On the third afternoon, she prepared to go hunting.

"At this time o' day?" Clara asked. "I wouldn't venture into those woods now. It's feedin' time for all them animals. And soon it'll be dark as Sam's skin."

Maggie dismissed Clara's concern and said she was looking forward to trying the new bow and arrows she had fabricated from rock, branches, and twine. She promised to return soon, with food.

"I wonder if she's one o' them Indians who turn into animals in the night," Clara said after Maggie had gone. "I've heard stories 'bout women turnin' into deer or bear, or men turnin' into snakes. Not that I believe them. But ye never know."

I reminded Clara that she had been with Maggie every night for the last couple of weeks, and I had been with Maggie for nearly two months. She had never transformed into a creature.

When Maggie returned with two rabbits, the sky was as dark as her hair, and despite the late hour, we roasted them on spits made from twigs which we'd soaked in Sam's beer. As we waited for the meat to cook, Clara came right out and confessed what we had been discussing. Maggie frowned at me.

"I never thought you were an animal," I said.

"Well, at any rate it sure seems like ye've got some sort of special power," Clara said. "I've only seen it a couple o' times, but it's like ye've got yourself some magic spells. Ye say ye're going huntin' and ye return with somethin' all the time. Why, I've known men who wander fer days lookin' fer food."

"That is because they do not know how to hunt," Maggie said.

After we finished eating, Maggie and I went to check on the horses, each of us carrying two buckets of water.

"I never believed Clara's speculation about you changing into an animal," I said. "But she also said there were legends about Indians having special powers. Are any of those true?" I followed her footsteps, knowing she could lead us safely in the dark. Without her I would have certainly tripped over a tree root or rock.

"Everyone has a spirit power," she said, holding a bucket for her horse. It drank with gusto. "You just need to know how to find it."

"Like knowing how to find meat when you are hunting."

"It is somewhat the same."

"So how did you find yours?" I offered a bucket to the horse that had become mine. Its ears wiggled in gratitude.

"When I first reached adulthood, I did as the other children before me had done. I went to the mountain to find my *wyakin*." She described this arduous journey, and to my surprise she had no one with her on this excursion. As she described her experience in detail, I envisioned a young Maggie in a small buckskin dress, setting traps for rabbits and building a tipi in the forest. It occurred to me, then, that our mutual recent endeavors had not been the first time she had overcome such adversity.

"And did you find your power?" I asked. The third horse whinnied, and Maggie set a bucket down for it. She combed her fingers through its mane before it finally lowered its head to drink.

"If the mind is ready, the animal spirit will come. The difficulty is being patient. It is not something to be rushed. I was not a patient girl."

Maggie had searched the mountain terrain with the hope of finding her *wyakin* quickly. She spotted deer and elk, osprey and loon, even mountain goat. None of the animals came to her when she called them or even noticed her presence. She spent three days and nights shivering and hungry, with neither blanket nor hide to keep her warm. So, as I came to learn, she had *not* caught rabbits or slept peacefully in the comfort of a tipi. The poor dear had nearly starved and frozen to death.

At some point on her quest, she began to have strange visions. On the fifth day, she awoke to discover that the trees appeared taller, the sky bluer. She also heard sounds as never before: deer chewing grass, fish fins paddling in streams. That evening, a giant shadow swooped directly over her as she lay in an open meadow, its wingspan at least as wide as her father was tall.

"That was when I knew what my *wyakin* was."

I combed my fingers through my horse's mane. It nudged its nose against me. "What? What was it?"

"Owl."

"An owl? Your special animal is an owl?" As fascinating as her story was, I was disappointed to learn it was just a big bird that served as her alleged guide. I had expected something powerful or regal. A wolf, perhaps. Still, I knew that one must accept whatever is important to the person one loves.

"This is why I was able to hunt the rabbits," she said.

Perhaps, I thought. There was some logic in that. But surely an owl did not help her kill the buffalo.

"Could I have a *wyakin*?" I asked. I could not imagine what mine might be. If hers was an owl, perhaps mine could be an eagle—another magnificent bird of prey.

Our conversation was interrupted by the sound of horse hooves on the trail below. These were not the hooves of Evalene's old horses, however, and there were no squeaky wheels accompanying the rush. We checked the tethers on our own horses, then retreated to camp. Maggie ran into the cabin; I retreated to our camp-fire, which soon cast light on two cowboys riding up toward me.

"Good evening, ma'am," one of them said, tipping his hat. I had a strong sense of déjà vu.

"Hello," I said, eyeing them warily as they dismounted. They were young men—boys, really, not much older than Maggie. They were groomed and clean. But I did not welcome their arrival, and I endeavored to reflect this sentiment upon my face.

"Sorry to bother you," one said. "We're looking for a place to board for the night. Do you know of any places in the vicinity?"

"There's a saloon a bit yonder." I turned and saw Clara now standing on the porch, our stolen rifle in her arms. She pointed it eastward. "Other than that, there's nothin' fer miles."

I wished she had not put it that way, pointing out our vulnerabilities so readily. Then she asked what they were doing in these parts.

One of the young men kicked at the dirt. The other said they'd been told of gold mining around there. "You hear of anything?"

Clara laughed. Although her cough had subsided, her voice—and particularly her laugh—still sounded like wagon wheels rolling over rocks. I suspected that had been her voice for a long time, given the way she loved those hand-rolled cigarettes, one of which she lit up now. "Son, if there was a gold mine around here, I wouldn't be standin' here talkin' to ye."

"How about Miners Camp? Isn't that near here somewhere? That's where we're heading."

Again, a laugh. "That depends on how ye define that word *near*. It's at least a few days ridin' east, if ye got good weather."

"Well, shoot. We've been riding all day. Any chance you could offer us a place to rest our bones and a hot meal? My name's Aaron, by the way." He approached the porch slowly, skirting around me, and offered his hand to Clara while keeping his eyes fixed on the gun.

"Ye'll have to ask the lady o' the place 'bout that."

He glanced back at me.

"You are welcome to sit for a while," I said, gesturing toward our camp-fire. "We can offer you some drinking water and a bit of cooked rabbit. But we have no proper accommodations for you."

"We'd be much obliged," Aaron said. "Come on over here, Rusty."

The men sat down by the fire, and I went to collect their drinks. Clara disappeared into the cabin. As I filled two cups, I questioned the sensibility of my wariness. Here were two nice young men looking to earn some money. Here we were, three ladies who could use some brawn. I decided to offer the men a proposition along with their water.

"We need to get a roof on a cabin out back," I said. Sam's boys had finished the walls for Clara's cabin, but they were now gone away for a few days, along with Sam and Evalene. "If you promise to help us with that to-morrow, we will let you stay here tonight. No roof, no heat, no furniture, but you may sleep within the four walls, and as such you will be somewhat protected from the elements."

Clara startled me. She had come back outside as silently as an Indian scout, and now—standing over me—she targeted me with a look of scorn, rifle still in her arms. In my naiveté, I was unable to read her thoughts.

"And we can water your horses for you," I said.

Clara went back inside again, this time in a huff.

"Are you sure that's not going to be too much of an inconvenience, ma'am?" the one named Aaron said before slipping a stalk of bunchgrass between his lips. He was such a handsome man, barely beyond his boyhood years. He would make a fine husband one day. I told him not to worry. And although a proper lady should never converse with an unknown gentleman without the presence of her husband—even one so much younger than she—I proceeded to engage in a delightful conversation with the both of them. The camp-fire was dancing, and I so enjoyed the interaction after having gone so long with no one but Maggie, and later Clara or Evalene, to engage with. One conversation led to another, and before I knew what I was doing, I offered them the last of Sam's beer and then described our plans for the land and buildings. The men seemed fascinated. But then, when I mentioned how exciting this was for me, having hailed from the big city of Chicago, they straightened and exchanged a quick, knowing glance. The conversation ended soon thereafter when each of them demonstrated their exhaustion with exaggerated yawns.

Maggie and Clara were both asleep when I came into the cabin, but I could not join them in peaceful slumber. The company had been too interesting, the conversation so welcome. And the sudden ending of the evening—puzzling.

The next day, the men honored their promise to me and undertook the installation of Clara's roof, under her close supervision. I watered their horses and made coffee and biscuits for them, and although they expressed appreciation, they seemed distracted and unwilling to interact much with me. Maggie stayed in our cabin, huddled in a corner with Clara's shotgun over her lap.

"You cannot hide every time someone happens by," I told her. "That will be no way to live."

"This is not supposed to be a boarding house for anyone who comes along. It is not supposed to be a place for men. You have broken our dream before it even had a chance to begin."

Her accusation struck me hard, and I felt utterly alone as I watched the men work. When their task was complete, the men refused my offer for more food and prepared to leave at once. I endeavored to remain hospitable, even if my feelings were bruised by everyone—even Clara had little to say to me that day—and after bidding farewell to the men, I ran to the top of a nearby rise. From there, as I watched their departure amidst a cloud of dust, I was overcome with a whirlwind of confusing feelings. I had, yet again, forgone an opportunity for rescue, but at the same time I was content with my decision to make a life here in the West with Maggie. Even so—even with the anticipation of a delightful life with her—I could not completely extinguish the spark of curiosity that she had ignited in me. I was now certain there was much more out there, beyond our little world, as I watched the riders' silhouettes disappearing into desolate, waning light.

When I returned to the cabin, Maggie was curled up like a cat beside Clara, who was working on a quilt. Upon hearing my entrance, Clara stopped her sewing—needle midair—and Maggie sat up quickly.

"I was just doing what any hospitable person would do," I said. "The same as what Clara did for us."

"Clara did not entertain the enemy. You should have sent those men away the minute they arrived," Maggie said.

I knelt beside her and wiggled her toes with my fingers. "They were not enemies, silly. They were two young men who helped us a great deal with Clara's roof. No one hurt you."

"You put us at risk."

"Maggie, not all men are bad."

"You are right. Only white men are bad."

Clara smirked.

"That is not true. I am sure there are Indian men who are also bad. Regardless, most men are not bad. Certainly not those boys—why, they must be no older than you are. They were kind and polite, and I could not send them out into the night without food or shelter."

"Did ye ask them what they're doin' out here?" Clara asked.

"You heard them. They are looking for gold mines. They seemed to me to be honest young men searching for good work."

"Well, they sure didn't look like the miners I've seen 'round here. And they sure didn't have any minin' supplies with them. Did ye happen to notice which way they went when they left?"

I most certainly recalled the two young cowboys riding away. "Westward. Into the sunset." It was such a powerful image, like the ending of a literary classic or poem. I resolved to sketch it in the morning.

Clara harrumphed. "They said they were on a journey toward Miners Camp. East o' here. Either they changed their plans, or they lied."

TWENTY-FIVE

Brooke

IT WASN'T JUST Hamlin's kind offer to drive me all the way back to Leila's. Or the coffee house music playing in his Subaru. It was everything about him.

We both avoided bear talk on the way to West Yellowstone. Or any mention of Palmer and his bizarre performance at the meeting. Instead, we focused on the greater Yellowstone area. I asked him a million questions about the weather and what there was to do around there. How long he'd lived in the area. Why he'd chosen Gardiner specifically as a place to settle. What he did for fun. I tried to make it sound like ordinary chitchat, but I was really doing research. For myself.

In the winter, Hamlin did a lot of snowshoeing and cross-country skiing. In the other seasons, he hiked, camped, and backpacked. He also kayaked. I asked about his favorite places for whitewater paddling.

"The closest water's probably the Madison. It's got some crazy drops just below the dam and Quake Lake, maybe a half hour or so from here. But you've got to know what you're doing. The big outfitters usually have you put in around Ennis. Ever heard of Kitchen Sink? It's a Class IV rapid, lots of fun. And then there's the Gallatin River out of Big Sky, or you can ride the Yellowstone out of Gardiner. And down south there's the Snake River. Out of Jackson."

Later, we talked about the people of the area and, as we drove into town, I asked him what he knew about Emily.

"Everyone knew Emily," he said. "And everyone loved her. She was a living monument to history, a regular walking archive. And the most giving person around. She came up to Mammoth frequently and wandered through the town, as if she belonged there as much as the elk did. People flocked to walk with her and listen to her stories, and hardly a week passed that you wouldn't find her lunching at the hotel. By the way, are you hungry?"

I was, so we stopped for pizza. He ordered a pitcher of beer. I didn't tell him I shouldn't have any because I was still, secretly, on oxy. One beer wouldn't matter.

I was actually more concerned about him having to drive all the way back to Gardiner after drinking. "You're welcome to stay with me tonight," I said.

He raised an eyebrow and smirked.

"I didn't mean it like that."

"I've heard that place is no-men-allowed."

I decided to let that one go. Actually, I wanted to get back to picking his brain about the area. Where I might want to go next. Whether I might just stay.

He grimaced after taking a long pull of the beer. "I've gotten so used to good microbrews that I have a hard time with the big commercial tap beers. We've got a new microbrewery in Gardiner. But the real place to go for good brews is Jackson. You've got your organic brewery, your Thai food pub and brewery, and—you'll like this—an all-woman-run brewery. I hear they've got the best designer beer in the West. You'd like it there, in Jackson."

I was more of a wine drinker, but all that talk about microbreweries was making me thirsty. I surprised myself by how much I liked this ordinary draft beer.

"I haven't been to Jackson in years. Decades," I said.

"Sounds like you need a reason to visit. I'll take you down there one day if you'd like."

A tempting proposition. In addition to this new friend sitting across the table from me, the reasons to stay in this area were stacking up. I asked how far Jackson was from Gardiner.

"Depends on time of year. When the park roads are open, probably three hours. In the winter, much longer than that. You wouldn't want to drive from one place to the other for just the day. Trust me, I know. I've done it for work. Bear business."

My phone rang, as if on cue. It was Palmer. "Speaking of the devil," I said.

"Why is he calling you?" Hamlin asked.

"No idea." After it rang three times, I picked up.

"Brooke, I need your help." Palmer sounded out of breath. "I need to go out of town. Important business, urgent. Urgent. I need somebody to stay at my house and watch the dog."

Row and I had bonded the weekend we went to J.P.'s cabin, and with Leila out of town I figured I could use the company. I also liked the idea of going to his house; I didn't like being at Emily's without Leila, even with Phoebe lurking about. When I replied to Palmer in the affirmative, Hamlin tilted his head, curious what I was agreeing to.

"Great," Palmer said. "There's a key under the front door mat." And with that, he hung up.

"I wonder what his urgent business is," I said to Hamlin after telling him about Palmer's request.

"I don't know, but he sure was an odd duck at the meeting today. You saw those scabs on his face and hands, right?"

I didn't tell him that I'd seen Palmer at the Lake Hotel when the injuries were fresh. I figured that would raise questions that I couldn't answer.

"Two rumors floating around at work. One, he got in a fight with a poacher. The other, he got in a fight with a bear. I guess both stories are believable given what he had to say today." He shook his head. "It's a sad story about that guy. I don't know him well, but I've heard he's been having mental troubles for years. The thing is, most of the time he's a likeable guy. And a good park ranger. And he's incredibly smart. But seriously unstable."

Although Hamlin's tone was compassionate, his words made me feel more sorry for Palmer than I already did. His kindness, his movie-star looks, his outdoorsy, sometimes folksy, appearance—all those traits had drawn me to Palmer, not romantically but just as a person. I hated to see him suffer. He needed help. The least I could do was offer a bit of friendship.

The pizza came. I lifted a slice of pepperoni from the pie and took a bite. It was so hot, it burned the roof of my mouth, just as I'd done when having pasta with Ruth. This was becoming a bad habit. I gulped more beer.

"Speaking of strange stories," I said, "what do you know about the no-men-allowed rule at Maggie...I mean Emily's place?" I was curious how Leila's version jibed with the greater community version.

"Not a whole lot, just the CliffsNotes version. As I understand it, that place was built more than a hundred years ago by one of Emily's ancestors. A couple of outlaws got killed there. And ever since then, men have been barred from stepping foot inside any of the buildings, or actually anywhere on the property beyond the front door of the main cabin. You've seen the sculpture just off the highway, right?"

"You mean that scarecrow thing? Yeah. It's creepy."

"Most men think so, too. Word is that place is haunted."

"So I've heard. Leila said it had something to do with a scalped posse."

"Could be. I heard there used to be a couple of heads hanging from tree branches to keep everyone out. Long time ago."

"*Lord of the Flies.*"

"Yep. Anyway, it's been understood for a long time that no man's welcome at Maggie's Place."

After all this time together, our conversation seemed to wane. Hamlin watched the football game on the TV above the bar. I texted Delaney, to see how she was doing after her big news. *Okay.* Did she regret her decision to drop out? *No!* Had Shane calmed down? *What do you think?* I knew him well enough to know he wouldn't have; I didn't need her to tell me. My text had been intended to be more like a sign, or maybe a confirmation, that she and I were still on the same team. I wasn't sure how to interpret her terse replies until her final text came through. *Can't wait to see you, Mom!* Followed by a trio of heart emojis.

By the time Hamlin and I finished our last slices, we were the last ones in the pizza parlor.

"I'd better get you to Palmer's dog," he said.

"Actually, I was wondering if we could swing by Leila's so I could get some of my clothes and things to bring over to Palmer's." And the last of my oxy. "It's out of the way—I'm sorry about that."

He kindly agreed to help me, but he stayed on the porch while I went into Leila's to get my things. When we got back to town, I again asked if he'd like to stay overnight. "On the sofa, of course."

"No thank you. I think I'd rather stay in a haunted house than in Palmer's domain."

His reply gave me pause. Should I have opted to stay at Emily's after all? Well, it was too late now.

Palmer's house was more of a rustic log cabin on the edge of town; although it was well past sunset, a floodlight on a nearby telephone pole illuminated the setting. An accumulation of split logs were jumbled on the north side of the house; an old-fashioned antennae rose from the roof. Two fir trees stood on each side of the door like sentinels. It was simple but, in its own way, inviting.

Hamlin held the door open for me. I maneuvered inside with my belongings while greeting a happy-go-lucky dog and a lethally wagging tail. I offered to make coffee. Hamlin declined. He asked if I was sure I'd be all right there by myself. I said I would.

After he left, the dog looked up at me, anxious for what, I didn't know. Taking care of a dog, I soon discovered, is like taking care of a baby you don't know. Did she want to eat? Go for a walk? Play? I freshened her water and found some kibble, pouring it into a bowl in the kitchen. She wolfed it down, then raced to the door. I let her out and, meanwhile, dragged my overstuffed overnight bag from the entryway—where I'd set it next to

Palmer's worn-out brown recliner and the dog's basket of tennis balls and toys—to the back of the house. There were two rooms. One was larger, its queen bed made up with a Pendleton blanket as a bedspread. The closet door in that room was ajar just enough so I could see men's clothing hanging from the rod. In the other room, a twin was covered with an old chenille spread, and a metal filing cabinet sat in the far corner. Room number two was clearly the guest room, so that's where I deposited my stuff.

I let Row back inside, and she wagged her tail in anticipation of whatever our next move might be. That's the thing about dogs, I quickly learned. They're always ready for an adventure. Sitting down on the sofa, I shivered, and I patted the seat beside me to invite her onto the furniture with me. I needed the dog's warmth. The house was cold as death.

I did not hear from Palmer for the next few days. As long as Leila was out of town and I was pretty much stranded, I tried to make the best of it. My relationship with the dog blossomed, and we soon became inseparable. We walked out to get the newspaper in the morning and sat in the kitchen's sunny nook for coffee. She watched over me, like a disciplined trainer, as I did my exercises on a mat in Palmer's living room, and she waited outside the bathroom door as I showered. A dog-walker named Nell came by the first afternoon and explained she did so every weekday. She left with an enthusiastic, energetic dog and returned an hour later with an exhausted one. Row and I both napped midday, and when she awoke she'd stand by her basket of tennis balls and bark until I'd acquiesce and toss them out the door for her, one by one. She clearly had a strong retriever gene.

We'd eat an early dinner—if you could call it that; Palmer had very little food in his cupboards or fridge, and his request to dog-sit was so sudden that I hadn't really given food much thought. Row would clean up any crumbs I dropped on the floor and then, around dusk, we bundled up and sat on the porch to watch the October sky fade from indigo to black. We both perked up when the owls hooted and the coyotes yipped, and I'm pretty sure we each felt comforted by the other as night folded around us. I couldn't remember ever feeling so at peace with anyone. Except for Leila.

On the third evening, when it was nearly dark, we walked a short distance away from the house. I'd been weaning myself from the meds yet again, and I couldn't make it very far until my leg started to scream at me like a wild banshee. When I stopped in front of a ramshackle garage, Row leaned toward it, sniffing the air and straining at the leash, her hackles raised.

"Come on, Row," I said, at first gently tugging at her leash to back away from whatever or whoever was lurking. But all one hundred-plus pounds of her stood firm, and the more I tugged on the leash, the more she dug into her position. I wasn't going to be able to get her to budge if she didn't want to. I recalled something about one of Newton's laws—equal actions and opposing reactions—but then my flash of brilliance exploded and died, like a light bulb burning out. So much for remembering high school physics. All I knew for sure was that the only way we were going to move, in either direction, would be if one of us were to give in to the other, let go of the oppositional force. It wasn't going to be me. Not with all those dark, foreboding trees all around. And whatever creatures might be hiding among them.

I yanked on the leash again; the dog still strained away. Time for bribery. "Cookie? Does Row want a cookie?"

The dog turned her velvety, triangular head toward me, while at the same time relaxing her stance. As I had still been pulling in the opposite direction, the shift of her weight broke Newton's law of oppositional forces and sent me tumbling backward onto my ass. Which hurt like hell.

"Damn it, Row! Thanks a lot."

She licked my face, eager for forgiveness. I organized myself into a vertical position, and together we retreated to Palmer's little house, Row pulling on the leash hard—probably worried I'd forget my cookie pledge if we didn't hurry. As she noisily gobbled down the treat, I ate the last two apples in the house, and then we courageously went back outside to the porch, but we never did figure out what had been out there. Nighttime in West Yellowstone was no different than anywhere else: it was full of suspense and secrets.

As we sat outside in the dark, Row and I contemplated the pile of kayaks and canoes stacked in the yard, and the recent weekend that had nearly ended in tragedy. But I also thought about how that outdoors aspect of my former life had been erased at the snap of two fingers when Shane and I got together. How little I'd understood about sacrifice when you get into a new relationship. How little I knew about love, too, and how it can steal you away from your true self. I thought about Grizzly Max, and what she'd said about looking into the eye—into the soul—of another living thing. I searched Row's eyes for her soul. The wind blew, colder now. The seasons were shifting, and so was I.

After listening to a few more nocturnal calls cutting through the air, and after my fingertips felt sufficiently frozen, we went inside. I rummaged through Palmer's kitchen, looking for something else to eat. If only I'd brought more of Leila's chocolate chips. Here, all I could find were condiments, coffee, and a couple of bottles of pinot noir—from my home state of Oregon, of all places.

I decided if I went to bed early, I could ignore my rumbling stomach. But just as I was crawling beneath the covers on the little bed in Palmer's second bedroom, my cell phone rang. It was Palmer. The connection was bad; wind roared in the background.

"Where are you?" I asked.

"Sorry, the service is bad here. Just out camping."

Camping? I thought he had *business* to attend to. And camping without Row? It struck me as odd, but that word *odd* had defined Palmer so perfectly on more than one occasion.

"Anyway, I'm going to be gone a couple more days," he said, shouting into the phone over the wind. "'Course I need you to stay on with Row. Until Saturday."

"Saturday?" It wasn't that I minded staying with her, but I was put off by his use of the word *need*, as if I had no choice. I was also completely out of food. Which I told him.

"Ask Nell to bring you something. I'll reimburse her when I get home."

An interesting idea, but one I probably wouldn't pursue. I didn't like to put people out, even though I'd clearly been imposing on Leila for weeks. Now, thinking about her, I recalled that she was coming home on Friday.

"I'll make do somehow, but please no later than Saturday. Friday would be better. I need to get back to Leila's."

I was still starving and knew it would be hopeless to try to sleep. I went back into the kitchen to double-check and see if I'd missed anything edible. I briefly wondered if I could make a smoothie with ketchup and seltzer water.

I rummaged through a bank of drawers I'd overlooked before. I didn't expect to find food in any of them—who keeps food in a drawer? But I was desperate. The top drawer had the usual scissors, tape, pens and pencils, notepad, stamps. The second drawer held a stack of placemats.

The third drawer was jammed shut.

I pulled on the handle several times, and the drawer rattled but wouldn't budge. I looked over my shoulder at Row, who yawned wide, unconcerned. I yanked on the drawer one more time, hoping to God the handle didn't fall off, because I didn't know how I could explain that away or fix it if it broke. But the drawer still remained stubbornly shut.

Row's tail thumped the linoleum.

I removed the second drawer completely from the cabinet.

A wad of paper had become stuck underneath its base. As I wiggled the pages free, I noted they were information sheets, the kind that accompany prescription medications. There was a big stack of these sheets in the third drawer, too. And beneath them were dozens of pill vials.

Abilify. Lithobid. Depakote. Symbyax. Haldol. Percocet.

They were either full, or at least partially full.

According to the information sheets, these meds—except for the Percocet—were mood stabilizers or antipsychotics, used to treat a variety of disorders. Most notably, all of the sheets mentioned bipolar disorder and, specifically, mania.

I tried to make sense of what I'd just found. Was Palmer bipolar? Why were so many meds here—unused? The prescriptions' dates ranged from a couple of years ago to a few weeks ago.

I'd previously figured out that Palmer didn't have Wi-Fi at his house, but a neighbor did, and it wasn't password protected so I was able to get on the Internet. I searched on my phone for whatever I could find about bipolar disorder.

Brain disorder...unusual shifts in a person's mood, energy, and ability to function...excessive energy, fast talking, and grandiose ideas...risk of suicide...men more inclined toward manic behavior...delusions, hallucinations, paranoia, and psychosis.

Bipolar disorder affected far more Americans than I ever would have guessed. People had posted comments beneath the articles and blogs telling how their lives were turned upside down from the disorder, either because they hadn't received a proper diagnosis or because they didn't want to take their meds. They lost jobs. They lost spouses. Some wound up on the street living under bridges.

One of the articles mentioned genetics. Another mentioned how abuse of recreational drugs, even marijuana, could trigger bipolar symptoms—which made me worry yet again about Carson. Another article said bipolar episodes could be brought on by traumatic or otherwise major life-changing events; date rape and going off to college were two examples given. Was dropping out of college a symptom of mania? I decided I'd better call Delaney again.

The most frightening thing I saw was a chart and article that discussed psychosis. The word *psychosis* brought that horror movie, *Psycho*, to mind.

I went into the bathroom to pee, wondering as I sat on the toilet if my bear incident, and Palmer having to deal with it there on the trail, had been a bipolar trigger for him. He'd already admitted it was traumatic.

Everything about him was now making sense. His arrogance, his unsolicited romantic advances toward me, his agitation. What concerned me was that, according to some articles, these manic episodes could go on for weeks or months, getting worse and worse, especially if the patient didn't take his meds. And sometimes the patient could become reckless, even violent.

As I popped his Percocet, Palmer's landline phone rang. I froze. It hadn't rung since my arrival, and I hadn't given any thought to whether I should answer it. How would I introduce myself to the caller? As Palmer's friend? His pet-sitter? His personal spy? I'd already been feeling guilty about rifling through his personal belongings. Maybe I could get a job at the NSA.

"Hello, Palmer's residence."

It was Jolene, his lovely ex-wife whom I'd met at the hotel party. I stumbled over my words as I tried to explain why I was there. She started to laugh.

"No need to explain."

By the chipper tone of her voice, I assumed she hadn't heard about the near drowning of her daughter. And I wasn't about to tell her. Not now, anyway.

"I was just calling Palmer to check in," Jolene said. "Taylor hasn't heard back from any of the messages she's sent him, and I wanted to be sure he was all right. Especially after what happened at the hotel and all."

I hesitated, wondering what I should tell her about his behavior at the bear meeting, his sudden departure, and what I'd just discovered. I decided I should honor his privacy. After all, she was his ex. They weren't still married—but even if they were, marriage didn't necessarily entitle you to knowing everything.

"I'll tell him you called. When he gets back," I said.

Now she hesitated. "Look, I don't know how much you know about him, but I should probably clue you in on the fact that he has some…issues. Obviously you're not responsible for him, but I don't want you getting roped into anything, with the dog especially, when he goes off."

It was one of those comments to which there was no safe reply.

"I don't really know much at all," I said. Shane popped into my head, nodding in agreement, always eager to mansplain things to me or otherwise remind me how little I knew about just about everything.

She sighed. "Palmer has always had a tremendous enthusiasm for life. And he's got a huge heart. I can see why you might be attracted to him."

Suddenly it dawned on me. "I think you've got the wrong idea. There's nothing going on between Palmer and me. I'm just the dog sitter."

"From his perspective, there's a lot more to your relationship."

"I'm married, Jolene. You know that. So does he." No need to elaborate on the status of that marital mess. "I'm sorry he feels there's something between us. There absolutely isn't."

"Unfortunately, when he learns there's been a misunderstanding, things could get even worse."

"By that you mean?

"Back in his mid-twenties, he sort of went off the deep end when a girlfriend broke up with him. That's when he was diagnosed with bipolar disorder—back then it was called manic depression. I didn't know him at the time; when we met he was taking meds and stable. Sometime after Taylor was born, things got wonky again. The meds didn't work anymore—or, to be more precise, he didn't like the side effects, especially the weight gain, and stopped taking them—and his illness took hold of him again, like the monster that creeps up from the basement in the middle of the night."

An apt, but frightening, metaphor. Suddenly I wondered if this house had a basement.

"He's been on and off meds, and in and out of hospitals, ever since," Jolene said. "And he has a tendency to disappear when the mania comes on. I was pretty sure something was amiss when Taylor and I were in Yellowstone. I'd never seen him so thin, not when he was taking his meds. And that whole episode—coming in with all those unexplained injuries. I tried to talk with him about it, but he wouldn't listen. And since we're no longer married, I don't exactly have any clout."

Of course I knew full well that being married didn't guarantee clout.

I went ahead and told her about his behavior at the bear meeting and how he later called me to take care of Row. She peppered me with questions. Together, we concluded he was more than likely experiencing a manic episode. I asked her what I should do when he did come home.

"There's not much you *can* do. You can't make him take his meds, and you can't have him committed. The only thing you can do is call the cops if he's a clear danger to self or others."

"Danger?"

"I don't mean to scare you," she said.

I heard her thoughts lining up carefully.

"He's never hurt Taylor or me. But he's been known to threaten people when he's in one of his dysphoric states. It's only happened once, but when it did, he went totally psychotic. Lost touch with reality. Started seeing things that weren't there and talking to invisible people. Believing things to be true that weren't. It's a terrifying thing to witness."

I couldn't recall the last time I'd had a phone conversation that was so exhausting. All I wanted to do now was lock the doors and sleep. Except that locking the doors wouldn't keep Palmer out of his own house. If Leila weren't still in California, I could call her. If Hamlin lived nearer, I could call him. I briefly thought about summoning the ghost woman for help, except I had no idea how to reach her. I didn't even know how to reach Nell.

"I hope I haven't upset you," Jolene said. "Remember, Palmer has a heart of gold. I'm sure you're safe. I'm mostly worried about him. Why don't you call me when he returns and we'll go from there."

After we hung up, I lay down on the sofa near the woodstove and pulled a blanket over my head. Row nestled along the base of the sofa beside me. The wind had kicked up outside, and the branches of those two sentinel trees brushed against the house. There was only one reason why going home to Shane made sense. At least whenever I was with him, I felt physically safe. Now, I felt more vulnerable than I had on the Mystic Falls Trail so many weeks ago.

TWENTY-SIX

Anne

MAGGIE WENT TO the river to catch fish. Clara prepared to sand down the floor of her cabin. I lightly touched her arm as she headed outside and asked if she and Maggie were feeling better.

"I'm all right. And as for Maggie's cough, I'm convinced she's getting better, too. But I suspect she's mighty upset with you, still, about invitin' those men here."

"I realize that. I have apologized and will do so again. But I saw the two of you whispering. Is there something else of which I should be apprised?"

"It's lady business. Not the type of thing a proper lady would want to hear."

"Oh." I felt myself pull away from Clara. She was correct; I had no experience discussing private matters with anyone else. But additionally, I was taken aback that Maggie would discuss something so delicate with Clara rather than me.

"Just tell me everything is fine," I said. I picked up the broom and began to sweep the floors.

"I don't think I can do that. She isn't fine. She missed a moon, as she puts it."

"Are you referring to her...monthly...unwellness?"

An alarm of clanging metal interrupted us.

"Confounded horses," Clara said. "I wish they'd stop kickin' that bucket 'round."

She went out to check on the commotion, and I continued to sweep. It bewildered me how so much dust could accumulate there each day. If only Sam would get back soon with those windowpanes. I daydreamed about my lace curtains, and a table set with linens, and then I found myself concerned with a more immediate situation, which was what to prepare for supper that evening. Maggie The Owl would be catching fish, and we could cook it over the camp-fire atop a bed of spruce branches, but we had little else to serve alongside. I feared if I ate another one of Maggie's sticky biscuits, I would begin to look like one, plumping out in all the wrong places.

When I heard the sound of horse hooves and wagon wheels, my heart skipped in joy. Finally, Sam and Evalene had returned! But when I saw a stage-coach lumbering along—a true sign of civilization—I was dumbfounded. I ran down our path to greet whoever it was, but my enthusiasm converted to confusion when I saw Aaron and Rusty again, mounted on their horses behind the coach.

Then I nearly fainted when Thomas stepped out.

As soon as he spotted me, his chin began to quiver. He whisked off a dashing top hat, which I had never before seen, and ran toward me. A piece of my heart must still have been branded with love, for I nearly swooned. When he wrapped his arms around me and rubbed his newly shaven cheeks against mine, our tears comingled and I began to recall who it was that I had become so enamored of years ago.

"My dearest Anne," Thomas said when he finally let go of me. "How I have worried. I could scarcely stand being without you. You have no idea how miserable I have been."

He pulled back, taking full stock of my appearance, which was most certainly far different from what he had remembered. Likewise I studied him. Slight creases now etched his forehead, and the hair on each side of his head had been dusted, as though with flour, since we were last together. Knowing all that he had been through in the intervening weeks made these changes in appearance seem like battle scars, and he appeared to me more striking than ever. I doubted he would see me in the same light, however. Although I wore the new dress I had made with the cotton Evalene had procured, it was a simple sheath of cheap fabric. My underpinnings were still entirely inadequate, consisting solely of yet another sheath. I wore no cosmetics, and my poor skin was dry and flaky after being in the mountain air for so long. I must have looked at least ten years older than when he last saw me.

I slipped my embroidered handkerchief out from my apron pocket.

"I think I have finally lost some weight," I said.

"Indeed you have." I could not tell whether this pleased him. He touched my chapped lips gently, with one finger, his eyes once again filling with tears. My heart beat like the wings of the bats that Maggie and I had seen.

Thomas then reached for my hair. "But what in God's name have you done here?"

I had followed Maggie's lead and cropped it short. Very short. "It is so much easier to deal with. Someday it will be the leading fashion. Do you like it?"

"I find it rather unbecoming. At least it will grow back," he said.

Then he kissed me deeply, his weight bending me backward as he leaned forward, but my batwings stopped midflight. Fool that I was, I had nearly forgiven him all his sins. When his tongue tried to break through my puckered lips, I pushed him away.

"Oh, Thomas. We have so much to discuss."

"Yes, my dear. And so much to do," he said, wiggling his eyebrows at me.

He would have to wait for that.

Aaron and Rusty had dismounted by now and come to stand behind Thomas.

"I believe you've met these boys," he said.

"Bounty hunters," a voice from behind me said. I turned, and there was my dear Clara, once again cradling the rifle like a baby. "Bounty hunters...an' liars."

She aimed the gun at Aaron, then turned to Thomas. "I suggest you tell these scoundrels to get out o' here. Now."

"And I suggest you back off," Thomas said. "No need to be so inhospitable. We mean you no harm."

"Like hell ye don't."

"Thomas, this is Clara. My friend, Clara. She has been of great assistance to me. Please be kind." I took his arm, then nodded at her. "Come, Clara. Let us show our visitors some hospitality."

"No thank ye," she said. "I think I'll just stay here awhile. Keep an eye on these boys. And the stage driver as well."

Glancing back at her over my shoulder, I led Thomas up the path and gave him a tour of the cabin without revealing its purpose. He did not seem impressed, even as I explained that we had built it ourselves, with only a little help from some local companions. I poured some coffee from the pot on the stove and offered him a sticky biscuit.

He took one bite, then spat it out. He spat out the coffee as well.

"Is it too hot?" Guilt immediately engulfed me, even as the memory of my own burn flared from that day when he'd been so angry with me.

"Dear God, no. But surely you do not consider that to be *coffee*. What has happened to you, my dear? You are nothing like the person you once were. Indeed, it seems you have even lost those fine boots I procured for you."

"And you have lost all your manners. This is my home, Thomas, and you have no right to barge in and insult me—or my coffee."

His upper lip curled as he surveyed the place again.

Just as a graceful doe feels when a powerful bull elk takes a fancy to her, my desire was to quickly flee. But I also desired to learn about his time with Maggie's people.

"Tell me about your experience since I last saw you, Thomas." I recalled how cooperative he had been when the Indians led him away. I had assumed his composure was related to what he deemed to be my best interests, but over time I began to tell myself a different version of the story, that my husband had been far more concerned with his own self-preservation than with his wife's survival. Perhaps he had cooperated only to save his own scalp.

"They were most civil to me," he said. They had released him, along with Mrs. Cowan and her young sister Ida, without injury, and Thomas had returned directly home from the encounter. He drank his coffee down, then sneered into the cup. "Awfully bitter."

"I have come to appreciate strong coffee."

After an unpleasant but necessary lull, he volunteered that the military personnel at Mammoth Hot Springs had forbidden him from going in search of me. "Far too dangerous for a civilian, they said. They assured me they would find you on my behalf. I remained in constant contact with the army and the park officials for several days. Nobody claimed to have seen even your shadow."

What about those two military men whom I had encountered right after Thomas was taken? Or those two rangers with whom I had engaged in a substantial conversation?

"I heard, by the way, that those heathens have finally been caught," Thomas said. "The chief surrendered near the Canadian border just last week."

Upon hearing this, my heart slipped to my knees. Poor Maggie. Her husband's people—whoever still survived—were now at the mercy of my government's army. A worse fate for them I could not imagine. I inadvertently glanced in the direction of the river, then noticed Thomas had followed my gaze like a posse pursuing tracks.

"Have you heard what will happen to the Nimi'ipuu that were captured?" I asked.

"The what?" He helped himself to our last sticky biscuit, frowned at it, then shoved the entire thing between the lips that had moments ago attempted to attach themselves to my face.

"The Indians," I said, as I used my handkerchief to wipe crumbs from the corners of his mouth.

"There's been some talk of shipping them to an encampment in Oklahoma," he said.

"Oklahoma! But that has nothing to do with the land they came from."

He squinted at me. "After all that has happened, you are worried about those savages?"

I forced my eyes to focus on him despite the ugliness of his words. I refrained from searching for Maggie although every bit of my being longed to see her. And I clenched my fists tight so that my hands would not slap him for calling my extended family a band of savages.

"Yes, as a matter of fact," I said. "I am."

I took his elbow. I led him back outside. I veered toward the path and escorted him down to the stage-coach, my luxurious moccasins skimming over the rocky ground along the way. He stumbled once or twice.

Clara still stood upright with her gun at the ready. Aaron, Rusty, and the stage-driver were settled on the ground, each leaning against a tree with arms folded across their chests and hats lowered over their eyes. I found it curious they had the audacity to nap in the presence of a lady with a gun.

"Thomas," I said, opening the stage-coach door for him. "It has been lovely to see you. I am relieved to know that you are well. And I am most grateful that you traveled all the way out here for a visit. But now I must get back to my work. And I presume you need to return to yours."

The sun lit only one side of his face; the other was covered in shadow. A fitting visage to remember.

"Are you joking, my dear?"

I lifted my chin. "Most certainly not."

Now he sighed and relaxed his stance, tilting his head as my father had done years ago in reaction to my youthful petulance. "You cannot possibly be suggesting that you are going to stay here. Not after I came all this way for you."

If I were to answer that question in the affirmative, it would be proof that I had indeed gone mad. What woman in her right mind would live in these conditions when she could go home to a warm, fully appointed house in the heart of civilization, and with a successful, smart, attractive man? What woman would surrender a marriage and the possibility of children in order to live the frontier life with an Indian girl? I recalled the conversation we had with Clara about asylums.

"Anne?" He wrapped his hand around my arm and squeezed. "My dear, I believe all this mountain air has touched your mind. Your notion of living here is not a natural one. What you need is a good deal of rest, somewhere cool and quiet where you won't be disturbed."

I felt strangely gleeful at that moment. He had just described these exact environs: cool and quiet. Clara, the woman who rarely showed emotion, grinned broadly. She looked younger now than she had all this time. Healthier, too. Her countenance strengthened me.

"You have neglected yourself," Thomas said. "You look as though you have been suffering."

"On the contrary, I have been more attentive to my own needs and desires than ever before." A wave of strength rose up from deep within my corporeal entity. It warmed me as a stove's fire warms a home. I settled my shoulders back and fixed my gaze directly on this man once known as my husband. I could not recall ever feeling so legitimate, before this moment. I was a fully-formed human being with a conscience and free will. "The only suffering I have known is that which I endured while living with you, beginning on our wedding night."

He blinked twice. I remained resolute. He squeezed my arm more tightly with one hand, his other one clenching into a fist. And then, without warning, he swooped me off the ground as he would a child, and wrangled me into the coach. I flailed ineffectively. He rushed into the coach after me and slammed the door closed. He whistled as though calling for a dog. All this happened so quickly, I was bewildered and momentarily dazed, and I became foolishly more concerned with my handkerchief, which I'd dropped in our tussle, than with his intentions.

"You have gone mad," he said, sitting across from me with each of his hands clamped onto my wrists and his legs on either side of mine. I attempted to kick free, but his strong thighs held me in place.

"I am not the one who is mad," I said, my teeth clenched.

In the shade of the stage-coach's dark interior, his eyes had turned black, and he seemed even larger now than he had when standing outside with me. It was he who had become a savage.

"Anne, this is not an invitation. You are coming home with me."

He whistled again as I struggled to free myself from his grip. Outside, the men were rustling. I heard the horses shuffling. I could not see Clara from where I sat.

"Let go of me! I am not going anywhere. Certainly not with you."

Thomas called out the window for Aaron. When he approached, he held up a set of manacles. I tried to free myself from my husband one last time, twisting and kicking and pleading. I tried to bite him, but his elbow met my nose. Blood gushed down my new dress.

"Seems you want to do this the hard way," Thomas said. Aaron reached through the window and affixed the manacles to my wrists.

"Clara!" I cried out.

For an instant, all was silent. And then, a single gunshot echoed through the woods.

Moments later, Clara appeared outside the stage-coach window, her gray hair disheveled, dirt on her face. Her hands were pinned behind her back by Rusty, who pushed her forward toward Thomas and me.

"Let her go," I said. "She has done nothing to you."

"Ready to cooperate now?" Thomas asked, his grin hideous. "Either you cooperate with me or this old hag will have more trouble with Rusty."

Clara shook her head at me.

"I cannot believe you are doing this," I said to him. I stomped on his foot but my moccasin was too soft to hurt him. "I am not your property."

"My dear, that is exactly what you are. My wife and my property. Now act accordingly."

"It is not my duty to surrender to you simply because we exchanged some vows, just as it is not my duty to scrub your repulsive undergarments in boiling water every week."

"Tie her up!" Thomas shouted to Rusty. The bounty hunter wrestled Clara to a nearby tree, but all the while her face reflected back to me the strength and defiance and craftiness I knew she possessed.

"I will be all right, my friend," I called out to her, even as blood still dripped from my nose. "Do not worry. Take care of...everything."

A cool breeze toyed with the gray tendrils that had fallen loose from her bun and blew them across her face. She nodded. She understood. But tears began to trickle down each side of a face that might have never before displayed such emotion.

Aaron handed a ring of keys to Thomas, then climbed onto his horse. Thomas reached his arm through the window and tapped the rooftop. Time to go.

The driver whistled and snapped his whip. The coach lurched forward. Tears sprang from my own eyes. Without my handkerchief, I could not dry them. But I did not care.

"Oh, stop your blubbering," Thomas said.

I seethed. "You might take away every other part of my life, but you cannot eliminate my sorrow."

"What about yer sketches?" I heard Clara call.

I poked my head through the window as well as my enslaved hands. "Give them to Maggie! And tell her I love her more than anything in the world!"

I twisted around to the rear coach window now and saw Aaron and Rusty following us on their horses. Behind them, Clara was still tied to the tree. And then another figure came into view. Maggie, in her buckskin dress.

"Wait!" I said to Thomas.

Maggie quickly attended to Clara's bondage, and Clara scrambled for her gun. She aimed it in our direction and shot three times.

Rusty slumped to the right of his horse. Aaron slumped to the left. I would never know where the third shot went. But now all the horses were charging ahead, and our coach swayed side to side. Thomas shouted at the stage-coach driver to get the hell out of there.

Maggie tried her best to catch up to us. Her knife shone like silver in her right hand as she pumped her slim but strong arms and sprinted as swiftly as an antelope. Still, she grew smaller and smaller in my rear view, and I strained to seal that image into my mind and heart forever: a desperate Indian girl with short black hair, running with all her might toward me across a golden, dusty, and ever-so-free landscape.

TWENTY-SEVEN

Brooke

ON FRIDAY MORNING, Palmer texted that he was on his way home. It was perfect timing, as Leila was expected to arrive around noon that day, and I didn't want to miss a minute with her. I sent her a text, asking if she could pick me up at his place on her way to Emily's. After packing up my belongings—and double-checking to be sure I'd put all of Palmer's paperwork and vials back in the kitchen drawer correctly—I sat down on the sofa to wait. Row barked when she heard tires crunching on the gravel out front, and I jumped up. When I heard his key in the lock, I knew how Row felt. If I'd had a tail it would've been wagging, too. But not because I was anxious to see Palmer. Mine would wag because soon I'd be back with Leila.

When the front door opened, it was immediately clear that we had a problem. For a moment, I thought it was Einstein standing there with his wildly disheveled hair. Palmer's jacket was caked with dirt and dried blood. He stank of who knew what. Row's tail thumped against the wall as she lovingly tried to greet her master, unconcerned with his appearance, but he nudged her right outside with his knee and practically slammed the door in the poor girl's face.

Only then did I notice what he was pointing at me.

"What's that...that thing?"

"A Glock. A baby Glock."

"A *baby* Glock?" I said, backing up into the room.

"A Glock 26 Gen 4 firearm. 9mm caliber."

"But what are you doing with a baby...Glock?" I'd never seen a real gun up close like that before. It was black and menacing.

Palmer glanced around the room, then came forward toward me. "Time to go."

"What's going on, Palmer?" I tried to keep my voice flat as I backed up toward the sofa. When my calf bumped it, I sidestepped, and he did the same, so that we wound up half-circling around the room as if dancing a waltz with a gun between us. Now, with his back to the sofa and mine to the door, I felt infinitesimally stronger, and my memory surged with images of those bipolar pamphlets. He had helped me once; maybe now it was my turn to help him.

"What's going on?" I repeated, then nodded at his jacket. "What's with all the blood?"

"I'll tell you on the way. All you need to do is keep one thing in mind. I did it all for you, Brooke."

First Shane, now Palmer. Why do men claim to do stuff for us when we don't ask them to?

"*What* did you do for me? Tell me you didn't hurt someone."

He motioned the gun toward the back of the house. "Like I said, I'll tell you on the way. Now get moving."

"On the way to where?"

Row whimpered from outside, then barked. I checked my watch; Leila would be here soon.

"I'm not going anywhere until you give me the gun," I said. "And then tell me exactly what you did and where you think we're going." My hand shook as I held it out for the weapon. I'd never held a gun.

Palmer's upper lip pulled back in a wolf-like snarl. I tried to assess what he'd do if I opened the door and ran. Jolene's voice surfaced in my mind. *I'm sure you're safe.* God, I hoped she was right.

"Palmer, give me the gun."

He held it out, then pivoted and aimed at something, or someone, that only he could see. He closed one eye and pulled the trigger. A loud crack, unlike anything I'd ever before heard: a bit like a firecracker, a bit like lightning directly overhead, a bit like the crashing of a garbage truck if it were in your living room. My hands shot up to my head and my blood pressure shot off the charts.

"Give me that thing before somebody gets hurt!"

Row barked again from outside, as if reinforcing my demand, and now that my ears had begun to ring, even the sound of her voice was painful. But it gave me an idea. Palmer showed no sign of acquiescing. When the dog barked yet again, I opened the door. She raced in, hoping to finally greet her master properly, and when she lunged at him with unadulterated canine enthusiasm, she knocked him off balance. The gun went flying.

Thankfully it didn't shoot again, and before I knew what was happening, I was the one holding that thing. It was cold and heavy, but also wet from

Palmer's sweaty hand. It was the ugliest baby anything I'd ever seen. I didn't know what to do with it; letting it hang by my side didn't feel right. Slipping it into the back of my jeans, the way they do on TV, would have clearly been an accident waiting to happen. For lack of a better idea—and maybe because the heft of a weapon like that can be remarkably empowering—I waggled it in Palmer's direction. I felt dirty wrapping my finger around the trigger.

"Sit," I said.

The dog immediately sat at Palmer's side.

"Not you, Row. Sit down, Palmer. On the sofa."

To my surprise, he did.

I looked him in the eye, trying to see his soul à la Grizzly Max. But his eyes were vacant.

"Tell me what you did," I said. "I'm not going anywhere until you do."

I had no idea what I'd do if he refused, or if he made a move toward me, or how I was going to get out of this predicament. The last thing I wanted to do was squeeze a trigger. Row pawed at his knee, as if she too waited for his reply.

"I killed them," he said, looking straight into me.

With these words, it was as if he'd shot my legs out from under me. Suddenly they didn't seem able to support all my weight. I reached for the recliner by the door to steady myself while still trying to hold the gun—its weight now seemingly doubled.

"Who? Who did you kill?"

"The bears."

"You killed…the bears?"

"Yes, the bears."

"Oh, God," I said. I slid to the floor, wondering if this was true and, if so, how many bears he'd shot. I recalled Max's story of the whimpering cubs. Row shifted her eyebrows as if she, too, were concerned.

Palmer began to rant about something, his words quickening and spittle spewing. I couldn't possibly keep up with his ramblings. Something about taking a stand and those fucking creatures and about the human race being in danger of eradication. "We won't be safe without total annihilation of those savages."

His words echoed the sentiments he'd uttered at the bear management meeting but also the stories Leila had told me about white attitudes toward her ancestors. Even famous men, like L. Frank Baum—the man who wrote *The Wonderful Wizard of Oz*—wanted to annihilate the American Indian. Granted, there is a difference between bears and people. But they're related—we all are. Bears and Indians were both inhabitants of the earth, and both populations had been exploited—and slaughtered—by white men.

"You can't mean what you say."

"Shut up!" He stood abruptly, his sudden movement startling both the dog and me.

Row—who had just lain down at his side—hurried over toward me like a child turning to her mother for solace. But along the way she distracted herself with that basket of tennis balls. She chose one and brought it to me. Ignoring her, I aimed the gun up at Palmer, propping my elbows on my knees for support.

"You can't just go around deciding who gets to live and who has to die," I said, knowing just how ironic it was that I held a weapon that could easily maim or kill while at the same time preaching about the very topic. I had no intention of using it, and Palmer probably knew that. But that's the thing about a gun; it creates suspense for everyone—especially the person holding it. I really didn't know what might happen, what I might do. "And don't tell me to shut up," I added in the toughest voice I could muster.

I heard an engine outside, the squeaking of brakes. Emily's truck. A bell rang on my phone, which was on the sofa across the room, closer to Palmer than to me. I assumed it was a text from Leila, letting me know she had arrived. Keeping the gun trained on him as best I could, I tried to envision how I might reach for the door, open it, and scream for help—all while holding the gun in position. I knew I couldn't outrun him with my physical limitations, and a scream could ignite something in him that could turn into a deadly skirmish. I did the only thing that came to mind. I carefully stood up, holding the gun at the ready with my right hand. I reached back down to Row and retrieved the ball from her mouth with my left. Then I opened the door and threw the ball out. It didn't go far, but Row chased after it anyway.

"What the hell are you doing?" Palmer asked. I ignored him, waited, then let the dog back in when she returned. I glanced outside; sure enough, there was Leila sitting in Emily's truck. Her mere presence steadied my heart. She waved but made no move to get out. And why would she? Palmer was the last person she'd want to see. She could wait out there for me, listening to music or podcasts, for hours.

I had to do something. Show her the gun? Palmer would figure out that Leila was out there, and anyway chances were good she wouldn't be able to see from that distance—or believe—what I was holding. Again I thought about hollering for help, but Palmer could surely react faster than she could. I needed to de-escalate the situation, not make it worse.

I transferred the gun to my left hand—risky but necessary. I wrestled the tennis ball out of Row's mouth with my right hand; this was my injured but dominant arm. I needed better aim this time. I drew back my arm and pitched. Bonsai. Row's slobbery ball hit the truck's windshield.

Row ran off to retrieve the ball. Leila got out of the car, her hands uplifted in a WTF gesture.

"Call 9-1-1!" I shouted.

She came running, which had not been my intention. I switched the gun back to my right hand, shook it once at Palmer, then waved it out the door. She stopped—still outside—and quickly punched a number into her cell. Then she cautiously came to the door, holding the phone to her ear and talking to someone, presumably 9-1-1. She took the gun from me with her other hand. That's when Palmer lunged for her.

"Sit the fuck back down," she said. I couldn't help but wonder what the 9-1-1 dispatcher thought just then. But Leila explained into the phone that she'd confiscated a weapon. Next, she pressed the speaker button on her phone. "Tell them what's going on," she said to me.

I gave the dispatcher my name, and Palmer's, too. Leila held the gun inches from his head, so he had no choice but to sit still and listen.

"I've been here for several days dog-sitting for Palmer," I said. My heart was beating so fast that my words tumbled out in a rush. "He came back about an hour ago, waving a gun around and ranting about how he'd killed some bears. He's terribly disheveled and not himself at all. I think he's bipolar. I think maybe he's manic or has somehow lost touch with reality. I think you should send an ambulance along with the sheriff."

The dispatcher said she'd stay on the line until the sheriff arrived. I set the phone down.

"If you're telling the truth," Leila said to Palmer, her voice shaking with an anger I didn't know she had, "and if you killed a single grizzly, you'll be sorry. Really, really sorry."

She had his attention. Mine, too.

"You want to know why? Because it's never wise to mess with someone's *wyakin*."

He stared at her, uneasily. He looked so discombobulated by now, I wasn't sure if anyone was home in his brain anymore.

"The grizzly bear is Brooke's *wyakin*, dumbass."

"My what?" I asked, totally caught off guard. I couldn't imagine why she'd think I would have a *wyakin*. Or why in the world it would be the very animal that had nearly killed me.

"Your animal guide. Your spirit guide," Leila said as if it should be obvious to me.

The grizzly was my spirit guide? *My* spirit guide? It didn't make sense to me, but nothing did anymore. Was that why I'd survived the attack, because it was my special animal? Was that why it had even attacked me in the first place? This whole idea felt foreign and prickly, like a pinecone rolling around inside my head. All of a sudden, I felt terribly important. Flabbergasted—but important. I, a white woman from Portland, Oregon, had my own grizzly bear *wyakin*! If only Shane could see me now.

"A woman with grizzly bear power is dangerous," she said, her attention turned back to Palmer. "And not only have you pissed off her spirit, you've pissed off the national park system."

"And the local sheriff," I quickly added, before acknowledging the magnitude of what Leila had said about me. I was trying to add levity, the way you laugh nervously when someone trips and falls. After what I'd read about bipolar people with delusional paranoia, I was tempted to mention the FBI and the CIA, too. But sensibility prevailed, and I kept my mouth shut.

Row came back to the front porch and barked. I let her in, and she brought her tennis ball to Leila.

"I thought I could trust you, trust you," Palmer said, his hands fidgeting in his lap, his eyes narrowing. He looked pathetic. I felt a familiar pang, guilt for turning him in—for betraying him—even though I knew he needed help.

When the sheriff arrived, I ended the call with 9-1-1. Row greeted him when he came in, tail wagging, and the sheriff called her by name. He then nodded at Palmer, and Palmer lifted his chin in reply. They all knew each other.

I gave the sheriff a Twitter-length version of what had transpired, my heart still racing and my story practically on chipmunk speed. Only after he handcuffed Palmer was I able to begin to calm myself. I took a couple of deep breaths and asked about the bears.

"I'll put in a call to the park." He nodded at Palmer. "He's so far out in left field right now. No sense worrying about what he had to say. My guess is that it's one big delusion and that the animals are all fine."

I hoped he was correct. "And the ambulance? Is it on its way?"

"They'll meet us down at the jail," the sheriff said. "Don't worry, we've done this with Palmer before."

"Be gentle with him," I said as the sheriff escorted Palmer out the door. "He's got a good heart." The sheriff, a soft-spoken man, said he would. I wanted to believe him about Palmer being okay. And the bears, too.

Sometimes it takes a touch of insanity to see what's truly sane and real. Max was right. What had happened to me was a gift of enlightenment. And Palmer clarified it all for me. Two months ago, I wouldn't have given a moment's thought to the plight of the grizzly bear. Or the American Indian, beyond what I'd learned during the Standing Rock protest. I wouldn't have seen how good hearts can be overpowered by other forces—in Palmer's case, by mental illness. I wouldn't have allowed myself the luxury of asking what was important in life or figured out that values and priorities can shift, that what one needs now might very well be different from what one needed twenty years ago. And maybe that it's okay if your needs no longer match your partner's because, after all, you're two separate people. Sometimes life brings you closer together. But sometimes it draws you further apart, and you need to go your separate ways.

My first order of business when we got back to Emily's was to read and reply to all the texts Delaney had sent that morning. After her first set of abrupt replies, she'd elaborated on her thoughts. She asked me to please tell Shane, if I heard from him, that she wasn't chasing boys, and to stop making stupid assumptions about her. Angry face emoji. That she wasn't like everyone else: she didn't think about sex all the time. Sideways-glance emoji. Finally, that she'd given a lot of thought to quitting school before contacting the dean, having been worried we'd think of her as a failure.

"But now that you've accepted my decision," she wrote, "I'm able to feel, for the first time in a long time, that my decision was right." The next emoji was of a mother and daughter. "Now it's time for Dad to believe in me." Her final emojis: a flexed arm, a thinking face, a woman. I had recently discovered an online emoji dictionary to help me decipher her symbols, so I understood those symbols were meant to depict her strength, her thoughtfulness, and her maturity. Pride for my daughter, and gratitude that she was back in my life, swelled inside me.

I floated into the kitchen to ask Leila if she was hungry—my way of suggesting that I was, without wanting to inconvenience her, although I knew she saw right through me. She offered to fix a sandwich. Meanwhile, I called Delaney.

"I'm so proud of you," I said. "Here my eighteen-year-old daughter has been able to figure out what's right for her before I've even figured out my own best path." An image of those microbreweries in Jackson flickered in my mind.

"Well, that's sort of what I wanted to talk about with you," she said. "Mom, listen to me. You were a new person when we came to visit you earlier this month. And you know what? I like that person way better than the old one. You're cool, more relaxed. You laugh now, and you're not all painted with makeup and stuff to impress anyone. You're prettier this way, Mom, in your jeans and sweatshirt and your stupid walking boot and crutches."

"I'm not on crutches or in my boot anymore."

"You know what I mean. You're more…you."

I'd had no idea that for so long, I hadn't been me. But once she uttered those courageous words, I realized I had indeed been someone else. For years—for years!—I'd been an imposter.

"I'm not quite sure what to say. I've had a crazy morning."

Leila sliced a sandwich into quarters, then handed a section to me.

"It's okay, Mom."

I took a bite of Leila's simple masterpiece: caramelized onions, thin apple slices, melted aged cheddar, and a handful of arugula, all piled between grilled multi-grain bread. I nodded at Leila and motioned for more.

"Mom?"

I mumbled to convey I was still there, on the phone, even though my mouth was stuffed with heaven.

"Just know that I want you to stay the way you are," she said. "In fact, I want you to stay there in Yellowstone. And I want to come be with you. At least for a while."

If the last week or so hadn't already earned an award for being the most bizarre, thrilling, wild time of my life to date, it now had.

"Mom?"

I quickly chewed and swallowed.

"Wow. I'm...at a loss."

I should've been doing a Snoopy dance upon learning that Delaney wanted to come to be with me, but something held me back. It could've been the delectable food I'd just devoured and my desire for more. Or it could've been Delaney's timing—just when I'd been thinking about starting life over—she surprises me with this. A mother should want her daughter with her, shouldn't she? Especially after all we'd been through? But then it struck me. I wanted—no, I needed—to be on my own.

"Have you talked to Dad about this?" I asked.

Of course she hadn't. And I sure didn't want to be the one to tell him. Especially when I wasn't convinced her proposal was right—for me.

"So what do you think, Mom? Isn't this a cool plan? We can have so much fun together."

How do you say no to your daughter? You don't. You affirm her. You assure her you love her. Then you evade the subject. I nodded into the phone. "I love that you're thinking so hard about your choices, Delaney. I'm proud of you. And I'm so grateful our relationship is mending—you know you mean the world to me. Let's give this some serious thought and talk more tomorrow. Okay?"

"Holy shit," I said to Leila after hanging up. "Just holy shit."

By now Leila was finishing the last of the sandwich. I asked if I could please have more, feeling like poor little Oliver Twist.

"We're out of bread," she said. Instead of offering something else to eat, she left the kitchen. *Weird*, I thought.

Later, while my stomach and I pouted, J.P. called to find out how I was doing. I lied and said I was fabulous.

"So you're off the oxy without any problems?"

"Problems? No, no problems." I needed to find another prescription. But I knew J.P. wouldn't be the doc who'd prescribe it.

He asked if I knew yet when I'd be returning home, to Portland. I said I still didn't have any definite plans.

"Well, when your life settles down, I hope you'll call me. I'd love to invite you back to the cabin, with me next time. I promise it will be an entirely different experience."

If only he knew.

I checked email on my phone. Hamlin had just sent one. The subject line was *Thinking of You*. The body of the message had no text, just a dozen or so links to various sites having to do with Jackson, Wyoming. One linked to a river-rafting outfitter. Another linked to a temporary employment agency's advertisement for local ski resort jobs. I couldn't recall if I'd mentioned that ski lift operator idea to him, and now that I saw it in words, I realized how delusional I'd been to think I could stand there in a blizzard, day after day, on my bad leg to check ski passes. For all I knew they might not even have human operators anymore. But the last link, to an article about pack-rafting in the Wild West, *that* I could really get into next summer.

I needed time to figure out how to reply to him. I also needed to figure out when and how to tell him about Palmer, not to mention Palmer's claim that he'd gone off and killed some bears. I decided to simply send him a smiley-face for now. I would deal with it later.

Nothing from Shane. No email, no text, no call. No Facebook message. Nada. Tomorrow I would write to him, too. Tomorrow I would tell him what I'd decided.

Leila crashed on the sofa in the living room with one of Emily's poetry books. I thought about sneaking into the kitchen in search of more food, but didn't want to appear ungrateful for that little sandwich. Besides, she seemed to have something up her sleeve. So I lay on the floor beside her. Row, who'd come home with us after the sheriff took Palmer into custody, stretched out beside me.

Someone knocked on the front door. Before either of us could move, the ghost woman walked in bearing a freshly baked pie. Cinnamon and brown sugar fragrances trailed her, and my stomach growled with joy. The dog and I both sat up, anxious for a slice. But Phoebe headed directly to the kitchen and returned empty-handed.

"Ready?" she asked.

"Ready as ever," Leila said. She hoisted herself off the sofa and extended a hand to help me up. "Come on, Brooke."

I assumed we were heading for the kitchen, for pie. But Phoebe led us right out the back door.

We trekked out to the forest, Row bringing up the rear. As we approached the mysterious lodge, my heart started skipping. Phoebe unlocked the heavy door with an old-fashioned iron key straight out of a fairy tale, then flipped on the interior lights.

There we stood, inside the most beautiful building I'd ever seen. Even more spectacular than I'd thought after peering in through the windows. The wood of the ceiling, walls, and floors glowed golden in the soft light. A fire crackled in the stone pit; the scent of pine permeated the air. Candles had been lit on the altar, and soft flute music—J.P. music—played through a hidden sound system.

"Go on," Leila said, gently urging me deeper inside. "Welcome to Maggie's Longhouse."

I felt their eyes on me. I now understood what this place was. It wasn't a spa. It was far more sacred than that.

"Come," Phoebe said, taking my hand. Hers was surprisingly warm for a ghost. "Let's show you around."

We started at the lounge and bar area I'd spotted from the tree branch that day. A glass pitcher was filled with amber liquid. Leila poured three cups from it and handed one to me.

"Tea," she said.

"Please tell me it's not kuding."

"An all-around blend of herbals. You'll like it."

"A Chinese philosopher once said, if you drink enough tea, it will take away your thirst, loneliness, and troubles," Phoebe said. "It will make you lighter. It will give you wisdom from the ancestors. On your seventh cup, it will hurry your wings to a sacred island."

"Or to the nearest bathroom," I said.

Neither laughed at my joke.

"Anyway, drink up," Leila said.

We moved clockwise around the room, heading past the entry door and toward the far end—the area that had been hidden from me on my earlier reconnaissance mission. There were two enclosed rooms. In the first was a small soaking pool, blue as the sapphire pool near Mystic Falls, with water trickling into it over an artistically arranged jumble of rocks. Thinking about those geyser pools in the park, I asked how warm the water was.

"Ice cold," Phoebe said. Which told me exactly what I needed to hear: the other room contained a hot tub. Oh, how I couldn't wait to slip into hot water and soak.

A smaller stone pit was positioned just outside the door to the hot tub room, its fire burnt low but hot. Five large rocks the size of dinosaur eggs roasted in the flames.

"What's this?" I asked at the threshold, like a girl trying to act surprised at her birthday party.

"Go on, take a look," Leila said.

I peered in through the door, and in the shadows made out an igloo-shaped structure, not even as tall as I, covered with fur hides. An odd hot tub enclosure, for sure. I huddled down and squinted hard. Through the igloo's opening came the scent not of chlorine, as you'd expect from a hot tub, but of sweet sage.

"I'm confused," I said.

"It's a sweat lodge," Phoebe said.

"Are you ready?" Leila asked, a terry cloth robe in her hands. I wanted to say that no, I really wanted some of that pie. And no, my leg hurt and could I please have some meds? But asking for food or drugs somehow felt wrong in a place like this.

For the next couple of hours, I sat in the sweat lodge, sweating. Profusely sweating, to the point where several times I thought I'd faint. Or die. The first time, Phoebe accompanied me. She wore a gauzy dress, like something you'd see on an angel in a child's picture book, but before I went into the igloo structure, she took my robe. I stood there naked, one arm across my breasts and the other hand covering my pubic hair. She waved an eagle feather over my head and all around my body—smudging me, she said—and offered a prayer to the Great Spirit and Mother Earth. She told me how to enter the sweat lodge, and where and how to sit—Indian-style, which was a terribly vulnerable position given that I was naked. She told me to face west, toward the spirit world—and then she placed one of the red-hot dinosaur egg-rocks in the empty fire pit. When she ladled water from a nearby bucket onto the rock, steam hissed like a thousand snakes.

"You are in a spiritual sanctuary. You were brought here for healing and guidance. If you keep an open mind and heart, you will find the answers you seek."

How could this ghost woman know what answers I sought? Or that I sought any answers at all? Skeptical thoughts kept popping up, like why didn't Phoebe know that what I really wanted was pie? But Phoebe kept offering more and more prayers, accompanied by an occasional chant or tap on a drum. Eventually my annoying thoughts subsided, at which point she handed me those bear claws that had been hanging in Emily's guest room. They looked exactly like the one Max had given me: smooth, long, and wickedly sharp.

Then she invoked my spirit guide to be with us. My *wyakin*.

I kept my eyes closed and fingered the bear claws like meditation beads. My heart rate rose, and my breathing shallowed. As she prayed and chanted, my mind bounced from one thought to another, from visions of a growling grizzly bear to sepia images of my ancestors. I tried to imagine myself floating on clouds but felt more like I was becoming drenched in a rain forest. I thought about that teeny sandwich Leila had made for me. I thought about Delaney and her comment about how pretty I was in the walking boot. If she saw me now, naked and sweaty, she might think twice about that. When Palmer's baby Glock appeared in my mind, I pushed it away as fast as possible.

Thirty never-ending minutes later, Phoebe told me to take a break and dip into the cold water bath. I practically pushed her over as I dove through the animal hide flap that served as a door. I raced out of the sweat lodge, gasping for air, and flung my body into the cold-water pool.

The shock nearly gave me cardiac arrest.

"So the goal here is hypothermia?" I called out.

Phoebe didn't reply. She came along a few minutes later, completely straight-faced, and said it was time to get out. She offered me a tall glass of ice water, even though I was covered in goose bumps and resembled an uncooked turkey taken out of the fridge on Thanksgiving morning. Hot cocoa would have been much better, as far as I was concerned. After I drank the water under her watch, she led me back into the torture chamber for the second round. This time, she told me to crawl clockwise to my spot and invoke the spirits with my own voice. I had no idea what to say, and I felt foolish asking an absent grizzly bear and my dead ancestors for guidance.

She placed another rock in the center. It hissed. Steam rose. Sure I would suffocate, I looked for a ventilation hole in the ceiling and discovered there wasn't one. No wonder I felt so light-headed.

Phoebe sat across from me with her eyes closed. I didn't understand why she was there—and not Leila. Leila would have known how hard this was for me. Self-pity engulfed me during this second round. I was in pain. I was beside myself with hunger and thirst. I felt betrayed, forcibly exposed to this stranger. All the while, Phoebe's prayers kept coming, louder and louder, as if she wanted to drown out my petty ruminations. By the end of this round, she had nearly won; I had joined in with her, chanting to a spirit from the north for courage, strength, and endurance.

I was also breathing more deeply and slowly, and sweating less.

Altogether, there were four rounds, each one lasting about a half hour, with a trip to the cold pool and a glass of ice water in between. More rocks, roasted with each round, more prayers offered. We prayed for knowledge and wisdom in the third round and for healing in the final round. By the end, I had grown to love the sound of Phoebe's prayers, her voice a flute humming softly at the low end of a treble scale. I had learned how to corral my thoughts. I felt safe there with her, safer than I'd ever been with anyone—even Leila. I felt as if I'd crawled back into my mother's womb. It was an experience wholly unlike any of the times I'd tried to meditate.

When Phoebe opened the flap for the last time, I didn't want to leave the volcanic rocks, or the sweat lodge, or any part of the experience. I didn't even want to leave Phoebe.

"Already?" I asked.

"Yes, already," she said. "Be sure to drink plenty of water."

Leila was waiting at the cold-water bath. I stepped into the water slowly now, more comfortable with my nakedness than ever before.

"What just happened?" I asked after submerging myself and then resurfacing. "At first I thought you were torturing me. I felt sorry for myself and mad at you. But I had all these weird thoughts and visions, and by the end I felt totally...at peace. Like I've been transported to some strange otherworld. Either that or I've taken some major hallucinogenic drugs. Was there something in that tea?"

"What happened is not meant to be explained," Leila said. "What happened is sacred, and different for everyone. Now just honor and accept it and go forward from here. But you're not quite done."

Curious, I stepped out from the water. Something felt different, but I couldn't figure out what it was. In fact, everything felt so different that I couldn't imagine what else could possibly lie in store. I wrapped myself in a fluffy robe, and Leila asked if I'd like her to braid my wet hair. This time, I accepted her offer. When she was done, Phoebe brought a piece of her pie, which I wolfed down.

"I could have used a bite of pie before all that," I said, my mouth still full. "Why did I have to wait?"

"It's more effective if you fast first. You find clarity earlier and more completely," Phoebe said.

"That's why you only gave me a smackerel of sandwich?" I asked Leila. She nodded.

After a second helping, they led me to the altar at the opposite end of the lodge. Above the altar hung what appeared to be a multigenerational portrait.

Seated in the middle was a very old, wrinkled woman—an Indian woman wearing a tan buckskin dress with a fringed hem, much like the one in Emily's trunk. In her arms, she held a sleeping newborn with a head of thick, black hair. Standing to her right was a woman of thirty or so with a violet silk blouse and a black pleated skirt, belted at the waist. And to the old woman's left was another elderly woman, not quite as old as the one in the center, her face also wrinkled, her hands freckled with age spots. She shared the same dark eyes as the other three, but her hair was brilliant red, and her skin porcelain white. I couldn't take my eyes off of her.

"That's my great-grandmother," Leila said.

"A redhead?"

"All families have genetic surprises. And now, no more secrets for you. Here's the story: Emily believed Maggie, her grandmother, was raped during the Nez Perce flight by a redheaded white man. That woman you see in the portrait, the one with the red hair, was Emily's mother. Jennie."

"Oh, dear God," I said, unsure what else to say. I couldn't help but wonder about my own ancestry and the coincidence that I had red hair too, and whether somehow, many generations ago, my relatives were related to the villain who raped Maggie. I couldn't help but feel guilt on behalf of him and all redheads, and on behalf of all white people for that matter, for what was done to Maggie and all the American Indians.

Leila took my hand. "Emily used to say that wartime rape has been around since the beginning of time. I think she was right; it's still happening, and it always will until we hold not just the individuals but also military organizations responsible. But Emily also used to say that, despite the pain it caused Maggie, future generations wouldn't have been alive if not for the rape. That didn't justify the rape. But it was always important to her that we honored Jennie, no matter her origin. And that we carry out Anne and Maggie's mission."

"Is Maggie's Place then primarily a place for victims of sexual assault?"

"No," Leila said. "We've been through this, Brooke. Maggie's Place isn't for any one type of woman. It's simply a place where women can feel free to be themselves and connect. Maggie believed that women provide compassion and understanding to one another in a way that men do not. Only through our uplifting support, regardless of background or current circumstances, can we be whole. Some women have come here periodically to recharge. Others, like Phoebe, have stayed for years. It's a place that offers whatever a woman needs. But yes, it also assures protection. Maggie believed that women are the protectors of life, and they deserve to feel safe, no matter what. Which is why she set this up as a place without men."

We stood there, side by side, studying the portrait for several minutes.

"And that's Emily." Leila pointed to the woman in violet. "Look at that hairdo."

Emily's hair was shoulder length and flipped up all the way around. "Circa 1960?"

"Close. The portrait was painted in 1958. The year Ruth was born."

"I still don't understand why you inherited this place. Instead of Ruth. I don't mean to be cruel, but she was Emily's child. Her blood relation."

"Aunt Ruth will always have a place here. But she's happy in Idaho, and she wanted me to have it. For my girls, someday, I think. Also, bloodline didn't matter to Emily or Ruth. 'Blood doesn't make the family. Love does.' That's what Emily used to say."

"So if that's Jennie," I said, pointing to the portrait. "And that's Emily, and that's baby Ruth…who's the old woman?"

"I'll give you one guess," Leila said.

"No. It can't be. Seriously?"

She nodded, grinning like a proud little girl.

"Wow," I said, incapable of any intelligent response to being in the presence of greatness, the same as when I'd first walked into the longhouse and the same as how some people feel when they walk into an old cathedral. Maggie was right there before me in that portrait. In her old buckskin dress. I felt an overwhelming urge to kneel.

Phoebe came up behind us and placed her hands on Leila's shoulders. "Come. It's getting late and we still have work to do."

She led us back to the center of the longhouse and gestured for us to be seated among the pillows around the stone fire pit. We sat facing one another and holding hands.

Kumbaya? I nearly asked. But this time I thought better of it and withheld my sarcasm.

"So here's the deal," Leila said. "Ruth and I have decided to not sell the property. And Phoebe has agreed to stay on as caretaker. But she needs help. She can't do it all herself." She squeezed my hand. "I know you don't want to go home, Brooke. And I realize you don't know what you want, really. But for now, Phoebe and Ruth and I would be grateful if you'd stay here. For as long as you'd like."

I hadn't seen this coming. I squeezed both of their hands. I was flattered. I was deeply touched. But this created an entirely new complication for me. This would mean I wouldn't be moving to Jackson for a while.

"Wow."

"You don't need to make any decisions tonight," Leila said, clearly aware I was flummoxed. "Sleep on it."

I was, indeed, too tired to think. I'd been waffling between Portland and Jackson, and now West Yellowstone was back on the table. I'd already told that artist in Jackson I thought I'd be moving there soon. She'd said she couldn't wait to photograph my scars. Her macabre desires, it appeared, would have to wait.

Phoebe produced a pile of fleece blankets and a couple of down pillows for me.

"Here? You want me to sleep here?"

After the incident with Palmer, and all the animal and ancestor spirits milling about, I wasn't sure how I felt about spending the night there alone.

"Phoebe will stay with you if you'd like," Leila said. "Oh, and here. Don't forget to look at these." She handed me the box of Emily's letters, which she'd presented to me at J.P.'s cabin.

After we said good night, Phoebe helped me get comfortable. As she did, I realized what had been different when I'd stepped out of the pool. My leg no longer hurt.

I fell asleep beside the fire, beneath the pile of blankets. The rest of my night was filled with bizarre Technicolor dreams. First, I was in the Wild West with Maggie and Anne, a baby Glock in my holster. Shane and Hamlin were there, too. In another dream, Jennie and I had our hair done in silly matching up-do's. A she-bear charged at me in another. The Wizard of Oz, and bulldozers chasing modern-times women and children across a prairie of wild grasses, were in others. I woke up in the wee morning hours perspiring, my heart beating so hard I considered calling 9-1-1 again.

And then came the nightmare after I fell back asleep. Delaney was an Indian girl, and I was her white mother, and it started as another ordinary nonsensical dream with buffaloes and cell phones—until a platoon of Gulf War soldiers showed up. One of them grabbed my daughter and threw her to the ground. I tried to pull him off but fellow soldiers held me back. I was forced to listen first to the ripping of her clothes and then to her screams for help. Once more a gigantic bear appeared. She stood on top of me, the full weight of her body pressing all the air out of my lungs. I could no longer shout. I couldn't even take a single breath. She opened her mouth wide—so wide she could easily have taken my entire head into her great jaws—and bellowed a pathetic, sorrowful cry.

TWENTY-EIGHT

Brooke

I WOKE FROM the dream, still in the longhouse, surrounded by pillows and blankets. The fire was now cold, its ashes black and gray. Row's face hovered over mine, her slippery drool dangling from her mouth and one paw on my chest. I navigated my way back to consciousness, first detecting the fragrance of syrup and melted butter and then noticing…Delaney! I couldn't imagine why she was there, and for a fleeting moment I thought this was just another dream. She looked so content there—almost angelic, her arms wrapped around her knees, waiting for me. I closed my eyes and opened them again. She was still there.

"Delaney?" Before I knew why, salty tears began to flow.

"Mom? Mom! What's wrong?"

"Nothing," I said, reaching out for her, laughing while I cried. She leaned in toward me, and Row was still holding her ground, so it turned into a three-way group hug, with each of us crying and laughing and slobbering over one another. The scent of pancakes will probably always remind me of that moment.

When we disentangled ourselves, I started to rise, and again noticed a void where the pain had been for all those weeks. Again I doubted whether I was truly awake, unsure of what was real and what wasn't. I pressed my eyes closed tightly, and wondered if, in truth, the bear had taken off my leg and all this rehab had just been one long dream. Or if all this time I'd had phantom pain, like soldiers whose legs are blown off in battle, and finally that had subsided. That image made me recall that horrible last dream with Delaney, and I shivered. Reluctantly then, I opened my eyes and looked down. My leg was still there. Absolutely free of pain, like a brand new leg. And my daughter was still there, too.

She handed a plate of pancakes to me, oblivious to how peculiar I felt after a strange and exhausting night of sweat and chants, cold baths, and perplexing dreams. As she knelt beside me, I wrapped my arms around her once again and squeezed so hard that the pancakes nearly slipped off the plate. She whispered for me to please let go. I did, unwillingly, and then took a bite of food. Leila's culinary talents did not disappoint. As I ate, Delaney explained how she'd traveled to West Yellowstone so quickly—a flurry of flights and ride-shares—and she confessed that now she was pretty much out of money. That, of course, assured me once and for all that I was no longer dreaming. I told her to have some tea. "Phoebe says it will make you wise."

"Does it work?"

"We have a lot to talk about," I said. "But I think it works. I'm seeing things much differently today."

Leila walked in, her perfect timing seemingly scripted. Her hair hung long and wet from her morning shower. As she presented us with the second course—a platter of cheesy eggs and the bottle of secret sauce—she asked how I was feeling.

"Marvelous. And weird. I don't know what happened yesterday. I don't know what happened last night. The pain is gone, and I feel lighter, but I also feel really odd inside. I can't explain it. Is that normal?"

She reached toward me and ran her hand gently down the scarred side of my face. "It'll take some time, but you'll make sense of it all before too long."

"I had really weird dreams. They were terrifying but, in a bizarre way, comforting. Do they mean something?"

She shook her head. "You're the only one who knows."

It seemed I knew nothing. Or maybe I knew everything. All that had happened with Palmer, with the sweat lodge, and even with those dreams seemed to be a perfectly orchestrated message from the universe that I couldn't decipher. I was at peace. I was a blank slate. It was both uplifting and unnerving to feel that way, especially on this last morning for Leila and me. I couldn't figure out if I wanted to scream or dance or sit cross-legged and chant *om* all day long.

The tip of my nose began to tingle; my eyes began to water again. I wanted to impress that image of Leila—sitting beside me in her pink tank top and sweatpants, her black hair trailing over her shoulders, her eyes locked onto mine—into my mind forever.

"Here, try this on your eggs," I said to Delaney, handing her the bottle of sauce and changing the subject for my own sanity. Nothing like food to get your mind off the tough stuff. "There's something mysterious in it. Leila won't tell me what it is. Maybe you can figure it out."

Delaney poured a drop onto her finger and licked it.

"Yum. It's juniper berry, Mom."

"Juniper berry?"

"Gin. Mixed with hot sauce. Right?" She turned to Leila for confirmation.

I poured the sauce onto my finger and tasted. "My underage daughter is a hundred percent right," I said.

Phoebe, who now stood in the doorway wearing an old peasant blouse and denim skirt and holding a pot of coffee and a stack of mugs, laughed out loud. The joke was definitely on me.

"It's awesome," Delaney said, grinning first at Leila and then at me as she doused her eggs with the sauce. I took the bottle from her and generously sprinkled it onto my own eggs. What the hell? I thought. How drunk could one get on eggs? Besides, I was off my meds and never felt better, thanks—I was certain—to the magic of the sweat lodge.

Leila sat down beside me. I asked if she thought Palmer told the truth about killing the bears. She saw the worry in my face and did her best to convince me it was all part of his delusion. Then she picked up the box of Emily's letters. "Did you have a chance to look at these last night?"

I mustered the courage to look directly at my beloved caretaker and friend, hoping I wouldn't fall apart right there in a new wave of tears and grief. I wanted to climb into her arms, even into her dark eyes, and stay there forever.

"I fell asleep last night. I'm sorry. I'll look at them later today, if that's all right."

"No worries, no hurries. But you should read them someday. You'll learn more about Anne and Maggie, and their relationship, as well as the plight of Maggie's people in those times, and the plight of women. They almost read like a novel when you follow them one after the other."

"Did they ever get together again?" I asked.

She waggled her index finger at me. "You'll have to read them to find out."

I whined that she wasn't being fair.

"What I *will* tell you," Leila said, "is that—if you haven't already figured it out—some of Emily's books, and that painting of bison above the sofa, were gifts from Anne. She sent them to Maggie years after she went back to Chicago."

"She left Maggie?"

"She was taken against her will. By her husband."

"I don't know anything about Maggie or Anne, but being kidnapped by your husband has got to be ugly," Delaney said.

"And heartbreaking," I said.

"Yes, it was," Leila said. "Ugly *and* heartbreaking."

She held out the box to me. I took it as if it were a newborn baby and gently laid it on my lap. Delaney leaned over, curious, gently running one finger along the edge. I briefly explained who Anne and Maggie were, and what the box contained.

Leila also produced the bear claw Max had given me. "I found this in your room and thought you might like it."

Delaney held out her hand. "Is that real? Awesome."

Leila placed the claw in Delaney's palm.

"By the way, I'm leaving the trunk for you, too," Leila said. "You were right; it belongs here." I had been holding my emotions together like fabric scraps basted loosely with thin thread, and when she placed her hand on mine, the thread failed and the scraps fell apart. I started crying all over again.

"Wow. This is so cool, Mom. Everything about this is place is incredible," Delaney said.

I took a long, deep breath. I exhaled it ever so slowly, as Phoebe had taught me the night before in the sweat lodge. It's hard to believe you have to be *taught* how to breathe. But you do. I scratched Row on the top of her head. "Yep. This place, and everyone here, is incredible."

I felt all eyes on me then, and I tried to contain my emotions long enough to say something. Anything.

"Thank you," I said to Leila.

After that, I didn't know what else to say. I hadn't consciously decided what my answer to her was going to be; I didn't know what my future might hold if I stayed there, or what it might hold if I moved on to Jackson or somewhere else. But images of a future Maggie's Place fast-forwarded in my mind: Phoebe tending the grounds, women walking alone or in pairs—in comfortable clothes and *sans* makeup—a toddler chasing the grumpy old cat. And a young woman who looked a lot like Delaney welcoming a newcomer on Emily's porch. The scenes blurred past too quickly to make sense of them, and I didn't see myself in those images, but nevertheless they somehow contributed to the one, maybe the only, thing I did know with absolute certainty at that moment: I felt wholly, unconditionally supported and loved in that place, a feeling I couldn't remember ever having had before. I also knew then that this was an experience I wanted my daughter to have, and one I wanted to share with other women who might show up at Maggie's Place someday, too—women who were black or white, Indian or African, young or old, gay or straight. Women who carried their own stories of sorrow and loss. Women who, like me, needed a special place to heal.

So, for the time being, I decided to stay.

GRATITUDE

Although writing is a mostly solitary endeavor, it's inspired by every day of life. As such, a page like this should be devoted to every person who made a mark on my life, no matter how big or small that mark might have been—or how good or bad—during the many years it took for this novel to finally see the light of day. But how long and tedious such a page would be!

So I will instead be brief, but I must start at the top: I'm grateful for Planet Earth and all her creatures. If only we could all learn to be kinder to her.

More directly, deep thanks to the numerous experts who offered guidance in my research, especially those Yellowstone National Park employees who took the time to share their expertise about grizzlies, the park's history, and medical evacuation practices.

I'm extremely grateful to my friend and first reader Christine Z. Mason, my editors Glenys Loewen-Thomas and Jennifer D. Munro, and my husband John—who lovingly endures all the exuberance, doubt, commitment, and angst that have become integral to my writing life. A loving shout-out to my sons, too: Dylan, Forrest, and Harrison.

A note of recognition to the Plums, a collection of friends from eons ago. You unwittingly inspired Maggie's Place one weekend in the Columbia River Gorge. Without you, this book would not have taken the shape it did.

Finally, let me not forget my readers. Thank you for trusting your precious time with me.

AUTHOR'S NOTE

This is a work of fiction. If you think you see yourself in these pages, that's on you. These characters were invented by me. But of course, some of them were inspired by people, events, and circumstances in real life that deeply moved me, one way or another. If you inspired me to write any portion of this book, congratulations.

Ursus arctos horribilis

The grizzly bear, an animal that has fascinated me for as long as I can remember, was my earliest inspiration for this novel. I respect its strength. I admire its lumbering grace. I relate to its preference for solitude. I also feel a sisterly kinship with the mother grizzly and how she fiercely protects her cubs. Today there are somewhere between 700 and 1,000 grizzlies in the continental United States, most of whom live in the greater Yellowstone region. Although they're considered "of least concern" on the official endangered species list, they're still at great risk. Their favorite snacks, the cutthroat trout and the highly nutritious whitebark pine seed, are getting harder to find thanks to climate change and anglers who introduced non-native species to the area. Their territories are diminishing as a result of land development. And the likelihood they'll be able to increase in number is remote, given that grizzlies are naturally slow to reproduce and hunting them is legal in some states.

I visited the Washington State University Bear Center for Research, Education, and Conservation in 2015, where I stood within inches of live grizzlies and where scientists study the grizzly's nutrition, ecology, physiology, behavior, reproduction, and cognitive skills. From their research, the scientists learn not only about the bears but also about humans. The more they learn, the more they see how the bear is not that different from Homo sapiens. Understanding bears can ultimately help us. For example, bears are able to retain bone density during sedentary hibernation, and understanding how this works could lead to important breakthroughs in helping sedentary humans remain stronger. Also, bears are important to the ecosystem. By eating fish that swim upstream from oceans, bears help move nutrients from the oceans to inland soils. The shrinking bear population, therefore, can have a detrimental impact on our entire ecosystem in the same way the near eradication of wolves or the shrinking population of resident killer whales have also changed the environment at large.

While I visited with one of the scientists, my oldest son engaged with one of the female bears, and she was equally curious about him, stretching her five-inch claws under the fence to gently touch the tips of his fingers. Nearby, two young cubs scrambled with each other in play. Later we toured the rest of the facility, and when we came to a door with a small window in its center, I stopped to peer in. There stood Frank, a large male grizzly. His fur was chocolate brown. His head was huge, his snout long. But he wasn't terrifying. In fact, it seemed that, when his eyes met mine, we connected with one another, not as predator and prey but as two living, sentient souls. Even as I was grateful he was helping scientists with their research, I wanted to open the door to his cage and set him free.

I grieve for Frank and for all the grizzlies struggling for survival, and for the tens of thousands of grizzly bears who have already died needlessly at the hands of mankind. I'd like to say I hope we'll come to our senses and learn to appreciate this remarkable creature—and protect it rather than destroy it—but such a hope would most likely be unfounded.

Nimi'ipuu

The story of the Nez Perce is a tragic one, like so many stories about indigenous people around the world whose circumstances tug on my heartstrings. By the mid-nineteenth century, white trappers and settlers had begun their migration west across what is now the continental United States. Although their spirit of adventure is glorified in many a history book or novel, the fact is that they, along with military men and missionaries, wreaked a great deal of havoc among the people who were already living in these lands. In 1855, the United States government signed a treaty with the Nez Perce, requiring them to deed over the 17 million acres in Idaho and Oregon they called home. In exchange, the government promised to set aside a 7.5 million-acre reservation and to offer the Indians a new lifestyle that included education, a different religion, and medicine. But before the treaty was even ratified, the reservation land was overtaken by white settlers, miners, and explorers. The government then downsized the reservation to roughly 750,000 acres. This did not make the Nez Perce happy.

So when the military tried to round them up, some of them basically said thanks, but no thanks. Instead, they packed up their families and belongings, left their homeland in eastern Oregon, and traveled east. Reports vary about how many were in this group, but it was probably about 800 people. The rest of their story foreshadowed many of the refugee stories we hear today: they faced incredible hardship, many died along the way, and those who survived had to accept a way of life far different from the one to which they were accustomed or the one they'd sought.

The saga is heart-wrenching, especially when one looks at the type of people the Nez Perce were. A peaceful and cooperative nation, they were known for salmon-fishing, horsemanship, music, storytelling, and hospitality. Like many other native people, they valued the earth and all its creatures. Contrary to the name assigned to them by French explorers, they did not customarily pierce their noses. The Nez Perce actually call themselves the *Nimi'ipuu*. Although I found various spellings of this name in the literature, I have deferred to the spelling used on the Nez Perce official website, http://www.nezperce.org/Official/Nimiipuu.htm.

I decided to set *Bear Medicine* against the Nez Perce story in part because it's a critical piece of history in the Yellowstone region, but also because native spirituality, in general, inspires me with its unique perspective about both the environment and personal growth—a perspective that ultimately helped Anne and Brooke find what they were looking for, and a perspective that I believe could help many of us, individually and collectively, in finding greater peace.

I wrestled with how to refer to the Nez Perce (or other people of color) in this novel when not using the *nimi'ipuu* name. During the nineteenth century—and well into the twentieth century—whites generally referred to native people as Indians, Injuns, or savages. They also often referred to African Americans as Negroes. Today, many whites use the term Native American for people of American tribal descent, but I've learned that some native people prefer the term American Indian over Native American because the latter can refer to anyone born in the Americas. My goal in this novel was to use the terminology most appropriate for the characters in question and the time period in which they lived, so in the end the terminology varies. It is my sincere hope that I haven't offended anyone with the choices I, and my characters, have made.

Women and abuse

This is clearly a book about women in search of self—a quest I believe has been universal for the female gender since the beginning of time and which certainly has been an ongoing, decades-long challenge for me. One could argue that finding one's identity is a universal search for all people, but women, and especially women of color, have had to deal with this question not only as an existential matter but as a real-life issue because so many others have tried to tell us who we are or who we should be. We have been treated as second-class citizens throughout civilization, and we still are to this day in many countries—both those that are still developing and those that consider themselves part of the first world. Except for a select few, women have also been largely ignored in our history books because our traditional roles, and the innate gifts of care and compassion that we bring to humankind, have been deemed to be of lesser value than roles that generate money or power—or that destroy the lives of others.

Along with the search for self—and for equality, of course—women have been struggling with psychological and physical abuse since the beginning of time. I'm grateful that physical abuse is on our society's radar nowadays, although it has by no means been adequately addressed or eradicated, and psychological abuse continues to impact women to an alarming degree. Whether it's a male presidential candidate looming behind his female competitor, or a husband undermining his wife's decisions or dreams, the effect of such behavior can be powerfully damaging. Moreover, women don't always recognize psychological abuse for what it is. And even when they do, it can be much harder to prove and remediate.

We clearly need more women in leadership positions. We certainly need to continue to educate boys about respect. We absolutely need grown men to model appropriate respectful behavior toward women. And, overall, we need to continue to generate awareness about the existence and insidious nature of abuse, because it's only through awareness that problems like this can ultimately be identified and addressed.

If you enjoyed *Bear Medicine*, please consider writing a brief review on Goodreads or wherever you purchased the book online. If you'd like to sign up for my newsletter, visit my website at www.gekretchmer.com.

ABOUT THE AUTHOR

G. Elizabeth Kretchmer grew up in Chicago, but yearned for the mountains and oceans throughout her childhood. She has lived up and down the West Coast for most of her adult life and now calls the Pacific Northwest her home. She holds an MFA in Fiction from Pacific University, and her short work has appeared in *The New York Times* along with other publications. When she's not writing, she's facilitating wellness-writing workshops, advocating for the environment, or working on her organic farm. Learn more about her at www.gekretchmer.com.

ABOUT THE ARTIST

Born and raised in Wyoming, Julia Hayes-Siltzer is an award-winning artist whose work can be found in regional galleries and field guides. She is currently studying for a Bachelor of Fine Arts degree at the University of Wyoming and hopes to design a career that merges art, traveling, teaching, and activism—particularly pertaining to domestic abuse and violence. Aside from art in all its various forms, she has a passion for growing exotic houseplants and listening to Duran Duran.

THE DAMNABLE LEGACY

Chapter One

LYNN VAN SWOL faced the lone gray wolf with a cold stare, mirroring the animal's own haunting gaze and confirming what I'd known all along. She was comfortable in wild territory, composed in the face of danger, unencumbered by fear. And she wasn't even fifty yet. In other words, she would be the perfect grandmother for a troubled teen like Frankie.

But there was much to be done before that day would come. For now, Lynn needed to get past this gorgeous and terrifying fur-clad adversary. When she first spotted it, she stopped immediately, probably assuming—as I had—that it was someone's dog whose owner would soon appear on the trail as well. But it only took a couple of heartbeats for me to realize this was no average dog.

It was a she-wolf, standing in the middle of Lynn's favorite running trail in the heart of Portland's West Hills, which wasn't exactly wolf territory. Its fur was thick and wet, mottled in shades of silver and gray, with a hint of brown at the base of the fur; its legs were long, its paws huge. And the eyes were a piercing, hungry shade of amber. A numbing April rain slanted at both Lynn and the wolf like pinpoint darts as they studied one another, sizing up the situation, neither of them showing a speck of fear. From what I knew, wolves don't want to be seen by humans; they might follow you from the shadows, lurking like cancer cells, but they're unlikely to come right out in the open. And most people will naturally experience a rush of fear in the face of a dangerous beast. But this must not have been your typical wolf, and Lynn was surely not a normal person. This was no doubt just another ho-hum instance of woman versus nature for Lynn. Another day to be patient, logical, calm.

Of course, we climbers are trained to be patient, logical, and calm. And when it comes right down to it, climbers and wolves have a lot in common. Both wait for opportunity. Likewise, it only takes one wrong move to ruin the plans of climber or wolf. I had big plans for Lynn that I'd set into motion before my death, and now that I watched from the safe distance of my empty afterlife, there would be nothing I could do to change those plans if the wolf interfered. All I could do was hope for the best.

A twig snapped somewhere. The animal's nose twitched. I don't know what it detected—I smelled only musky, wet fur. It lifted its nose upward and for a moment I thought it sensed my presence. But of course it couldn't do that; I knew by now I was invisible to the living. The wolf took a few steps forward, so that it stood only a few yards from Lynn.

It was time for Lynn to take charge. She slipped the straps of her cinch bag off her shoulders and pulled out a Clif Bar. When she ripped the package open, the scent of peanut butter and chocolate erased the smell of wet fur and tantalized me. The wolf, too, apparently. It sniffed the air again and perked its ears. It licked its lips. What did Lynn think she was doing? For a slick second, I decided she was insane, until she flung the bar into the forest. The wolf startled, and I figured this was the end.

They both watched the food's trajectory, then returned their gazes upon one another. The wolf took another step toward Lynn.

"Okay, then let's try this," she said, her voice strong, steady, and deep, not wavering in the slightest.

After retrieving a polyurethane bottle from her bag, she took a long swig of water—another luxury of the living—while keeping her gaze directly on the wolf's eyes. I wondered if that was the right thing to do. With some animals, you're supposed to avoid any such exchange, even a glance.

"You're probably going to destroy this," she said to the wolf. "But here you go anyway." She turned away from the animal and hurled the bottle into the forest in the same direction as the Clif Bar, her pitch athletic and firm. The bottle thwacked against the trunk of a Douglas fir, then ricocheted off. "Now go on," she said. "Go on!"

When the wolf lunged, I nearly fell back in fright. But it headed away from Lynn, into the dense brush to sniff out its prize. Lynn watched for a moment and then, seemingly unfazed, picked up her cinch bag and hung it from her shoulders. She licked the sticky residue of the energy bar off her fingers and began to run again, in the same direction she'd been heading all along. She didn't turn back, not even once, to see if the wolf followed.

WOMEN ON THE BRINK

Alligator Poetry

I LAY SPRAWLED across my new king-sized Ralph Lauren duvet—another gift from Hugh—trying to figure out why Sylvia Plath chose the oven and Virginia Woolf decided to drown, and also where on earth Charlotte Perkins Gilman even found chloroform. Meanwhile, the phone rang: more pleas for money.

I liked giving my husband's money away. I also enjoyed talking to the telephone solicitors, most of the time. But not today. Today I felt like that woman in Ezra Pound's poem who was *dying piecemeal of a sort of emotional anemia*. What if *I* committed suicide? What if I, like Virginia Woolf, just disappeared one day? Would anyone even care? Sometimes I wondered if I was going mad when these thoughts, and the darker ones beneath them, ambushed me. They were mean little SOBs, these thoughts. Opportunistic predators.

It was that nasty e-mail from my younger sister Veronica that got me riled up this time, a venomous missive that pinched nearly as badly as those real pinches from forever ago when we shared a small bedroom, adorned with frilly lavender bedspreads and curtains. Every night after the lights were turned out, Veronica would reach across from her twin bed to mine and pinch the skin of my forearm so hard it would make me cry. Mother always said Ronnie was jealous of me, but I never understood why.

And now, four decades later, the jealousy—and the pinch—hurt as badly as ever, but Mother was no longer around for comfort, so on days like this I turned to the likes of Woolf and Plath for whatever pitiful solace they had to offer. Which wasn't much. I rolled over and woke up my laptop to reread the e-mail thread. First, the one I'd sent to Veronica.

From: Gillian Blake-Moore
Subject: We're Disappearing
Date: September 18 2:27:13 PM PDT
To: Veronica Berg

Ronnie,

I just read another article about the disappearing middle class, and I'm so sick of all this. It sounds like we're just going to be Photoshopped out of life. Deleted. Poof! One day we're here, the next day we're gone.

Here's a link for you if you feel like getting depressed. www.broadviewreporter.com/tag/disappearing-middle-class.hi52587.htm

Speaking of depression, I've been thinking about you all day and figure you must be beyond your wits. Was Sissy really suspended? Well tell her Aunt Gillian says she'd better snap herself into shape. Or else.

I'm reminded of a Kenneth Koch poem, *One Train May Hide Another*. Here's a line for you to think about while you're dealing with life's woes:

"When you come to something, stop to let it pass
So you can see what else is there."

Hugs,
Gillian

What was wrong with that? But here's what my beloved sister wrote in reply.

From: Veronica Berg
Subject: We're Disappearing BUT YOU'RE NOT
Date: September 18 2:41:10 PM PDT
To: Gillian Blake-Moore

Gillian, obviously you won't be poofed out of anywhere! I immediately read that article you sent (although I have far more pressing concerns) and the writer made it perfectly clear that anyone earning more than $250,000 will be just fine through all this financial mumbo jumbo! Which, of course, means you. (Don't try to tell me Hugh doesn't make that much; I know for a fact he rakes in a lot more than that.) So please at least call a spade a spade. <u>You're not middle class!</u>

If you're worried about me, say so, and I'll tell you thanks but no thanks. Please just don't try to pretend you're still one of us. When was the last time you made chicken soup from a carcass to stretch through the week?

Veronica was so tense these days! I was just trying to help, to let her know I'm here for her, to listen or maybe even offer financial advice. And while my husband did indeed earn an embarrassingly large salary, I certainly didn't think of our family as *rich*. Upper middle class at best. More importantly, I thought of myself as the same person I was way back when, just a simple middle class gal from the Hoosier state, and I didn't see why Veronica couldn't think of me that way, too.

On a more important matter (from my perspective, at least), you haven't heard the half of our problems! While I was out on the back porch talking to Legal Aid about Sissy getting caught with pot, that damn daughter of mine vanished. Ran off with her backpack, that anthology of poems you sent her last year, and those awful big black boots she wears everywhere. All gone. Just like that. Lingerie: gone. Socks: gone. Of course she left her school books strewn across her desk. And she didn't even leave a note. So I'm sorry to report that I won't be able to share your "concern" (or was it a threat?) with her.

Sorry to sound so harsh. I'm just so stressed. This is the sort of crap those of us who live in the <u>real world</u> have to deal with. We don't have time to get depressed.

By the way, stop sending us poetry.
V.

Well, well. Of course Veronica's life was challenging. But did I really deserve to be dumped upon like this? And what was that comment about not sending poetry anymore? Was Veronica the only one who had the right to read or share or discuss poetry, just because she was an English teacher? Or was she somehow blaming me for Sissy running away, since she took the book I had sent her? Here we were, two sisters living thousands of miles apart, each one still derailing the other, whether intentionally or not. It felt like our relationship was becoming more and more diluted, like a cube of bouillon dissipating in a pot of boiling water.

I heard something, and when I sat up and looked out the picture window, I discovered what it was. Seattle raindrops were plinking off the surface of our swimming pool down below. I hoped Rosa would remember to shut all the windows before leaving. I lay back down and tried to recall the words from that Rachel Wetzsteon poem. The only line I for sure remembered was about petals scattering in the wind, "like versions of myself I was on the verge of becoming." What was it that I had been on the verge of becoming before marriage and children and wealth? I couldn't remember any more.

Jackson. That's what I could do. Write to my brother. Maybe he would explain what was going on with Veronica.

> From: Gillian Blake-Moore
> Subject: Veronica
> Date: September 18 2:50:53 PM PDT
> To: Jackson Blake
>
> Hey bro,
>
> How are you? I'm sorry I haven't been in touch lately! We have just been so busy, what with Henry's college apps and Sarah's application to the National Youth Orchestra and little Mulu Ken's soccer games every weekend. Hugh's been traveling a ton, too, mostly back and forth to South America. Oh, how I wish I could go with him, but there's just so much to do.

That last line was a lie; I had no desire to travel or do much of anything these days. And I really wasn't all that busy, either; Henry and Sarah had reached that age where they didn't seem to need a mother anymore. But Jackson didn't need to know these truths.

I'm worried about Veronica and thought you might know what's going on. Obviously Sissy's a big part of the problem; did you know she's run away? I feel like picking up the phone and calling our sister, but no matter what I say or do I always seem to upset her. Have you noticed the same?

I've been thinking about you and Wanda a lot lately, too, and wish I lived closer so I could help out. How are Wanda's treatments going? Please give her my love and tell her I suggest she read Joan Halperin's poem, *Diagnosis*. She might find it comforting to know she's not alone.

Also, I'm wondering if you'd like me to send you a link to an article about the disappearing middle class. I already sent it to Veronica.

Hugs from your big sis,
Gillian

I decided to haul myself off the bed and face the day before the kids got home from school. Making my way down the curved stairway step by step, I absentmindedly trailed my fingers along the cherry balustrade and instinctively checked for dust. I think I was subconsciously hoping that, for just this once, there'd be something wrong or dirty or out of place around here. But of course there wasn't, and for a fleeting second I looked around to see what I might do to upset this little world of perfection. I stopped momentarily, on the fourth step down, and gazed out through the foyer's arch-shaped window, through the gray drizzle and over the rooftops of the lower elevation, smaller houses to the crowded highways and the lines of school buses. My children would not be on those buses.

Why? Because they had always *refused* to ride them. I didn't understand why; they were perfectly adequate methods of transportation when I was a school girl. But my children wanted me to drive them to and from school, and while I didn't like their propensity toward snobbishness, I did, for the most part, delight in the role of mother-chauffeur-slave. It meant I got to spend more time with them. Until Henry turned sixteen.

Hugh had insisted on getting our son a BMW, overruling my desire to have our children live like normal kids. Then Henry—a child who always had craved responsibility—insisted on driving himself and the other kids to and from school ever since. So I got fired from that job.

In fact, Henry and Sarah were doing so much for themselves these days that I sometimes felt like I was slacking off. It was as though my little family's universe had shifted but still remained in holistic balance. And while some parents can't wait until their kids aren't as needy as they once were, I was having the opposite problem. I was bored. I had become a human vacuum, wandering through this hazy thing called life.

I started to recall Charlotte Perkins Gilman's words, right before she'd killed herself. *When all usefulness is over*—until I was interrupted.

"Goodbye, Miss Gillian!"

Rosa's call, echoing from somewhere else in our sparkling, cavernous house, brought me back to my right mind, thankfully before I missed a step and tumbled to the marble foyer floor and—what? Before I tumbled to the marble foyer floor and killed myself? Maybe it would have been a blessing.

"See you tomorrow!" Rosa called again.

"Wait!" I called, and I hurried down the rest of the steps, but by the time I made it all the way down the hall to the mud room, which never had a trace of mud in it either, Rosa was already out the door.

That's the trouble with such a big house: You can't even say a proper goodbye.

It wasn't that I was ungrateful; sometimes I just longed for that little two-bedroom house where I grew up in the Midwest, even if it did have Formica countertops instead of slab granite, and linoleum floors instead of hardwood and marble. Even if I did have to share a bedroom with Veronica. At least we could find one another.

I stood at the window and watched Rosa backing her rusty little Ford Focus out of the driveway, and my heart felt as though it were weighted down with a thousand of our cold marble tiles. Rosa had been with our family since before Sarah was born, since before we'd adopted Mulu Ken, since before my mother died. Rosa had been like the big sister I never had, there to celebrate good news or offer comfort in times of sorrow.

"There, there, Miss Gillian," Rosa would say whenever I got upset, and she'd set down her dust cloth or her mop and sit down to listen to all my *rich life woes*, as Veronica would call them. Or sometimes Rosa would read a poem I'd just penned. She never asked what the poem meant or suggested any changes, as Veronica would. She also never charged for the extra time. She was far more than a maid, which was what Veronica had called Rosa last month when she left that spiteful message on voicemail.

I hadn't picked up when the phone rang that day either. Like today, I'd been in bed with a bad case of what I called the alligators, those dark thoughts that swarmed about, closing in, snapping their big sharp teeth at me, much like they had been today. I had never told anyone about these feelings, or the way I thought of them metaphorically as primordial reptiles. They'd think I really was loony. But I knew I wasn't. Just as Sylvia Plath described her own depression as an owl's talon clenching her heart, my dark thoughts reminded me of alligators.

And on that particular day when Veronica had left that scornful message, the alligators had been circling my bed and I'd let the phone ring because I knew I couldn't talk to my sister and act like everything was all right. But listening to her voicemail wasn't exactly chicken soup for my despairing soul, either.

"Are you trying to tell me you're *too busy* to pick up my call?" That was the first thing Veronica had said, and normally, when she made comments like this, I could let it slide. But then she said something about how I obviously wasn't busy cleaning the house, because I had *Rosie the Maid* for that. It was only then that she revealed the real reason for her call. Dad was in the hospital. *Maybe you'd like to come visit if you can tear yourself away from your poems.*

Okay, so maybe I wasn't Maya Angelou. Maybe I hadn't even published anything yet. But I still had a right to write, didn't I? And was it my fault that Hugh and I were financially comfortable? Did I really deserve it whenever my sister unfurled her scorn at me?

I sat down that very afternoon and wrote an old-fashioned snail mail letter to my sister, and I was so upset I kept a copy of it, which I've reread so many times that I now knew it by heart.

Dear Ronnie,

I'm sorry you are so jealous of me. You seem to forget that we were both born and raised in the same middle class home where we did our chores and said our prayers and practiced the golden rule. Just because we each grew up and took a separate path, and mine led me to a man with a lucrative law practice, doesn't mean I'm a different person than I once was. I am still your sister, and I wish our differing financial situations didn't have to drive such a wedge between us.

And just because I have a housekeeper instead of a job doesn't mean I am some sort of spoiled rich bitch. It's not as though I just sit around take, take, taking from the world and not giving back. Obviously I could have been doing my own dusting and sweeping and dishes and vacuuming and mopping all these years. I could have been doing all that quite well, thank you very much. Or I could have been working in an office somewhere. Did you forget I have a business admin degree? But instead I chose to spend my time, and my resources, doing other things.

Like adopting Mulu Ken, who you may recall was once a starving orphan in Ethiopia. And employing a needy Hispanic woman who is far more than a housecleaner, by the way. She's a lovely woman. And don't forget that Hugh and I have donated quite a bit of money to higher education and other charities.

As I wrote the letter, I actually thought about letting Rosa go just to prove a point to my sister that I *could* do my own housework. But I loved Rosa too much to do that. And Rosa did need the money; she'd been trying for so long to hoist herself over the ledge of poverty and I was happy I could help her. Another option, of course, would have been to convince Hugh to downsize. But that would be crazy to do something like that just to please my sister. Besides, he'd never go for that. He needed to uphold an image for professional purposes, he often said.

I am so tired of being resented. If only people understood what it's like to be me. If only at least my own sister understood.

I never heard back from Veronica in response to that letter. Now, as I watched Rosa's little car disappear down the hill, I longed for her to come back. I wanted to tell her about today's e-mail from my sister. Or maybe what I really wanted was to forget about Veronica and listen to one of Rosa's stories, about her family back home, about the border crossing, about the struggles she'd faced ever since coming to America. To listen to Rosa, a woman of meager means, tell her stories with such love and gratitude and hope in her eyes.

But she was gone, and the putt-putt sound of her dying car was soon replaced by the booming bass sounds from Henry's Beamer. The floor vibrated beneath my bare feet, and my heart felt like it was vibrating, too. Now that I'm not driving them to and from school anymore, the highlight of my day is when they come home. I hurried into the kitchen, hoping it would look like I'd been busy doing something productive today, and began to set a platter of food out for the kids: Beecher's Honey Blank Slate cheese, local Honeycrisp apples, gluten-free rice crackers, and organic chocolate almond milk, of course, to drink.

Sarah sashayed into the house first. She had a dreamy look in her eyes.

"Guess which ninth grader just got invited to Homecoming?" She twirled in a circle, the sides of her lacy cardigan fluttering around her like angel wings. "By the captain of the football team!"

Before I had a chance to race through the list of how a mother is supposed to feel when her only daughter gets invited to her first dance—by an upperclassman—Henry sauntered in and tossed his backpack on the table.

"Hello, Mum," he said. He'd been perfecting his British accent ever since he visited Oxford last spring break. He gave me a kiss on my cheek.

The thing is: every afternoon was like this, a present day version of Ozzie and Harriet—which I only knew from reruns, given that I wasn't old enough to have watched it the first time around. Three perfect kids who greeted me warmly, washed their hands before sitting down at the table, and were willing to spend a few minutes with me to tell me about their day. I knew I didn't deserve this, and I knew I should be grateful that this is what I had. There was no excuse for my alligators.

"Wait, where's Mulu Ken?"

"Oh, sorry Mum," Henry said. "Forgot to mention that MK's gone home with his pal Alex." I watched his Adam's apple bob as he swallowed his apple slices. "I cleared it with Alex's mum. No worries. She said she'll have him home right after dinner."

Utterly perfect kids. If Virginia and Sylvia had been in my shoes, might they have lived longer, happier lives?

The phone rang then, for the umpteenth time that day. I ignored it. I didn't want to interrupt this precious time.

"Aren't you going to answer that?" Sarah asked. When I shook my head, she lunged for the phone and hit the speaker button.

"Hello, this is Children With Hair Loss calling to—"

Sarah hung up.

"Why did you do that?" I asked. Sarah and Henry looked at one another, then both rolled their eyes.

"Are you kidding?" Sarah said.

Henry walked to the desk at the edge of the kitchen and picked up my mom's old Longaberger basket. "She hung up because of this, Mum." The basket was overflowing with mail, including free return address labels,

American flag pins, and even coins—with requests for money from all sorts of organizations.

"What about it?" I asked.

"Mom," Sarah said. "You're becoming obsessed with giving away money. It's not that it's bad to give to charities. But some of these people are just scam artists." She tightly wrapped the remaining cheese in Saran Wrap and set it in the fridge. "Besides, you've got to find something else to do with your life besides answering junk mail. Go out and get a job or something. Find your passion."

She stood across from me, exactly my height, and met my eyes with hers. Her expression was not cruel, but those last three words were as sharp and serrated as the knife that remained on the cheese cutting board. Didn't she understand that she, and her brothers, and her father, had been my passion? Didn't she give any credit to my previous, albeit short, life as a bookkeeper, or to my desire to write my own poetry? Maybe I wasn't that good yet. Maybe I wasn't winning awards with my words the way she was with her music. But still. I was flabbergasted, and at a loss for words, too.

She turned to wash the cutting board and knife at the sink, and Henry cleared the rest of the snacks from the table. I simply stood there and watched them as though I was a mere audience member and they were the important actors on the stage. When they completed their tasks, Henry said they were heading upstairs to do their homework.

Why? I wondered. Why did they have to be so goddamn perfect? Why did they have to clean up every crumb in the kitchen? Why did they have to study so hard and get straight A's? I watched them go and found myself resenting my own children. Being around them had made me feel unnecessary, inferior, and lonelier than I had before they'd come home. How sad was that?

Just as Veronica was jealous of me—her own sister—I had become envious of my own children. And maybe I was also a bit jealous of Veronica, too. At least Veronica's life was normal.

"Dinner at 6:30?" I called after the kids. "Spicy jambalaya? With Rosa's jalapeno cornbread recipe, and homemade peach cobbler for dessert?" At least I could still cook.

"Sorry, Mum. We've got to head back to school at 6:00 for a Homecoming meeting," Henry called back. "Mandatory."

A mandatory meeting at dinnertime? I watched him take the stairs up two at a time. Damn it! I had been looking forward to dinnertime; it had always been the highlight of my day, when I could produce a fabulous meal for my family and feel like I'd accomplished something. But not so much anymore. My perfect children were too perfectly involved in school and in their own lives.

Well at least Hugh would come home to appreciate my efforts.

I began to busy myself in our bright and airy Tuscan-style kitchen. The rain had stopped and a ray of light filtered in over the sink. I set the butter, sugar, eggs, and cornmeal out on the island, and chopped peppers on the end-grain cutting board, and then decided I'd text Hugh to confirm he'd be home by 7:00 p.m.

As I waited for his reply, flipping through the mail Rosa had left on the counter, a new e-mail came in on my phone.

> From: Jackson Blake
> Subject: Veronica
> Date: September 18 3:22:08 PM PDT
> To: Gillian Blake-Moore
>
> Hey Sis,
>
> Sarah's joining the National Youth Orchestra? Don't know what that is, but it sounds impressive, and way out of my league. But then I wouldn't expect anything less from your kids.
>
> Regarding Ronnie: I don't know what your problem is with her. She acts fine to me. Obviously it's upsetting when your child gets caught smoking weed in the school parking lot and then runs away. On top of Walt losing his job. I think it's just that she has so many problems to deal with, something she figures you'll never understand.
>
> Wanda says hello and will call you sometime when she's feeling better. This chemo's taking a harder toll on her than the last one, but some say that's a sign it's working.
>
> Jackson

The house phone rang then. My mother used to say dinnertime was the busiest time of day for interruptions. I answered it quickly, thinking it would be Hugh calling instead of texting, saying he wanted to hear my voice. But it wasn't him.

"Hello, this is the Society for Diversity in Landscaping calling."

The Society for what? Although I was indeed curious, Sarah's words were still echoing in my mind, so I hung up, and then immediately wished I hadn't. What she didn't understand was that it's lonely, living way up here on the hill in our huge house with my housecleaner and my perfect little world. It's lonely being in the top one percent. At least all these solicitors give me an opportunity to have an uplifting, even hopeful conversation with someone.

I looked back at Jackson's e-mail. What exactly did he mean when he referred to *my* problem with Veronica?

I tried to ignore Sarah's words. I tried to ignore Jackson's. But they were like Tolstoy's proverbial white bear in the forest. The more you try not to think of it, the more you do. Anger began to bubble up inside me, and I began to take it out on the cornbread batter, beating it harder than I know I should have. I whipped and whipped until my forearm cramped.

Damn it, Jackson! You're the one who has it *all* wrong. *I'm* not the one with the problem.

I shoved the cornbread into the oven. Next, I started slicing peaches with a vengeance. It's a wonder I didn't slice off a fingertip. Thankfully, I put down the knife when a text came in.

Hugh: *Bad news. Must work late. Don't wait for dinner. Love.*

Really? This could not be happening. I wiped my hands on a towel.

Me: *Hugh! I asked you this morning about these dinner plans. Can't you just go to work early tomorrow? I can hold off till 8 for dinner.*

Hugh: *No can do. Sorry, sweet pea. Love.*

This was not good. I did not want to be alone tonight. My anger was quickly replaced with a heaviness, the debilitating weight of marble again. The alligators were congregating and threatening to move in, perhaps closer than they had ever before.

I'd been trying to hold them at bay all day by visiting my favorite bookstore in the morning, taking a bubble bath at noon, indulging in a glass (or was it two?) of pear cider—which I rationalized was fine since it had less alcohol content than wine—and I'd lain down with Sylvia Plath. But it had all been for naught. Rosa went home. The kids were busy. Hugh had important things to do. Only the alligators were here for me.

And now they were rumbling. Bellowing. Growling. They sounded ravenous. I wondered if maybe I did need to get some professional help.

I looked into the oven at the cornbread, then imagined what position Sylvia had sat in. I turned the oven off, leaving the half-baked cornbread inside. I threw the peach slices and pits into the compost bin under the sink, ran upstairs, and dove under the covers. I prayed for sleep to come, but it didn't, because sleep never comes when you really need it.

I waited for Mulu Ken.

Finally, I heard him come in through the front door. It was dark inside and out by then. He was much later than I'd expected. But I couldn't be angry with him as I listened to him whistling his way through the kitchen. MK somehow always gave me a jolt of energy and hope, this time just enough to haul myself out of bed. I put on my happy Mommy face and went downstairs.

"How was your day, MK?"

I kissed him on the forehead, and he retrieved the imaginary kiss in his fingertips and placed it in the front pocket of his jeans.

"It was good, Mama Gill."

It had been seven years since we'd adopted him, but he still insisted on calling me that. I understood why; his African birthmother, now deceased, would always be his true mother. But just once I wished he'd use the word *mom* for me.

"Did you get enough to eat at your friend's house?" I asked.

"Mm-hmm. And I finished my homework while I was there, too."

"Then let's go up," I said, and I shepherded him up the stairs. I lay on his bed, waiting as he took his evening shower and brushed his teeth, studying the posters of Africa he'd hung on his wall and wondering what his life would have been like if his mother had lived. If he would have been happier there, with her, than here with me.

After he was tucked into bed, I sat by his side and listened to him recount more about his day, his black arms skinny as licorice crooked behind his head, his smile stretching his cheeks wide.

"I got a B+ on my marine wildlife report," he told me. "Mrs. Taylor says my writing's getting better."

I smoothed his hair back from his forehead.

"And a girl in my class said she thinks I'm cute."

I felt the same pang I'd felt earlier when Sarah told me she had been asked to the dance. Was I already losing MK to girls and the rest of the world? "What did you say to her?"

"I thanked her," he said.

I laughed. "Well, she's right. You are cute. Very cute." I gently wiggled the lobes of his ears, a secret gesture of love we shared with one another.

"Now tell me about your day."

I was caught off guard by his request. I could not tell him that I'd lain around all day being depressed. Or that my sister and I were having a spat about trivial matters. I couldn't tell him the alligators had been to visit. Before I had a chance to figure out what to say, he had something else to say to me.

"Oh, Mama Gill, I forgot to tell you about the dinner Alex's mother prepared for his family. It was fantastic. We should have it sometime."

I thought about the cornbread, now cold and abandoned in the oven, and the peaches in the trash. I recalled Hugh's text and Henry and Sarah's oh-so-important obligations. I did not really want to hear about somebody else's family dinner, but I didn't know how to stop him from going on.

"It was fried chicken from a place called KFC," MK said. "Finger-licking good, they say. And it was." To prove his point, he licked his fingers even though any remnant of batter, meat, or grease would have been washed down the shower drain. "Could we have that for dinner sometime, Mama Gill?"

KFC?

I laughed. Every day I lovingly labored over sometimes-complicated, always-savory and healthy recipes for the family, never once having thought about serving fast food to them. I hadn't had KFC since I was a young girl, but now that I thought of it, I remembered how exciting it had been whenever Dad would come home from work with that big red and white bucket, along with sides of coleslaw and sweet buns. Ronnie and Jackson and I would practically trip over one another on our way to the kitchen, and we always fought over who got the last drumstick. The family sat around the table laughing and talking and doing what families are supposed to do at dinnertime: connecting over a meal.

I kissed Mulu Ken good night on the forehead, watched him stuff the invisible kiss under his pillow, and retreated to my own room once again. I sat down at my vanity with the gilded mirror and began to brush my hair, one hundred strokes before bedtime, as I'd done ever since I'd been a child. Maybe, I thought, happiness is inversely related to money, and that was really my whole problem. The families I'd known with money tended to get divorced or fight over estates or otherwise lose touch with each other. Maybe the ones without much money—the ones who ate KFC for dinner—were a whole lot better at staying put, dealing with whatever life throws at them, and appreciating simple things. Like buckets of crispy chicken legs.

I then began to remove my makeup with Noxzema, like Sylvia Plath had religiously done every night, and just when the cream was slathered over my eyelids, I heard Hugh's voice.

"Sorry, love."

I kept my eyes closed as he took the cleaning pads from my hands and gently wiped my eyelids for me.

"Keep your eyes closed for one more minute," he said. "I brought something home for you."

I couldn't imagine what it might be. Another diamond necklace? A new tennis bracelet? I didn't want another bauble as an apology for a missed dinner. I heard a whimper then, and he released his hands from my eyes.

A black Labrador retriever puppy was sitting on the floor next to him, a blue leash held down by one of Hugh's feet.

"My admin's dogs had pups," he said. "They're from a perfect lineage. Show dogs. I told her I wanted the best one for you. That's why I was late."

I was not simply speechless; I was thoughtless, too. Completely blank, as though I had not only wiped away the makeup from my skin but also the thoughts beneath it. Yes, the puppy was adorable, and yes, Hugh was a dear for thinking of me and for surprising me. But I didn't want a dog from a perfect lineage. I didn't want any more perfection, period. If I'd wanted any dog, it would have been the sickly runt of the litter. But I didn't even want that. As I tried to figure out what to say, I heard an alligator rustling.

"I'm tired, Hugh. Let's talk about this in the morning."

He hesitated. No doubt he was startled that I hadn't oohed and aahed over the puppy. He leaned over and kissed me on the forehead, then led the poor thing out of the bedroom.

The next morning, I got up to make blueberry pancakes for everyone. I cleaned up the dog pee and poop that landed just beyond the newspaper I'd set out for the puppy. I listened to Hugh regale me with his upcoming calendar commitments.

And I read the astonishing e-mails that came in from my beloved relatives.

> From: Sissy Berg
> Subject: (no subject)
> Date: September 19 8:34:17 AM PDT
> To: Gillian Blakemore
>
> Dear Aunt Gillian,
>
> You may have heard about some trouble I got in. It was really stupid what I did and I'm sorry for all the trouble I've caused. Anyway, Mom talked to a lawyer last night who thinks she can get me off the possession charge but we can't afford her. Mom said forget it but I wondered if maybe you'd be willing to help? She (I mean the lawyer) wants a

$4,000 retainer and I promise someday I'll pay you back if you decide to help. If you could just send me some money through PayPal, I'd really appreciate it.

Love from your niece,
Sissy

PS Please say hi to H, S, and MK for me.

So. Sissy had returned home, and Veronica wanted money from her rich sister for legal fees, but was too cowardly to ask for it herself so she put her daughter up to the stunt. Was that all I was good for these days? Charity?

From: Jackson Blake
Subject: Middle Class
Date: September 18 8:52:20 AM PDT
To: Gillian Blake-Moore

Hey Sis,

I finally checked out that link you sent Ronnie. You're right, things are getting worse. What I'm most worried about is that my employer is talking about more radical changes to our healthcare coverage. It all started with Obamacare and it's gotten worse ever since. Wanda and I are nearly as worried about finances as her cancer. You have no idea.

Yeah, I think the middle class will disappear in our lifetime. What I'm not sure about is whether it's better to be one of the peasants or the aristocrats. Good luck to you and your kids! LOL.

Jackson

And what, exactly, was that supposed to mean?

The puppy whined, which was what I felt like doing, too. Hugh had sequestered it inside a dog crate, and clearly it wanted to be out and about. I let it out. It sniffed around the kitchen, then lifted its tiny hind leg and peed on the corner of the island.

Go ahead and pee, dog. LOL.

Hugh, who had gone upstairs to shower and get dressed, came back down.

Somebody said, "I don't want the dog."

It was my own voice that had spoken the words, although I didn't even know the thought had been forming in my head.

Hugh looked at me as though I'd said I didn't want him. "You don't?"

"No."

Something hung in the air between the two of us. It felt a little like guilt, but not exactly. It might have been freedom. I wasn't sure. He poured himself a cappuccino. I watched him do it.

"So, love, what *do* you want?" he asked me.

"I don't know, but not a puppy."

"You seem unhappy." He was still handsome after all these years: his shoulders broad, his abs strong, his butt firm in those designer slacks. He still had a full head of thick hair, and his face was tanned and unblemished. I hated him for all that. Whenever I looked in the mirror, I saw old, fat, grumpy—even if I've just had my brows waxed and my nails done. He, on the other hand, was more dashing than ever.

He was right: I was unhappy. But to admit that was to admit weakness. You don't just walk around telling people you're unhappy when you aren't even sure why you are. Especially when you have a virile, successful husband who would give you whatever you want, and three fantastic kids, and a beautiful home, a housecleaner you adore, and abundant financial resources. When you and your family are perfectly healthy. You don't go telling people about alligators.

But as it turned out, I inadvertently had.

"What does this mean?" Hugh asked. He pulled something out from the back pocket of his slacks. It was an envelope, one with a clear window on the front, the kind bills come in. His brows were furrowed.

"How should I know?"

Then he flipped it over, and I saw what it was. Yesterday, I'd jotted down some thoughts. A poem. About alligators. Those words hadn't been meant for public consumption, not even for his eyes. Especially not for his eyes; he wouldn't understand. I must have left it on the nightstand, along with some poetry collections, by accident.

He handed it to me, and I reread what I'd written.

Alligators

They come every so often,
Catching me by surprise.

Slowly, stealthily,
As though they smell my blood.
They feed on my raw
Desire to love
Or be loved,
To give
Or be given to.
To live.
They surround me.
They drown me.
One day
They will
Devour me.

Not exactly Plath, perhaps.

"I'm worried about you," he said.

"Me, too."

"I want you to see a therapist," he said.

"I'll think about it." But I knew I probably wouldn't, because as long as I lived in my perfect house with my perfect family, there would be nothing the therapist could do or say that would change anything. You can't fix perfection.

After Hugh left for work with the puppy, and the kids left for school, I wandered back upstairs, each footstep feeling as though someone had strapped twenty-pound weights to my feet. I didn't even know why I was going upstairs, or what I would do when I got there.

Our house was deathly quiet.

Maybe I should just do it, I thought. If there is no purpose in life, why live it? The truth was that Hugh and Henry and Sarah no longer needed me; they didn't even seem to care if I was around. Mulu Ken did, but he didn't think of me as his real mother, and with the way his brother and sister doted on him, I knew he'd survive. As for Rosa? Yes, she would miss me, but she'd light a few candles at her church and say a few prayers and then she'd be all right.

Veronica and Jackson? Fuck them. I had been starting to wonder lately if I'd ever had a good relationship with them. Maybe I'd been deluding myself all these years.

I went into the bathroom and stripped off my clothes. I took a long, steamy shower, morbidly musing that at least they wouldn't have to wash down my body upon my death. I slipped a comfortable flannel shirt and leggings on, skipping the bra. Who needs a bra when you're about to die? Did Virginia Woolf wear one when she wrote she was "doing what seems the best thing to do?"

I opened the medicine cabinet and began to pull various bottles down from the crowded shelves—vitamins, Tylenol, expired antibiotics, Hugh's over-the-counter sleep aid. The phone rang.

Let it ring, I decided. Let it ring.

But the damned answering machine didn't kick in, and eventually it felt like the phone was taunting me, keeping me from figuring out my recipe for death.

"Hello?" My mouth was dry, my voice hoarse.

"Good afternoon. This is Pacific Northwest Wildfire and Disaster Support—"

I was about to press END, but something stopped me. Maybe it was the name of the organization, someone who'd never called me before. Or the smooth, friendly, almost timid voice of the woman on the other end of the line. She was not a professional solicitor.

"I'm sorry to bother you. I'm sure you're busy."

Yes, I thought. I'm so, so terribly busy.

"This calling program is highly unusual for us, but in light of the disaster we're facing, we're reaching out to residents of select zip codes in the Pacific Northwest with the hope they'll be able to help us."

Select zip codes, right. I knew exactly what that meant. They were reaching out to those with affluence. Veronica wouldn't get this phone call if she lived around here. Or Jackson. All this woman needed from me, all anyone needed from me, was money. And it wasn't even money I'd earned. It was Hugh's money. I was just the clearinghouse.

"Disaster?" I asked.

"Yes, the massive wildfires raging throughout Central and Eastern Washington and Oregon. They're unprecedented in size, and we're only ten percent contained. Communities have been ravaged, and we're looking for folks who can help in any way possible. Donations, of course, are always helpful."

Of course.

"But even more than that," she said, before I had the chance to hang up or offer a pledge, "we're looking for manpower. Or womanpower, I should say." There was a hint of humor in her voice. A tasteful, subtle hint. "We're actually looking more for time and talent than money."

What an odd thing for a telephone solicitor to ask for. What was the catch? I hesitated, thinking that I certainly had time. All the time in this big old lonely world. But talent? I shook my head as though she could see me. Sorry, I had no talent that anyone valued. Not anymore; it had been nearly two decades since I'd held any sort of job, such as it was—bookkeeping for a local restaurant chain. And it was clear that my lame attempts at writing poetry didn't demonstrate any talent, although, even if they had, I wasn't sure how poetry could help put out the fire. But there was one thing I could do, for whatever that was worth.

"I can cook."

The woman paused, and I realized then how foolish I had sounded. I was about to tell her I'd been joking.

"Really?" The tone of her voice had perked up. Then she let out a small laugh of what sounded like relief. "You're the first person who's offered any sort of talent since I started making these calls. Everyone else just wants to donate money and get off the phone."

I looked out the window. Another gray day in Seattle, where wildfires were merely an abstract idea. A pair of mallards flew into the yard and landed in the pool. A happy couple.

Everyone else wants to get off the phone because they have things to do. They have more purpose in their lives. Or, more accurately, they have a sense of self. That's why they don't want to listen to this woman talk about out-of-control wildfires. But because I was feeling more and more like a blank sheet of paper in a half-used spiral notebook—a notebook from which all the used pages had been ripped out, but which still contained a healthy number of pages waiting to be filled—I had the time and the interest, or perhaps the bona fide need, to listen to what she had to say.

"So what exactly would you want me to do?"

I listened closely to the woman's voice on the other end of the phone, telling me about the firefighters who had come from all over the country to fight the blazes. This organization was looking for volunteers to tend to the firefighters' needs: lodging, laundry, medical.

"And food." My heart started beating wildly, the way Mulu Ken had flailed the first time he'd jumped into our pool. Yes, I could cook. I could do food. I could tend to the tired and hungry stomachs each morning and each evening, filling them up with delicious nourishment while they, unknowingly, filled me up with purpose.

I could do this. It would just be for a while, just for as long as the fire lasted. Those medicine bottles would wait for me.

"It's hard to say how long you'd need to be here," she said after I'd asked. "We'll take however much time you can give us."

It was a mutual feeling. I'd take however much time they could give me.

After hanging up with her, I began to pack my casual clothes, first filling one suitcase and then another, all the while trying to figure out how I'd tell the family what I'd decided to do. I imagined MK's bright smile as he remembered the volunteer organizations that had come to help his fellow villagers. I envisioned Henry and Sarah looking at me with pride for coming up with a passion and something to do. I anticipated Veronica's hesitation on the phone when I called to tell her and her inevitable question of why in the world I'd go off and do that sort of thing. And then I saw Hugh's look, first of confusion, and then a bit of a pout that I'd be leaving him for a while, and then his concern about whether there would be a suitable place for me to stay way out there in the middle of nowhere.

This was when I knew, for sure, this was what I had to do. My decision to leave wasn't just to help remedy disaster for a community ravaged by wildfire. It was to address the disaster that had become my life.

I dragged the suitcases out of the closet and into the bedroom, and I felt something behind me. I turned; there was nothing there. But I knew what I'd felt. The alligators. They were lurking there, somewhere, and I realized I wouldn't, and couldn't, wait for the family to come home to tell them about my plans. I had to go now.

I sat down and wrote them a letter.

Dear Hugh, Henry, Sarah, and MK,

I know this may come as a surprise to all of you, but I have made a decision to go away for a while. You may have suspected I've been unhappy lately. In truth, I have felt as though I'm on the brink of something—something that I can't quite name. All I know is that I need a change, and right now I'm heading to eastern Oregon to volunteer in support of the firefighting efforts there. It's urgent, which is why I've decided to leave right away.

Don't worry about me; I will call you when I get there. I know you'll all be fine here. I love you and I will miss you all.

Love you,
Mom

PS Hugh, please don't send me any money.

I took off my diamond ring and earrings and locked them inside the safe in our closet. I placed the letter on Hugh's dresser, next to a wooden bowl filled with his cuff links. And I only glanced at all those dead poets stacked on my nightstand.

By nine o'clock that night, I had traded in my Jaguar XKR for a Ford Explorer with nearly 100,000 miles and gotten cash back. I had stopped in Walla Walla for dinner at a KFC. And I had found my way to eastern Oregon. I was still twenty miles out from my final destination, and probably forty or fifty miles from any fires, when I pulled the car over onto the highway's shoulder to stretch my legs.

There had been an early snow, and the ground was completely white. I got out of the car and, although the air was vaguely smoky even at this distance, I felt more clearheaded and alive than I had for so very long. I trudged through the snow into the woods, blazing a path among the trees where no one had yet walked. It was remarkably peaceful there, and far less lonely than back in the city where I'd lived for most of my adult life. I listened. A bird—perhaps an owl—flapped enormous wings. A clump of snow dropped from a branch and softly plopped onto the ground beside me. But there were no other sounds, no other movements, and as far as I could tell, there were no alligators for miles around.